Sloan rose fro
started toward her

Willie thought she'd never seen a more dangerous-looking man. He stopped just inches from her.

She stared at the ridges of his belly and the line of dark hair tapering into the top of his pants.

"Go," he rumbled, "or I'll do something we'll both regret. And there won't be any taking it back. Only guilt and confusion and heartache. That's the only promise you'll get from me."

He reached around her for the door handle and tugged it wide. She felt the heat of his arm as it stirred the air over her skin.

"Run," he bit out. "Run before I make you disreputable as hell."

And she did. For the first time in her life, Willie fled from a man...!

Dear Reader,

Kit Gardner has written seven terrific historicals for Harlequin, but many of our readers also know her for her equally exciting historicals from Dell written as Kit Garland. This month's story, *The Untamed Heart,* a Western with a twist, has a refined English hero who happens to be an earl, and a feisty, ranch hand heroine who can do anything a man can do, only better. Don't miss the sparks as these two opposites fight their very strong mutual attraction.

This month also brings us a new concept for Harlequin Historicals, our first in-line short-story collection, *The Knights of Christmas.* Three of our award-winning authors, Suzanne Barclay, Margaret Moore and Deborah Simmons, have joined forces to create a Medieval Christmas anthology that is sure to spread cheer all year long. Author Susan Amarillas's new book, *Wild Card,* is the story of a lady gambler who is hiding in a remote Wyoming town, terrified that the local sheriff will discover she's wanted for murder in Texas. And talented newcomer Lyn Stone is back with *The Arrangement,* a unique and touching story about a young female gossip columnist who sets out to expose a notorious composer and winds up first agreeing to marry him, *then* falling in love with him.

Whatever your tastes in reading, we hope you enjoy all four books, available wherever Harlequin Historicals are sold.

Sincerely,

Tracy Farrell
Senior Editor

Please address questions and book requests to:
Harlequin Reader Service
U.S.: 3010 Walden Ave., P.O. Box 1325, Buffalo, NY 14269
Canadian: P.O. Box 609, Fort Erie, Ont. L2A 5X3

KIT GARDNER

THE UNTAMED HEART

Harlequin Books

TORONTO • NEW YORK • LONDON
AMSTERDAM • PARIS • SYDNEY • HAMBURG
STOCKHOLM • ATHENS • TOKYO • MILAN
MADRID • WARSAW • BUDAPEST • AUCKLAND

ISBN 0-373-28990-1

THE UNTAMED HEART

Books by Kit Gardner

Harlequin Historicals

KIT GARDNER

at one time in her life masqueraded as an accountant. These days she considers herself a writer and a mother. When she's not pounding furiously on her computer keyboard, she now can be found on her knees in her perennial gardens, bellowing on the sidelines of a soccer field or blubbering over anything Jane Austen. She's an eternal enthusiast for all things English but has been known to spend entire Sunday mornings watching reruns of "The Wild, Wild West." She lives with her husband, three sons and a golden retriever near Chicago. She loves to hear from readers. Write to P.O. Box 510, Plainfield, IL 60544.

Prologue

Nebraska
April 1880

Sloan Devlin, fifth Earl of Worthingham, held four kings and an ace. The smooth-handed gentleman seated to his right slid his entire pile of bills and coin into the center of the table, raising the stakes well above four thousand.

"I call, tenderfoot," the man drawled. Beneath the brim of his low-crowned black hat, his mouth twisted into a grin that would have sent any well-seeing female to the floor in a faint. "Lay them on the table, gents."

Across the table two railroad businessmen with bulging bellies and whiskey-ruddied cheeks tossed their cards onto the table. The one who called himself Hyde rolled his cigar from one corner of his mouth to the other and glanced from the black-hatted man to Sloan. The other, Strobridge, gulped from his glass and glanced nervously around the otherwise deserted railcar. Over the tops of their brown bowlers a barren wash of gold whizzed past beyond the windows. The car's wooden floor vibrated beneath Sloan's shoes, each clickety-clack of the rails registering the locomotive's westward trek across the prairie.

The gentleman cheat, who'd neglected to mention his name, stared at Sloan. The man had resorted to deceit as though he'd done it countless times before. But a gambler down on his luck was never too hard to recognize. Sloan had known several in his thirty-five years, men who utilized their quick hands to stack the deck or deal crookedly, fluttering the cards up like a flock of quail and neatly assembling them as they wished. A man had no chance against those fellows, unless luck played her hand, and Sloan had always found luck at the gaming table. Elsewhere—well, that was another thing altogether.

At first glance Sloan had registered the gambler's baby-smooth hands, and the finely made, high-heeled French leather boot he crossed over one knee. Maybe only a few years younger than Sloan, he'd been graced with the good looks and bold manner that marked him as part of the dashing American West Sloan had traveled from England to discover. His skin and hair were of the same sun-burnished hue as the landscape beyond the windows. He wore his fresh-from-the-tailor's-iron linen and broadcloth with an elegance common to the men who occupied London's most fashionable gaming houses, and yet his eyes remained wary as if he'd seen enough to expect the worst of people.

He obviously hadn't expected to be outwitted by the be-spectacled Englishman he'd marked as an easy dupe.

Sloan spread his cards faceup on the table. "Four kings and an ace." It was an unbeatable hand. All eyes swung to the gambler.

He was staring at Sloan's cards with the kind of passive, cheek-twitching calm that in Sloan's experience typically indicated tremendous distress. He lifted lifeless eyes and Sloan felt every muscle tense.

The gambler spilled his cards onto the pile of chips in the center of the table.

Hyde coughed. "By damn." His eyes angled at Sloan. "Where'd you say you were from?"

Sloan drew off his spectacles, folded them and slid them

into the breast pocket of his topcoat. "Cornwall, England." He indicated the booty. "I take it this is mine."

Hyde pushed the pile of bills toward Sloan and began filling a sack with the coins. "They play poker over there in England?"

"Not exactly."

"That where you learned to cheat, gent?" The gambler surged to his feet, toppling his chair.

Calmly Sloan folded a stack of bills. He could feel the man's angered heat radiating from his chest. Sloan glanced at the hand lingering near the open flap of his waistcoat, fingertips perhaps inches from cold steel. Sloan kept folding bills.

"Now hold on there," Strobridge crowed, bouncing out of his chair. "We're all civilized gentlemen here. My friend Hyde here and I have come all the way from Boston without encountering any fuss, or any Indians and we don't need any trouble now. Peaceful business in Denver is what we're about. Just peaceful Union Pacific business in a lawless land. There's no need to draw your gun, Devlin."

"I wasn't intending to," Sloan said, stuffing the wad of bills into his pocket. "I don't own one."

All three men stared at Sloan.

Sloan shoved his chair from the table and rose to his full height, which, as chance would have it, was a good two inches taller than the gambler, high-heeled French boots notwithstanding. Their gazes locked.

"In Cornwall," Sloan said, "there's a saying that any man who calls another a cheat in a game of chance is doing so because of his own guilt in the matter. It's not the winner who must defend his well-earned victory but the loser who can't stomach his failure at deception."

The gambler's eyes were as bleak as a dead man's. Sloan's stare was just as uncompromising.

"Dammit, now, shake hands," Strobridge sputtered with a forced laugh. "Go on. Then we'll open ourselves a fine bottle of brandy. We can drink to the success of the Union Pacific railroad and to all the silver ore flowing out of the Rocky Mountains. That's where the fortunes are made, gents. Not on one game of cards. Go on, now. We're civilized men, remember.''

Sloan extended his hand to the gambler. But swallowing pride was too damned difficult for some civilized men. To others, indeed, what was a bit of lost pride next to needless loss of life? Sloan had learned that lesson firsthand and it had been a costly one.

So costly, he'd left Cornwall and the tinners he'd championed against the mine owners. So costly, he'd left Devlin Manor, his tenants, his estates, and all the responsibility that came with a sudden inheriting of a title.

Sloan's belief in a peaceful settling of differences had ended with his father taking a stray lead ball in the chest and dying just steps from Devlin Manor's door. After witnessing that, only an idealist who was a fool would still cling to the idea of men resorting to diplomacy over violence, a handshake over pistols at dawn.

So he was an idealistic fool, but Sloan wasn't ready to abandon his faith in the human spirit. It was because of it that he'd set out from Bristol on the Cunard steamer to embrace the American frontier in all its unbridled splendor, to see its vast and varied landscape with its climatic excesses, its giant herds of buffalo, its Indians, its bold pioneers who were in the process of writing a stirring chapter in history, a saga of heroic proportions. Until now, he'd viewed the West through the eyes and canvases of the European painters who imagined it. Now he would experience it, and somewhere on this vast land he would rid himself of the burden of putting his father into the line of fire, and restore his worthiness of the title. Maybe then he could return to assume the responsibilities.

''Get the brandy,'' the gambler ordered, clasping Sloan's hand in his woman's smooth fingers. ''And get the gent a glass.'' He settled himself in his chair as the two railroad men scrambled below the table, producing a bottle and several glasses, which they filled and set before Sloan and the gambler.

"To silver," Hyde said, lifting his glass. "May no one-horse, shantytown dare to stand in the way of progress."

"And to all the lily-white, land-owning virgins that ever called those one-horse towns home." The gambler displayed a flash of teeth and drained his glass. "May they forever turn to a man in times of great need. And may that man be me." His chuckle spilled slowly from his lips as though he savored a thought. "That, gentlemen, is all the fortune I'll ever need."

Hyde and Strobridge echoed his laughter. "If you're on your way to Denver, Devlin," Strobridge began, as he filled his third glass with a less than steady hand, "I know of a saloon in a town called Deadwood Run, couple stops before Denver. The Devil's Gold. I have a special lady there. I always pay her a call once I finish up my business in Denver. This trip will be no different. Dakota Darby's her name. She'll show you how to spend that money you got there, and it won't be on cards."

Sloan set his empty glass on the baize. "I'll remember that."

"Looking for great enterprise, eh?"

"Rather the opposite. Preferably off the railroad line."

Hyde puffed up his chest. "There isn't a place worth seeing that isn't on the Union Pacific line. Nothing except stretches of prairie waiting for the track to come through and make them into something. And no one worth knowing, either, especially the fools that think they can hold out on the march of the iron horse. It's the coming of industry. You're a smart fellow. You can understand that. But some folks are too stubborn to see it no matter how much money you wave under their noses."

Sloan narrowed his eyes on Hyde. "Money for their land."

"It isn't for their mules."

"Or their tarantula juice," the gambler muttered into his glass. "One gulp of that homemade brew is enough to make a hummingbird spit in a rattlesnake's eye. I prefer my drink like my women—smooth, unspoiled and mighty pure.''

Again the railroad men sniggered their agreement. After a moment Strobridge glanced at Sloan. "All the land for the asking and they sit tight, refusing to budge."

"Maybe they think they've good reason," Sloan said.

"Sure they do. It's their pride, the same damned pride that saw them westward seeking their fortunes in the first place."

"Fortunes you promised them."

Strobridge's glass poised at his lips. "I'm no swivel-tongued promoter, spouting empty promises."

Sloan puckered his brow and fished one hand then the other into the inner pockets of his topcoat. "I believe I read something that sounded like a promise in a Union Pacific prospectus I was given in New York. Or was it Chicago? Something about the paradise awaiting development west of the hundredth meridian. It must be in my valise.

"According to your verbiage, gentlemen, if I remember correctly, the frontiersman is an idealized figure, his plow a sacred symbol, your railroad a harbinger of progress. Gold and silver were the thematic notes sounded endlessly in this brochure with land, open space and freedom tinkling in counterpoint. That sounds like a vision of the new Eden and promise enough for a man to abandon his share of a family farm in the East and pack up his family and head west."

Hyde jerked his head at the window. "Look out there, Devlin. All you'll see is an endless bonanza. The Union Pacific firmly believes in the natural process of individual enterprise. Any determined man can share in the good things if he works hard enough. And the railroad's going to be there to provide it for him. If he's smart."

"Damned right," Strobridge said. "I'm not saying you'll find fools everywhere, Devlin. Most enterprising folks wouldn't dare come up against the power of a company like the Union Pacific." He punctuated this by shoving one finger skyward.

"You'll find all the crazies you want in Prosperity Gulch," Hyde added, chomping on his cigar. "Most damned impertinent bunch of poor cusses you'll ever meet. Eking out a living from the South Platte on less than twenty cents a day. After the big mine exploded last year and killed a handful of them, you'd think they'd all just pack up, head back east, and give it up. And yet nothing short of the cavalry will get them out of our path."

"They'll move," Strobridge snorted. "Our line needs to go through that land if we're going to get track around the mountains to the rich mining towns in the deeper valleys. This time, they'll move. They'll have no choice."

"Threats never moved pride," Sloan said, remembering all too clearly the beleaguered tinners in Cornwall standing firm with their demands in the face of threats from the mine owners. All threats had accomplished was bloodshed.

"Money should move pride, Devlin, and it hasn't. I'll be damned if I return to my boss in Boston when this month is out without clearing the way for our line."

"By driving the people from Prosperity Gulch."

"After our business in Denver I'm sure as hellfire going to try, even if it means calling in the cavalry to do it. We'll just have to convince those folks that when their town collapses, as it surely will, their lots will have no more market value than town lots on the moon."

"Where is this worthless town?"

"Ten miles straight north of Deadwood Run." Hyde jerked his chin at the gambler who dozed in his chair. "Our gambling friend can't abide smooth liquor, Devlin. I wonder if it's the same with smooth women."

Gathering up his winnings, Sloan bid Hyde and Strobridge good-afternoon and left their railcar for his own some three cars back. Curiosity had drawn him from the overcrowded heat of his car several hours before and had delivered him to the railroad men's poker table. He was glad it had. He now had an idea where he might be getting off the line.

Dare to make a difference.... His father's words seemed to echo from the rhythmic click of the rails as he moved briskly through the cars. He'd dared once to champion a cause for the beleaguered against the mighty and had failed. Opportunity was again here. Was it a cause worth championing? Perhaps. The mighty couldn't get mightier than the Union Pacific Railroad, and the people any more beleaguered. Were they worth closer scrutiny? Absolutely. It was all waiting for him ten miles north of Deadwood Run. He could turn on his heel anytime and leave that town and those people. He had no ties to bind him there.

Just as he stepped between the last two cars, something jabbed him in the back.

"I'll take what's mine now, gent." The gambler's snarl rose above the roar of the train.

Sloan went still. Heat billowed up from the train's belly. "Is this how you show thanks in the American West, stealing from the man who covered your cheating hide?"

"You're right about that, gent. I'm going to steal from you what I should have won. But in the West we go one step farther with English gents we don't like."

Sloan felt the gun nudge deeper against his back. "I didn't take you for a coward."

"Turn around then," the gambler growled. "I'd rather look into your eyes when the bullet finds your liver. Slow and easy. Just turn around."

With hands hanging loosely at his sides, Sloan turned in the cramped space.

"You're a queer bird, gent," the gambler muttered as he rid Sloan of his sack of coins and the folded bills in his pocket. Tucking these into his topcoat, he squinted at Sloan's embroidered plum waistcoat and starched cravat made of the finest French linen. His eyes hardened on the ruby stickpin nestled in the linen folds.

Sloan flicked his eyes over the gambler's shoulder into the railcar, where several passengers loitered. "You'd best shoot me now before the passengers begin to suspect foul play. You'll have the small matter of my body to dispose of, you know.''

Profuse color climbed from the gambler's collar. ''The prairie's as good a place as any for you, gent. The crows and buzzards will pick your bones clean before anyone knows you're there. A wagon might not come by for a week or longer.''

Sloan allowed a hint of a curve to soften his mouth. ''Then what are you waiting for?''

The gambler's eyes narrowed. Doubt, suspicion, chagrin swept over his handsome features, but not a fierce desire for blood. Sloan had suspected as much. This man was no killer. To Sloan's way of thinking, the gambler needed a small push over the edge of his rage. And he was betting the man would resort to fists first over his gun.

Sloan's voice rumbled low and distinctly ominous even to his own ear. ''You're as soft as you look, sir.''

The gambler took an instant too long to throw his punch. With lightning deftness, Sloan deflected his fist with an upward slice of his forearm, smacked the pistol from his hand with the other, then brought both sides of his hands cleaving into each side of the gambler's thick neck before he could draw another breath. The gambler went rigid, groaned, then fell back against the side of the railcar and slid to the floor. Sloan bent and retrieved his winnings. Twisting one fist into the gambler's shirtfront, Sloan hauled him to his feet and shoved him against the railcar.

''In the future,'' he said silkily, ''you would do well to leave us queer birds to our business. Perhaps, then I will leave you to yours.'' Sloan turned and, with one flex of his arm, tossed the gambler from the train. With grim satisfaction he watched the gambler land and roll into a thatch of bleached grass that lined the track in deep gullies on both sides and swept in unbroken, breathtaking beauty from horizon to horizon.

Straightening his cravat with a jerk of his chin, he smoothed his double-breasted frock coat, tugged at the velvet cuffs, drew a deep breath, flexed his massive hands and turned to enter the last car. As he did so, the polished tip of his pointed shoe nudged the gambler's pistol. Bending, he retrieved the gun and, for several moments, stared at it, feeling the weight of the cool steel in his palm. His finger brushed over the ivory grip, curled around the trigger, traced the length of the scroll-engraved silver barrel. And then he threw the gun over the side of the train and pushed open the door to his railcar.

Chapter One

Prosperity Gulch, Colorado
April 1880

"Classin' up the place again, Miss Wilhelmina?"
J. D. Harkness, owner of the Silver Spur saloon and dance
hall, hoisted a crate of clean glasses onto the bar. Swiping a
thick forearm over his brow, he dissolved like falling bread
dough onto a bar stool and glanced around the deserted saloon.
Midmorning sunlight slanted through the windows, capturing
the dust that hung in the air. Deep in one corner, beside an
upright piano, an old man dozed under his hat. Just outside
the double doors two men perched on overturned barrels, taking turns spewing streams of brown goo at a cuspidor set in
the middle of the street. A handful of folk drifted past the
front windows. The day wasn't looking promising for business, but today wasn't any different than any other.

Harkness swung his weary gaze to the flame-haired young
woman polishing glasses beside him. "What the hell are you
doing here, Willie?"

Wilhelmina McKenna Thorne slanted eyes the color of summer leaves at Harkness. Several fingers slipped beneath her
high lace collar, directly at the spot where the lace itched most.

With the other hand, she poked at the knot on top of her head and wished she hadn't stuck the pins in so far. "Why, Uncle Jeremiah, I've come to help."

"I was afraid of that. No, don't touch another glass. Just get on home, Willie, where you belong." Harkness jerked his head to the corner. "And take Gramps with you."

Willie grabbed an apron and swung it around her whippet-narrow waist. "There's nothing to do at the house for me or Gramps. I haven't had a boarder in over six months, not since—"

She bit off her words. A flush crept to her hairline and memory blossomed with relentless fury. She swung her face away from Harkness before she betrayed it right there—her secret, the one she intended to take to her grave.

She found herself staring at the portrait of a young woman, ripe and lush and naked, hanging above the bar in framed gilt. Willie closed her eyes and tried her best not to think about the things men wanted to do when they looked at a woman's naked breasts and round hips, the love words they whispered that made a girl forget that her mama had told her never to take off her clothes except for her husband, and then only in the haven of a shuttered bedroom. Certainly not on a grassy knoll at midday when the sun would heat bare skin with a fever.

Willie forced her eyes open. "Besides, Rosie had her baby last night."

"And a fine boy he is. Looks just like his pa did. A shame he didn't live to see him born. Ah, hell, go home, Willie."

Willie jerked the apron ties into a stiff bow. "Gertie left this morning to see her sick mother in Denver."

Harkness grimaced. "Gertie's got more sick relatives than any widow I know. And she always comes back to work wearing a sassy smile that doesn't belong on a travel-weary woman. I 'spect she's got a gentleman friend in Denver."

"She might not come back this time."

Harkness snorted then levered himself over the bar and produced a bottle and two glasses. Splashing the brew into each glass, he slid one over to Willie, eyeing her as if he suspected she was up to mischief. "I can run the place without my girls and you damned well know it."

Willie worked her glass between her fingers. "True. But without them, where's your draw?" She jerked her chin at the portrait. "She's not enough. Even for tired miners who can't see and travel-weary folk who've lost their way. And if the cowboys come through town off the pass as I suspect they might today, all biting at the bit to spend their hard-earned pay, you wouldn't want them to choose the Devil's Gold Saloon in Deadwood Run over the Silver Spur just because they believe the whiskey tastes sweeter when it's served by a woman."

"They want more from the women at the Devil's Gold than sweet whiskey. And they get it there."

"Some, maybe. But not all want what the Devil's Gold has to offer. Besides, Deadwood Run's another ten miles further off the pass, a bit far to ride if a man only wants to look at a face that doesn't grow whiskers."

"I don't know many cowboys that would be content with only that."

Willie smiled, a soft easy curve of her lips that made Jeremiah Dagwood Harkness blush every time she swung it on him. "Sure you do, Uncle Jeremiah. You just can't think of an argument."

"The hell I can't. And don't call me 'uncle' again, dammit. Quit your smiling. You still have to tell me the whole of it. Start talking. All of it. The truth this time."

Willie felt her smile fade a bit and wished Jeremiah Harkness hadn't known her since the day she fell off her pa's wagon over ten years ago and wandered into Harkness's saloon. He'd taken her home that day and became her Pa's best friend. Prosperity Gulch had been nothing more than a tent town then. "All of what? I'm here to help. We both know Prosperity Gulch needs the business. So does the Silver Spur."

"What about you?" Harkness waved his glass at the room. "A few turns around the floor, a buck here for a dance, two bucks there, especially if you smile." Harkness lifted a smug brow that inched higher in direct proportion to the deepening of Willie's flush. "Admit it. You're broke."

"That has nothing to do with—"

"I can loan you anything. All you had to do was ask."

"No." Heat pulsed through Willie in angry surges and she laid a hand on Harkness's arm as he dug into one pocket. "No, J.D., no loans."

Harkness set his jaw. "You call me 'uncle' easy enough because you feel so God almighty friendly with a man just about old enough to be your pa. But when you need me most you treat me like a damned stranger. You're as blind proud as your pa was."

Feeling every bit of her feisty nineteen years, she shoved her chin up at Harkness. "Fine. Then I'll leave."

"Dammit, Willie—" Harkness caught her arm as she attempted without success to maneuver her bustled, knife-pleated, obscenely narrow skirts around and brush past him. "You're better off in britches and boots. Suits your temper better, too. But I have to say you look damned pretty just the same. Mighty grown-up all of a sudden."

Willie squirmed. "I itch. I haven't worn this dress in years. It took me three hours to iron it." She fidgeted with the lace collar then drew a breath, feeling the fabric pull taut across her breasts. "It makes me look—young."

Harkness seemed to release a breath. "If the cowboys come through you're sure to make a small fortune."

Willie glanced up at him, hope sputtering to life. She tried very hard not to look as desperate as she felt, even though Jeremiah Harkness was the closest thing to a father she had right now. Even he could guess she was desperate enough to do just about anything, short of leaving Prosperity Gulch. Dressing up in her best clothes and high-heeled shoes and dancing with a few miners and cowboys was nothing. Even

Gramps understood that. No, they'd have to tie her up and gag her to get her out of town, starving and all. No McKenna or Thorne had ever abandoned a dream without one hell of a fight, even if the dream wasn't theirs but their pa's, even if chasing that silver dream had seen him dead and buried in his pine box just a year past, alongside her four brothers and a handful of unlucky miners.

What little money Richard Thorne hadn't invested in his quest for the big strike was now gone. Any sane person would pack up and move on to a town where enterprise flourished and money was being made hand over fist. A town like Dead-wood Run. Her pa hadn't, no matter the temptations or the trials. Then neither would she, no matter how desperate she became.

Six months ago she'd been desperate enough to pin all her hopes on a handsome East Coast businessman passing through. He'd promised to return to Prosperity Gulch and make her his wife. Six months later she'd realized his promise had been made after he'd taken her to that grassy knoll beside the river and laid her on the blanket he'd stowed in his shiny black buggy with the red-spoked wheels. The sun had been warm that October day, heating her skin when the tears of shame had spilled to her cheeks and splashed to her bosom. She'd been a fool to believe Brant Masters would keep his promise and come back for her, even the part about him staying on at the farm once he'd returned East to tidy up some business. She might not have believed him if Mama had still been with them.

Harkness slowly shook his head. "If any of those miners or cowboys even breathe wrong around you, by God, I'll—"

What was left of his promise was driven from him when Willie threw her arms around his neck and nearly toppled him from his bar stool with her vehemence. Harkness's huge hands caught her around the waist to keep his balance.

"Nothing's going to happen," she promised, pressing a

smacking kiss on Harkness's cheek. "I know you don't like trouble in your place. Not one glass will be broken."

"That's what your pa used to say when he'd bring your brothers in on Saturday nights and break damn near every glass. Hell, Willie, he'd have skinned me alive years ago if he knew one day I'd let his only daughter serve whiskey in my saloon."

Willie reached for her glass. "I took care of four wild brothers for over nine years by myself. I know how to handle whiskey and men." *Not all men,* a voice in her head whispered as she drained the whiskey. "Besides, I always have this." Bending, she slid the pleated hem of her dress up past her silk-stockinged knee and a frilly white lace garter. Tucked into the garter was a short-barreled Colt Peacemaker.

She grinned up at Harkness, expecting his nod of approval. After all, the man had taught her how to drink whiskey and shoot like a man to defend herself while her father and brothers were away at the mines all day and night. But his look was far from approving. His usual soft brown eyes were hard, fixed on the gun strapped to her thigh, and his squared jaw flexed with a rhythmic tick that typically boded trouble.

Willie's brows quivered. "You don't think I can get to it fast enough, is that it? Well, I can. These stockings are made of silk and they're very slippery. See, they come up clear to here—" She turned sideways, lifting her hem past the point where the stockings rode high around her thigh. "Damned uncomfortable things—"

She glanced up when Harkness's chair scraped against the wooden floor. With long, lumbering strides he moved down the length of the bar toward the back room.

"Where are you going?" she shouted at him, planting her hands on her waist. In reply she received a grunt. Shrugging, she turned to finish polishing glasses. Some men just couldn't abide an enterprising woman. Funny, but she'd never thought J. D. Harkness to be one of them.

* * *

The frontiersmen are freeing America from stifling European models and laying the groundwork for a flourishing democracy destined to climax in national greatness.

Sloan had penned those words in his leather-bound journal somewhere in the middle of the Atlantic aboard the steamer he'd boarded in Bristol. The words had flowed effortlessly from his pen, his theory fired by the tales told of the triumph and majesty of the great American West, and his thirst to discover and record it all on paper.

It seemed his theory had soared a bit high in the cushy and comfortable trappings of first-class stateroom accommodations, thousands of miles away. High, maybe, but he refused to believe it unrealistic. No matter that his pocket had been picked in New York and again in Omaha, both times by young boys who looked as if they hadn't seen a bath or a meal in weeks. No matter that he'd had to throw a man from a train to save himself from the same fate.

Triumph and majesty, innocence and spectacle. Not tragedy, wretchedness, guile. Pocketing his journal and drawing off his spectacles, Sloan stepped down from the wagon and squinted against the late-afternoon sun blasting from out of the snow-capped mountains, straight down Prosperity Gulch's single dirt street. On either side of the street, weather-beaten storefronts huddled together, looking as if their builders had slapped them up haphazardly in anticipation of disassembling them just as quickly. Only a handful of pedestrians lingered on the street. A livery stable marked the edge of town not fifty yards to the east. Beyond that the street seemed to run off into an endless sea of yellow grass.

At the farthest point west, a small building crouched. Three men on tipped-back chairs with boots braced on the hitching post loitered beneath a sign that read Jail. One dozed with his chin on his chest. The other two watched Sloan. Gun belts rode at their hips. Sunlight glinted off the star pinned to the burly man's vest.

"This is it, mister." The toothless wagon driver extended

a thumbless palm at Sloan and squinted up at him from beneath the dusty brim of his hat. The man looked and smelled as if his body played host to an appalling number of lice and fleas. At regular thirty-second intervals he let fly from his lips a stream of brown spittle that Sloan assumed was the remnants of whatever he jawed with lazy circular chews. Grimy fingers snapped closed over the coin Sloan pressed into his hand.

"Cain't yet figure why you English folk come all the way out here 'cept to hawk the railroad or shoot buffalo. Course, there's no more sport or danger or skill in shootin' a buffalo than in shootin' an ox. Ain't no tellin' the English folk that. They come fer the sport. But there ain't no buffalo no more in Prosperity Gulch, mister. Or men, neither. They's all been kilt."

"Where can I find accommodations?" Sloan asked.

The driver deepened his squint. "Nobody comes and stays in Prosperity Gulch 'cept the folks who's fool enough to live here. You sure you ain't lost, mister?"

"A hotel would suffice."

The driver scratched his head, glanced off down the street then gave a toothless smile. "Anythin' a man be wantin' he can git in a saloon. Try the Silver Spur. Couple paces up the street. Maybe you'll find a bed that don't squeak an' a saloon gal who don't mind bein' rode hard. Most don't mind atall, 'specially by a fine-lookin' mister like yerself."

Both men turned at the sudden rumble of horses' hooves, preceded by a wall of dust billowing down the street. Hoots and howls accompanied the revelry as a dozen or more men reined their mounts in just twenty paces up the street. Dismounting, several fired their guns skyward, startling the horses. Others lifted bottles to their lips, tipping their heads back to drain what remained of their brew. In a dust-choked, animalistic surge, they entered the double doors of one building.

"Cowboys is here," the driver said, wiry brows arching when yelps and yowls suddenly erupted from the establishment. He spat into the dust. "Gertie must be workin' tonight. That's one helluva fine lookin' woman. More than enough there ta keep a man warm at night. I first saw her at the Silver Spur after she lost her husband when the mine blew. She's right particular, though." The driver shook his head, as though amply impressed. "It ain't every night she takes a man up to her room." Slitted eyes flickered up and down over Sloan's travel-weary attire, settling on the stickpin at his throat. "You just might be the lucky one tonight, mister, in a room fulla hard-ridin' cowboys."

Something about the odd glitter in the man's eye stirred a faint wariness in Sloan. Tenderfoots provided great sport for frontiersmen. Sloan had to wonder how often strangers wandered down the sun-bitten streets of Prosperity Gulch.

Retrieving his valise from the wagon bed, he bid the driver good-day and headed for the Silver Spur. The sounds of revelry grew more pronounced the closer he came, bursting over him in a cloud of smoke and heat as he shoved open the saloon's double doors and stepped inside.

He paused to draw his top hat from his head, allowing his eyes to adjust to the dim lighting. The place was small. Every table bulged with cowboys and hard-bitten men, most engaged in card playing. The air hung thick and oppressively hot with the stench of smoke, drink and bodies gone stale. Candles dripped wax from two cheap gilt chandeliers hanging overhead. In one corner an old man hunched over a piano, struggling out a tinny tune. A cowboy jostled heavily against Sloan, belched, then stumbled out the door. Behind the bar a shiny-pated, massive barkeep in white shirt and suspenders splashed whiskey into an endless row of glasses, then turned and disappeared through a back door.

On the wall above the bar hung a garish portrait of a copper-haired woman reclining naked amidst lush grapevines. One leaf rode conveniently high between her plump thighs. Demure fingertips brushed at the base of her neck. A secretive curve graced her small lips, promising the world. Her belly was full, pink and smooth, her breasts like firm, ripe, overgrown white melons. Sloan's eyes narrowed on the large, rosy peaks and his belly tightened. A feast for any man's fantasy.

His blood seemed to heat.

He saw her then at the bar, carefully arranging full whiskey glasses on a tray. Gertie, copper haired as the lady in the portrait, peach skinned and luminous in a sheath of white. For some reason an unexpected jolt jarred through Sloan. Perhaps because she looked too young to have experienced widowhood already. The way she moved reminded him of a girl not yet fully a woman: the willowy, long-limbed, rangy sort of un-selfconscious movement common to prepubescent girls. Not to widows, or to women who took men up to their room for a hard ride on a squeaky bed because they had no other way to feed themselves.

Cornwall's brew houses were full of women whose husbands never returned from the mines or the sea. Scrub-cheeked, freckle-nosed women of all shapes, ages and sizes, yet all had the same dead look in their eyes, a look that made a parody of the seductive words they whispered in a man's ear and the breast they offered for him to fondle, all to lure him to their bed for a few shillings.

Sloan had become a champion for those forgotten miners' widows. The stipend Cambridge sent him for his contributions to their publications had retired many a widows' debt on her brew house and freed them of their servitude to the mine own-ers. Sloan had come to know those women well enough to recognize that Gertie was not one of their lot. At least not yet.

She turned from the bar, tray balanced in her hands, hair sliding from the knot on top of her head. She focused on the whiskey sloshing out of the glasses with eyes uncommonly large and uniquely slanted. Her tongue peeked out of one cor-ner of her mouth as she attempted to maneuver among the tables. The bustle seemed to be causing her some navigational problems. The dress was all wrong—high-collared, rose-sprigged, virginal white, at least one size too small. Sloan had

seen dresses like that several fashion-years before on girls going to church in London.

Sloan watched her hips swing around one cowboy's chair.
Uncomfortable though she might be in her clothes, she possessed a fluidity of movement uncommon to most young
women. In that dress she looked like a beautifully tapered
white lily.

A subtle fullness settled deep in his loins.

She lifted the tray over her head and turned sideways to
shimmy through a narrow path between tables. The movement,
unconscious as Sloan was certain it was, offered up her more
visible assets like a feast to a roomful of starving men. Every
eye in the place seemed to rivet on her. A sudden hush descended over the room, save for the piano's off-key tune.

A seated cowboy turned, licked the spittle from his lips and
ogled her bosom with a lascivious intent that fired a long-
dormant but staggering fury in Sloan. He took a step, watching
the cowboy's dirty hands.

Another cowboy slid his chair into Gertie's path, trapping
her with the tray balanced above her head. Her smile cut like
a knife through Sloan. It was the smile of a child, a guileless,
slightly mischievous smile that had no place in the Silver Spur
around these men. She belonged in a sun-dappled, tightly
sealed parlor with all the other virgins of the world, working
a needle through cloth and dreaming of the noble man who
would love her.

The first cowboy rose from his chair, his lean, muscular
body not a hairbreadth from Gertie's. Narrow hips jutting,
broad chest straining at his shirt, he braced his muscled thighs
wide and poised his sinewy, sun-hardened arms to crush
around her. Sloan could smell the man's thoughts. Those
slitted eyes had already stripped Gertie of her sheath and laid
her on that squeaky bed.

Sloan moved through space without volition or thought to
consequences. All he could see was Gertie turning in profile
to face the cowboy. Her eyes widened as he spoke to her and

realization swept over her. Her lips parted in silent protest.
She wasn't strong enough to defend herself against a man gone
rabid with need. His cohorts would cheer him on. She had
only one champion in this room.

Shoving a cowboy from his path, Sloan shouldered between
two others and then he burst upon them.

Gertie's head snapped around. Her gaze froze him midstride. He saw the helplessness in the quiver of her brows, the
desperation in the heightened color in her cheeks. He knew
only that the upward curve of her breasts brushed against the
cowboy's chest with her breaths.

"Madam Gertie," he rumbled as he surged past her, "I will
handle this matter for you. Step aside."

"But—"

The cowboy's eyes met Sloan's long enough to register the
challenge issued. But his fingertips got no further than his gun
belt. With a lightning-quick slice of his hand Sloan slapped
the cowboy's trigger hand away, blocked a wild punch with
his forearm and easily ducked another. In two strides he drove
the cowboy back against the table and the table up against the
wall. The cowboy raised his hands beside his ears in wide-
eyed, dumbfounded surrender.

"I jest asked her ta dance, mister," the cowboy sputtered.
"Ain't no laws against dancin' in a public place."

Sloan shoved his nose an inch from the cowboy's. "Is that
what you call it here? Where I come from, we call it something
else, and we conduct it privately. I doubt very much the lady
would have consented to what you suggested."

"The hell she didn't. I was gonna give her two dollars!"

Sloan stared at the man as the grumbles of agreement rippled through the crowd. He turned and found Gertie standing
directly at his back. Hands on her hips, one brow arched with
disdain, she didn't look the least bit grateful for his interven-
tion and saving of the day. She looked…as if he'd muddled
her plans.

"You don't know what you're doing," Sloan said, suddenly

very much aware that he towered over her and that the air seemed to grow instantly thicker between them. And hotter. Her skin was of the most astonishing shade of warm apricot.

Her emerald eyes dropped to his tailored topcoat, then narrowed on the stickpin at his neck. Suspicion lurked in her voice. "Who are you?"

He found himself watching the slow descent of one thick copper curl onto her shoulder. "Sloan Devlin, madam, late of—"

"You're from the railroad." An icy shadow fell over her features.

"Indeed, I came from—"

"Get the hell out."

He bit off his reply as Gertie turned abruptly and made her way through the swarm of men. Sloan's attempt to follow was instantly thwarted by the bulging chest of one particularly foul smelling man with only a handful of teeth to register his sneer. Sloan set his jaw wearily. "Don't make me move you."

"D'ya hear that, fellas?" The man spread his sausage legs wide and punched one fist into his palm. "This gussied-up railroad gent says he's gonna move ol' Reuben. Better take off yer fancy coat, railroad gent. Don't wanna mess up yer Sunday best with yer blood."

"No chance of that." Sloan's eyes slid over the man's shoulder. Gertie stood at the bar, arranging whiskey glasses on a tray. Another young cowboy stood at her side, feasting on her every movement.

Oddly enough, none of the brew-house maids he'd championed had ever rejected his help so recklessly, so defiantly, so damned foolishly. Virgins couldn't afford to.

"Leave him be, Reuben," a leathered old man wheezed from one table nearby. "He ain't even got a gun."

A chorus of jeers went up. Two men began shoving at each other. Several others exchanged heated words. Someone stuck the old man's nose into a glass of whiskey.

"My wife run away last year with one of them fancy railroad gents came through after the mine blew," Reuben snarled. "Left me with four kids an' her own ma who cain't even cook. I been lookin' fer revenge ever since."

"A bath might have served you better," Sloan replied, attempting to shoulder past. Reuben shoved him in the chest. Sloan stood his ground and met the man's bleary but antagonistic gaze. Sloth, filth and a marked penchant for fighting. Nothing encouraging to be found so far in Prosperity Gulch, save for Gertie. A peculiar, almost overwhelming desire to talk to her took hold of him.

"I don't want any trouble," Sloan said. "Let me pass."

Reuben stepped from his path with a travesty of a bow. "Whatever you say, fancy gent."

Sloan took two steps and realized his mistake an instant too late. He'd allowed distraction to get the better of him only once before, and a bullet meant for him had found his father. He thought he'd learned that lesson well. Apparently not. Reuben put all his weight behind a punch that caught Sloan in his ribs and drove the breath from him. Sloan doubled over, spun to the left and swung his left leg in a blinding arc into the side of Reuben's thick skull. Like a mighty oak felled by the single stroke of an ax, Reuben toppled to the floor.

"I didn't want to do that," Sloan muttered, stepping past the man's motionless body, one arm pressed to his ribs. It was then that Sloan realized every man in the place was engaged in a fistfight. He stepped over one fallen cowboy, ducked as a chair flew past, and narrowly missed being crashed over the head with a whiskey bottle. Fists met flesh everywhere he looked. Blood spurted. Curses spewed. And above it all the piano belched out its gay tune as if playing to a room full of civilized people.

He made his way to the bar. Gertie had disappeared. His eyes flickered to the stairs. She wouldn't have gone up there with that young cowboy...or had she?

The shiny-headed barkeep met him in front of the bar, ham-like hands braced on his hips. He was a formidable-looking man, powerfully built, but the glint in his eyes revealed far more than a lust for a bloody fight. There was something distinctly possessive in the man's stance, a protectiveness that extended beyond the tables and chairs in the place. Sloan was fairly certain the man didn't easily lose his temper.

"Where is she?" Sloan asked.

"You're goin' nowhere but out that door, mister. And you can take your fancy fightin' with you. It won't do you any good against a Smith and Wesson."

"We've no quarrel between us. Where is she?"

"You leavin' or do I get my rifle?"

"I want to talk to her."

"I'm going to start counting, mister."

"Sloan Devlin's the name, late of—"

The man moved one step closer. "If you don't leave my place, I'll kill you."

"Yes," Sloan said, looking deep into the man's eyes. "I believe you would." Again his eyes shot to the stairs. "I'm leaving. Just tell me, is she up there alone?"

A growl came up from the man's broad chest, bursting from his lips in a bellow of rage. And then Sloan knew beyond a doubt that this giant was deeply in love with the reckless Miss Gertie. A part of him must have understood that, must have forgiven him his vulnerability, because he didn't strike out when the man clamped his fists onto Sloan's shirtfront and shoved his face close.

"She's never been up those stairs with a man, mister," he snarled. "And she never will, least of all with another fine-looking, smooth-talking gent who'll give her nothing but empty promises and another broken heart." The man released Sloan and rubbed an unsteady hand over his brow. The creases around his eyes seemed to deepen and the glitter of rage faded as he glanced around his saloon. "Now get the hell out of my place."

With a curt incline of his head, Sloan tugged his topcoat smooth, turned on his heel and maneuvered his way to the

saloon's double-doored entrance, retrieving his valise along
the way. As he stepped into the late-afternoon sunlight he
passed the bandy-legged wagon driver who'd pressed his face
up against the saloon's front window and worked his jaw in
a circular motion.

Sloan had just stepped onto the wooden boardwalk opposite
the saloon when gunfire exploded through the Silver Spur. A
moment later two cowboys crashed through the beveled glass
front door, spraying the street with tiny shards.

An odd hush fell over the saloon and the street. Even the
piano fell silent. One by one the cowboys crept out into the
street, some rubbing bruised jaws, others limping, most with
blood streaming from flesh newly laid open. Sloan leaned a
shoulder against the corner of one building, drew his journal
from his valise and flipped it open. He squinted out into the
street as the saloon owner emerged from the Silver Spur with
a long-barreled rifle.

Sloan's gaze ventured up, drawn to the rooms above the
saloon. At the windows, white lace curtains stirred in the soft
breeze. The curtains hung motionless now, like the dust hanging heavy and still over the street. There was no breeze to be
found. Lace at a window would stir if someone moved past
them.

He glanced down at the journal and wrote, *Women allow
themselves the privilege of a broken heart only once. After
that, they never fully part with it again.*

Chapter Two

"**Y**ou from the *Independent?*"

Sloan snapped his journal closed and glanced over his spectacles at the man standing at his elbow. The fellow jerked his eyes from Sloan's journal but there was no apology in his gaze, no chagrin in the set of his jaw beneath his sweeping black mustache. There was also no gun belt around his waist, just a black walking stick in one hand. He wore a starched white shirt and black trousers common to men of decidedly civilized occupations. Sloan found himself taking an immediate liking to him despite his palpable animosity.

"No news in Deadwood Run today, eh?" The fellow eyed Sloan with increasing suspicion, particularly the stickpin at his throat. "Or you fellas run out of all those epithets and insults you've been hurling at us? I've been called a loathsome creature one time too many by that louse you call an editor over there." The man jerked his chin at Sloan's journal. "I'll tell you right now, mister, there's room in this town for only one newspaper and that's the *Lucky Miner.*"

"They've been lucky then," Sloan said, folding his spectacles into his pocket and tucking his journal under his arm.

The man snorted and waved an arm at the motley collection of men lingering on the street. "Where'd you hear that? The miners of this town do nothing night and day except drink fiery liquids and indulge in profane language. Sure, the miner you see today loves whiskey, cards and women, just like the cowboys. But compared to the forty-niner of California, or the fifty-niner of Colorado, he's a hollow mockery." The man frowned at Sloan. "And you can quote me on that. It'd be the first time fancy didn't get the upper hand of fact in the *Independent*."

"A common malady when there's a dearth of news." Sloan watched the color creep from the man's wing collar. "Truthfulness is not the hallmark of frontier journalism, no matter the paper."

The newspaperman puffed up his chest. "You give folks what they want to read if you don't intend to close up shop. Let's just say most editors in these parts have become masters of the exaggerated news story. Based on the facts, of course."

"Of course."

"Hell, about a year ago some poor fella from back East came through town, muttering something about the Indians he'd seen east of here. By the time he'd driven to the other edge of town I'd put his wagon through an Indian fight that to this day has no parallel in history. Folks liked it well enough."

"It's a wonder they didn't all flee town," Sloan said.

The newspaperman looked squarely at Sloan. "Folks here aren't afraid of Indians. They're scared of one thing, and that's being driven off their land by the railroad. They didn't knuckle under ten years ago when the railroad said there'd be no town without a rail line through here, and they won't now. Course, you know all about that, don't you? The Union Pacific's used the *Independent* for spreading its propaganda for years."

"I'm not from any newspaper," Sloan said, extending his hand to the newspaperman. "Sloan Devlin, late of Cornwall, England."

"Lansky," the man said after a moment's hesitation, pumping Sloan's hand. "Tom Lansky. Editor and proprietor of the *Lucky Miner*. That's a damned fine set of Sunday bests you've got on there. You must be one of those orators who travels around spreading the word about politics and the finer things of life. Funny, but I took you for a writer. Only writers carry a pencil and a journal in their finest coat pocket.''

Sloan's lips curved in a rare smile. "I'm no orator. And as far as I know carrying a pencil and journal never qualified a man to think he had something worth writing about. Or that anyone might care to read it. I've found it's not the desire to put words on paper that makes a man a writer, but the difference he can make by doing it, the pleasure he brings to his readers.''

Lansky grunted. "Whenever people can learn to walk on their eyebrows, balance ladders on their chins and climb to the top of them will an editor be found who can give pleasure alike to rich and poor, honest and false, respectable and low. I'm just a poor fella who empties his brain to fill his stomach.''

"Don't underestimate the power of the printed word," Sloan said, flipping open his journal where he'd tucked a folded handbill. He snapped it open. "This is only one brochure that I encountered in New York. And all of it enticing people westward to make their fortune. They tell a man to come, rush, hurry, don't wait for anything to buy lots, sight unseen. I visited one of these prophetic cities just outside of Omaha, fortunate as it was to have a depot. I found that this city of grand houses and shady trees contained not a single human habitation, and the only shade to be had was that thrown by the stakes pounded into the dry dirt. It was a paradise, lacking only water and a larger measure of good society. A fortune is being made, but not by the frontiersmen.''

"It's a story, all right, but if you're looking to make a big difference somewhere, you'd best go on back to England while there's still no Union Pacific buying up all the land there.''

"There's nothing for me in England at the moment.''

Lansky squinted up at him. "You looking to stay on?''

"If I find good enough reason.''

"Fine. You've got one. I'm offering you a job. Editorial

column every couple of days. Anything you want to write about. Stir things up a bit. If there's a town bleeding for a champion, it's Prosperity Gulch."

Sloan squinted out into the sun-bitten street where only a handful of people meandered past. Set against the majesty of the snowcapped mountains, the town huddled like a shriveled old man. *Leave it alone...stay a few days...move on....* "How many people live here?"

"A hundred, give or take, though folks keep to their homes when the cowboys come through. Twice that number called the place home a year ago before the Lucky Cuss mine blew. The dirt was still fresh on the graves when the railroad men rode into town waving ready cash. Guess they thought fifty cents on the dollar for land would sound good to widows with children. Now we got the damned vigilantes trying to burn everybody out."

Sloan glanced sharply at Lansky. "The widows?"

"Everybody. They've come a good handful of times in the dead of night. Torched Widow Gray's house and barn and shot all her cows and pigs. The only reason she was spared was because she had the good sense to hide in her hope chest. It helps that the Widow Gray's a small woman. She sold out two days later. A good twenty more followed her the next day."

"Do these vigilantes work for the railroad?"

Lansky shrugged. "You tell me."

"It's become a matter of pride," Sloan muttered, half to himself, remembering the tinner's immovable pride in the face of the powerful mine owners. "Pride more than the land."

"Damned straight. Of course there's some miners who still think they're going to strike that big vein in the South Platte River. There's a group of them determined to find it, no matter what the railroad does to try to run them out. Some folks think the railroad men know all about that big vein and are hoping to get the land cheap before the strike and lay their track right through town. Those folks are sitting tight, thinking their land values will triple then. Others still believe they can make their livelihood in Prosperity Gulch, strike or no strike. Some are afraid to sell now, thinking they'll get ambushed by the miners before they can get out of town, if the vigilantes don't get them first.''

"What about the mine that blew?"

"It's common knowledge the owner was a fool. Had too much charge with him one day and she blew. Killed him, his four boys, handful of other men. There's been nothing there for years. I'll tell you, though, no matter who you talk to, tempers are running high. There's a lawlessness in the air, Devlin. I can smell it. And the victims are the common folk, the folks who've sunk their lifeblood and their savings into land, homes and businesses.''

Proud, angry and desperately in need of rallying around a common cause if they were to stand a chance against a foe like the powerful Union Pacific and its rogue vigilantes. The town needed a heralding cry, and what better than the newspaper to corral tempers and focus energies?

"Where can I find a hotel?"

Lansky's lips jerked into a smile. "You'll find the softest bed and the best cooking at Willie Thorne's boardinghouse. Second farm on the right about a mile west of town. I'll tell you what. I'll pay you fifty cents for every column—''

"I don't want your money, Lansky."

"Whatever you say, Devlin. You think about my offer."

"I plan to." Sloan picked up his valise and turned east along the boardwalk.

"Hey, Devlin, Willie's place is due west. Where are you going?"

"To buy a horse."

"Get yourself a breastplate while you're at it. I ask only that my editors be responsible for defending themselves against folks who don't like what you have to say in the paper. And there's bound to be some. Last editor I had was horse-whipped and run out of town by a fella for something he wrote about the fella's wife. Something about her dimensions giving her the appearance of an ambulatory cotton bale. Wouldn't hurt to oil up your gun. You just might need it."

"I'll remember that," Sloan said, turning on his heel and heading for the livery.

The ax blade whizzed through the air then cleaved into the log, cleanly splitting the wood into pieces that would fit neatly into the stove. Willie tossed the pieces onto a pile that reached to her knees then hoisted another log. Taking up her ax, she aimed, drew a breath, swung the ax and drove it into the log.

"Fancy man," she hissed through her teeth, swiping a forearm over her brow then tossing the split wood onto the pile. "Gussied up and dandified. Damned shiny-toed shoes and pleated trousers. Too damned tall for decency—"

Again she bent, lifted a heavy log and braced it against her belly as she slid it atop the wide tree stump she used for wood chopping. Smacking her hands clean against her blue-denimed hips, she braced her boots wide, took up her ax and swung it in a powerful arc.

The last time she'd looked so far up into a man's clean-shaven face had been seven months ago when she'd all but run over Brant Masters with her wagon. He'd been wearing the same sort of finely made coat and trousers, the same high linen collar. He'd even stuck one of those jewel-headed pins into his tie and his shoes were shiny and new. Now that she thought about it, Brant had smelled clean and spicy, a scent that had made her knees go wobbly and her belly flutter every time he passed within six inches of her. That scent had seemed to fill her nostrils for weeks after he went back East.

The fancy English gent had smelled like that. Refined. Educated. Thinking himself too good for the likes of Prosperity Gulch. But the English railroad gent's eyes weren't dark and sparkling like Brant's. They were icy blue, shot through with silver, and seemed as deep as she imagined an ocean could be. Against the midnight blue-black of his hair they were startling.

Willie threw the wood aside. "Railroad weasel."

"The man sure could fight."

Willie glanced up, pushed her hat back on her head and met Gramps's cockeyed grin with a puff that blew the stray wisps of hair off her forehead. "I don't know who you're talking about, Gramps." She bent to retrieve another log.

"Same fella you've been grumblin' about, Willie-girl. That English gent."

Willie swatted at a mosquito and grimaced in reply.

"You're cuttin' enough wood for the whole damned town."

"I'm mad." She swung the ax high.

"Thought so."

The log cracked into three pieces. "What's he want?"

"Hard to tell."

Willie flung the wood aside with a snort. "I'll tell you what he wants. He wants to stir up trouble. Divide and conquer, like Pa used to say. He's no better than the vigilantes. Just a fancy, dandified version. Instead of torches and threats, he uses that accent and his fine suit coat with the velvet cuffs and fancy fighting methods. He might not even be from England. He could be some out-of-work actor from New York sent by those men at the Union Pacific. If you ask me, I say he's a fraud. At the very least he's up to no good."

"Could be." Gramps tipped his broad-brimmed hat back on his head and leaned heavily on his cane. "Course, I never seen fightin' like that. Reuben had to be carried out of the Silver Spur. I heard him mumblin' somethin' about forgettin' about revenge for the time bein'."

"See there?" Willie planted her hands on her hips, lips pursing with her mounting indignation. "His scheme is working already. Even Reuben's ready to give up the fight. It didn't take burning his house down. Just one kick to the side of his head." She set her jaw and stared out into the woods that fringed her farm on three sides. The sun had just disappeared behind the mountains, throwing her land into sudden shadow. The air grew instantly cooler. "Maybe he'll just move on."

"Maybe he won't."

Willie glanced sharply at Gramps, recognizing the admonition in his weathered stare. At times he looked so much like her pa her heart squeezed in her chest. Like her pa, Gramps was fashioned of the long, rangy limbs, broad shoulders and proud carriage common to generations of Thornes. Her brothers had all inherited the same tall, wiry build, the dark, stern features, and all the blind determination and pride that went along with being a Thorne. And though Willie had been graced with an abundance of the Thorne arrogance and pride, only she bore the marks of a true McKenna: the heavy mass of copper gold hair and a body of such startling womanly proportions she could barely fit into the Levi's and shirt she'd worn just a year before.

"Your mama ever say anythin' to you about gettin' more bees with honey than with vinegar?"

Willie gaped at Gramps. "You're asking me to be friendly with that…that…"

"You sound like your pa, chock-full of damned fool's pride."

"Pa was no fool," Willie retorted. "He stood up for what he believed in—his land, his family and his dream to make Prosperity Gulch a thriving town without the help of any double-crossing railroad that wanted him to pay for the privilege of the track coming through town. So they laid track through Deadwood Run and thought they'd kill off Prosperity Gulch by doing it. But they didn't, not ten years ago, and not now.

"Pa had vision, Gramps. It was enough to rally several hundred people around his cause and keep Prosperity Gulch thriving. He never lost sight of that, no matter who tried to stop him. And he would never have turned coat and pasted on a smile for a man he didn't trust just because doing so would have put money in his pocket or a meal on his table for a few more days. And neither will I, even if I have to dance every night with cowboys to do it."

Gramps narrowed his eyes on the mountains to the west.

"If your pa had to do it over, he'd have kept his dreams to himself and your mama in her house in Illinois where she belonged. He wouldn't have dragged her out into a wasteland a hundred miles from nowhere, and left her alone night and day while he worked in that mine. When the sickness came she didn't have the spirit to fight it off. Not every dream should be chased."

Willie's gloved fingers tightened around the ax handle. Even now grief wrapped like invisible ropes around her and tightened, compressing her lungs in her chest. "I won't give up on his dream, Gramps," she said, her voice husky with emotion. "If I do, if Prosperity Gulch sells out to the railroad my pa fought for so long, he'll have died for nothing, and my brothers with him."

Gramps looked hard at her with the unwavering, grizzled stare that probed right to her soul. "You never were half as selfish as your pa. Are you plannin' to waste your youth tendin' to an old man and choppin' wood and chasin' vigilantes out of town? Or are you waitin' for Brant Masters and all his promises to come ridin' down the lane in that black buggy of his?"

Willie stiffened, knowing by the glint in Gramps's eyes that her cheeks had turned a traitorous red. Still, admitting naiveté was not something even an unselfish Thorne would find easy to do. "I've completely forgotten about him," she said, a little too breezily. "Too busy, I guess."

"Yep. We're damned busy out here on the farm." Gramps rested one bony elbow on a fence post and squinted at the farmhouse in the distance over an unsown field swaying with tall grass. "Not a boarder to be had since Brant last propped his shiny boots on your kitchen table and watched you scrub your floors. Yep. You're too damned busy to remember all that."

Willie felt her shoulders droop and the fight seep out of her. Gramps saw too blasted much. Just like her pa always had.

"Well, I'll be damned."

Willie glanced sharply at Gramps then turned, her gaze following Gramps's. The weather-beaten house huddled among tall sycamores, all thrown into impenetrable shadow. Still, as her eyes strained into the darkness, Willie was almost certain a deeper shadow moved beside the house. Her fingers reached for her short-barreled Peacemaker stuffed into the back waistband of her Levi's. "How many?"

"Just one. You won't need your gun."

Willie glanced at Gramps, even as she drew the Peacemaker into her hand and slipped her finger over the trigger. "You'd best go get the repeating rifle. We don't know his business."

"Put the gun away," Gramps softly said.

"Put the gun away?"

"Yes."

"Gramps—"

"Willie-girl, I think you got yourself a boarder."

"A boarder—?" A sudden warmth spilled through her and brought a smile bursting from her lips. "How can you be sure?" She turned. The man had turned from the house and was leading his horse through the field of grass toward them. Her heart almost burst from her chest. "It's Bran—" The name stuck in her throat and her heart plummeted. Chagrin flooded over her, followed by a deeply felt contempt for the part of her that still clung to feeble dreams spun by untrustworthy men.

As much as that part of her might wish otherwise, she didn't recognize the stranger's fluid gait, the breadth of his shoulders or the tall black hat he wore. His coat was long and tailored, with tails that flapped when he walked. He was so tall the grass that caught Willie thigh high reached only to his knees. His legs cleaved through the grass with an animalistic grace, so different from the rough-and-tumble pack of hard-fighting, hard-drinking brothers she'd shared her first eighteen years with.

Something began to stir in her the closer the stranger came, but it wasn't fear. Though shadow hid his features, there was a disturbing familiarity about him. Something in the set of his shoulders, the way he moved.

"Oh, no," she whispered, and lifted her gun.

The young man Sloan assumed was Willie looked up at him from under the shadow of his oversized hat and shoved his gun at him.

"Stop right there, fancy man." A boy, not a man. The voice was pitched far too high and carried a huskiness common to pubescent youths. Sloan drew up short, realizing a youth's inexperience and exuberance often got the better of good sense, particularly when that youth gripped a gun in his hand, a remarkably steady hand that bespoke of familiarity. Beside the boy, a rangy old man watched Sloan with an odd glint in his eye.

"Willie Thorne?" Sloan said.

"You got that right, fancy man." A youth, certainly not a man, with hips and thighs still so rounded with baby fat his waist looked unusually narrow. Sloan deepened his gaze. Something wasn't right. Youths were narrow chested, full stomached. This boy's white shirt stretched taut where Sloan least expected it to, directly at midchest. Sloan stared at the fullness there and felt heavy heat fill his loins.

Beneath the shadow of the hat, full pink lips parted in a grim version of a smile. Sloan went instantly, uncomfortably rigid. No woman in his experience had ever looked so blatantly, arousingly female.

For an instant Sloan thought of his father's Oriental man-servant Azato, who had spent years developing mind-over-body principles in Sloan since the day he'd first come to Devlin Manor as part of the cargo his father had acquired on a voyage to the Orient when Sloan was only a boy. These principles demanded that Sloan resist all physical pain and all adversity in his effort to achieve the art of mystical self-defense. Without question, a master of these techniques should be able to resist a woman's best efforts.

Still, looking at the amply proportioned Willie Thorne, Sloan couldn't help but wonder if even Azato would have given as much thought to being mighty if women the world over began to pour themselves into men's trousers and skimpy shirts.

The girl took several steps toward him, braced her boots wide and leveled the gun at his chest. "Get the hell off my land, mister."

Sloan's gaze shot past her to the pile of split wood and the ax protruding out of a stump. It looked as if it had been solidly plunged there by a strong hand. The bearded old man looked incapable of lifting the ax, much less his cane. The farmhouse had been deserted when Sloan had peeked through one lace-draped window. Only two cups sat on a table freshly cleared of dinner plates. She obviously lived alone with the old man. Alone, she tended to the farm, split the wood, mended the fences.

Admiration stirred in Sloan, despite the beleaguered look of the place. And in that instant she embodied struggle and triumph, desire and adversity, every paradox he'd hoped to find on his journey. He wished she'd take off her hat so he could see her eyes and her hair. "I'm looking for accommodations, Miss—"

The gun jerked. "Don't—move," she said slowly, taking another step. "And don't try any of those fancy fighting maneuvers. I'm a quicker shot than Reuben Grimes. And a hell of a lot more accurate. I could shoot that stickpin right out of your collar." She thrust her chin at him, a slightly clefted, determined chin. Her lips pursed with disdain, and then he knew. He should have known the moment he spotted her across the field of grass simply by the peculiar reaction she stirred in him.

Gertie. Willie. Something didn't fit. Without question, she was at home here on this run-down farm, in her trousers and boots, ax in hand and dirt up to her elbows. At the saloon, he'd sensed a helplessness in her, a distinct undercurrent of discomfort despite her best efforts to show otherwise.

Sloan had seen enough adversity in his life to know that desperation led many down a path that they wouldn't typically choose. All desperate people had a price, one Sloan was not above finding, particularly if it would keep her out of the saloon and away from cowboys with itchy hands.

"What do you want for a room?" he asked, reaching into his trouser pocket and withdrawing the fat wad of bills he'd won on the train. He thumbed off several bills and glanced up at her. She was staring at his hand with such intensity he could almost hear her tallying all that his money would buy: the paint for the house, a new fence, even a plow to turn this field of grass into wheat or corn. Perhaps something as simple as food. Or a dress that fit her properly.

The old man narrowed his eyes. Sloan didn't blame them for not trusting him. But only a fool would refuse help when in such need.

"Put your money away, fancy man. I've no rooms to let you."

Sloan heard his teeth click. Bloody impertinent female. Quickly he recalled the price of meals and lodging in New York, at the grand and luxurious American Hotel. And then he doubled it. "Fifty dollars a day for a room and the pleasure of your company at meals."

The gun wavered. Her skin grew unearthly pale. She tipped back her hat and blinked at him with eyes as wide and fathomless as the sea beyond Cornwall's far western headlands. "You're bribing me," she said, her voice chilled. "You can't do that."

"Seventy-five," he said softly. "Do you cook, Willie?"

"Better than her mama could," the old man muttered under his breath.

Willie shot him a look that would have stopped an army.

The old man merely shrugged. "Your mama was a fine

cook, Willie-girl. Like I always say, a skillet and a pail of grease are the essentials to any recipe.''

Willie let out a wheezing breath. "State your business, fancy man."

"Sloan," he said, tipping up one corner of his mouth. Pocketing his money, he extended a black-gloved hand over the top of the gun. "Sloan Devlin, late of Cornwall, England."

She barely extended her fingers when Sloan leaned forward and enveloped her small hand in his. Her eyes briefly widened, deepening in color.

He expected to feel nothing through the fine leather of his gloves. After all, he'd spent his youth pounding his fists into tree trunks day after day to thickly callus his hands against pain or feeling. And yet he could feel the warmth of her, the pulse of her, the vital, womanly essence of her seeping through calluses and leather and skin. He relinquished it at the first tug of her fingers.

"I've come to see the elephant," Sloan said.

She seemed unimpressed, and her voice rang with contempt. "That's what all the English folk said when they came and shot the buffalo. Now there's nothing for them to shoot. Who sent you? Union Pacific? Kansas Pacific? A couple years back some fancy English gent was following the Kansas Pacific's survey parties, drawing pictures. Maybe you're one of them. Or are you Denver Pacific?"

"I came by rail," he replied, "and shared several games of poker with some fellows from the Union Pacific. But that's the extent of my association with the railroad."

Her eyes narrowed, as if she gave the idea of believing him some consideration. "You're a gambler."

His laugh rumbled from his chest. "Not on my luckiest day."

"You still haven't told me why you're here."

"I'm a writer."

"They pay writers good where you come from."

"No true writer writes for money."

"Then why do it?"

"I want to make a difference."

"Have you?"

"Not yet. At least not enough. I suppose that's why I'm here."

"To stir up trouble."

"I prefer to walk away from trouble."

"Good. The road back there leads all the way to Denver. Just point your nose west and start walking." She headed for her ax. For an instant, Sloan found himself staring at her backside. Women as lushly formed as Willie should have been legally banned from wearing men's trousers.

An odd compulsion to throw her over his shoulder swept over him. He took a step, tugged his dozing excuse for a horse behind him, then drew up as she swung the ax in an arc that stirred the air right in front of him. She'd set her jaw with grim determination. Sleek muscles strained in her bare forearms. A grunt came from her lips when the ax plunged into the log.

Sloan felt the tension mounting inside him. "How many nights will you spend in the Silver Spur to earn anything close to what I'm offering you for a single night's accommodations? A week? A month? All I'll ask from you is a smile every morning."

The ax whistled through the air, again keeping him at a good distance. Wood chips sprayed into the air.

"I don't trust strange men with velvet cuffs and shiny-toed shoes, Devlin."

Ah, the broken heart finally betrayed itself. So the thief of her heart hadn't been a cowboy. A gambler, perhaps?

Sloan glanced at the old man. "Is she typically this difficult?"

The old man spat into the ground. "Yep. I keep tellin' her she'd best get more likable if she's ever gonna find herself a husband."

"Reasonable would suffice for now," Sloan said, watching

the color creep up from her neck and up under the brim of her hat.

Willie plunged the ax blade into the stump, whirled and advanced on Sloan with hands braced on her hips and green eyes blazing. "Eighty-five a night, one week in advance, non-refundable. Meals, bed and outhouse privileges included."

"That's reasonable." Sloan pulled out the money and peeled off twelve crisp one-hundred dollar bills. "I'll pay for two weeks of services—" Just as she reached out to snatch the bills, he lifted them beyond her fingertips. She arched up after it, her eyes darting to his, and in them he saw desperation and blind hope all twisted up with pride. "And the pleasure of your company, of course," he murmured, startlingly aware of her in the most base physical sense. She stood just inches below him, emanating a womanly warmth, smelling of grass and mountains and freshly chopped wood.

Her brows quivered. "Whatever that means. I live here." Lightning quick she plucked the bills from his hand and, without counting them, tucked them inside the open neck of her shirt.

Sloan's mouth went instantly dry.

Again she turned to retrieve her ax but Sloan was much quicker this time, reaching around her and taking up the ax.

She angled her eyes at him and pursed her lips. "Give me that, Devlin, before you hurt yourself."

With one arm, Sloan lifted a log onto the stump. Bracing his legs, he glanced sideways at her and tossed her his horse's reins. "Stand back."

She didn't move. "I don't need your help, Devlin. I don't need any man."

"No," he murmured, looking directly into her eyes. "I don't believe you do. Now that we both understand that, stand back."

"I don't—"

Sloan swung the ax. Willie jumped back just as the ax plunged through the log, shattering it into five pieces. Sloan looked at Willie. She stared at the ax blade buried five inches deep in the stump then slowly looked up at Sloan. Her lips parted. Color bloomed into her cheeks. She looked like a rose bursting open beneath the sun.

"I—I'll take your horse to the barn," she said.

"Thank you."

She hesitated. "And I'll get you some dinner." She glanced at the old man, flushed a deeper crimson, then whirled around and strode toward the house.

Sloan watched her until the shadows swallowed her.

Chapter Three

The skillet slammed onto the hot stove. A chair scraped. A cupboard slammed. Butter sizzled in the skillet. Eggs cracked against the side of the pan—plop, plop, plop. Willie stared at the eggs bubbling in the butter and considered reaching for another. Her neck had hurt when she'd looked up and met Devlin's gaze square. He was taller than Brant by a good three inches, and seemed substantially thicker, despite the elegant drape of his fancy clothes. Brant had always taken three eggs each morning. She cracked another egg into the pan.

Satisfied, she turned to the peeled potatoes, took up her knife and whacked with an efficiency honed by years of serving up fried eggs and potatoes to four hulking brothers. Walt, Wynn, William and Wes. The knife lay idle against the chopping block as she glanced at the table, imagining them sitting there, dust covered, exhausted and ravenous.

Walt, the oldest, had always sat opposite Pa at the far end of the table, straddling his chair, his face stern. Somehow, even then, he must have sensed his tragic fate but he'd never let on, not even to Pa. Buried deep somewhere inside him he'd had other plans, dreams of his own that had nothing to do with the mine and silver and his father's dreams for Prosperity Gulch. Walt had the simpler dreams of a twenty-four-year-old man, dreams of being a husband to pretty blond Melissa Cutter and following her family out to California for a better life. A new start.

But Willie hadn't found all that out until the funeral, when Melissa had told her of Walt's dreams, and the tears had washed over her face without stopping.

Willie gritted her teeth against the burn of tears in her eyes. She wondered if Gramps had told Walt that all dreams shouldn't be chased. Walt always minded, even when he hadn't wanted to.

Willie reached for an onion. In a flurry of whacks she chopped the onion into superfine pieces. Wiping a forearm over her eyes, she swept the onion and potatoes into another skillet of bubbling butter then reached into the open neck of her shirt and retrieved the folded bills. Slowly she counted them, then counted them again, rubbing her fingertips over the crisp edges. She drew them to her nose. The bills smelled new, untainted.

Moving to the window, she lifted aside the red checked gingham and peered into the darkness gathering over the fields. Two dense shadows moved through the grass. She watched the taller of the two. Apprehension wriggled in her belly.

Sloan Devlin wanted something from her. No man handed over twelve hundred dollars without wanting something more than a bed and warm meals in return. They'd both known it. So why was she getting all jittery inside wondering what fancy-man Sloan Devlin wanted from her? Maybe because something about him reminded her of Brant Masters.

Boot heels thumped on the porch steps. One set of boot heels. And no scrape of a cane. Willie whirled from the window, lunged to the stove and shoved a wooden spatula into the pan of fried eggs just as the door creaked open. She stared at the eggs, working the spatula beneath each one as the door gently closed. The fine hairs along the back of her neck stood up.

Without looking over her shoulder, she jerked her head to the table. "Have a seat, Devlin. Coffee's in the pot."

His rumble of thanks seemed to shake the floorboards under her boots. Reaching for a plate, she felt a peculiar chagrin at the crack meandering through the fired stoneware, considered searching for one that wasn't cracked or chipped, then thought the better of it. Lifting the skillet, she swept the eggs onto the plate, followed that with the fried potatoes, then turned and set the plate on the table.

She glanced up at him through a fringe of loosened curls and felt a jar clear to her soul.

He stood behind a chair and watched her, his eyes mirroring the yellow glow of the single candle sitting on the table. His hair was sleek and short, combed close to his head from an arrow-straight part. For some reason, Willie felt as if he sucked all the air out of the room with his presence. He was oddly compelling and just a bit frightening. Willie was not a woman easily frightened.

He quirked one black brow. "I don't eat alone."

"You will tonight."

"The terms of our arrangement are specific regarding the pleasure of your company."

Willie felt her belly sink. "You mean at the table."

"Yes, and elsewhere, of course."

She swallowed. "Elsewhere." The word gurgled past her throat. There was only one elsewhere that she could think of when she looked up into his eyes. Without his coat, he seemed massive and possessed of an energy that seemed tightly reined. His voice was laced with the same seductive promise that Brant had used just before he'd pushed her back onto the soft grass. And his eyes bored into hers as if he had the power to read her mind and bend her thoughts to his will.

Or was she imagining it all? She swallowed, remembering how easily Devlin had driven the ax blade deep into the stump. Somehow she'd never expected that of a dandified gent wearing a tall silk hat and soft leather gloves.

She glanced at the open door at one end of the kitchen, the door leading to the bedroom that Sloan Devlin would occupy for at least two weeks. Fury and pride and every ounce of Thorne self-righteousness erupted within her. She'd made a mistake because of blind naiveté once. She wasn't about to again, no matter how desperate she was.

Holding out her hand, she loosened her grip on the crumpled bills and they fell to the table like dry leaves. "Take it. I don't want any of it. We have no agreement, Devlin. After you eat, get the hell out of my house."

Turning, she shoved a chair from her path, and would have fled her own house if he hadn't blocked her path. She stared at his embroidered burgundy silk vest.

"Wait," he said softly. "It's becoming increasingly obvious that you don't understand."

"I understand." She jerked her chin up at him so vehemently her tightly coiled hair sprang from its knot and fell down her back. "I might not have realized it at first because I was so—so—" *Desperate.* She set her teeth. "That doesn't matter, because I understand now, mister. I know damned well what you want and you're not going to get it here. Try the Devil's Gold Saloon in Deadwood Run. You can get a room and a half-dozen girls' company for a fraction of your twelve hundred dollars. And a damned better tasting meal to boot."

Devlin arched a brow. "What the devil would I do with a half-dozen women?"

Willie's face went instantly hot. "I—how the hell should I know? But the cowboys always talk about—" Her breath left her in a sharp spurt. "Never mind. Quit changing the subject."

"I don't believe I've ever spoken of pleasure and a half-dozen women in the same breath. You did. My dear girl, you've run far afield with this." He bent to look directly into her eyes. A hint of a smile curved his mouth and for some blasted reason Willie was tempted to believe every word he said. Up close, he looked less like a gentleman and more like a man who'd seen much in his life. He had a weathered, almost beaten look to his face. Much like her own father had.

"Odd as it might seem," he said, "I'm not after the pleasure of your company in my bed."

Suspicion narrowed her eyes and thrust her jaw out another fraction. "No man would ever admit that outright."

"No, I don't suppose they would. Underhanded methods suit some men far better. I'm pleased to say I know little of that. But, rest assured, if the notion ever struck me, I wouldn't use either money or underhanded methods."

"Or a grassy knoll," she murmured, flushing again when she realized she'd spoken her thoughts. Devlin was watching her with such sudden intensity she wanted to squirm. Instead she turned abruptly for the sink. "You'd best eat before it gets cold."

After a moment, the chair brushed against the floorboards. Had it not, she might have thought he still stood at her back. He moved as silently as a soft wind in leafless trees. Most men she'd known made constant noise, especially in a house, banging their way around furniture and through rooms and meals, devouring food and tidiness like a pack of wolves. Forks in constant clatter, glasses thudding, knives scraping on plates, all amidst a grunted sort of chewing. When they left, as suddenly as they'd come, the room seemed to expand again to allow fresh breezes.

"Willie."

She blinked and wondered how long she'd been staring out the window into the darkness. Her reflection in the windowpane suddenly jumped back at her. She looked...haunted.

She uncurled her fingers from the edge of the sink and plunged her arms into the water. "Did you need something?"

"Your name. Wilhelmina, isn't it?"

"I don't like it."

"It suits you."

Her mother had always said that. Loneliness suddenly crept into her heart. "My mother named me after her grandmother, the notorious Wilhelmina McKenna. According to family legend, she was an Irish hellion who birthed twelve children to three husbands, all of whom died of mysterious causes.''

"The children?"

"No, the husbands. My mother used to say I had Grandmother Wilhelmina's hair."

"A blessing, indeed." Something in his voice made Willie's hands go still in the water. She listened to the thumping of her pulse as he added, "You could have inherited her tragic legacy with men."

Swiftly Willie worked a rag against the bottom of the skillet. "It's too soon to say. I've never married."

Willie glanced at Devlin. He pushed back his chair and, with empty plate in hand, moved toward her. Her throat seemed to close up.

"Coffee?" she asked, turning away from him and snatching a rag from a wall peg. She moved around the table and reached for the coffeepot on the stove beside him.

"I'm in your way."

"No—you're not." She just hadn't wanted to move between him and the table to reach the stove. There was something oddly disturbing about being in close proximity with this man. Aware that he watched her and that he had guessed at her reason for avoiding him, she poured two cups and slid one toward him on the wooden counter. "I hope you like it strong and black."

"It seems de rigueur." He caught her quick glance over the rim of his cup. A disarming smile deepened the creases around his eyes. "Local custom. I haven't seen tea since I left the steamer in New York, and the only words spoken in this country after the word *coffee* are 'strong' and 'black.' I'm pleased to say there's remarkable variation in the taste. You outdo the Pullman Palace car, Wilhelmina."

She hesitated, pondered her pinkening cheeks, then lifted her chin. "That's no compliment."

"It should be. The berth in first-class cabin accommodations

aboard a Cunard steamer are less comfortable than the berth
in a Pullman Palace car. It seems Mr. Pullman has taken as
much care in the decorating and furnishing of his railcars as
French decorators do in decorating the dwellings of the very
rich. Were he up to dealing with the shoddily laid track in
England, Mr. Pullman could revolutionize railway travel there
and at the same time enrich himself beyond the dreams of
avarice.''

"Then he will. All Eastern capitalists want richness beyond
the dreams of avarice. All men do.''

"Not all men. To some, the ultimate rewards lie elsewhere.''

"Ultimate rewards begin to mean very little when food is
scarce. Noble dreams die swift deaths when there's no money
and no work. Just ask any miner.'' She stared up at him, realizing he was waiting for her to continue. Something about
him made her want to keep talking, as if what she said and
felt and thought was valid, worthwhile. And she wanted to
spew it all out for him, all the misery, the loneliness, the guilt
and the inevitable despair.

For one startling moment she knew a vulnerability that she
hadn't felt since the day her mother had died.

"I'll show you where you'll sleep,'' she said, her voice
taking on a chill. With head lifted, she led him to the front
bedroom as if she were Mr. Pullman himself, stopping just
outside the open doorway. Her first thought as she glanced
into the room was that Sloan Devlin's feet would hang off the
end of the bed.

"Breakfast is at six,'' she said as he leaned past her to peer
into the room. Pressing herself against the doorjamb, she drew
in her breath just as his sleeve brushed against her bare forearm. "Supper at one. Dinner at six. There's a water pump out
back for washing up.'' She stared at the back of his head
where a dark leather cord bound the thick length of his blue-
black hair. Unbound, she imagined it would fall past his shoulders.

He turned and faced her and her knees gave a sudden wobble. "Where do you and your grandfather sleep?"

Her eyes skittered across the kitchen to a shadowed corner and the narrow steps there. "I sleep upstairs. There's three bedrooms there. Gramps sleeps in his chair in the front room."

"You're alone here."

Damn his gently coaxing voice, smooth as warm honey. Brant's voice had been even smoother, when he'd wanted it to be.

She lifted her eyes to his and gripped the doorjamb at her back. "My mama died when I was ten. My pa and my brothers all went when the Lucky Cuss blew last year. Now it's just me and Gramps and Huck, the dog. And the boarders."

"Do you get many?"

"We get some." It wasn't a complete lie. They got a boarder every six months or so.

"People must not know what they're missing."

Something inside her went weak. Smooth as honey, just like Brant. So much like Brant and yet somehow so different. Hadn't she lingered just like this outside the room with Brant that first evening, mesmerized by his charm, captivated by his smile? Less than a week later she'd lain beneath him on the soft grass and watched him lean over her, blocking out all the sun.

Like a frightened rabbit she scooted past Devlin, tossing over her shoulder something about seeing to Gramps. Devlin's softly spoken "Good night, Wilhelmina" followed her out onto the porch and halfway across the yard before it leapt up into the starry sky and vanished.

Noble dreams die swift deaths when there's no money.

Sloan looked up from his journal and stared out into the moon-splashed darkness. The field of grass rippled like ocean waves in the milky moonlight, extending from the porch to a sweep of trees more than a mile out. Beyond that, rising from the earth like a majestic beast, loomed the blue-white peaks of the mountains. The moon seemed to hang just inches above the tallest peak. Sloan listened to the rustling of the grass, breathed in the scent of wildflowers and scanned the horizon from east to west before again lifting his pencil.

The senses are at once quickened and overpowered by the limitless space. Those who people these vast tracts of land should enjoy a freedom far better than that of a wanton breeze, balmy with perfume. I feel a deep longing that the thousands who earn a precarious livelihood in England by tilling the soil of their taskmasters and lords could somehow come to a place where the strength of their arms would win them a comfortable subsistence and would enable them to possess the land which yields them their daily bread. But here, too, noble dreams die.

He lifted his head and stared at a tree standing alone in the field. Its branches glowed with silvery light. What dreams remained unreachable for Wilhelmina Thorne? She was far too young to spend the rest of her life with a look of haunted longing in her eyes, far too compelling to live out her days here, a treasure hidden and undiscovered where the grass met the base of the mountains.

There was a loneliness about her that reminded him of the tinners' widows. But where despair would have found a comfortable home long ago grim determination resided. Willie was searching for something, something to squelch her discontent. He wondered what her broken heart had to do with it.

A dim light from above cast a sudden splash of gold onto the porch. Sloan looked up at the window and watched a slender shadow move behind sheer curtains. Above the rush of the grass he heard her humming, husky and low. The curtain billowed, whispered apart, and he glimpsed pale womanly roundness and white skin as she leaned near the window, unaware.

The curtain stilled, but her shadow remained. Her humming seemed to swell and fill the air. Sloan felt his breath compress in his lungs as the breeze again stirred through the curtains.

He saw a splash of white lace, a cascade of copper curls and then the lamp was snuffed.

He didn't realize he'd held his breath until it left him in a wheeze. Despite the cool breeze, perspiration suddenly dotted his forehead. He swept his palm through his hair then stood, pencil and journal gripped in one hand. He pondered the darkness. His room had smelled like citrus, the sheets like hot sun and starch. He wondered if Willie's room smelled the same.

A young heart was broken on a grassy knoll in Prosperity Gulch.

Turning, he climbed the creaking porch steps to his room.

Willie awoke before the cock crowed, when dawn had barely lightened the night's mantle a shade. Toes curling against the chill of the planks, she scooted from her bed, moved to the window and pushed the curtain aside. Something besides the creeping of dawn had awakened her. Her eyes probed the gloom. Her ears strained above the predawn silence. The moon had long disappeared over the mountains. Stars still hung low in the sky, winking at the morning. All was as it should be. Her eyes shifted and sought movement among the shadows.

She saw him the instant she heard him. Or was it him? Something moved in the far corner of the field where she'd chopped wood. A man, tall and shirtless, stood motionless at the edge of the woods, staring out into the trees. But the sound echoing out over the valley and up into the trees was inhuman, primal, savage. Like the haunting cry of a wolf.

Gooseflesh swept over Willie's arms and prickled at her cheeks. Strange though it might be, a man howling into the woods was hardly reason to be frightened, especially since she'd chased wolves off her property many times over the years. But she understood the wolves and their reasons for venturing too far from the thicket. She knew nothing of Devlin, or his howling. Surely he wasn't howling at the wolves? Talking to them...

She gritted her teeth, appalled at the odd turn of her thoughts. Men didn't talk to wolves, not even peculiar Englishmen out to see the elephant. No man would be so foolish as to attempt to lure a predator out of its den. Then again she'd seen no fear in Devlin's eyes when Reuben Grimes had threatened him or when the cowboy had attempted to draw his gun. She suddenly wondered if anything would scare Sloan Devlin.

Or was he simply ignorant of the harm that could befall him at every turn?

Whirling from the window, she yanked her night rail over her head and reached for the Levi's and shirt folded over the back of a chair. Before she left the room, she grabbed the repeating rifle in the back corner.

Gramps stood at the foot of the stairs, coffee cup in hand, staring out at the field. He didn't look up when she bounded down the steps. "What the hell's he doin'?"

"Howling at the wolves."

"The hell he is. I heard a bear once sounded like that. He was dyin', real slow. He cried just like Devlin's cryin'."

Willie checked the rifle, aware that her limbs felt jittery. Tossing her hair over her shoulder, she glanced at Gramps. "He's not crying. He thinks he's talking to the wolves."

"You goin' to kill him?" A strange twinkle lit Gramps's eyes. "Or you gonna try to scare him?"

Willie set her jaw. "I haven't made up my mind."

"He's like the wolves. He won't scare easy."

"I know." Tucking the rifle under one arm, she pushed open the door. Huck awaited her at the foot of the porch steps, shaggy black tail pumping back and forth, tongue lolling out of one side of his mouth. She didn't pause to ruffle his ears. "C'mon, boy."

In long, loping strides, she set out across the field, Huck hunkering low into his trot right at her side. Dew clung to her boots and dampened her pants clear to her knees. The air hung still, chilled and eerily calm, the silence broken only by the swishing of her boots through the grass. And then he howled again and the fine hairs on the back of her neck stood up. The sound echoed up into the trees like the wail of a dying animal.

She quickened her pace, bursting into the clearing with the rifle gripped at the ready. She went instantly still. So did Huck beside her.

Devlin stood with his back to her, straight and still as a hundred-year-old sycamore, swathed in some mysterious cocoon of unawareness. He wore nothing except a pair of very tight black pants that looked as if they had been cut off to grip just below his knees. His legs were exceptionally lean and long muscled, nothing like the tree trunks that had powered her father and brothers through the mines for years. But though she'd seen her brothers in all stages of undress throughout their youth and into manhood, she'd never been so suddenly and completely fascinated with the shape of a man's legs, the tapering breadth of his bare back or the meaty muscles of his buttocks.

Not even on the knoll.

The sun rising over the treetops colored his skin coppery gold and set his unbound black hair aflame with blue. Despite the air's chill, his shoulders glistened with a smooth, dewlike sheen. All along the curve of shoulder and bicep, his muscles rippled below the thinness of skin even as he stood motionless. Willie bit her lip, disturbingly aware of a desire to feel the heat of all that skin and sinew beneath her palms. Her blood hammered a pulse in her ear. Her mouth went dry.

Lightning quick he moved. One leg arced up at an inhumane angle toward the nearest thick tree, stirring the leaves that hung above his head. It was an explosion of energy and movement in the span of one heartbeat. Had she blinked she would have missed it. Had he misjudged his distance or his angle, he would have driven his bare foot into the thick, gnarled trunk.

She didn't breathe. He paused, again motionless, soundless, and yet he stood as if every muscle poised at the ready to respond to some invisible enemy. His scream erupted, blood chilling and eerie. And then in an explosion of movement, he lunged at the tree, legs arcing, arms firing. With fists and feet he beat into the bark, spun, then jumped in a frenzied attack, punctuating each blow with a low, guttural shout that seemed to bring a surge of power to each strike.

Willie watched in horror, expecting blood to be streaming from his hands, legs and feet. But there was none. The man was crazy. Still, as Willie watched, her horror became fascination. There was a mystical beauty to his movements, something she couldn't comprehend or define. He was more animal than human, more mysterious than the wolf, more dangerous.

Willie drew the rifle against her chest. She took one step back. A twig cracked beneath her boot. She froze.

Devlin spun toward her and went instantly still. Hell's fire blazed in his eyes. His chest barely moved with his breaths. Fists clenched against his thighs. Arm muscles popped. His legs braced wide, gripped and taut, ready to strike again.

In that moment, he was everything wild and hungry and beautiful that Willie could have ever imagined. And he was all male, his masculinity so blatantly displayed by his skin-molding britches she felt her legs turn to water and the blood rush in her ears. The rifle slipped from her hands.

He moved toward her with great powerful strides and all she could see was the sun reflected in his eyes and the curl of his lip, like that of a ravenous wolf. She whirled, tripped and felt the ground tip under her feet.

Chapter Four

Sloan caught her arm and lifted her back against him. "There's nothing to fear here, Wilhelmina. Except your gun, and it's on the ground. Can you stand?"

She spun around in a whirl of coppery curls that fell to her hips. "Of course, I can stand," she snapped, shoving up her chin just to make certain he could see the determination in her eyes. His touch had obviously driven the fear out of her. She took one step back, then another, blinking as if she didn't know what to do with her eyes. Skittish, not naive. The broken heart had no choice but to cloak itself in a thick wall of defense. As he watched her draw the black dog close against the side of her leg, he wondered if she had good reason to hate all men, or fear them.

"I heard you howling. I thought you were calling to the wolves. But you weren't."

He felt an unexpected surge of satisfaction. She was more curious than afraid. "Wolves howl to confuse an enemy."

She glanced at the tree. "Is that what you were doing?"

"It's called a kiai." He watched her lips move in silent repetition. Perhaps she could understand what others never could. Maybe she would see beyond labeling him a madman and a peculiarity. "The kiai brings power to a blow and can confuse an assailant."

"What assailant?"

Sloan inclined his head at the tree and watched her. "My imaginary opponent."

Her eyes narrowed. "You were fighting a tree."

"I could spend an entire lifetime perfecting my movements and mental awareness fighting that tree. I've fought many before, straw pads before that, even wet sand."

"That's why your hands don't bleed." She watched him extend his fingers along his thighs. "Do all men fight trees in England?"

"None that I've known."

"It's like an art form."

"As much as any other."

"You could kill someone with your hands."

He looked into her eyes and saw a spark of suspicion flare. "I never have."

"But you would."

"The way of the empty hand is not to kill, but to defend, even to the death."

"The empty hand. You mean, no gun."

"No weapon."

"That's unheard-of here. Everyone carries a gun."

"That's why everyone needs to. I've never felt a need to prove that I can fight. I still believe disputes can be solved peaceably. Many battles are won without firing a single bullet."

"Not here."

"Not even in England." He watched a bird soar high overhead. "It's always better to walk away from trouble, even if it's the tougher course."

"Trouble inevitably follows."

"Then you deal with it, efficiently." His gaze rested on her. "You're not satisfied."

"I'm never satisfied."

"I believe it. Maybe you wish to learn."

Her face lit with the wonder of a child untainted by grief

or despair. In an instant, the defenses vanished. He felt something twist in his belly, a pain and longing so deep his breath caught.

"You can teach me to move like you do?" she asked.

"Not in one day, or a year. It's part of the ancient ancestral heritage of an island race in the Orient, based on the teachings of the monks that live in the mountains in a place called Ryukyu."

"You were born there?"

His fists flexed. "I've never been to Ryukyu. To become a fighting master, I had to be put to a test of courage." He paused, watching her. "I learned from Azato. He's a great master. My father saw him demonstrate his skills for royalty in the Orient when he traveled there over twenty years ago. He brought Azato back with him to England."

"Your father traveled so far."

"My father was a vagabond, in search of a higher meaning to his life." He paused and felt the silence press in around him. The sun inched up over the stand of trees to the east, promising heat to chase away the morning chill. Promising so much where the eye could see forever over a sea of grass to the east, enough to stir a man from his grief. A heavy weight compressed in his chest, still, no matter what he did to ease it. He glanced at her, and in her eyes he saw dwindling hope, forgotten dreams and promises broken.

"A higher meaning." She snorted and glanced out over the horizon and the majesty of dawn. Her face remained impassive, unmoved save for the caustic twist of her lips. "You can't find it in a mine, though you can't tell folks that. I guess we're all looking for it somewhere. Aren't you?" She looked up at him as the breeze played through her hair and the sun turned her eyes the gold-green of a cat.

Heat washed over Sloan, a deep heat that fired his blood and plunged directly to his loins. Never in his life had he been so profoundly aware of a female in the basest, most physical sense. When he looked at Willie, when she looked at him, the barriers dissolved between mind and body, and his desires became his needs and his obsession.

"I've been looking for it all my life." He stared at her, his arms suddenly aching to protect her, as much from broken dreams as from himself. He took a step, involuntarily reached for her, and she drew back, one hand going to the base of her throat in an instinctive gesture of defense.

"Don't," she said, low, husky.

He went completely still. "I won't."

"That's what Brant said."

"Then he was a fool to jeopardize your trust."

"He didn't want my trust, Devlin."

"Twice the fool."

"No, he was a master. I was the fool."

A knot tightened in Sloan's chest. He'd never known possessiveness, or a sudden need to crush a man he'd never met. "Wilhelmina—"

"I'll get your breakfast," she said, bending to pick up her rifle. She drew it close and looked at him as if she weren't beyond using it. "Shirts are required at the table." She seemed to swallow. "And—normal pants."

He cocked his head. "As you wish."

Her face hardened. "You'll never know what I wish, Devlin."

He watched her walk all the way back to the house, the black dog loping at her side. In the rosy sunlight her hair rippled like a shimmering length of watered silk and her hips moved with an age-old female sway. But beneath the soft, womanly exterior lay a soul touched by grief and hardened by far more than one man's broken promises.

Within strength is found weakness, within hardness, softness. Azato had often spoken of alternating forces being indestructible, inexhaustible. In contradicting one another they complimented. And captivated.

Before he turned to head toward the house, he took a path

that led deeper into the woods, toward the faint murmur of water washing over rock.

"Ya look like that teacher fella came around 'bout a year ago," Gramps said, glancing up when Devlin's shiny-toed shoes scraped on the kitchen floorboards. Willie kept her eyes glued to the list she was writing of "things needed." The list was long. Two of those crisp bills would buy enough to fill three wagons. A second ago she couldn't write fast enough. Now, suddenly, her mind was blank.

His footfalls seemed to shake the house. She stared at her list and her mind fogged with the image of Devlin coming out of the woods a short time ago, his hair and skin glistening with water, his pants plastered to his thighs and hips. From the kitchen window she'd watched him walk through the field, even after the onions started to burn in the skillet.

The stream lay at least a mile back of the woods, in a deep ravine that fed down from the foothills over several treacherous waterfalls. Unless a man knew the terrain well, he'd never know where to find it. So how had Devlin?

Gramps's chair scraped. "Remember that gussied-up teacher-fella, Willie-girl?"

Willie muttered something and stared at her list, trying her very best not to notice the tangy scent that had swept into the room along with Devlin. Beneath her elbow the table trembled as Devlin scooted his chair close.

"Yep," Gramps continued. "He came into town drivin' his oxen by shouting Greek and Latin phraseology. Least everyone said it was Greek and Latin. Course, any man what can quote a few phrases of an unknown language is qualified to be a schoolmaster in my book. Got a hatful collected on his first pass around, more than enough to build a schoolhouse."

"An enterprising fellow," Devlin rumbled. "I take it he was a fraud."

"I reckon he might have been. Kept a quart of whiskey and a leather quirt in his desk. Course, the whiskey was strictly for him. The quirt was for the students. He disappeared the day after the mine blew. Some folks think he had something to do with it, even if he could speak Greek and Latin.''

"The mine was sabotaged?''

Willie blinked at her list and felt every muscle tense.

Gramps snorted. "Some folks 'round here would believe anything, Devlin. Just depends on the day.''

"What do you believe?''

Willie slanted her eyes up at Gramps. He stared at the table, then shrugged. "She just blew. There was enough powder charges down there to blow a hole clean through the mountains. They were risking their lives for weeks to tunnel through rock and found no sign of color anywhere. They'd been warned, but they didn't listen.'' His voice dipped low and deep. "Damned fool never did listen, 'specially to reason. Always sayin' his big strike was behind the next rock.''

"Some become as much obsessed by the hunt as by the prize.''

Willie glanced at Devlin and instantly wished she hadn't. He was watching her as if he knew she'd look up at that precise moment, and suddenly she knew the innuendo she imagined in his words was real. Damn, but she should never have told him anything about Brant. What was it about him that tempted her to forget that he was a stranger, and quite possibly, the enemy?

The enemy. It was hard to imagine him capable of anything dastardly dressed as he was in a high-collared white linen shirt and lemon-colored kid gloves. His Prince Albert coat and trousers were of a rich mahogany brown, and his lemon-colored waistcoat was embroidered with lilies of the valley, red rosebuds and violets.

She'd never seen anything like it. On any other man the ensemble would have looked ridiculous. But on Devlin, the clothes draped with a stylish elegance that in some odd way accentuated his dark masculinity.

Willie was completely baffled, especially when she felt his

stare penetrate clear to her thoughts. She stuck her nose in her list and wished he'd finish up and be on his way.

"My boy was restless," Gramps muttered into his coffee. "Some even say a bit flighty in his imaginings."

"Pa wasn't crazy, Gramps," Willie said, distinctly uncomfortable with Gramps discussing her pa with Devlin. She angled Gramps a meaningful look and gently reminded him, "The horses need tended."

Without even glancing at her, he leaned over his coffee and regarded Devlin from beneath shaggy brows. "Packed us all up one day and said we were goin' on a merry outing on the frontier. Had a helluva farm in Illinois with a fancy parlor and a shiny buggy and nice dishes for Vera, his wife. Fine woman. He was a veteran cavalry commander in the war, a damned hero. He could have just sat on his porch and enjoyed his life. Vera even had a maid."

Willie scooted back her chair. "I think we'd best get to the horses now, Gramps."

"But one day, 'bout ten years ago, he told me and Vera and the four boys to just pack it all up an' head out. That first night we had supper served on a clothed table with champagne. That was for Vera. After that she never had any more champagne. Willie-girl was barely old enough to remember."

"I remember," Willie muttered, pocketing her unfinished list. "I was nine."

"With two pigtails down to her butt."

Devlin had stopped eating and was watching her. Resisting the urge to squirm, she regarded Gramps from beneath ominous brows. "Ready, Gramps? I've got to get to town early."

"You go on."

Willie set her teeth. "I need you to come with me."

"You never needed an old man's help before, Willie-girl. I'm sure J. D. Harkness will be more than happy to help you load up the wagon. Ain't nobody in the Silver Spur this early."

Devlin's chair scraped against the floorboards and he surged to his full height so suddenly Willie's breath caught. "I'll accompany her," he said. "I'm going to town myself."

Willie thrust out her jaw. "That's not—"

"If you say so," Gramps said to Devlin.

"It's no trouble."

Damn them both for behaving as if she weren't there.

"Watch yourself, Devlin," Gramps said as Devlin settled a tall black silk hat on his head. "The fingers of low-life gunmen get itchy at the sight of a stovepipe."

"I didn't know Prosperity Gulch had any low-life gunmen."

"Never can tell anymore. I seen decent fellas turn low-life awful fast when times are hard."

"Yes, I suppose they can." Devlin drew up and held a hand for Willie to precede him out the door.

Determined not to let her exasperation show, Willie strode out of the kitchen one pace ahead of Devlin, muttering over her shoulder, "I'm riding on the wagon alone."

"As you wish," he murmured. "I'll saddle my horse."

She thought she felt the heat of his breath on her neck and scooted quickly ahead and into the heat of the day before the shivers again whispered over her skin.

Sloan's nag would have been laughed off the block at Tattersall's in London. Even men like Sloan who didn't live and die by their equipage would have known at first sight that the horse wasn't worth a shilling, much less the ten dollars the livery owner had asked and gotten Sloan to pay for him. He'd been the only horse the man had for sale, as second rate as the shoeing the man was doing on another horse. Sloan could merely wonder if most of the tradesmen and practitioners who occupied the frontier towns were impelled there by a lack of success back East. After all, even he had been drawn here by all the promises, hoping to find some peace on the frontier, hoping to forget his own failures.

Dismounting, he looped his reins around the hitching rail.

Willie was tending to her own horse, her back turned toward him. The horse's sleek lines suggested that he had come with them from that prosperous farm in Illinois, and had probably descended from her father's cavalry. His eye lingered only briefly on the magnificent animal. Willie moved around the horse and wagon with brisk efficiency, nose jutting even when she was looking down. She'd left him in the dust of her wagon wheels and hadn't spoken to him since she'd breezed past him in the kitchen.

Sloan touched his fingers to the brim of his hat and nodded as two women ventured past on the wooden boardwalk. They didn't return his greeting. He glanced up and down the street. Townsfolk lingered on the walks, outside of the stores, some sitting on overturned barrels, others leaning against the buildings, still others ambling along as if they had no place to be in a hurry. Most were watching him with a kindred suspicion. In this they were not divided.

Trust would be difficult to earn here, especially since it had obviously been misused by someone. Most probably the railroad, the Eastern capitalists, invisible in their comfortable offices far removed from the hardships of their corporate endeavors. One act of betrayal was all it took to put that hard, fathomless look in people's eyes and suspicion in their hearts.

He wasn't used to being on the outside, wanting to get in.

He watched Willie climb the steps to the general store and followed after several moments, catching the door by his toe when she pushed it closed behind her. The place was small, crammed from floor to ceiling with wares. Willie was at the counter, reading to a short, mustached man from a list. Sloan lingered beside an aisle of shelves piled high with dry goods. At the end of the aisle, a hard-worked woman stood beside a table stacked with bolts of cloth and skeins of brightly colored ribbon. Sloan watched her knotted fingers fold a length of ruby satin into pleats then drape it over her plain skirt. Her face, worn and rough as the clothes she wore, illuminated with pleasure at the splendor of the material.

Sloan moved to the counter, well aware that Willie's voice broke off suddenly when he paused behind her. He got a good look at her list an instant before she crushed it in her fist. Over the top of her head he gave the stony-faced merchant a cordial nod then lowered his head and said, "You've nothing for yourself on your list, Wilhelmina."

"You can start with the sacks of flour and sugar, Mr. Lewis," she said, sending the merchant off toward the back of the store. She turned and nearly ran smack into Sloan's chest. "Devlin, you're in my way."

"So sorry. Hair ribbons are over here."

She pursed her lips and looked as vexed as she might look with a bothersome fly. When he moved a step back, she slipped past him in a wave of warm lilac. One arm waved in a vague direction. "Why aren't you off writing somewhere?"

"I've nothing to editorialize about just yet." He followed her down the far aisle. He paused when she paused to scan the shelves. "I'm still observing."

"Observing?" She reached high on tiptoes, fingers outstretched, backside curving one way, breasts thrusting the other. Sloan stared at her for several moments then quickly retrieved the cans she needed. "Thank you." She blinked up at him then frowned. "What's to observe?" Without awaiting his reply, she again brushed past him and disappeared around the corner of another aisle.

He followed, pausing beside the woman who lingered over the bolt of ruby satin. He offered a brief smile. At once a veil of suspicion shadowed the woman's features and Sloan could see every trial she'd borne over the years mirrored in her eyes.

"The ruby satin becomes you, madam." He touched his fingertips to his hat. Just as he turned, he saw a spark flare in the woman's eyes and she drew the satin again over her arm.

If a few simple words from a stranger could lighten one woman's burden, there was hope for Wilhelmina yet. Maybe even for all of Prosperity Gulch.

The bell above the door tinkled and the burly owner of the

Silver Spur lurched in and drew up short. His eyes beneath his hat at once found Willie at the counter. Nodding a greeting to Lewis the merchant, he ambled over to her, eyes strangely hopeful, like those of a young man courting his girl.

"I'll help you load up, Willie." His features visibly hardened when he spied Sloan at the end of the aisle.

Glancing over her shoulder, Willie pursed her lips at Sloan as he moved down the aisle toward them, then shoved a hand into Harkness's chest just as he lunged at Sloan. "J.D., no."

Sloan thrust his hand at Harkness and offered a grim smile he didn't particularly feel at the moment. "Sloan Devlin."

"I remember," Harkness said, ignoring Sloan's outstretched hand. "Tell me he's not with you, Willie."

Willie's eyes slanted at Sloan then lifted to Harkness. "I can't. He's my new boarder."

Harkness growled something under his breath that sounded like an expletive.

Sloan glanced between the two, already certain of the answer to his question. "You're related?"

Willie shook her head and patted Harkness's bearlike chest much like a daughter would with her father, or a niece with her favorite uncle. The problem was that Harkness seemed to go instantly, uncomfortably still at her touch. "J.D. was my Pa's best friend. He looks after me—even though I don't need it." The smile she lifted to Harkness would have made birds sing in the winter. Gripped with an odd need to twist Willie's little chin away from Harkness, Sloan swung a cool smile on the other man.

"I'd wager she needed more looking after than she received last night, Harkness."

"No glass broke till you showed up, Devlin."

"You would have had worse than broken glass on your hands and you know it."

"Worse? Hell, if twenty cowboys want to put up their hard-earned money to dance with Willie, and she says it's all right, then I believe her. Listen, Devlin, she took care of herself well enough long before you rode into town. And she will long after you ride out.'' Chest puffed up, fists flexing, Harkness loomed over Willie like an immovable fortress. But when she looked up at him, even Sloan could feel the man's insides turn soft as fresh coddled cream.

She was an innocent, no matter what had happened on that knoll. Innocent and completely unaware of what she did to men. There was no guile in her, at least not yet. She'd been spared that even in heartache. Not that Sloan hadn't been tempted to think otherwise at least a dozen times since he'd had his first glimpse of her in trousers. But even that was a stroke of guileless genius, and innocent folly. Sloan grew more certain of it as he watched her slip her arm through Harkness's and draw it close against the side of one breast. When she leaned close to Harkness, her hair brushed beneath his chin and Sloan felt it as acutely as if she inflicted the torture on him instead.

The woman had been raised in a house full of men. She'd obviously grown comfortable around them. Too comfortable. At least with Harkness. Certainly not with him.

''He's a writer,'' Willie murmured to Harkness.

Harkness's eyes narrowed. ''You from the *Independent?*''

''I'm working with Tom Lansky, at the *Lucky Miner.* An editorial column.''

''What about?''

''I haven't yet decided. Wilhelmina's helping me.''

Willie turned to look over Harkness's shoulder at something in the store window. Her movement, simple and unstudied as a child's, brought the fullness of both breasts brushing against Harkness's arm. As quickly as she did it, she turned back again, repeating the motion. Harkness's face seemed to drain of color.

''I'm not helping him,'' Willie said, her eyes darting up at Sloan. ''He's just following me and getting in my way. Oh, there you are, Mr. Lewis. Here, just take them out to the wagon. Devlin, you can get the rest.''

The merchant hurried past, twin sacks perched on each shoulder. The door tinkled and Willie hurried after him, leaving Sloan and Harkness to stare in silence at each other.

"We should talk, Harkness."

"I'm not thinking about talking, Devlin." One hand slid to the pistol riding low at one hip. "You'd best just finish up your business and head back to where you came from."

Sloan tugged first on one glove, then the other, stretching his fingers into the supple leather. "I'm afraid that won't be for quite some time. There's something here that needs tending."

Harkness took two steps and shoved his face into Sloan's. "Stay the hell away from Willie."

"She's not a child, from either of our perspectives." Sloan arched a brow. "I don't want to argue with you, Harkness. You have my word, I mean Willie no harm."

Harkness snorted. "Your word."

"Where I come from that still means something. And it doesn't require a gun to prove it."

Harkness squinted at him then glanced at his high starched collar. "I don't trust you, Devlin."

"Good. But you will." Turning to the counter, he hefted several brown paper packages and tucked them under his arm. "Where's the mine?"

"The—?" Harkness frowned as he scooped packages into his arms. "The Lucky Cuss is a couple miles west of town past Willie's place, in the Hangman's Gorge, but you can't go there."

"Why not?"

"Mine's closed. Has been since the day she blew."

Sloan shifted the packages under his arm. "Who closed it?"

"The owner. Rocks are too unstable for anyone to be down there. Hell, the gorge has walls two thousand feet high on both sides. It's barely wide enough to let a thread of river water through. Too dangerous even for a mountain goat." Harkness arched a caustic brow. "Might scuff your shiny shoes."

Sloan ignored the gibe, certain more were to follow. "How did the miners manage it?"

"They laid track through there and fashioned a car to take them down into the gorge every day."

"Enterprising."

"Damned stupid, if you ask me."

"It got the job done."

"They didn't find the lode, Devlin."

"Thorne knew it was there."

Harkness scowled. "Maybe he did. But he didn't find it soon enough. And that ain't news around here, Devlin, if that's what you're thinking to editorialize about. Won't sell any more papers. You sure you're not from the railroad?"

Sloan glanced sharply at the other man. "They're curious about the gorge, I take it."

"Always asking to go down there, every time they come through town waving their money."

"The owner won't let them."

"Damned straight."

"They've offered to buy him out."

"Couple hundred times."

"Stubborn fellow."

"Can shoot a man through the heart at a tall man's hundred paces."

"I suppose that's helpful here. I'd like to meet him."

Harkness's eyes narrowed. "I'll bet you would."

The bell over the door tinkled and Willie strode in, slipped between Sloan and Harkness, and scooped up the remaining packages from the counter.

"I thought you were here to help," she muttered, cat eyes slanting up at Sloan. Her cheeks were flushed, and her eyes sparkled with a vitality that would have captivated any man.

"Devlin wants to see the Lucky Cuss," Harkness said. "Meet the owner, maybe convince him to let him have a look around."

A copper brow inched up. "How's he plan to do that? The owner's a stubborn cuss. Doesn't much like tenderfoots."

"I say they settle it over a bottle," Harkness suggested. "Whoever's left standing wins."

"That sounds fair."

Willie and Harkness stared at Sloan, obviously surprised that he'd agreed so readily.

He shrugged. "I've enjoyed my share of smuggled rum." He watched a smile flirt with Willie's lips and felt compelled to add, "I didn't smuggle it myself. I merely enjoyed the spoils of a scuttled French ship. I don't suppose that would give me an unfair advantage."

"I doubt it," Harkness muttered. "The owner's never backed down from a wager, especially a drinking one."

Willie nodded. "Not that we know of."

"Interesting fellow. Have him meet me at the Silver Spur in an hour."

Willie seemed pleased with this. Her eyes twinkled with a childlike mischief Sloan was hard-pressed to ignore. Even Harkness's smile was genuine. "I'll do that, Devlin."

"I can make it back to the farm," Willie said as she turned to the door. "You go on, Devlin. Tom Lansky's waiting outside for you."

With Harkness lumbering along behind him, Sloan followed Willie to the wagon, helped load the last of her goods, then glanced up and down the street for some sign of Lansky. "Lansky's not a patient man," he muttered, adjusting his hat low against the glare of midmorning sunlight.

"The press is three blocks up the street on the left," Willie said as she brushed past him. "You can't miss it."

Sloan watched her walk to her horse and offer him something from her pocket. Softness fell over her features as she murmured to the animal and pressed her palm beneath his muzzle. Her voice rang low and deep like the soothing strains that had drifted out into the night air from her open window, revealing a startling depth of feeling for a horse that had obviously meant much to her father. She glanced up at Sloan and, as quickly as it opened, the window slammed closed, curtained behind a mask of indifference and suspicion.

"Good luck, Devlin," she said, then turned to Harkness. Something about that didn't sit well with Sloan at all.

Reaching for his reins, Sloan moved to his horse's side and mounted. The horse instantly reared to his hind legs, pawed the air with his forelegs and gave a piercing scream. Sloan gripped the reins with one hand, grabbed at air with the other and fell against the horse's neck when his forelegs met with the street.

An instant later, the horse bucked, lunged deep then bucked again. Sloan jarred heavily in the saddle, hauling back on the reins with one arm and trying to keep his seat. He snarled a command and jerked hard on the reins. The horse froze then rose up to paw at the skies. Before his feet touched ground he plunged at breakneck speed down the street.

Chapter Five

Willie watched the stallion streak past in a cloud of dust. Devlin clung to his back, his Prince Albert coat snapping.

"Where'd you find the horse?" Harkness asked.

"At the livery," Willie replied. "Lansky took him there late last night after he saw a drunk cowboy trying to mount up on him. The cowboy wanted nothing for him. Said he found him without a herd somewhere. He's too wild for anyone to ride. Lansky gave him two dollars for his trouble."

"Two bucks well spent. How many men did it take to get a saddle on him and tie him to that hitching post?"

"Five. It was Lansky's idea. Not mine."

"You taking a liking to Devlin?"

Willie glanced quickly at Harkness. "I just don't want him hurt because of some tenderfoot prank."

"You've never worried about any of the other tenderfoots we've run out of town. Most of the pranks were your idea."

Willie resisted the urge to squirm. "Some of them. And only because I was fairly sure they were railroad men. But none of my pranks ever involved an untamed horse."

"Or a fancy Englishman." Harkness paused, awaiting a response Willie refused to give him. Finally he said, "He'll be back in time to drink himself under one of my tables."

Willie bit her lip. "You're sure he'll come back?"

"You saw him fight last night. What do you think?"

Willie bent and picked up his black silk hat crushed into the dirt. She brushed off the rim then pushed her fist inside to straighten it. The silk lining was warm and soft, untainted by greasy hair tonic. She rubbed the silk between her fingers. Quickly she turned to the wagon and found Harkness watching her. Her cheeks went unexplainably hot and she tossed the hat up onto the seat. Shoving her hands into her pockets, she looked off down the street. Through a curtain of dust, she spied a bandy-legged man hurrying toward them, arms pumping like locomotive pistons in his crisp white shirt. Her partner in crime.

"Did you see that?" Lansky asked when he reached her. His face creased with a grin, he took several deep breaths then turned and squinted into the distance. "I've never seen a horse run that fast. Devlin was still on his back when he reached the edge of town. I don't think he'll stop till he makes Omaha."

"That would leave you without an editor," Willie mused.

Lansky swung on her, his smile turning chilled. "And you without a boarder, Miss Willie. But that's a risk we must all take to test the man's mettle."

"Or to humiliate him. Call it what you want."

Lansky set his jaw. "I call it good sense in troubled times. A few days ago I'd wager you did, too. Hell, if it were up to me, we'd put all the slick-tongued gamesters that ever came through here on a wild mule and send them off with a whack on the rump. We should have done it a year ago with that phony teacher. We should have done it with Brant Masters."

Ire roared to life in Willie. "Brant was not a—" Well, he was slick tongued, no question. Smooth as honey on silk. She jerked up her chin. "He wasn't a gamester."

Lansky cocked a cool brow. "Is that so? Couple fellas I know in Deadwood Run say different. Of course, you'd know the truth, wouldn't you, being his fiancée and all. Expecting Brant anytime now, aren't you?"

Willie flushed. Throughout her childhood, she'd refused to

learn the womanly arts, preferring shooting, riding and whiskey swilling. Had she been thinking like a man, she never would have gushed about Brant after he left, leading all the townsfolk to believe his promises, just like she had. They'd all stopped asking about him when six months had passed. By then, she'd stopped gushing. And believing.

The skin under her shirt collar felt hot. "Every man I know has had his turn at a gaming table and there wasn't a gamester among them. One day Brant's going to ride down that street and you won't be smiling so smug."

"I hope you will be, Willie. You deserve—" Lansky's voice caught. He blinked off down the street. "Is that—?"

Willie heard it, too, the muffled drum of hoofbeats. From out of the low-hanging mantle of dust came a lone horse and rider. Her heartbeats quickened. The horse was a vivid chestnut, his powerful forelegs churning in the dust. Twin coattails flapped behind the rider. *Devlin*—

The thought startled her. Every day for six months she'd looked up this street and imagined a broad-shouldered man on horseback riding back into town for her with coattails flapping. For six months her first thought at seeing any well-dressed stranger on a horse was that Brant had come back. Until now.

"I'll be damned," Lansky muttered.

"He doesn't look like a runaway anymore," Harkness grunted, obviously not pleased. "The tenderfoot's not so tender, Tom."

Willie battled a strange compulsion to grin. The closer the stallion came, the tighter her chest grew until her breath compressed in her lungs. She drew back a pace when Devlin pulled the lathered horse to a halt and dismounted, slinging the reins over the pommel. The horse blew furiously, danced lightly sideways and showed Devlin the whites of his eyes. Devlin grasped the stallion's bridle, murmured something to him, then briskly rubbed his muzzle. His movements were unstudied and marked him as an experienced horseman.

His knees were dusty and covered with tumbleweed, his

gloves soiled, his hair half-pulled from its leather strap. Dead grass hung from the bottom of his topcoat and dotted his back. He'd obviously been thrown at some point. Mild satisfaction whispered through Willie followed by a surge of admiration. Somewhere east of town, in a sun-parched wash of prairie grass, Devlin had managed to catch the stallion and remount. Most men would have been happy to see the horse go. Most men would have walked back into town, or moved on to the next town. But Devlin was no ordinary man.

His hair was windblown, his skin swarthy with exertion, and his eyes pierced through each of them like the thrust of a silver blue blade. Willie's heart thudded when his gaze settled on her. He remained impossible to read. "To whom do I owe for the privilege of testing the firmness of the prairie with my backside?" His eyes slid to Lansky then to Harkness. "Gentlemen?"

Harkness cleared his throat.

"It was my idea, Devlin," Lansky blurted, taking a step forward as if he expected to receive a sound dressing-down. "It was—a prank."

Devlin's eyes flickered to Willie. "I see." She believed he did indeed see, down to every last trace of her involvement in the prank, and her odd disquiet about it all. One hand delved into his trouser pocket. "What do you want for him, Lansky?"

Lansky blinked. "What?"

"I want to buy him. What's your price, give or take that worthless mule I bought yesterday for ten dollars? I thank you for disposing of him for me."

Lansky opened and closed his mouth three times. "I—uh—I don't see why you can't just have him, Devlin. No charge."

Devlin's eyes glittered in the sunlight like brilliant diamonds. "Contrition makes a man do odd things."

Lansky hesitated. "I—uh—I suppose it does. Hell, Devlin, you understand, of course."

Devlin smacked the dust from his thighs. His lip curled with the subtle bite of his words. "Of course. The fine people of

Prosperity Gulch believe the true test of a man's character is his ability to sit a wild horse. Rather unusual, gentlemen, even where I come from.''

"Now hold on there, Devlin," Harkness sputtered. "We're not that easy to convince. Hell, in some towns that's enough to get you elected sheriff. But not here."

Devlin stared for a moment at Harkness then added, "I'd best tell you now, I don't own a gun and I've never shot one, nor do I ever intend to. So if you're thinking to test me on that front, don't."

"I don't believe that's necessary," Harkness said.

"Folks are still talking about the way you leveled Reuben Grimes at the Silver Spur," Lansky added. "Rumor has it you've all the weaponry you need right there in your bare fists."

Devlin swung his eyes over the crowd gathered on the boardwalks watching them. "Notorious already," he murmured, as if the idea didn't at all sit well with him. Then he turned and looked straight at Willie. "It's a strange way to earn someone's trust, isn't it?"

Willie went instantly still. He was talking about Brant again, as if he knew precisely how irresistible honey-whispered promises could be to a girl on the verge of becoming a woman. Somehow, he knew exactly how Brant had earned her trust, and that of an entire town—a dazzling smile, a confident manner, elegant clothes and charm enough for an army of women. Quickness with a gun had helped win over the most suspicious old men and the more dour of the widows.

She should have learned her lesson with Brant. She thought she'd built a wall around herself too thick for any man to penetrate. So why was trusting Devlin becoming so damned easy, and disliking him increasingly more difficult?

Willie turned and headed for the wagon. "Beau's missing a shoe," she said to no one in particular. "I'll be at the livery stable."

Harkness moved as if to accompany her. Her sideways glance stopped him in his tracks. "I can do it alone, J.D."

Climbing up onto the wagon's seat, she tossed Devlin his hat, took up the reins and slapped them against Beau's back a bit harder than she'd ever done before. The horse leapt forward with a startled whinny. Willie sat ramrod stiff on the wooden seat, feeling every jar of the wheels over the ruts in the street. She blinked against the dust, shoved a hand across her watery eyes and wondered how she'd let a fancy English gent upset her. By the time she'd reached the livery stable, she'd vowed never to let it happen again.

The pioneer is something a lot less glamorous than a man in a bear coat with a long rifle over his shoulder and keen blue eyes studying the horizon for a red-skinned savage to drop in his moccasin tracks.

Sloan glanced up from his journal at the three miners sitting at the Silver Spur's bar. Slumped in their chairs, with grimy hands wrapped around their respective bottles and trousers inching down their scrawny backsides, they'd spent the last half hour alternately belching and spewing strings of profanity. In the past several minutes, they'd tempered both to some extent. Sloan assumed this was due to the appearance of a dark-haired woman behind the bar.

Judging by the men's comments, this was the infamous Gertie, just returned from several days in Denver. Beneath her powder, lip rouge and the low-scooped, high-bustled gown, Gertie was strikingly reminiscent of the brew house maids in Cornwall. Like them, she treated the regulars with a contempt borne of familiarity, her face a study in cloaked hauteur. She ignored their more ribald comments, replied only when she chose to, in a low monotone that oozed disdain. With hips swaying and bosom barely contained by her dress, she served up their drinks and tended to her work briskly and efficiently.

Crossing one boot over his knee, Sloan watched her and wondered if she was thinking about opportunities lost, and the prospect of growing old wiping down the bar at the Silver Spur after the miners had left. Her face had the pinched, sunken look of a woman embittered. She must not have found what she was looking for in Denver. Had she, he doubted she'd have come back.

He caught her eye when she moved around the bar and began to arrange clean glasses on a tray. She seemed to hesitate, then started toward him, her face transforming with each step. A soft smile tipped her eyes and wiped every trace of bitterness from her mouth. She was unquestionably striking, tall and extravagantly proportioned, with a long neck, ivory skin and a waist narrow enough to accommodate even a small man's hands. All three miners swiveled around in their seats to watch her walk across the room.

She stopped when her skirt brushed against the toe of Sloan's boot. "You're that fella everyone's talkin' about." Her voice was exceptionally low. "Devlin, isn't it?"

"Sloan Devlin."

"Sloan." She wore a thin gold band on her right-hand ring finger, and red polish on her long fingernails. She smelled of jasmine and desperation. With no more than a kind word and a quick smile, Sloan was certain Gertie would follow him wherever he'd lead her. He could be anyone, as long as he didn't reek of a week's worth of sweat.

The exploitation of the pioneers went far deeper than the slickly worded prospectuses that had first lighted their passion for the West. He wondered how many mornings Gertie had rouged her lips and polished her nails, hoping to buy herself a way out of town. He wondered how many times she'd climbed those stairs with a well-dressed stranger at her heels and a dwindling hope in her heart. He was obviously among those few who warranted more than casual disdain.

"You alone?" she asked.

"I'm waiting for someone."

"Gents like you always are." She braced one bare arm on the table, leaned closer and smiled. Her breasts arched out of her shallow bodice. "Who is she, Devlin? Maybe I can convince you your time would be better spent elsewhere."

"It's business," he said, lifting a glass to his lips and watching her over the rim. "About the mine."

Her face went instantly flat and she jerked upright. Her eyes spat accusations. "You're from the railroad."

Sloan took several deep gulps then set the glass beside his journal. "That seems to be the prevailing opinion whenever I mention the mine."

"Nobody but the railroad cares about that worthless shaft."

"Especially the widows."

Her throat worked and she drew her right hand against her belly, fiddling with the gold band on her finger. She blinked several times and Sloan could almost see her defenses crumbling.

One kind word…

He reached to pull out a chair. "Sit down, Gertie."

She waved a hand over her shoulder. "We've got customers. J.D.'s not going to—"

"Those miners will be nursing those bottles until the sun sets. Sit down."

Her eyes met his. In that instant, he imagined she took notice of far more than a tailored topcoat and a ruby-headed stickpin, enough, at least, to wipe the last of the suspicion from her eyes. Sweeping her skirts aside, she dissolved into the chair, then drew a lace handkerchief from her pocket. Head lowered, she worked the linen between her fingers. "I lost more than my husband to that mine. Every dream I ever had went with him. I don't know why anyone would care if the shaft caves in."

"Someone obviously cares or they wouldn't be trying so hard to run everyone out. There could be silver there."

Gertie's harsh laugh could have cut glass. "Richard Thorne thought there was and he got everyone else who was fool enough to believe him. What man wouldn't chase a promise like that, and Richard could sure promise a man the moon.

That's what we all came out here looking for. I left a fine house in Cincinnati for this." She glanced quickly over her shoulder at the three transfixed miners. At once her voice dipped conspiratorially low but her eyes filled with a calm, cold certainty. "You want to know what I think, Devlin, I think the railroad blew that mine."

"You think it was sabotaged."

"It was more than sabotage. It was murder."

"You sound certain."

Gertie leaned over the table. Her voice dropped to a hoarse whisper. "I don't run around throwing out accusations like that, Devlin, unless I know what the hell I'm talking about. I can't afford to. A vigilante gang could come and burn down my house to get me to shut up. These days you don't know who your friends are, or who's in league with the railroad." She paused and drew slightly back, her penciled brows quivering. "God knows why the hell I'm telling you all this."

"You've told no one else?"

"Oh, I told J.D. But he wouldn't even listen. Told me to worry about things worth worrying about."

"And murder's not worth your time."

"J.D. was like a brother to Richard Thorne. If anyone would want to clear Thorne's name, it would be J.D."

"Maybe he's too afraid of the railroad to try."

"Isn't everybody?"

"So why tell me, Gertie?"

"I guess you look nothing like a railroad man."

"Or a vigilante."

Gertie's lips twisted. "I haven't seen you with a black hood over your head yet."

Considering this, Sloan leaned his forearms on the table and dipped his head to hers. "Tell me how the mine blew, Gertie."

She hesitated, watching him for several moments as if she weighed the risk of confiding in a virtual stranger, no matter how trustworthy he might look. She leaned her arms on the table and began twisting the lace between her fingers. "Thorne

might have been working with half a story but he never took
more than enough charge to clear where they were working.
He left the rest well back of the mine, locked up somewhere.
Sam—my husband—said Thorne was always careful like that,
like he knew he couldn't trust everybody. And what with the
kids all running down there sometimes, he just couldn't leave
charges lying around.'' Her eyes lifted. ''Two days before the
mine blew they'd stopped blasting.''

Sloan watched her carefully. ''You're saying they had no
charge in the mine with them when it blew.''

''None.''

Sloan glanced at the three miners watching them. ''Who
else would know that?''

She shrugged. ''Miners' widows. Maybe a couple fellas
who were lucky enough not to be down there when she blew.
Course, no one's ever said anything about it. Folks are too
scared. Maybe they don't want to believe those men were murdered. It's much easier to blame a dead man's foolish fancy.''

''Thorne,'' Sloan said, thinking of Willie's stiff-backed defense of her father.

''At least it doesn't keep you up at night, thinking. Folks
here aren't stupid, Devlin. What good would come of stirring
up trouble against the Union Pacific?''

''What does the sheriff have to say about it?''

''Cochran?'' Gertie snorted a laugh. ''He can't even stop
the vigilantes. The last time they came through town waving
their torches and scaring everyone, he was in Deadwood Run
with his deputies. Cochran's got himself a whore over at the
Devil's Gold Saloon.'' Gertie tossed her head. ''Her name's
Dakota Darby. If you haven't heard of her, you will. All the
men folk know her, in some fashion.'' Her painted lips tightened. ''Whoever blew that mine—and I think it was the railroad—could have done it at night and shut it down. But they
did it during the day, when all those men were down there.
They murdered them all and for what?''

''Silver.''

Gertie's eyes flashed. "If it's there the railroad doesn't want it. They want the land. And they don't want a fight. So they thought they'd scare the fight out of us by killing those men. And they have. Couple more vigilante raids and another handful of widows will go. They'll take whatever the railroad gives them for their land. And they won't give a damn about avenging the murder of their husbands." She crushed the handkerchief in one fist and seemed to swallow with some difficulty. "Tell me, Devlin, why is it that the common folk never win the game?"

Sloan covered Gertie's trembling hands with one of his. "The common folk don't make the rules."

"Maybe they should."

"Precisely my thoughts."

Gertie glanced up and over his shoulder as the saloon door opened. At once a veil of cool disdain drifted over her eyes and hardened her features. Her lids drooped and she leaned forward, laying her lavish bosom on the table for Sloan's leisurely perusal. There was suddenly something of the seductress in her movements, as if she were putting on a bit of a show for someone. "You want to know about that mine, Devlin," she murmured, angling her eyes over his shoulder. "The owner just walked in."

"Right on time," Sloan muttered, rising from his chair. He turned and found Willie staring at him from just inside the saloon's new beveled glass door. She was alone.

It struck him then. Willie owned the mine.

She walked toward them with the long, sure strides common to boastful young men, arms swinging, chin lifted. She exuded a confidence unknown to half the men Sloan had met in his lifetime.

She stopped and leveled a cool look on Gertie. "A bottle of whiskey and two glasses."

Gertie hesitated, glanced at Sloan then turned in a swish of skirts.

"You look surprised, Devlin," Willie said, brushing past him and sliding into the chair opposite.

"I am. But I should have guessed you were the owner."

She took off her hat, then slouched back in her chair and tucked her fingers into her trouser pockets. She oozed reckless bravado yet looked so guileless Sloan was completely captivated. "Around here men divide women into two classes— the reputable and the disreputable."

"The good and the bad." He watched her through hooded eyes. "The good don't drink whiskey."

A corner of her lip tipped. "What do you think?"

Sloan leaned his forearms on the table and surged forward in his chair, aware that she seemed to shrink slightly back into hers. "What reason do you have for feeling disreputable today?"

Her eyes widened, and in those vivid emerald depths he glimpsed hard fear. "I don't need a reason," she said too quickly, laying her forearms on the table between his. "I'll bet you can't guess how many men I've sat across from at this table." The purr in her voice could have charmed a snake. "Men just like you, who said they wanted a closer look at the mine. I think they just wanted to drink whiskey with a disreputable woman. Maybe that's all you want, Devlin."

Her lips parted over a smile that stirred fires long banked and cooled in Sloan. A humming urgency stirred in his belly. He watched her tongue move between her teeth and yearned to peel away all the layers of her until he laid her soul open. "What did you do out there on the knoll, Wilhelmina, that makes you want to be disreputable?"

Her eyes darted to his glass and she reached for it. "What are you drinking?"

His hand shot out and wrapped around hers. She tugged, he gripped; she resisted, he held.

"Let go—"

"You're no more disreputable than my maiden Aunt Genevieve."

Her eyes narrowed. "Does she drink whiskey?"

"Rum. The fine smuggled stuff from Spain. And beer, at least a pint a day. She lived alone in a small cottage in Falmouth on top of a hill that overlooked the quay. She sewed heaps of linen and talked about how disreputable she'd been in her youth."

"She never married?"

"Never. She fell victim to a broken heart."

"Is that how she died?"

"Quite possibly. She was, without question, the finest, most upstanding disreputable woman Falmouth has ever known. Or me, for that matter. Until now." Her hand seemed to tremble beneath his then slipped free.

With a visible relief, she glanced up as Gertie plunked a bottle and two glasses on the table. Sloan nodded his thanks and reached for the bottle, splashing a draft in each glass then sliding one to Willie. He toyed with his glass, watching the amber liquid slosh against the sides. "This isn't necessary," he said.

"Afraid, are you?"

"Hardly. I have what some might call a consuming interest in disreputable women, and their drinking habits."

From beneath the veil of her lashes she glanced toward the bar where Gertie lingered, watching them. Sloan knew enough of women to sense that something had come between these two. A man, judging by the visible thrust Gertie gave to her bosom.

"Then you should talk to Gertie," Willie said. "Let's get this over with. I have a wagon to unload." She lifted her glass and her eyes met his over the rim.

Chapter Six

"The mine was sabotaged."

Willie drew up rigid and jerked her head toward Gertie. "So, someone's been spewing honey-tongued theories about the mine, and God knows what else. Listen to me, Devlin, I don't care if the whole damned town wants to blame my pa, I know he didn't purposely blow—" Her voice clogged in her throat when Devlin surged forward over the table like an advancing storm.

"No, he didn't, but someone did."

She blinked at him, startled that he would believe her father wasn't to blame. Just like that. "You know nothing about it, except what Gertie's told you?"

"Gertie has her theories. If I go down there, I'll know more than anyone."

"That's what one of the railroad men said. I'll tell you what I told him. No one's going down there." She set her jaw but felt her defenses crumbling when Devlin's eyes turned icy silver. She stuck her nose in her glass.

"You don't want proof," he said.

She gulped from her glass, exhaling deeply against the fiery burn that settled in her belly. "Proof of what? That my pa was an eccentric nonconformist who saw himself as the founding father of the next New York City? Or will you tell me that he pursued his dream recklessly, risking his own life and others' by blasting through rock every day for years and finding nothing? I know all that. I don't need you to tell me anything.''

"You don't believe that he's not to blame."

Her throat went dry with a guilt that made her soul ache. She lifted her glass but Devlin caught her hand. She stared at his long fingers in his buttery gloves. "I don't know what to believe. Every now and then my pa used to say he was getting restless. He wanted to go somewhere that had wealth for the digging of it. But he didn't want to be rich. He had an urge for the excitement of being right up against the earth, trying to coax the ore out of her. If he'd ever found it, I think he would have given it away. He had a passion for owning a rich mine, but he wasn't greedy. That's hard for folks to believe. It's easier to blame."

"And to bear the blame."

She lifted her eyes. "Not really."

"Then don't. Let me down there."

So much sincerity in his eyes, so much promise. Promises. She'd believed in them before. "You can't help, Devlin."

"One time."

She cocked a brow and indicated his glass. "First under the table loses. That was the wager. You win, you see the mine."

"And if you win?"

She felt her lips part with her surprise. She leaned over the table, reckless. "Fine. I win, you leave town."

"You're that afraid of the truth."

"I just don't like strangers." She lifted her glass against his. "Drink up, Devlin."

He did, draining his glass in short order. With no outward sign of discomfort, he set the glass on the table and Willie felt a clammy dread begin to coil in her belly. Surely she hadn't underestimated him. Again. The horse was one thing. But a rum-sipping fancy man wouldn't know the first thing about stomaching rotgut whiskey…or would he?

"We're going to need another bottle," he rumbled, silvery eyes hooded. "Or would you like to change your mind?"

Willie drew up stiff. She'd never backed away from any challenge. She certainly wasn't going to now with Devlin, not with the stakes so high. "No chance of that, tenderfoot."

She drained her glass and let him refill it, once, twice, three and four times. And then she lost count. As she'd done in the past, she ignored the dull buzz in her ears, blinked through the haze that seemed to drift over her eyes, and set her will against the creeping feeling that she'd fallen into his trap when he ordered another bottle and regarded her with eyes keen and sharp and a grim smile twisting his mouth.

Any other man would be weaving a path out the door by now, shaking his head, muttering under his breath. Not Devlin. He'd doffed his coat and gloves and sat across from her looking ridiculously elegant given the nature of their business.

The bottle scraped against her glass as he poured with a steady hand. "I probably should tell you that I'm a master of the mind-over-body principles," he said.

Her tongue seemed to momentarily refuse command. "Did you learn those principles drinking whiskey with the monks?"

His laugh was deep and genuine. "Azato believes in purity of body and spirit. He's never touched a drop of liquor."

Her chest jerked with a hiccup. "You have." She licked the thin sheen of perspiration from her lips and tried her best to glare up at him. "You've tricked me."

"Giving up?"

She thrust out her jaw. "I didn't say that."

"You don't have to." Before she could think, he took her glass and shoved his chair back from the table.

She reached for her glass but he was too quick, moving around the table and lifting her out of her chair with one hand clamped around her upper arm.

"Ow!" she sputtered, tugging at her arm.

With barely a flex of his arm he yanked her flush against him. Willie instantly turned to stone. "That's better," he softly said. "We can do it your way if you want the whole town to know what happened here. But something tells me you wouldn't like to be the subject of any more gossip, no more than you like your father taking the blame for something he didn't do. Do it my way, and no one need ever know that you lost our wager."

"I could have won," she muttered, squirming against his ironclad hold. Yes, he was like one tall, thick band of sculpted iron. Funny that she was so keenly sensitized to him when she seemed whiskey-dulled to everything else around her.

"Tuck your hand under my arm."

She tried to slant him a suspicious look. "How do I know you can walk?"

"You'll have to trust me. I know it's difficult."

It should have been. But for some damned reason it wasn't.

He muttered something to Gertie, retrieved his coat and led Willie out of the Silver Spur. They passed J.D. on the boardwalk. Something kept him rooted to his spot, watching them. Without any fuss, she let Devlin help her up onto the wagon seat, even clinging a bit longer to his hand than she might have liked to. He seemed so strong and able.

Damned thoughts, but she didn't have the will to battle them just now, especially when he mounted up close beside her and took the reins in his broad hands. She thought the heat of him would swallow her up. He glanced down at her.

"Don't fall off," he rumbled.

Slipping her hand under his arm, she lowered her eyes and found herself staring at the length of his thigh pressed against hers. The sunlight glistened in the woven wool of his trousers. Beneath the cloth his leg looked hard, like finely whittled oak.

The wagon jolted forward. She jostled against him and jerked his arm against her breast to keep her seat. She might well have been struck by a red-hot branding iron. The wagon jolted again over a deep rut, and she gripped his arm close like a vise. And why not? He was like a sturdy tree trunk offering harbor in a river of rushing water.

She closed her eyes and the earth spun. She'd felt these sensations before...once before. They'd sucked her so deep beyond herself she'd only whispered her resistance when her skin was laid bare to the warmth of the setting sun.

Once they reached the edge of town and smoother road, Devlin muttered to Beau and the horse lengthened his stride. The road lay like a smooth ribbon ahead of them. A breeze cooled Willie's cheeks, filling her lungs with the fragrance of spring bursting into bloom. Beneath her the wagon settled into a sway. She slumped against Devlin, surrendering the last of the fight when she leaned her cheek against his arm and closed her eyes.

When she opened her eyes she found herself staring at the beamed ceiling over her bed. The shade had been drawn and her white cotton coverlet pulled up over her Levi's to her waist. She lifted one hand to the top buttons of her shirt, finding them secure. Relief washed over her followed by a chagrin so profound she groaned.

What the hell had happened?

Her boots sat at the foot of the bed. The door had been closed, and one window left open to catch a cooling breeze.

So he was considerate. A gentleman. Maybe.

And she'd been a fool. Worse, a drunken fool. It wasn't so difficult for a man to look good when a woman behaved as she had.

Scooting from the bed, she reached for her boots and snapped up the shade. The sun had just sunk over the mountains. Already the chill was creeping, promising a cool night.

She splashed water from the washbasin over her face and neck, smoothed her hair into a single plait and grabbed her hat from a tall-backed chair in the corner. She found Gramps in the kitchen leaning over a deep pot on the stove. He glanced at her then back into the pot. His grizzled face registered no surprise that she'd gotten herself so soused she'd had to sleep the afternoon away. Such a lack of response usually meant trouble.

Willie directed her attention to tugging on her boots, certain that she smelled hearty beef stew. Her mouth watered. "Smells good, Gramps."

"Yep."

She moved to the stove, lifted the lid and peered into the pot. "Wagon outside?"

"Nope."

"Where is it?"

"In the barn. Emptied."

Obviously Devlin had unloaded it. Of course, she'd left him no choice. Any man would have known Gramps couldn't heft fifty-pound sacks of flour and sugar. Silence swelled as Gramps stirred the stew.

Willie set her jaw and slammed down the lid. "Say it."

Gramps lifted innocent brows. "Say what, Willie-girl?"

"Fine." She pushed the checkered curtain aside and peered from the window into the gathering dusk. "Where's Devlin?"

"I reckon he'll come soon enough."

Letting the curtain fall over the pane, she glared at him, hands finding her hips. "Fine. So I learned my lesson."

His eyes angled at her from beneath wiry brows. "Did you?"

She shifted her shoulders uncomfortably and replied, "I won't drink whiskey with him again. But I'd like to know why the hell you're turning traitor on me."

"Ain't no fight goin' on as far as I can see. No sides to take."

"The hell there aren't. Since when did you trust a stranger?"

"I like him."

"You like him."

"So do you."

Willie felt instantly hot. "I do not. I don't like anything about him."

"He's not Brant Masters."

Willie felt her mouth sag then snapped it shut. "Now why the hell would you say that?"

"Devlin would never make a promise he couldn't keep and you damned well know it."

"I don't know anything of the sort."

"If Devlin said he'd be back in six months to marry you, he'd be back in four. Hell, he'd never leave in the first place. He'd take you with him."

"Really?" Willie cocked a brow, her voice ringing with the strident tones...of a woman defending her man. If Gramps meant to imply that Brant Masters hadn't intended from the start to come back for her...well, even if part of her considered that from time to time she certainly wasn't going to let anyone know it! "I wouldn't go anywhere with Sloan Devlin, back East or otherwise, no matter what he promised me." Ire sufficiently raised, she turned, took two steps and skidded in her tracks. Devlin stood in the doorway, arms folded over his chest, one boot crossed over the other, as if he'd been standing there listening for much longer than Willie would have liked.

He watched her, as if he knew she'd flush to the roots of her hair. Which she promptly did. Even after a day's work his linen shirt looked crisp. His hair was sleekly combed back into its leather thong. A day's growth of black stubble shadowed his face and neck, and he'd rolled his shirtsleeves to his elbows. His hands and forearms looked like they belonged to a mountain man, not a dandily dressed gent.

Something dissolved like melting butter deep in Willie's stomach. When he moved into the room, she felt her knees wobble and all her ire evaporate.

"Feeling up to sleuthing?" he asked, dipping one hand into a bowl of berries on the table. He popped several into his mouth, casual as could be, gentleman enough to pretend he hadn't overheard a thing.

"Sleuthing," she parroted. "You mean the mine."

"Yes." A glitter sparked in his eyes. "Now."

She blinked up at him. "We can't—"

"You own it."

"Yes, but—"

"Don't you trust me?"

She almost said she did. "It's too dangerous even when the sun's at its peak."

"Then it shouldn't matter if it's on the wane, should it?"

She had no reply in the face of his logic and his grin, which made him look entirely too handsome to suit Willie's mood.

"Fine. You won the wager." She tried to brush past him but he blocked her path with a shift of his shoulders.

"Berry?" he asked. One brow lifted innocently. The berries nestled in the center of his large palm, plump and ripe, a perfect shade of red. Her mouth watered as it had in Lewis's store when she'd first spotted them.

It was a peace offering, one she could hardly deny herself. She bit out a thank-you, gingerly took a berry by her fingertips and lifted it to her mouth. Her eyes met his as the berry burst in her mouth. Sweet juice dribbled to her lips and she swept her tongue over the rim of her mouth, hesitating at the last moment when she realized he watched her mouth with an intensity that would have shaken a hundred-year-old oak. She bit into her lower lip and felt the blood rush to her loins.

Horrified, she averted her eyes and brushed past him. Her shoulder nudged his as she passed, and tingles raced up her arm, as if his fingers had reached for hers to stop her.

"Where's she going?" she heard Gramps ask as she yanked the back door wide and burst into the welcoming cool.

"To get a lantern," Devlin said. "We're going to need it."

They saddled Beau and Edgar, Sloan's new stallion. Sloan accepted a pair of men's denims, a cotton shirt, leather gloves, a wide-brimmed black hat and pointed-toe boots from Gramps, declining a pistol. The pants were tight, the shirtsleeves two inches too short, but the boots, the hat and the gloves fit. When he stepped from the house, Willie glanced sharply at him, at

Gramps, then turned her back on both of them and secured a lantern to her saddle. He watched the end of her thick braid sway at the high curve of her backside and wondered which of her four brothers had worn these clothes. Before she mounted up, she tucked a rifle into the saddle scabbard, slanting Sloan a look that dared him to tell her otherwise.

They rode in silence. Sloan kept Edgar several paces to the left and rear of Beau. Willie seemed to prefer it. She rode with the stiff-backed carriage common to the young debutantes who frequented Rotten Row in London's Hyde Park. Nose jutting, back arched, bosom proudly upthrust, she would have caused a sensation in any city, even without the benefit of a bustled silhouette. Little wonder Brant Masters had been captivated.

But if the man had appreciated even half of her, he'd never have left her dangling for six months on a promise. Gramps had been right about that. From beneath the shadow of his hat, Sloan watched her and felt his chest tighten. Men didn't make promises they didn't intend to keep for no reason. And if they did they wanted something in return, something that a woman would want to save for the man who promised he would be her husband.

Willie pulled Beau to a stop at the entrance to a dark ravine. Crudely laid track led from the path and disappeared in a steep grade down into the ravine. Willie pointed to a bluff overlooking the gorge. A tree stood alone on the bluff, aglow in the rays of the setting sun.

"Pa's buried up there," she said. "He always said he wanted to be laid to rest in a place so that his spirit could overlook the spot where he'd lived the merriest days of his life. My brothers are there with him."

Sloan looked up at the tree. "My father is buried on the far western headlands of Cornwall, at the edge of a cliff overlooking the sea. He knew too few merry times there. And far too much strife." He caught himself, knowing he'd said too much about a subject he had no wish to discuss.

She was watching him. "He died recently."

"Four weeks ago yesterday." Looking at her, he wanted to say more, so much more, but the idea of spilling his soul to anyone had been either bred or beaten out of him. The instinct to shutter himself and his feelings against the world was too strong. He nudged Edgar forward.

"No," Willie said, catching hold of Edgar's bridle. "It's too dangerous to ride into Hangman's Gorge. I don't think the horses could manage the grade. We'll walk from here."

They left the horses in a grove of thicket and with Sloan holding the lantern and Willie the rifle, they started down the tracks into the mouth of the canyon, Willie in the lead. Darkness instantly swallowed them. The air hung chilled and eerily still, echoing the crunch of their boots on the gravel. Weeds choked the tracks. Overgrown thicket alongside snagged at Sloan's shirt, growing more dense and impenetrable the deeper they moved into the canyon.

Straining to see into the encroaching gloom, Sloan couldn't shake the feeling that they were descending into a bottomless pit. Sheer walls of rock swept to the sky on either side of them but these were soon blocked from view by a canopy of thick bramble that hung so low and heavy Sloan had to duck beneath the branches. The track curved to the right, hugging a moss-covered wall of rock. It sloped steep, very quickly.

"Is this the only path to the mine?" Sloan asked, bracing his legs against the steep pitch of the track. Willie skidded and groped at the wall with one hand until Sloan caught her arm. This time she didn't attempt to tug free.

Her nails bit into his forearm but she didn't glance back at him. "It's the only path that I know of. There could be others, but none any more navigable than this. Why? This one too much for you, fancy man?"

She skidded again and jerked her rifle arm into the thicket. Sloan tightened his fingers around her arm and pulled her back until her hair brushed under his chin. "Is that your way of asking me to lead, Wilhelmina?"

She drew up suddenly, bracing herself back against him.

Sloan peered over her head into the fathomless pitch and tried not to think about the fullness of her backside pressing against his loins, or the scent of wild clover that stirred from her hair when he bent closer. Around them, darkness draped like a thick velvet curtain.

"I think we need the lantern," he murmured, his voice taut. He should have been thinking about getting to the mine. But what the mind dictated the body was apt to want otherwise, especially when he moved to light the lantern and she pressed herself deeper into his chest, as if she wanted to wrap herself in him. Desire plunged through him as if shot from a cannon.

It was then that he realized she was trembling, not visibly, internally. And she was strangely quiet, except for her breaths which came shallow and fast.

His lips brushed the air beside her ear. "You're afraid."

"Light the lantern."

"We forgot the flint."

"I have matches. They're in my pocket."

He waited for her to move. A hawk screeched somewhere high above their cocoon. "The matches, Willie, where are they?"

"I—I can't—" Her voice cracked. "I'm afraid to move."

Sloan had seen men paralyzed like this by fear, barely able to breathe.

"Where are they?" he asked.

"M-my left shirt pocket. I don't know why I can't move. I'm sorry—"

No one was more sorry than he. Mind over body. A fine time for it all to desert him. Without the benefit of a glimmer of light, he would have to feel his way into her pocket, the left pocket, which lay, if his memory served, over the curve of her breast.

"Easy," he muttered, as much to himself as to her.

"I can't move my legs and I'm shaking—I need to see—"

"Quiet," he murmured, "I've got you." Slowly setting down the lantern, he slid his hand along the length of her arm.

Her fingers instantly gripped his. Her palm was damp, clammy and cold. "You're going to have to release my hand."

"I can't."

He pressed his lips close to her ear. "You can. I won't let you fall."

She squeezed his fingers with a strength that startled him. "It's like the mouth of a giant black furnace, ready to swallow me. The last time I was here, the mine still burned so hot we had to turn back…before we could find any of them. It was—" Her voice caught, like that of a terrified child torn with grief. "I—I had a dream once after that, just like this."

Sloan felt as if a woman's gentle hand wrapped around his heart and squeezed. "I won't let you fall."

"I hate this."

Yes, he imagined she had done everything she could to vanquish her fear. She had to in order to survive alone. "Irrational fears aren't weaknesses," he said.

"Is that what this is? It feels like weakness."

"When I light the lantern, the fear will leave you. If it doesn't, we'll go back. I promise." His hand curved around hers. "Trust me. Now let go just a—that's it." The instant her fingers relaxed he slipped his arm around her waist, anchoring her back against him. He braced his legs, taking her full weight, and the gravel gave slightly beneath one boot. It spilled down into the void, ominously silent in its trek. He closed his eyes. Against the bunched muscles of his thighs she felt like a sweet bit of heaven.

"Easy." He curved his other hand over her shoulder, fingers tracing her collarbone, judging distance. Her cotton shirt was damp, the skin beneath it overheated by some inner source. Her ribs expanded against his other arm with her agitated breaths. She knew nothing of the torture she inflicted on him. She saw only the maw of the furnace, gaping wide, eager to consume her as it had her father and brothers.

Any sane man would move swiftly. No sense in prolonging

the torture. Slip into the pocket, retrieve the matches, done. He hardly needed to touch her.

His fingertips seemed to pulse. He laid his palm flat on the first upward curve of her bosom. Beneath the cotton her heart fluttered like the wings of a frightened sparrow. His fingers splayed downward, tips brushing over the cotton and the firm fullness beneath, seeking the edge of the pocket. His chest swelled as his breath compressed in his lungs. Blood rushed ominously in his ears, plunging into his loins in rhythmic surges. His fingers inched lower...there. He slipped two fingers beneath the edge of the pocket, closing them around what he assumed was the matchbox. He curved his fingers, scooping up the box. It was then that his knuckle brushed the distended peak of her breast.

His breath left him in a slow hiss. Before he gave into every savage instinct he harbored, he snatched his fingers out of her pocket, flicked the box open and struck a match. Pocketing the remaining matches, he bent for the lantern and lit it.

In all his years of training with Azato he couldn't remember a torture that had pitted his mind against his body more handily than extracting matches from Wilhelmina's breast pocket.

Lifting the lantern high, he peered over her shoulder and down a plunging length of weed-choked track. It disappeared into a cave of overgrown blackness not a hundred yards farther. He felt the tension spill out of her, which surprised him. Their path looked no less daunting lit by the glow of their lamp. Perhaps even more so. Richard Thorne had been wise to lay the track through this canyon. Wheeled cars would have managed the grade easily. Sloan could only wonder why a man would expend so much effort if he didn't believe the mine held a prize worth taking.

"That's never happened to me before," Willie said quietly.

"I'll lead." She offered no resistance, her hand curling small and warm in his.

With boots braced against crumbling gravel and thighs

bunched against the pitch of the track, Sloan stepped carefully down the track.

"You know what you're looking for?" she said after a time.

"I'll know when I see it."

"You've seen many mines?" She sounded doubtful.

"I've seen more than my share of unstable mines overhanging the Atlantic breakers several hundred feet below. And more than my share of exploited and imperiled tinners—they mine the tin and copper in Cornwall, near a town called Redruth."

"They feed empty promises of riches even in England."

Sloan lifted a low-hanging branch out of their path, letting it fall when Willie eased past. "The tinners don't work for themselves. They're employed by the mine owners, very wealthy men who keep them on pittance wages and send them into mines that should be closed down. I've seen what's left when a mine blows because of too much charge. I know what becomes of a man when a rocky headland finally gives way beneath the ancient mine he was sent into." He swallowed the hot bile in his throat. "I know the faces of the widows. And I know how difficult it is to make it right." His voice echoed around them with a haunting melancholy. He might have imagined it but Willie's fingers seemed to tighten around his.

The path leveled off abruptly. "We're getting close," Willie said. "The entrance to the main cave should be just ahead, around the next curve."

Sloan lengthened his stride, and she followed at his heels, her hand still tight in his. He watched the glow of the lantern bounce off the wall of brush surrounding them. Alone in this solitary haven he knew a peculiar need to tell her more. Perhaps because she didn't press, her silence coaxed far more from him than he would have ever thought to tell her.

"My father died taking a bullet intended for me," he said tonelessly. And suddenly the words couldn't come fast enough. "He was shot by a mine owner during a riot brought on by an inflammatory editorial I wrote for the Cambridge papers. In it I championed the doomed cause of the tinners and laid the blame for their strife where it belonged—with the mine owners. The tinners revolted. Riots broke out. They stormed the house—''

"That's why you're here," she said. "To forget."

"I'll never forget, Wilhelmina."

"No, but you could forgive."

Her words stirred a peculiar feeling in Sloan, one he had little time to contemplate. They rounded a curve and Sloan drew up swiftly, dousing their lantern in the span of a heartbeat. Willie bumped smack into his back, opened her mouth, but before she could speak, Sloan spun, yanked her up against him, flattening himself deep against the wall of rock, then clamped his hand over her mouth. Her breaths came hot against his palm. No, she wouldn't like that in the least.

He lowered his head, easing the pressure of his hand at the curve of her back. His lips brushed her temple.

"There's a light just ahead—someone's here—" His blood began to pound in his ears. And it had nothing to do with whatever covert business someone was carrying on in the mine. Warning bells clamored in his mind. Standing this close to her in a secluded canyon was tantamount to mental suicide. His mouth brushed her temple. He tasted the salt on her skin and murmured, "Don't speak." Lifting his hand from her mouth, he heard her suck in her breath, felt her hands grip his biceps.

Fear. Nothing more.

He turned his head the precise moment she lifted hers. Her breaths played against his mouth. No. His palm flattened against her back, slid lower, gently pressed. In a sinuous whisper of movement, she came up and into him. Above the evening hush came the crack of a gunshot.

Chapter Seven

Devlin lit the lantern. "Stay here."

Willie frowned. "The hell I will. I've got the rifle. And it's my mine. Whoever they are, they're trespassing."

In the soft lamplight, Devlin's face was thrown into grim shadow. "I'm afraid they're doing more than that."

Something went cold inside Willie but before she could brush past him, he caught her arm. "Stay behind me," he muttered.

"I don't—"

The pressure of his fingers increased around her arm. "Where I come from, women have the good sense not to chase danger. Even if they did, their men wouldn't allow it."

Her heart seemed to do a flip-flop. "I'm not your wom—"

"Behind me." He curved one hand around her waist and slipped past in a rustle of air and a play of shadow.

She glared at his broad back, feeling oddly contrite and not understanding why. Before darkness swallowed him, she hurried after him, hands tight around the rifle. They crept silently, crouched low. When Devlin paused, she placed a tentative hand on his shoulder and strained on tiptoes to peer around him. She stared into fathomless pitch.

"Are they gone?" she whispered.

A match flared and Devlin lit the lantern. The light illuminated the clearing that marked the cave's entrance.

"All but one." He moved to one shadowed corner of the clearing. There, in a dark pool of blood, was the body of a man.

Willie stared at the bloody hole beside the tin star pinned to the man's vest. "It's Virgil Brown," she said as Devlin bent and pressed a hand to the man's neck. "One of Cochran's deputies."

Devlin straightened. "Not anymore. I want to know why."

Willie shuddered and rubbed her hands briskly over her upper arms. "That's easy. Brown discovered someone nosing around on my property. The man was killed for doing his job. It's railroad men, Devlin. They killed him."

"That certain, are you? Everyone seems too damned eager to blame the railroad. I opt for the less popular theory." He turned, his heavy brows dipping as he stared into the brush encircling the clearing. "There's obviously another path somewhere. Our murderer did escape without our notice."

"But how would anyone know—?" She blinked. "You mean someone's been coming here, without my knowing it?" She bit off her words when Devlin muttered something, turned and strode into the cave. With a hesitant glance at Virgil Brown, Willie followed.

Chunks of gray rock lay strewn about, some with sides smooth and sheared, as though a knife had sliced through them to separate them from the cave walls. Willie picked her way among the boulders, unable to shake the mantle of grief settling over her. She hadn't been to the mine in over a year, not since the day J. D. Harkness had found what was left of her father and brothers. She'd kept herself away, hoping to keep the sorrow buried deep with the rock...and all the bodies of the men they'd never found.

"It's impassable," she said when Devlin reached a wall of boulders that reached to the cave's ceiling. "The entire mine collapsed when she blew. It's solid rock all the way into the mountain.''

His silvery eyes slanted at her. "So everyone's been told.''

"Most folks believe what they're told.''

"That's their first mistake." He reached for her rifle, glanced up, then shoved the butt of the rifle into the ceiling. Dust and tiny bits of rock showered over them. Willie squeezed her eyes closed and ducked just as Devlin swept her against him. A moment later a chunk of rock thudded to the floor of the cave, right at her heels. "The truth lies somewhere between what you're told and what you're never told." His voice was oddly soothing, rousing in Willie a desire to curl into his arms.

Willie blinked the dust from her lashes and lifted her head. She was at once startlingly aware of the heat of him pressing against every womanly soft inch of her. She felt herself go weak. His eyes fastened on her mouth.

"Don't believe so easily," he rumbled, "except with me."

"Odd advice. You're different from everyone else?"

"I'm not Brant Masters."

Her heart fluttered so wildly in her breast she was certain he could feel it thudding against his chest. "Yes," she whispered. "You're just like him. Now let me go."

He lowered his head. "Not yet."

Her fingernails dug into his arms even as she arched against him at the gentle pressure of his palm at her lower back. "Devlin—no—"

His mouth hovered over hers. Their breaths came deep, in unison, bringing chest up into chest, belly rippling against belly, loins warm against loins. Willie trembled.

"What's this?" He rubbed his thumb over her cheek then narrowed his eyes on the smudge of gray on his thumb. Lifting his hand into the lantern light, he turned his thumb back and forth into the light.

"Dirt," she said.

"I wonder if your father thought so." Gently he brushed

his thumb over her other cheek, back along her jaw, then slowly over her lips.

Breath held, Willie waited for him to examine his hand. His gaze deepened. His thumb nudged her lips apart. "I want to kiss you, Wilhelmina."

"You want more than that."

"I'll content myself with far less."

"You don't deny it then."

"Only a fool would deny it."

Willie swallowed, part of her so eager and willing to lay all her trust in him...just as she had when Brant had asked for one innocent kiss...and then another.

Her lips trembled open. "I—I know what happens when—"

"Do you?" His eyes glittered like a thousand stars.

Her cheeks went hot. She felt the warmth of his fingers curling around the back of her neck, the gentle pressure of his thumb tipping her lips up a fraction. They parted a hairbreadth beneath his, trembling with a sudden wild eagerness to know, to taste, to feel and delight—

She knew the instant his mouth closed over hers: he wasn't Brant. She'd expected a sweet, coaxing exploration, something befitting of a fancy English gent with violet-sprigged waist-coats and lemon-colored gloves. Something that would tempt her resistance out of her, bit by agonizing bit, allowing a long moment's hesitation, confusion, before the final, breathless surrender. These were the only kisses she'd known.

She wasn't at all prepared for a consuming sensual on-slaught, a savage release of primal male sexuality. She wasn't prepared for being devoured by the flame of a man's passion. And she'd never imagined the sensory power of a man's splen-didly rigid body, the heady rush of complete awareness of her femininity.

She pressed both hands against his shoulders and their mouths parted with a gasp. His eyes narrowed and he leaned toward her as if he meant to kiss her again. Confusion crashed over her and she twisted out of his arms, drawing the back of one hand to her lips. Against her skin her mouth felt hot.

"We can do nothing more tonight," he said, his voice laced with a hushed intimacy that made Willie breathless. "I'll get Brown. Follow me with the lantern."

Relief washed over her but, as she watched him walk out of the cave, she felt a hollow sense of loss, as if opportunity had presented itself and she had chosen to run from it.

Brown was a big man, sturdily built, with the paunch common to lawmen who spent most of their daylight hours spitting at cuspidors outside their jailhouse, and their nights in saloons swigging whiskey and beer. Devlin hoisted his body onto his back and began to climb up the steep grade to the horses. Willie followed, holding the lantern high. Though Devlin managed with no outward signs of distress, by the time they reached the horses, she was struggling for breath. Leaning one arm against Beau, she rubbed one thigh and glanced up at Devlin. He barely looked winded as he lay Brown's body over Edgar's back.

"I'll take him to the sheriff," he said, loosening Edgar's reins and mounting.

"You're not going alone," she said breathlessly. "Cochran might think you killed him. They hang men here for walking funny. Cochran might not stop to ask questions."

She felt the heat of his stare from beneath the shadow of his hat. Silvery moonlight spilled over him. "Can you make it?"

She jerked upright, forcing a shrug through her shoulders. "Of course, I can make it," she snapped, biting her lip against a sudden surge of ineptitude. Grasping Beau's reins, she mounted.

"Here." Devlin held out a canteen.

She'd brought the rifle. He'd thought of water.

Lifting the cap, she drank deeply. Devlin watched her lower the canteen from her mouth and wipe a trickle from her chin.

"Thanks," she said, her voice oddly husky. She handed the

canteen to him, wanting to look away but strangely unable,
particularly when he lifted the canteen to his mouth. Strange
sensations whispered through Willie as she watched the thick
column of his throat work with his swallows. In the milky
moonlight he looked dangerous and magnificent.

And Willie again tasted the heat of his kiss, just as he
seemed to relish the taste of her on the mouth of the canteen.

Awash in a surge of indecision, she reined Beau around and
dug her heels into his flanks, sending him speeding at a full
gallop down the road, back toward town. She had to get away
from Devlin before she forgot about shattered dreams and a
broken heart and allowed it all to happen again.

Sloan drew Edgar up in front of the jail and dismounted
just as the door creaked open. A large, barrel-chested man
emerged, a rifle hanging loosely from one hand. The tin star
pinned to his chest winked in the moonlight. Cochran. Willie
followed at the sheriff's heels, strides long and sure, chin assuming its stubborn perch. She reminded Sloan of Edgar. No
matter the leather strapped to his back or the bit forced into
his mouth. Beneath it all beat a heart untamed.

He stared at her, waiting for her to give up the fight and
meet his gaze. J. D. Harkness stepped out of the jail right
behind her. He watched Harkness curl one paw around her
arm in a possessive declaration. Cochran walked over to Edgar, grasped Brown by the scruff of his shirt and threw him
to the ground.

"It's Brown, all right." Cochran spat into the dust then
squinted at Sloan. "Found him in Hangman's Gorge, eh?
What the hell was he doin' there?"

"I was hoping you could tell me that, Sheriff." Sloan extended his hand.

"I know who the hell you are," Cochran said, ignoring
Sloan's hand. This time his spit landed between Sloan's boots.

"Maybe you can tell me what an English gent's doin' in the mine? That's private property, mister."

"I was there with the owner's consent. Your concern, Sheriff, should be with the men who killed your deputy."

Cochran chewed, slow, lazy, and watched Sloan. "I know who they are. It's railroad men. Brown musta been followin' railroad men up to no good."

"What railroad men?"

Cochran stared at him, his mouth going still.

Sloan arched a brow. "Where are all these men everyone finds it so convenient to blame for everything that happens in this town? I'm the only newcomer the town has had in some time. Where are these men staying if not here?"

Cochran shrugged. "Deadwood Run's the nearest town. They could be there. But they could be anywhere. Menfolk around here don't need nothin' more than a bedroll and a campfire to call a place home, fancy man."

"Fine." Sloan couldn't temper the sarcastic bite in his tone. "Now that we've established these Eastern capitalist businessmen from Boston are making their home out on the prairie, what do you think they were doing down in that mine?"

Cochran grunted. "Damned if I know. Ain't nothin' down there but rock."

"Indeed. Then why go there at all, much less at night? And why take a path unknown to anyone else? I took the rail path down there. No one had been on that path in months. It's common knowledge the mine's closed up. But for some damned reason your deputy knew that those men were going down there tonight by way of another path, Sheriff. A bit odd, don't you think? Unless, of course, he wasn't following those men. Indeed, he might not have been following anyone."

"What are you saying, Devlin?" Willie asked, stepping from the porch and from beneath Harkness's hovering shadow.

"Are you saying Virgil Brown was in cahoots with whoever was down there?"

Cochran snarled a curse. "Nobody hated railroad men more than Virgil Brown. He'd have nothin' to do with them."

"My point precisely. Those aren't railroad men going down there every night. And Brown knew that."

"Then who killed him?" Willie asked slowly, a spark of fear and realization igniting in her eyes.

Sloan's teeth met. "Not railroad men, I can assure you."

"Now hold on there, Devlin," Harkness said, moving past Willie. Hamlike fists clenched at his thighs, he paused nose to nose with Sloan. "Sounds to me like you're meaning to stir up trouble here."

Sloan met his stare. "The trouble started when Virgil Brown was murdered. I'm looking for justice. I would think you would be, too."

Harkness's lips bared over his teeth with his low snarl. "You're sniffing after something, fancy man, but it ain't the truth. It's what's standing over there on that porch. Look all you want. But if you lay a hand on her, I'll kill you."

Sloan couldn't blame the man for his descent into obsession. Wilhelmina seemed destined to stir such feelings in men.

"Leave it alone, Devlin," Cochran muttered when Sloan turned and mounted Edgar. "My boys and I will handle it. But the last thing I want to do is stir up another vigilante attack. Folks is scared enough as it is. We'd best just sit tight for now."

Sloan heard the bite in his tone. "Inaction never solved any problem." Sloan watched Willie murmur something to Harkness. Rising on tiptoes, she kissed Harkness's cheek and slipped away from him, innocent as a child.

"Find those railroad men, Sheriff," Sloan said, as Willie mounted Beau. "That will solve half your problems. My guess is that they don't exist."

"What else you guessing at that's none of your business?"

Sloan tipped his hat at the sheriff. "I'll let you know."

"Leave it alone," Cochran said again as the horses turned to head back out of town.

Only when Sloan lay back on his bed a short time later, and watched the moonlight play through the lace-patterned curtains at his window, did he recognize Cochran's words for what they were: a threat, thinly veiled, but a threat just the same.

Before the first traces of dawn pierced the night sky two days later, Willie slipped from the house and started across the field of grass toward the forest. It had been a restless few days and nights. Devlin had spent all his time in town, "observing and editorializing," until long after she retired each night, while she drove herself into physical exhaustion during the day erecting a new fence for the perimeter of her property. She'd expected to sleep like the dead. Instead, she'd tossed and stared at the ceiling overhead until her eyes watered. For some reason, she couldn't turn off the hum inside her, a tingly awareness that something was going to happen.

And she couldn't wait for it another minute.

She'd slipped on her Levi's over her night rail and her boots over her bare feet. The morning chill roused shivers along her bare arms and drew her nipples taut against the thin cotton. Her hair hung in a loose tangle of curls to her hips, brushing against her arms with her movements. She listened to the swish of the grass, felt her thighs brushing together like hot irons. She tasted the dampness of the falling dew on her skin and licked her lips. They felt swollen, sensitive, eager.

Like they had when she'd kissed Devlin in the cave.

She knew the path through the woods by instinct, needing no light to guide her through the overgrown brush. It didn't occur to her to be afraid. Fear was for the timid of heart.

Besides, she'd tucked her Colt Peacemaker into the back waistband of her Levi's. One shot would scare off any vagrant wolves.

The forest lay eerily silent, as if all its creatures waited for her to pass. She moved stealthily, each step firing her need to find the surcease she knew awaited her.

The muted hush of rushing water quickened her step. She paused, judged her position and parted several branches. The sky hung like an indigo curtain over the clearing. A quarter mile north, water cascaded over a rocky cliff, feeding the stream that wound through the woods clear to the South Platte. She'd tested the falls once, a long time ago, and had found the water far too cold, even in the heat of summer. Thirty feet of sheer drop below her, a still oval pool reflected the starry sky. Smooth cliffs surrounded the pool on three sides. On the remaining side, a shelf of rock hung over it. Willie would swim beneath the rocky ledge and stay there until the last ripple left the water, and all sign that she was there vanished. Only then would the forest come alive with sound.

After the mine blew she'd spent most of her days here...until Brant Masters came to town and changed her life. Odd that she hadn't been here since Brant had pointed his buggy east and ridden out of town.

She stepped through the brush and paused, her boot tips poking over the cliff's edge. Filling her lungs with the morning air, she eased open the buttons of her Levi's and looked up into the sky. Already the dawn was chasing away the night, filling the sky with apricot hues. Slipping off her boots, she tugged her night rail free of her Levi's and eased the denims over her hips, wriggling her bottom until they slid down her legs. A moment later she slipped the nightrail over her head. Letting it fall to the branches, she kicked her feet free of her denims.

She felt pagan, reckless and wanton. Pressing both palms to the curve of her belly, she closed her eyes and felt the surge of her pulse beneath her hands. Her fingertips brushed up over the indentation between her ribs, traced the underside of her breasts then cupped the fullness. She felt the weight of them. Tentatively her thumbs brushed the peaks. Her gasp echoed through the clearing. A shameful flush pounded in her cheeks even as her hand slid over her belly until her fingers brushed the damp curls between her thighs.

Without another thought, she lifted her arms over her head and dove thirty feet through the air and into the pool. She surfaced with a gasp for air, filling her lungs then diving beneath again with clean, powerful strokes. She dove straight to the bottom of the pool, gathered her feet beneath her and pushed up to the surface. Laying her head back in the water, she stared at the skies overhead. She floated until the pool grew still, her hair fanning out over the surface, her breasts lifting up out of the water like a pagan offering. Arching her head back, she smoothed her hair from her face then set out toward the rocky overhang with clean strokes. Shadow obscured the space beneath the ledge but she knew it was there, waiting for her.

She arced up, lifting her torso and bottom out of the water and again dove beneath the surface. Hands outstretched for the wall of smooth rock ahead, she realized she was beneath the shadowy ledge because she could see nothing here, just pitch as thick as a black velvet curtain.

Her fingertips brushed something and instinctively retreated. Whatever it was felt oddly like smooth rock but somehow different. She fanned her arms to the side, paused, then kicked once to surface, arching her back. That simple movement brought her breasts, belly and thighs brushing up against the entire length of a man.

She knew it was a man, not a rock. There was no mistaking certain physical attributes, arms and legs being the very least of them, and, more particularly, those attributes more impressively sized. She broke the surface with a terrified gasp and was instantly clamped hard against him.

Before she could think to scream, his voice rumbled out of the darkness, close to her ear. "No, Wilhelmina. Stay. Just for a moment. Stay with me."

Chapter Eight

Sloan set every ounce of his will and steel-honed fortitude against male instinct. And knew he would fail. It was as if she'd dropped from the heavens at the bidding of an angel who'd decided to have mercy on him.

She felt like heaven. Every inch of her cleaved into him, kept there by the clamp of his hands around her waist. Only a fool would submit himself to this torture and expect to rise above his most primal urges. He should release her. A gentleman would. A master in control of his body would.

At the moment he felt, quite contentedly, like neither.

"I think you ought to know something, Devlin." Her breaths came shallow against his neck. In the dim light she was a wispy silhouette, a deeper shadow against the lighter shadows. Her features remained obscured.

He felt her ribs beneath his thumbs, the gentle bob of her breasts high against his chest, the curve of her thighs, the heat of her loins. She had to know what she did to him. It lay in irrefutable evidence against her belly.

"Tell me," he rasped.

"I still think of myself as engaged."

Sloan felt a chill creep into his blood. "To Masters."

"Yes, of course."

"For some reason I thought he'd left—"

"He did. He's—coming back. Any day now."

She must have lifted her head because he felt her breath against his mouth. "He is," she repeated softly.

"You're waiting for him."

"As long as it takes. I gave him my word."

Sloan needed much more at the moment to convince him. He slid one hand up the curve of her back and felt her skin ripple in response beneath his fingers. Burying his hand in the heavy tangle of her hair, he curved his fingers around her head.

She stiffened. "Devlin, we shouldn't—"

"You're quite right. We shouldn't."

"I'm going to marry Brant when he comes for me. I won't be the one to go back on my word."

"You gave him more than your word, didn't you?"

"I—" Her breath caught when he lowered his head and pressed his mouth to her neck, tasting the dewy essence of her. He drew her scent deep into his lungs and felt his blood fire with such savage desires his head spun. She jerked, unconsciously pressing her breasts deeper against him.

"Did you give him this to seal your promise?" With one flex of his arms he lifted her higher and lowered his mouth to the valley between her breasts. Beneath his lips her skin quivered, warm beneath the cool water, slick as satin, ripe as sweet fruit. "Did you swim in this pond with him, Wilhelmina?"

She trembled in his arms. "N-no—never—I wouldn't—"

"No, you wouldn't have left your clothes on that cliff if you knew I was down here watching you."

"You were hiding."

"I come here every morning to meditate. First, in the waterfall where the water runs coldest, then here. I could easily believe you followed me...if I didn't know you better." He slid his mouth lower, to one arching peak.

Her fingertips bit into his shoulders. "Please—don't."

His breath fell ragged on her skin. It took every ounce of his will to lift his head. In the gathering light of dawn she blinked at him, her lashes long and spiky, her eyes enormous, brimming with wariness.

"I won't," he said softly. "I wouldn't want you to feel as if you have to marry me because of a few favors I took."

Her mouth snapped open then clicked shut. "It wouldn't matter what favors you took. I'd never marry you. Or anyone else, for that particular reason. I'll marry for love."

"Ah. You love him."

"I— Let me go."

He realized the futility in arguing a point she refused to see, at least at the moment. Things might not look so fuzzy when they'd both found their clothes. He released her, and in a ripple of water she slipped away, leaving him clutching fistfuls of nothing. With long strokes he swam after her toward the center of the pond. The sky overhead bloomed with lush pink and apricot hues. The face of the western cliff glowed with the first burnished gold rays of the sun, throwing shimmery light onto the pond. Sloan felt the heat on his shoulders and face. He kept several strokes behind her, watching her hair fan out like a copper gold curtain into the pool, until she suddenly turned. Her brows met in a scowl.

"How do you suggest we do this? You know—get dressed."

"Ah. I don't suppose you thought of that when you left your clothes up there."

"I wasn't thinking about you being here."

He watched the color creep into her cheeks. He wondered what thoughts had prompted that. His lips softened into a smile. "I promise not to look."

Her scowl deepened. "I don't believe you."

"You might have a problem with misplaced trust, my dear, but it isn't with me."

Her brows quivered. "Why do I always get the feeling you only say a fraction of what you mean?"

"For that reason you listen closer than you would otherwise."

"No. I get confused and irritated. By tomorrow I'll stop listening to you completely. Where are your clothes?"

"Offering to get them?"

She set her jaw, deepening the cleft in her chin. "And you have this annoying habit of answering questions with a question. Is that something peculiar Englishmen do? No—don't bother to answer that. You haven't answered me straight once."

He inclined his head in a mocking bow. "Forgive me, my dear. The last thing I wish is to confuse, irritate and annoy you. They're on a rock by the waterfall."

"What are?" She closed her eyes, shook her head and pursed her lips with obvious vexation. "Fine. You'd best go get them."

"Why? I'm in no hurry to leave. You're remarkably talkative this morning. Very insightful."

"I'm cold. And getting very hungry."

"Ah."

"Ah. What does that mean? You say it all the time. Ah."

"Consider it a token of appreciation."

She looked dubious. "For my hunger?"

"Absolutely. You have a remarkable appetite for a woman. Two eggs each morning with biscuits, butter and jam, coffee with three large spoonfuls of sugar and a generous dollop of cream." He resisted the urge to grin when she closed her eyes and blushed to the roots of her hair. Damping a need to gather her into his arms, he added softly, "It becomes you."

"Gluttony has never become anyone."

"You're a woman of extremes. It comes naturally to you."

"I know."

"Don't let it trouble you. I find it quite fascinating."

Again she gave him a wary look. "Something worth writing about, I suppose."

"Without question. A king's ransom more than I'm finding in town. You don't know how captivating you are, Wilhelmina. The fires under you burn hot and bright. You make other women look as if they're on a perpetual low simmer.''

Her chin inched up defiantly. "You're talking about ladies. English ladies. Proper ladies, like the wives of the Eastern capitalists.''

Without thinking, he moved closer until he could feel the ripple of water she stirred with her legs. ''It has nothing to do with reputable and disreputable. I'm talking about a woman's capacity to captivate. A man wouldn't grow bored watching you.''

She slanted him a sideways glance and turned to swim several strokes away. ''A man with nothing better to do, maybe. Are you going to get your clothes or not?''

''As you wish, my dear.''

Willie tried to ignore the gentle chiding in his voice, just as she tried, and failed, to suppress the feeling that he found great delight in toying with her. Not that she was enjoying it. No, not at all. Play, that's what this was. Meaningless fun for a man with nothing better to do than make a mockery of the town and its folk. Well, that wasn't quite true. The other night he'd seemed genuinely concerned about the mine. And Virgil Brown. And her. What *was* his purpose here?

She heard the splash as he levered himself out of the pool, and she jerked her eyes completely away from him. Humming a nervous tune, she stroked and kicked with great vigor as if this required serious concentration. No, she wouldn't look at him walking up that rocky incline. She wouldn't even glance at his back and shoulders and legs and magnificent backside. If he looked anything like he'd felt under water, she might be struck numb with terror. She'd just never imagined a man could feel so god-awfully imposing.

A proper woman on low simmer wouldn't look. Then again, a woman on low simmer would have had the good sense to keep herself out of this sort of situation. Low simmer. It even sounded dull. She lowered her lids, angled her head and took a swift, hesitant peek through the curtain of her hair. Not an outright, bold-faced look. Nothing extreme. Just a peek. But that was more than enough.

Her throat went bone dry. She blinked, focused, deepened her stare. She thought she'd known what to expect. Eighteen years with four strapping brothers should have educated her well. Apparently not well enough, because Sloan Devlin resembled a great, bold, rutting stallion much more than any man she could have conjured even in her most intimate imaginings. And the need he fired in her was different from anything she'd known in reality or fantasy.

He paused to retrieve his clothes, turning in profile then fully front to face her. She gulped and sank beneath the surface, wishing just this once that the water was icy enough to chase away the heat pumping through her blood and making her loins feel heavy and swollen. She swam beneath the surface to the edge of the pool and groped for the rocky ledge. Levering one arm against the ledge, she brushed the water from her eyes then gave a startled yelp when Devlin loomed directly above her.

"Stay here," he said. "I'll get your clothes."

"That's not—"

But he'd already turned and had begun to climb the face of the cliff. It had taken Willie many days to find the easiest path up the cliff among the small ledges that provided the safest foothold. Devlin had obviously mastered his own path in only three days. He wore nothing but his odd black knee britches that fit him like a second skin. She found herself cursing herself for finding such fascination with his muscled backside. By the time he'd returned with her clothes, she'd worked herself into a state of complete self-contempt.

It didn't help matters when she looked up and saw his massive hands clamped around her night rail. "Put them—"

He placed the clothes on the ledge, just at her fingertips. She curled her fingers into the denim.

"Thank you, Devlin." Her eyes skittered about as he hunkered down. The breadth of his shoulders blocked out all sunlight. Droplets glistened in the smooth fur that blanketed his chest and swept low over his belly. Her own chest felt oddly tight. "I—I'll see you at breakfast."

"Not this morning. I'm going into town early. I'll be there most of the day helping Lansky assemble his new press."

For some damnable reason Willie's belly seemed to sink. "Unless you need me here."

"No," she said quickly. "Why would I? Gramps and I will be mending fences all day."

"No time for lunch?"

"There's always time to eat, Devlin."

"Good. Meet me in front of the Silver Spur at noon."

"Gertie's a terrible cook," she couldn't resist saying.

"We're not eating there. I was thinking of trying the Devil's Gold Saloon in Deadwood Run."

She craned her neck to squint up at him. "What are you up to, Devlin?"

His lips curved into a smile that made the sun-dappled skies pale in comparison. "We have to do something about your suspicions."

The look in his eyes made her heart roll over in her chest. "And if I can't spare the time? We've a good five miles of fencing that needs fixed."

"It can wait and you know it."

Her teeth clicked when he turned and started back up the cliff face. His confidence was truly grating. "Don't wait for me if I'm not there by noon," she called at his back, her voice ringing with a false conviction she prayed he wouldn't recognize. "Those fences needed mending months ago. Besides, why would I purposely go looking for trouble?"

"Because you're more curious than you are afraid." His voice echoed out over the valley as he paused at the top of the cliff and glanced down at her. "I'll see you at noon." And then he disappeared into the brush.

In their heedless pursuit of everything the American spirit hungered for and their desire to overrun the virgin wilderness

*with the utmost dispatch, the settlers of the West found them-
selves exploited by the villains more than they were vanquished by the land. The financiers, promoters and Eastern
capitalists lured thousands to fill the open spaces only to dump
them without preparation, equipment or money on hostile
prairies whose ecology couldn't support either farming or
ranching. Was the golden spike that linked the first transcon-
tinental railroad ultimately the spike driven into the heart of
the American dream?*

"Whatcha got there, Devlin?"

Sloan snapped his journal closed and glanced up.

Lansky leaned one shoulder against the door to the newspaper office. He shoved the stump of his cigar to one corner
of his mouth and smiled. "Looks like an editorial to me. Let
me read it. I'll set it in agate type to make tomorrow's paper."

Sloan tucked his journal into the inner pocket of his topcoat
and stretched his legs, crossing one ankle over the other.
Squinting against the midmorning glare, he studied the faces
of the women and children meandering about town, those who
wore their broken dreams more obviously than anyone else.
A restless need to make a difference stirred in his belly, along
with a brief flicker of hope that he could, this time, make it
right. He'd paid once for his bravado with his father's life.
He'd never again underestimate the power of the written word
to stir hatred and greed, pride and passion to feverish and fatal
heights. Perhaps that was the reason he didn't hand his work
over to Lansky.

Azato had taught him nothing about fear for others.

"It still needs work," he muttered.

"You running scared?"

Sloan glanced sharply at Lansky.

The newspaperman shrugged. "After what happened to Virgil Brown, word has it you brought trouble with you into
town."

"I didn't kill him."

"Course, you didn't. You just happened to be down there. Coincidence is a funny thing to try to explain to people. There's a reason the sheriff told you to leave it all alone."

Sloan narrowed his eyes. "You're advising me to?"

Lansky snorted. "Hell, you're talking to a man who makes his livelihood stirring up folks to improve circulation. I say write what you need to write, and say it straight. So Cochran throws you into jail for a night for trying to cause trouble. Could be worse." Lansky rubbed his jaw. "Course, someone might take a shot at you. But I warned you about that. That's why I carry this here." Lansky hefted his ivory-handled cane, upended it and shoved the butt at Sloan. "Loaded with Colt shot. Fires when I press on the lever here, by the handle. Just in case. You get a gun yet?"

Sloan swung his gaze back to the street. "Tell me about the teacher who came through town about a year ago. The one who vanished right after the mine blew."

Lansky chomped on his cigar. "I can tell you right now, Devlin, don't waste your time. Nobody wants to think about those men dying down there anymore. Folks have made their peace."

"Blaming the wrong man."

"That'd be tough to prove seeing as Richard Thorne is dead."

Sloan sat forward and rested his forearms on his thighs. He squinted into the street. "The mine blows. Everyone in town runs there to try to save those men, right?"

"Sure. Who wouldn't have tried to help those poor cusses?"

"The man who blew the mine. He's the one running away with a pocketful of money. Like you said, Tom, coincidence is a funny thing to try to explain."

"That teacher's long gone, Devlin."

"Whoever paid him isn't."

Lansky sucked in a breath. "Don't write that in your editorial, Devlin. I'd like to keep my job."

"Sounds like you're afraid of someone, Tom. Your Eastern capitalist railroad employer, perhaps? Or someone else?"

Lansky's Adam's apple jerked in his throat. "I—I'm not afraid of anybody. I just don't—"

"You're promoting something here, aren't you?"

Lansky yanked his cigar from his mouth. "What the hell—?"

"I've read several back issues of your paper, Tom. Your editorials reek of Eastern capitalist propaganda, the sort of balderdash that lured these people out here for nothing but railroad gain. The words didn't sound like yours. That's because they weren't."

Lansky blinked furiously. "Th-that was before—"

Sloan rose from his chair. "Before?"

For whatever reason, Lansky took a step back into the shadow of the doorway. "Before the mine blew. Before Thorne proved we could have a thriving town without the railroad running through here and making it so. Before that idiot editor in Deadwood Run opened up his own shop—"

"And became the railroad's new voice. The track ran through there and you lost your worth to the railroad. Is that the 'before' you're talking about, Tom?" Sloan watched Lansky chomp on his cigar so savagely his mustache jerked. "You were paid to open a press and produce a paper before there was even one building to throw shadow in the dust or more than a handful of people to read it. You were sent here to be the mother's milk to this infant town. Your paper did nothing but sing the praises of the community for the benefit of anyone out of town who would read it. You claimed no more desirable place could be found in the state of Colorado. I wonder if you still believe that."

Lansky twisted his neck out of his high collar. "And if I did, it was my job, dammit, and they paid me well at first to do it. Folks who settled here didn't mind the publicity."

"Deceptive as it was."

"Folks don't much care for the truth when their livelihood

depends on the effectiveness of my promotion. If they got dissatisfied, they might have done to me what they did to that editor over in Medicine Lodge, Kansas. Invaded his office, hauled him outside, coated him with sorghum molasses and sandburs then rode him around town on a wooden rail. Cuss sold the paper shortly after that and left for parts unknown. But like I said, that was before. Things change, Devlin. Folks here have changed. I've changed.''

"Indeed. You've gotten a conscience, I take it?'' Their eyes met, held. ''Or is it that you simply have nowhere else to go now that the railroad's finished with you? Or do you plan to somehow get in their good graces?''

"What are you suggesting, Devlin?''

Sloan shrugged and offered a slow smile. ''Just thoughts, Tom. I told you, nothing fit for publication just yet. Forgive me, I theorize far too much for a stranger.''

Lansky grunted his agreement.

"So tell me, Lansky, how many strangers have been through town and stayed on for more than a night in the past year?''

"Hard to say. That teacher fellow. Before that, couple of railroad gents. But they come through from time to time and don't stay longer than a night. Course, there was Brant Masters. He stayed around awhile, up at Willie Thorne's, long enough to get her engaged to him. Course, then there's you.'' Lansky looked straight into his eyes. ''How long you planning to stay?''

A sudden vision of Devlin Manor bloomed in Sloan's mind. More than guilt awaited him on that barren, sea-swept headland. Duty would inevitably begin to tug at him. Perhaps it already had, each time he looked into a child's face and saw the miners' orphans in Cornwall and the beleaguered tenants on his father's estate...*his* estate. He was the Earl of Worthingham now, with a mountain of responsibilities and obligations awaiting him. He should be thinking about getting back. "It's difficult to say," he muttered, then quickly added, "Other than Masters, where did these men all stay?"

Lansky jerked his head at the Silver Spur across the street and west several blocks. "J.D.'s."

Sloan's eyes followed. Harkness stood on the wooden boardwalk just outside his beveled-glass double doors, watching them. "He's not married," Sloan said half to himself, thinking about the look Harkness got in his eyes when he looked at Willie.

"His wife died six months ago. Doc said she just gave up."

Sloan glanced at Lansky. "She was ill?"

Lansky shrugged. "Her spirit just gave up. About five years back Lily was thrown from a horse. Couldn't walk after that. Docs could do nothing for her. Hell, J.D. had every doc from Omaha to Denver come look at her. It was a tragedy. Lily was a fine lady. Never had any children. Only folks ever saw her after that was Bessie Lewis and her mama, who visited Lily every day, rain or shine, and that was only because they're the nebbiest busybodies in town. There is nothing those two women don't know about folks in this town. Can't keep anything from them. Other than Bessie and her mama, J.D. kept Lily pretty much closed up in a room above the Silver Spur. She died there."

"Six months ago," Sloan murmured.

"Right about the time Brant Masters came into town. You want to talk about him, too?"

"No." Sloan checked his watch. Fifteen past noon. He looked west down the street. No sign of Willie. Damned impertinent female. He'd go get her, if he had to, and pry her away from all her fences.

"Where you headed?" Lansky asked.

"Deadwood Run."

"Looks like you'll be going by yourself."

The hint of mirth in Lansky's tone drew Sloan's scowl.

Lansky lifted a brow. "I'm not saying I blame you, Devlin,

not one bit. Willie's a fine woman. She'd make any man a helluva wife. A pity Brant Masters put his stamp on her.''

Before he realized, Sloan twisted his fists into Lansky's crisply pleated white shirtfront. ''She bears no man's stamp,'' he growled. ''Especially not Brant Masters's. Understand?''

Lansky went pale. ''Tell *her* that, Devlin. I'm not the one you need to convince. She's set to marry the gent.''

''We'll see about that.'' Releasing Lansky, he snarled an apology, straightened his topcoat, turned on his heel and set out toward the Silver Spur.

Chapter Nine

Willie reined Beau up at the Silver Spur. J.D. stopped sweeping the boardwalk and watched her dismount. Devlin was nowhere to be seen. He'd obviously left for Deadwood Run without her. What had she expected? After all, she'd dallied at the farm and kept Beau's pace slow to town, and for what reason? To test Devlin? To prove something to herself, like maybe she wanted him to care enough about her going with him to wait an extra fifteen minutes for her? She'd proved something all right. Her heart felt as if it had sunk to the pit of her belly.

"I brought you something, J.D." Looping Beau's reins around the hitching post, she held up a basket covered with a red-checked napkin. "Gooseberry muffins." She stepped onto the boardwalk, a frown worrying her brow. Sometimes J.D. looked so sad her heart wrenched. "Maybe it will make you smile." Rising on tiptoes, she kissed his beard-stubbled cheek.

Just as she was about to draw back she spotted Devlin exiting the Silver Spur. Something about the way he looked at her made her close her eyes, press her cheek to J.D.'s and linger there longer than she would have otherwise. She felt J.D.'s hands encircle her waist and press her tight against him, too tight. Confusion spilled over her. Flustered, she glanced up at J.D.

"Willie," he said hoarsely. He was staring at the open neck of her shirt. She touched the buttons and realized she'd left one too many unhooked.

She'd done it before when she'd dressed in haste. So why was she suddenly so embarrassed? Turning, she slipped the button through the loop. Her heart thudded like a hammer in her chest.

"You're late," Devlin said, grasping her elbow and taking the basket. Shoving the basket at J.D., he steered Willie toward Beau. As she turned, Willie spotted Cochran ambling toward them.

"Where the hell are you taking her, Devlin?" Harkness asked.

Willie mounted up. "Deadwood Run. It's Gramps—" Willie swallowed. "He needs—" She glanced at Devlin sitting tall and elegant in his saddle. He watched her, an amused look on his face. Midday sun winked in the diamond-headed stickpin at his throat and glistened off his black silk top hat. "A hat," she blurted. "Gramps wants a new hat. You know the shebang in Deadwood Run has hats all the way from England."

Harkness looked at her so intently Willie wanted to squirm in her saddle. "Gramps wants a hat from England," Harkness said slowly, as if he knew damned well she lied.

Willie jerked her head at Devlin. "Just like his."

Harkness stared at her. "I could have taken you."

"I know, J.D., but I thought I'd take Devlin along. Keep him out of trouble." She bit her lip, wondering why the devil she'd said that.

Harkness's eyes angled at Devlin. "Seems to me trouble's what he's looking for."

"I was thinking more along the lines of dinner," Devlin replied in his smooth tone. "Perhaps at the Devil's Gold Saloon. Care to recommend anything, Harkness? Sheriff?"

Cochran sidled up next to Harkness, his eyes fixed on Devlin. "I recommend you keep to your own business, Devlin."

"Does that include any railroad men I might find there? Perhaps, you'd care to accompany us. After all, a murder was committed in your town two nights ago and you've made it clear you believe the railroad responsible. You even suggested these men could be as close as Deadwood Run. I'd wager your constituency will want to know what you intend to do about catching them before the next election."

Cochran's girth seemed to puff up and over his low-riding gun belt. "You suggesting I'm not doing my job?"

Devlin's lips tipped up. "Now why would you think that?"

The air suddenly seemed to crackle. Willie sucked in her lower lip when Cochran's hand inched toward his gun. "Let's go, Devlin," she said briskly, reining Beau around and digging her heels into his flanks.

"As you wish, my dear." Devlin tipped his hat at Harkness and Cochran. "Gentlemen. We've a hat and some dinner to find."

"You didn't need to do that," Devlin said when they'd reached the edge of town.

Willie acknowledged several women who stood on the boardwalk in front of the livery watching them ride past. "What did I do?"

"Lie."

Willie stuck her nose up. "It wasn't a lie. Gramps has always wanted a top hat. I try never to fib, Devlin."

"That's wise. So sorry. I thought you'd sensed what I had. It seems I was wrong."

They rode in silence for several moments. The sun beat down, hotter out on the open grasslands than in town. Wind billowed through the grass in great sweeps. Clouds scudded across a sky that swept for an eternity in all directions. Finally, when she couldn't stand it another moment, Willie glanced over at Devlin. "So what did you sense?"

His eyes met hers and her heart seemed to trip along. "You tell me," he said. "Never ignore instinct, Wilhelmina."

Instinct. She stared over Beau's ears and felt the squirming start in her belly. Until today she'd never felt uncomfortable with J.D. Today there'd been something in his eyes that had never been there before. Even Devlin had seen it. But Devlin saw everything.

"J.D.'s very lonely," she said quietly. "Ever since his wife Lily passed on, he's so sad. I suppose he needs a wife."

Devlin laughed, the first outright burst of enjoyment she'd ever heard from him. She couldn't help but stare at him, at the wide grin, the crinkled eyes, the creases in his skin that made him look like he'd experienced life for centuries. A knot tightened in her chest.

"I know of many a miserable new husband who would disagree with you, my dear Wilhelmina. In London there are gaming rooms that cater to gentlemen of misfortune who once thought that taking a wife would bring joy and peace into their lives and soon learned otherwise." He glanced at her, silvery eyes twinkling with deviltry. "Don't get angry on me, now. There are just as many good-intentioned young brides who have devoted themselves to proving that a woman can bring a man true happiness."

Willie drew up rigid in her saddle. "You don't sound as if you believe they can. Is that why you're not married?"

"Believing it and finding it are two altogether different circumstances."

"You haven't found a woman in all of England who can make you happy? Perhaps you haven't tried hard enough."

"Perhaps she isn't in England."

Willie's heart jumped like a startled rabbit. Jerking her eyes from his, she dug her boot heels into Beau's flanks, lengthening his stride to a gentle lope. With only a murmur from Devlin, Edgar matched the pace and drew alongside, so close Devlin's leg touched hers.

"I'm a dreamer, Wilhelmina," he rumbled. "Just like you."

Her throat swelled. "I'm not—"

"You're clinging to broken dreams just like your father did.

You're waiting for a man who isn't worthy of you to come back and marry you, and he never will.''

"I'll never forgive you for that."

"If he was fool enough to leave you he's not coming back."

Willie shoved her heels deep into Beau's flanks. Edgar stayed right alongside.

"We're dreamers," Devlin rumbled above the thud of the horses' hooves. "We learn nothing from our mistakes or the mistakes of those around us. If anything we cling all the harder to our own high-flown ideals. Hell, I watched my parents make each other miserable for years before my mother ran off with a man who never could have made her happy. She died miserable, just like my father. Any other man would have little faith in the power of love after experiencing that. But for some reason I'm clinging to my ideal even harder because of it.''

"Then you're a fool." Willie reined Beau sharply to the right, along a path that skirted a small mountain ridge. In three strides, Devlin pulled alongside her.

"I'll catch you no matter how fast or recklessly you ride," he muttered. "The horses can't keep this pace for ten miles. You'll break them both." His gloved hand shot out and grasped Beau's bridle just as he tugged back on Edgar's reins. Both horses skidded in the grass so sharply Willie had to stand in her stirrups to keep her seat.

"What the hell are you doing?" she snapped. "Let me—"

Quick as lightning, he grasped her upper arm and lifted her entirely out of her saddle and up against him from chest to hip. The startling contact trapped her voice in her throat. But not his. Never his.

"Let you what?" His voice simmered with something deeply felt, something that sent a wild shiver through Willie. "Let you plunge recklessly where you wish? Sorry, but every dreamer needs to be reined in before they do something stupid."

Her mouth snapped open. "I'll tell you what's stupid. Stupid is riding off with a man I know nothing about to chase trouble in a town full of no-good, railroad-greased cusses who don't give a damn about Prosperity Gulch. Stupid is letting that same stranger come between me and J.D.''

"The only thing standing between you and Harkness is your lack of feeling for him.''

"That's not true. I love J.D. He's like a father—''

"Indeed. A pity he doesn't share your sentiment.''

She gulped and tried to ignore the tingly awareness pulsing through her. "J.D. cares for me—''

"I don't doubt that. But when he looks at you he doesn't see a child.'' His voice dipped low and husky. "He sees a woman, full-grown and ripe as a peach, ready for the taking. When a man looks at a beautiful woman, when she touches him on the arm, when her body brushes against his as she kisses his cheek and smiles up at him, do you know what a man thinks about, Wilhelmina?''

"I—'' Willie swallowed, mired in confusion. It was a tiny bit difficult to think about anything when Devlin talked like that, when he looked at her mouth like that, when her body responded to his beyond the call of her will.

She knew what a woman thought about at moments like this, when wantonness robbed her of logic, and her breasts tingled and her loins felt heavy. She thought about what lay under his fine clothes, she thought about running her hands over it...she thought about what she'd seen when he turned to face her at the pool's edge, when he'd worn nothing at all....

His chest pushed into hers. "I'd wager you know very little about it, no matter what you think happened beside that stream with Masters. For a woman who's been familiar with men her entire life you have innocence written all over you.'' With a flex of his arm, he forced her head back and her mouth under his. Her hat slipped from her head, her hair spilled down her back, and her resistance crumbled. "There's nothing disreputable about you,'' he rasped. "And, therefore, no reason that I can think of for you to marry Masters.''

She licked her lips, twisted her fingers in his topcoat and

clung to one last vestige of reason, even if it was a long reach. "I love him."

"You might think you do. Giving a man a few kisses doesn't mean you owe him your heart, or the rest of your life."

"Yes, but—"

"Don't argue with me, Wilhelmina. Let me prove it to you."

Devlin's lips were warm and firm, his kiss so tender something melted inside of her like butter over a low fire. A pitiful moan struggled from her throat at the first gentle thrust of his tongue, and she opened her mouth for him, eager and frightened at the same time. And she wanted more, so much more.

Devlin lifted his head. Her lips throbbed, swollen, wet, wanting. She felt the pressure of his fingers digging into her arm, saw the tension in his face, the flare of his nostrils.

"There's a world of difference between lust and love. You'd do well to remember that."

He might as well have dumped her in an icy stream. Her eyes flew wide with spurred rage and she shoved her fists against him. "*Lust?* Is that what you think this is?"

One corner of his lips tipped upward. "No? Then you must be in love with me."

She gaped at him. "You're despicable."

"Arrogant, yes, but despicable? Remember, you hardly know me."

"I know enough." Thoroughly annoyed, she yanked her arm out of his hand and righted herself in her saddle. Then she saw her hat on the ground. "You might think you know everything," she huffed, dismounting to retrieve her hat. Twisting her hair back into a knot on her head, she shoved her hat on and remounted. "And you might think I need to learn a lesson or two and maybe I do. But I can tell you this, I'm not marrying Brant Masters out of any guilt over what might have happened on that knoll beside the stream one afternoon—" She bit her lip. He watched her.

"Have you considered the small matter of you kissing me back?"

All business, she wrapped Beau's reins around her wrist and stood in her stirrups to test their length, unnecessary at this point but she couldn't look at Devlin. "I'd rather we both forget this."

"Ah. A triviality."

"Yes, that's it."

"Perhaps to some women."

"To the disreputable sort, yes. You just accused me of being lustful, didn't you?"

"Passionate."

Willie swallowed and urged Beau into an easy trot. *Passionate, with hot fires burning under her.* Her saddle creaked as she shifted uncomfortably. Devlin drew alongside her. She lifted her chin a notch and squinted out over the horizon, feeling his eyes on her, feeling…uncomfortable. No, not quite that. Fidgety. Self-conscious. Giddy. She felt as if she were blushing from the inside out.

Brant had looked at her like that. But something about the way he'd watched her and touched her, something about the way he'd pushed her back on that knoll had made her feel…

Disreputable.

She pushed the thought from her mind. They rode the rest of the way in uncomfortable silence.

Sloan thanked the man behind the counter and exited the hotel. He paused on the boardwalk beneath a sign that creaked in the wind, and squinted across the street at the Deadwood Run general store. Through the glass and between several fancy dresses on display in the window he spied Willie. Actually, he glimpsed only the curve of her backside, but even at this distance he knew it was her. She turned and disappeared behind the window display, as if she'd stopped to look at those fancy dresses and hold the pleated and flounced hem against her arm…dreaming.

The prettier of the two dresses was an ivory-and-emerald striped taffeta evening gown trimmed with emerald bows and flowers. The bodice draped low and nipped tight at the waist, then flared into a soft bustle. The cap sleeves would ride just off her shoulders, leaving her arms bare.

He felt a strange tightness in his chest. She should have that dress, and a dozen others to hang in her empty armoire. She should have parasols and shoes in every shade. She should never pound a hammer into fence rails again.

If only someone could convince her.

She stepped from the store and adjusted her hat low against the glare of the setting sun. Its rays seemed to capture her and set her aflame. She looked...young, not altogether innocent at the moment and too damned ripe, as if she would blossom through her clothes with her next breath.

With something very close to hunger Sloan watched her descend the steps to the boardwalk and pause to glance up and down the street. She seemed oblivious to the lingering looks she received from the men who passed her. She halted three well-dressed men midstride, sent several lively female conversations into abrupt silence, and nearly caused a collision between a stagecoach and a wagon loaded with chickens when each of the drivers found more interest in her than in the street.

When one well-dressed young man paused beside her and tipped his hat, obviously intent on conversation, Sloan bolted into the street and through the tangle of crisscrossing traffic. He caught her arm and sent the young man on his way with a well-directed scowl. Odd, but he'd never resorted to a snarling offense. She frowned up at him, obviously displeased with his untimely interruption.

"Did you tell him you were engaged?" he asked.

She turned on her heel, thumping him in the stomach with her hatbox as she did so. "He didn't try to kiss me, if that's what you're asking."

Sloan watched the sway of her backside and followed behind her, feeling like a protective maiden aunt. The thought prompted a scowl. Again he caught her arm. "No, this way. We're going to the Devil's Gold Saloon for dinner."

"What are we looking for there—other than food."

"Dakota Darby."

Her head snapped around and her eyes narrowed to glittering slits. "That's why we came? To see her?"

For some reason her mild irritation made him chest-puffingly pleased. "You might say that."

"You didn't need to drag me along to do it."

"To do what?"

She pursed her full lips. "To do what men do with women like Dakota Darby. She's the reason men come to Deadwood Run."

"All's the better. By the way, no sign of any railroad men at any of the local hotels. Then again, according to Cochran, they're sleeping on the ground out in the middle of the prairie."

She frowned up at him. "Why are you doing this, Devlin...whatever it is you're doing?"

"Chasing trouble, remember? I've never heard the truth mislabeled as trouble by so many who claim themselves in search of it. Maybe that's what bothers me so much."

"Why should it? You have no stake in Prosperity Gulch. You should ride off, just like—"

Their eyes met. "I'm not Brant Masters, Wilhelmina."

"You're not like any man I know."

His smile seemed to burst from deep in his soul. "Good. I intend to keep it that way."

"Don't you have anywhere to be?"

His scowl settled into place far too easily. "I could be in England. Actually, I should be there. I have what my father used to refer to as rather pressing responsibilities, responsibilities he tended to neglect. They've become infinitely more pressing since he died, and no doubt have further fallen into complete chaos with each passing day."

"You've family there?"

He shook his head. "Only Azato, but he needs no one. I have tenants."

"You're a landlord."

"In a manner of speaking."

"Then you'll go back."

Again their eyes met. "Eventually," he said. "There is an inevitability to duty we must all face at some point."

"It sounds like you're running from something."

"I prefer to think I'm searching for something." He scowled over the heads of the pedestrians crowding the boardwalk, distinctly uncomfortable with the turn of his thoughts. "Ah. There it is. A busy place."

"J.D. would give his soul for business like this." She seemed to slow her pace the closer they came to the Devil's Gold Saloon's double doors. The raucous sounds of the crowd cramming the saloon drifted out over the street. Smoke billowed from the place. A lively piano tune sang above the din. "You didn't need me here with you," she said, her voice tight.

Sloan drew her close as several cowboys wove erratic paths down the boardwalk and paused to leer at Willie. "True. But I want you here." She smelled like summer fresh meadows and wide-open skies. And when she lifted her eyes to his in unspoken question, he felt the vise clamped around his heart grip a bit tighter. He took her elbow and pushed open the double doors. "Stay close."

What the Devil's Gold lacked in refined patronage it more than made up for with its elegant decor. Three enormous gilded chandeliers threw a smoky golden haze over the throng. The walls were deep burgundy tapestry, the floor carpeted in the same color. A mahogany bar occupied the center of the expansive room, serving up drinks in crystal glasses and stemware. Barmaids in elegant burgundy evening gowns made their way among the tables with trays balanced over their coiffed heads. The establishment was filled to capacity with a mixture of cowboys, gamblers and disreputable-looking women. The entire back third of the place was occupied by a wide stage, draped in the same dark velvet and gold braid. Patrons crammed chairs, one all but atop the other around the stage.

"Show's in five minutes," a mustached barkeep offered when Sloan paused at the bar. "Best get a seat now. You ain't seen nothing till you seen Dakota Darby and her feathers."

"Two whiskeys," Sloan muttered, retrieving a stool just vacated by a mumbling cowboy. "And two house specials." At Sloan's nudge, Willie sat, pulled her hat low over her eyes, and stuck her nose into the glass the barkeep slid in front of her. The barkeep lingered as Sloan stuck one hand into his trouser pocket. "I'm looking for some friends of mine." Sloan tossed several coins on the bar. "Hyde and Strobridge are their names."

The barkeep picked up the coins. "You ain't from around here."

"Neither are my friends. They're out of Boston." Sloan tossed several more coins onto the bar.

"I ain't seen 'em."

Sloan pressed a bill flat on the bar and slid it to the barkeep. "But they've been here before."

"Everybody comes here, mister." The barkeep pocketed the bill and coin. "Specially railroad men from back East. They come in here every night when they's in town promoting their interests." The barkeep jerked his head to a large round table in a corner near the stage. "They sit right over there, waitin' for Dakota to come talk to them. Hyde and Strobridge. That's what they call themselves."

"And they're alone?"

"Sometimes they have a couple fellas with them." The barkeep's eyes flickered over Sloan's waistcoat and high-knotted cravat. "Gents like you who wear their money."

Sloan kept his face impassive.

The barkeep turned to a nearby tray and retrieved two platters of rare meat and potatoes swimming in watery gravy. Sliding them in front of Sloan and Willie, he jerked his head toward the stage. "Show's starting."

Sloan watched the barkeep amble off then glanced at the table in the corner, occupied by five swarthy-skinned men in evening clothes. Their conversation seemed to bounce off the walls surrounding the table until the houselights dimmed and the gas footlights on the stage were lit.

An expectant hush filled the saloon. A moment later the piano struck up a haunting melody. All eyes, including Sloan's, riveted on the stage and the shimmery curtain where an oval spotlight danced, waiting.

"Hyde and Strobridge."

Sloan glanced at Willie, knowing at once by the set of her jaw and the fire leaping in her eyes that she'd convicted and hanged him in an instant, without explanation.

His fingers clamped around her arm to keep her there should she get any ideas otherwise. "I met them on the train," he said, looking deep into her eyes. "You know I'm not one of them."

She gave a harsh laugh. "Really? You dress like them. You sound like them. You call them your friends. In another minute you're going to tell me to sell and get the hell out of the path of progress. That's what they said the last time they came to the farm. Only they weren't smiling."

"I'm not your enemy, Wilhelmina."

"Then why am I so afraid of you?"

"You've nothing to fear from me," he said softly. The air between them seemed to compress and thicken. Sloan cupped his hand around her shoulder and battled an urge to draw her deep into his arms. She seemed to sway closer to him, and he to her, until the brim of her hat brushed beneath his chin and her scent wrapped like soothing arms around him. He barely heard the roar of the crowd around them as the curtain swept up.

"Oh, my God," she whispered suddenly. "They're pink."

Chapter Ten

Dakota Darby's notoriety did not stem from the shocking shade of her feather fans. It was the ingenious ways she used them to hide all the uncovered areas of her body while she moved around the stage singing ballads in lusty tones. That such a talented performer had descended on a town in such dire need of drama had been a source of wonder for all of Deadwood Run. It had also enhanced Dakota's aura tenfold.

Though Willie had never seen Dakota Darby, she'd heard a great deal about the woman from her brothers, particularly the youngest, Wes, who had professed himself smitten with the singer at first sight. She'd overheard more vivid descriptions of Dakota's talents from the miners, in particular her nightly exits from the stage without the benefit of her feathers. Knowing this, Willie ducked her head against Sloan's chest and tried her damnedest not to peek at the stage. It was an impossible feat for a girl as curious as Willie.

"I want to go," she muttered, glancing at the stage and feeling heat prick at her skin. Dakota, she noted with profound regret, was quite pretty, not overly done, as Willie had expected, with a cloud of apricot blond hair that seemed to lean toward a pale shade of pink. Her arms were round and ivory smooth, her shoulders gently sloped and womanly. Beneath the sweep of the fan her legs were slim and shapely. A heart-shaped face framed enormous blue eyes and her cupid's-bow mouth was painted a ripe, rosy pink. The sultry words she sang promised only a fraction of what her voice and body offered. A vision of everything lush and female, she captured and held every eye in the place. Willie felt conspicuously un-womanly.

And then Dakota's heavy-lidded eyes met Sloan's.

Willie swallowed and glanced up at Sloan. His face was masked in indifference, but he looked all the more imposing and handsome because of it. Jaw tight, brows low, his eyes reflecting the gas footlights, he watched Dakota Darby with an intensity that made Willie go cold. She turned to flee but was met with the unbending pressure of his arm around her waist.

"You're not going anywhere." He sounded ominous.

"D-don't make me watch this."

"That innocent, are you?"

"Yes—" Her head snapped up. Her gaze locked with his. "Is that why you brought me here? To prove some theory?"

"Your kiss was all the proof I needed." He lifted his eyes to the stage.

Willie licked her lips and stared up at his profile. Her kiss. His had tasted of raw, untamed passion tightly reined.

A chorus of whistles and shouts rose around them. Dakota's voice dipped extraordinarily low in a final, drawn-out note that dripped with sensual promise. Sloan's eyes narrowed on the stage, on Dakota, on the wispy tips of her feathers brushing over her soft skin. And Willie, drowning in embarrassment and curiosity, couldn't help herself.

Daring another peek, she felt her throat close up when Dakota folded her fans in front of her and turned her bare back and lush backside on the throng. Willie knew she should tear her eyes from the stage but she couldn't. With saucy sways of her hips, Dakota moved to the back of the stage, turned slightly and, with a sly wink that sent the place into an uproar, lowered one fan to offer a glimpse of one large, pink-crested breast, then disappeared behind the curtain.

Several men stormed the stage and the three hulking men who guarded the entrance backstage. Others bellowed for an encore. Several threw punches at each other, overturning a table.

"Close your mouth." Sloan nudged her beneath her chin with the tip of one gloved finger. "Come on. I don't think either of us is hungry." Without waiting for her reply, he grasped her fingers in his and tugged her along behind him through the crowd toward the stage. He mounted the side steps and found his path blocked by one of the hulking men.

Willie clutched the hatbox to her belly. "Devlin, I don't want to go back there—"

Ignoring her, he fished into his trouser pocket then muttered something to the man. In reply, the man peered around Sloan at Willie. Eyes averted, Willie flushed to her hairline when Sloan snatched her hat from her head and drew her into the glare of the gas footlights. The man gave her a quick yet startlingly thorough once over, then jerked his head toward the rear of the establishment.

"What did you say to him?" Willie asked as Sloan pushed the curtain aside and tugged her along backstage.

Sloan plunked her hat on her head. "I told him you were Dakota's sister."

Willie glared at the back of his head, tugged her hat low and, in the process, stumbled over a coil of rope. "The hell you did. You paid him, just like you paid the barkeep."

"And if I did?"

"I wouldn't trust anyone whose loyalties can be bought."

"I don't want their loyalty. I want information."

"From Dakota?"

"Especially from her."

"Anyone can be paid more to keep quiet."

"Not if I'm one step ahead of the game." Sloan led her

down a narrow set of steps into a long corridor with a door at the very end.

"A game," Willie huffed. "That's all this is to you."

"It helps to think of it that way. They are."

"Who is?"

Sloan didn't break stride or glance back at her. "Whoever doesn't want us to find out who really blew that mine."

"You mean the men who blew it."

"Or someone with something at stake if we find out the truth. I'd tell you not to trust anyone but that would be a bit repetitive, wouldn't it?"

Willie shrugged off a chill, but her fingers wrapped tighter around Sloan's as he ducked down another corridor. A bite laced her tone. "You've been here before?"

Sloan laughed. The sound echoed warm and mellow against the dark chill of the corridor. "No, never here, but all theaters are alike backstage. There's a familiar scent."

Willie wrinkled her nose. "It must be Dakota's perfume. A musty scent, isn't it? Like an old woman."

"More like tarlatan costumes and rice powder and resin."

Willie froze and yanked on her hand. "You're from the theater, aren't you? I knew it the moment I spotted you in your fancy clothes. Admit it. You're an out-of-work actor from New York."

Sloan turned, his eyes sparkling with a strange mixture of mirth and admiration. "My dear suspicious girl, I spent half my childhood backstage at Her Majesty's Theatre in London. My mother was a singer. She was quite well-known, notorious, actually, and somewhat of an anomaly since she refused to give up the stage when she married my father."

"Why should she? Marriage shouldn't confine anyone."

His gaze deepened. "No, it shouldn't. But in England, some things just aren't done. People must live by certain rules, especially if they're peerage." At the quiver of her brows he added, "By day my mother was Lady Catherine Devlin, Countess of Worthingham. By night she was Cat, the famous singer.'' He leaned nearer, his eyes sparkling with deviltry. ''A woman of the theater,'' he murmured. ''My father's inability to reconcile the two led to the demise of their marriage. Well, that and a certain Italian tenor from Naples.''

Willie felt her belly flip-flop and chagrin flood through her. ''That means you're a count.''

''Fifth Earl of Worthingham actually. Of course, you don't believe me.''

Willie narrowed her eyes. ''What should I call you?''

He drew her hand to his lips. ''Something endearing would do. 'My darling Sloan,' perhaps?''

Willie fought against a smile, pursing her lips to accomplish it. She felt his breath on her fingertips and yanked her hand away. ''What do they call you in England?''

''I'd rather not say. I've made a few enemies there among the mine owners. My tenants fondly refer to me as 'His Lordship.' Always in the third person, even when they're speaking directly to me. Not that they mean anything untoward by it. It just makes me feel a bit too high-flown and self-important. I'd prefer Worthingham.''

Willie considered it. ''I like Devlin better.''

He tucked her hand in his and continued down the hall. ''Fine. We'll work on the endearments.''

When Sloan paused at the door, Willie drew up stiff just as he lifted a hand to knock. ''I'm not going in there with you.'' She looked up. *And I don't want you going in there, either.*

''I'm not leaving you out here alone.''

''What could she possibly have to tell us that's worth anything? She's just a—'' Willie bit off her words.

''Just a what?'' His eyes went icy silver. ''Some women will do anything to keep a roof over their head. Some sing. Some dance with cowboys for two bucks. Some even imagine themselves in love with the first man they kiss on the edge of a stream. That doesn't necessarily make them disreputable, does it? Maybe she's waiting for something just like you are.''

Willie felt her cheeks burn.

Sloan jerked his head back toward the stage. "She could have any of those men out there. We know it. You can bet she knows it. And yet I'll wager she's alone. Waiting."

"For who?"

"Not for just anybody. Remember that, Wilhelmina."

Before she could reply, he turned and rapped on the door. Several moments later the door burst open. "Dammit, I told you not to bother me—" Dakota Darby's mouth snapped closed. Baby blues traveled a path from Sloan's chest clear to his eyes. She seemed to melt into her words and into the door at the same time. "Why, hullo, gent." Without taking her eyes from Sloan, she jerked her pink blond head at Willie and pressed ruby red fingernails to the deep vee of her pink satin wrapper, precisely where the folds gaped over her bosom. "Who's the sister?"

"I ask only a moment of your time," Sloan rumbled.

"Give me more than a minute," Dakota drawled, drawing deeply on a cigarette then exhaling swiftly through her nose. "You might change your mind."

Sloan tipped his top hat and introduced himself and Willie, who tried very hard not to notice that Dakota Darby in all probability wore nothing beneath her wrapper. The satin clung to her breasts and the lengths of her tapered thighs. Willie glanced up at Sloan, certain that from his vantage he had an unimpeded view of Dakota's lavish charms. But he gave no hint of it. His face remained pleasantly impassive, his voice cordial and ringing with the cultured tones of an aristocrat.

An earl, no less, come to save Prosperity Gulch. Or was it, as he'd said, merely a game? A sick, demented game for an aristocrat bored with his responsibilities and out for a bit of fun.

Willie glanced up at him again and felt something twist inside of her when he said something to Dakota and smiled. For one breathless instant, before she realized, every suspicion she harbored was vanquished and trust blossomed in her heart.

"Thorne." Dakota squinted at Willie through the smoke of

her cigarette. "Any relation to the Prosperity Gulch Thornes, the ones who died in that mine?"

Willie met the woman's gaze squarely. "My pa and my four brothers died when the Lucky Cuss blew."

Dakota drew on her cigarette, her powdered face unmarked by emotion. "I knew your brother Wes." She squinted through the smoke. "Anyone ever tell you you look like him?"

Willie felt a tightness in her throat. "My mama. But that was a long time ago."

Dakota waved her cigarette. "It's in the eyes. Something...but he looked sad, and you—" Dakota glanced at Sloan. "You got him, don't you, sister?"

Willie blinked furiously. "I don't have—"

Dakota's eyes narrowed on Sloan. "You from Denver? The Pinkerton National Detective Agency's got an office there. They've been through here a couple times looking for some bank robbers."

"Or mine saboteurs," Sloan said.

"No, they'd leave that one alone."

Sloan's voice was smooth as warm butter. "Why should they? It's a mystery begging to be solved."

Dakota sucked hard on her cigarette then tossed it to the floor and crushed it beneath her slippered foot. Glancing swiftly down the corridor, she stepped back into her room and muttered, "Nothing to solve."

Dakota tried to push the door closed but Sloan shoved his fist into the wood. "I'll pay handsomely."

"It won't be enough," Dakota said. Drawing her wrapper high and tight at her neck, she added, "Listen, Mr. Devlin, take your woman here and get the hell out, before—"

"Before what?" Sloan's tone was soft, and yet an ominous chill crept over Willie. "Whatever they're promising you for your silence won't be worth anything from the inside of a jail."

"I don't know what the hell you're talking about, mister—"

"You're an accessory to a crime. Sometimes knowing and saying nothing is as bad as committing the crime. I'd wager a mob of angry townsfolk won't bother to ask why you did it before they hang you. Neither would these Pinkerton detectives if someone were to alert them to you. Listen—'' Sloan grabbed Dakota's hand and pressed something into her palm. "I'll be at Thorne's Boardinghouse if you change your mind."

Dakota snatched her hand into the pocket of her wrapper. "You'll be waiting a long time, mister. Or you'll be dead first." Dakota's eyes darted to Willie. "And so will she."

"That's not likely," Sloan said. "We'll catch them first."

Dakota snorted. "You two?"

Sloan cocked a brow. "That many of them, are there?"

Dakota flushed and tried to slam the door.

"There's a theater in London," Sloan began in a low, hypnotic voice, "with a stage four times as large as this, and an auditorium that could seat a few thousand. My mother performed on that stage for years. In fact, I'll be returning there shortly, by Cunard steamer out of New York. I intend to visit the theater owner. He's always looking for hungry talent."

Dakota blinked up at Sloan and Willie saw a flicker of hope spark in her eyes. "Get the hell out of here," Dakota snarled.

Sloan's fist met the door. "One name," he rasped.

"One name and I don't see the next sunrise. It happened before to someone else who knew too much. She wasn't guilty of anything. And look what happened to Brown."

"Another innocent?"

"Hardly." Dakota caught herself. "I learn quick. Good night, Mr. Devlin." The slam of the door shook the walls.

"That did not go well," Willie said.

"Better than you might think. Come on." Sloan grasped her hand and tugged her along back up the corridor. "Frightened?"

"You should be, too."

"What sort of protector would I be then? Ah—'' Abruptly Sloan ducked around a corner, shoved open a door, and drew

Willie into the cool early evening air. He paused, glanced around what appeared to be the rear of the saloon and headed for a narrow alley that skirted the saloon on one side. "This way. The horses are in front."

Willie hurried along after him, hatbox thumping against her thigh. "I want you to know that I don't need a protector. I never have and I never will."

"Then you don't need a husband."

"Needing and wanting are two different things, Devlin."

"Ah. And you know all about wanting. And husbands. Stop."

He drew up so swiftly at the corner of the building, Willie bumped into his arm. Curious, she peered around him and tried very hard not to notice the male scent of him. The length of his bicep brushed the side of her breast and she jumped as if touched by flame.

Without thinking, she whirled away from him around the corner and onto the boardwalk. She spied the horses tethered in front of the Devil's Gold and hurried toward them. She thought she heard Sloan call out to her, was certain she felt the heavy thud of his footsteps on the boardwalk behind her. In another second he would wrap her in his heat.

She quickened her pace. Darting past several gentlemen, she grasped Beau's reins, threw them over his neck and had just reached for the saddle when someone grabbed her around the waist.

It wasn't Sloan. The touch was too hard, too rough. It made her think only of escape, not surrender.

She whirled, jabbing with one elbow and swinging her hatbox. Both connected. She heard a grunt, a brutal expletive and then a black sack was shoved over her head, pinning her arms to her sides. Her bellow of outrage was squashed in her chest when she was hoisted over a man's shoulder like a sack of flour. Hatbox thumping, feet thrashing, she felt the wind sucked from her lungs as the man turned and ran. He took only three or four steps then grunted and fell to his knees.

Willie landed flat on her chest, rolled to her back and struggled to get the sack off her head. An instant later it was whisked over her head. She gulped a clean breath and found herself staring up into Sloan's glower.

"Taking care of yourself, eh?" he snapped.

Her reply clogged in her throat when he brushed a tangle of hair from the corner of her mouth with one finger. He loomed over her, blocking all but the starry indigo sky, and she was possessed of a sudden need to reach her arms up around his neck and draw him close.

His gaze lingered on her mouth. "Catch your breath."

"I've got it." She shoved up to her elbows, expecting him to rise. He didn't. She lifted her eyes and felt the warmth of his breath on her mouth and the heat of his body leaping into hers. "Help me up, Devlin."

He even found her hat and the hatbox. "Do you know him?"

Willie stared at the man sprawled on his back in the street. His dusty boots pointed skyward. "You didn't kill him, did you?"

"Hardly. Is he a friend of yours?"

Willie stared long and hard at the man's whiskered face, the dusty denims and worn hat. "I've never seen him."

"I thought so. Some men will do anything to find themselves a wife." His gaze met hers. "And some women a husband."

Willie felt her mouth snap open. Sloan turned and strode toward the horses. Willie stomped after him, pushing past several onlookers who had gathered around. "What the devil do you mean by that?" she demanded, hands finding her hips.

He retrieved a length of rope from her saddle then turned and looked her over from head to toe in a way that made her go hot from the inside out. "You're begging for trouble in clothes like that, Wilhelmina. You have been since we rode into town. Why the hell do you think I wouldn't let you out of reach in that saloon?"

Willie ignored that. "What's the matter with my clothes?"

"Nothing. It's the fit. Or rather the lack of it."

He tried to move past her but she shifted her shoulders, blocking his path. She glared up at him, feeling her cheeks throb with her flush. "You think I'm fat."

His eyes seemed to darken. "No. I think women formed like you are not meant to wear men's clothes."

She thrust out her jaw. "Because you think I'm fat."

He leaned perilously close to her. "If you'd like, my dear, we could debate the merits of every inch of your lovely body at great length, anytime you wish. But right now, I think justice would be better served if we find out exactly why this cowboy tried to kidnap you—much as I'd prefer to think he had only matrimony on his mind. Help me tie him up and then we'll—"

A gunshot rang out. A bullet whizzed past Willie's ear and pinged off the hitching rail. She spun toward Sloan and was met with the force of a brick wall. She fell heavily to the dirt, pinned beneath him, her face crushed against his chest.

"Get to the horses," he growled, levering himself up, wrapping one arm around her waist and flipping her to her belly. "Crawl," he rasped close to her ear as another bullet slammed into the dirt not three feet to her left. "On your elbows. That's it—faster—I'm right here—"

Willie blinked through sweat and dust and matted hair, swallowed her fear and a good bit of dirt, and scrambled toward the horses. Bullets sprayed around them. People scurried from the street with frightened screams. Pressed against her back, Sloan scrambled with her, then hauled her to her feet just as they reached the horses. Before she could grasp Beau's reins, Sloan lifted her onto the horse's back, mounted Edgar and, with a shouted command, sent both horses off at a full gallop down the street.

It wasn't until they were a mile out of town that Willie realized she'd left the hatbox in the middle of the street.

Chapter Eleven

About two miles outside of Deadwood Run, Sloan pulled Edgar to a stop in a small grove of trees and dismounted. Beau skidded behind him, chest lathered, sides heaving.

"We can rest them here," Sloan said, tugging off his gloves.

Willie looked over her shoulder. "They could be following us."

"Not likely." Stuffing his gloves into his coat pocket, Sloan slipped Edgar's reins over his head. "Rather ardent admirers, aren't they?"

Willie's head snapped around. "They weren't admirers. You know that. They were warning us to stop asking questions." She slipped from her saddle. One hand clutched the rifle in its saddle holster. The other gripped the saddle horn. She stared out over Beau's back into the endless stretch of moon-washed prairie grass. "They've got something to hide—something worth killing for. They killed my family. Now they want to kill me."

Sloan looped Edgar's reins around a tree and moved toward her, ignoring the warnings in his mind to keep safe distance. A woman in need didn't know what she was doing in her vulnerability. And he—true, he considered himself a gentleman incapable of exploiting vulnerabilities to suit his own purposes. But he didn't think he could maintain his head alone in the moonlight with her.

He stopped at her back. The breeze stirred, lifting her scent to him. His arms ached to wrap around her. "They could have killed both of us on that street and they didn't," he said softly. "They just didn't want us to talk to that cowboy."

"He was going to kidnap me."

"Probably for a few hours."

"But who knew we were going to Deadwood Run?"

"Tom Lansky. Cochran." He hesitated. "Harkness." She seemed to draw up stiffly. "Anyone could have seen us ride out."

She sagged against Beau. And then she turned and curled into Sloan's arms. Her hat slid from her head. Her hair fell like a thick copper curtain around them. Sloan drew her deep against him, tucking her head under his chin and stroking the curls from her face. He stared over her head and felt her heart thumping madly against his.

"They murdered my family," she whispered. "And they let my pa take the blame. They let everyone believe he was a fool. They let me believe it, too—I didn't want to—but I did, Devlin. Part of me believed that he'd blown that mine out of his own reckless need to find silver that was never there. I wanted to blame him for that, for everything he'd done to my mama...for the dreams he stole from my brothers, from me—" Her voice cracked, deepened. "I was the fool."

"No," Sloan murmured.

"I'm just going to give it to them...whatever they want. The farm, the mine, the house. It's lost all its worth to me—" She lifted her eyes and moonlight shimmered in her tears.

Sloan's chest felt tight. "Listen to yourself."

"I am. I can't live like this. I can't expect Gramps to. I'll sell out to the next cuss who walks up the road. I mean it—" She blinked and tears spilled to her cheeks and quivered on her lips. "I do," she whispered again.

Sloan lowered his head and glimpsed the despair in her soul. "I won't let you. I'll find those men, Wilhelmina."

She lifted her face and closed her eyes. "Yes," she breathed, "I know you will."

He heard the warning bells going off in his mind and ignored them. Tenderly he lowered his mouth to hers. Her lips parted and she arched up and into him with a need that drove the last of the reservations from his mind. He told himself to be gentle, even as he tasted her tears, thrust his tongue deep into her mouth and crushed her in his arms. He reminded himself that she was an innocent, vulnerable as a child, even as he curved one hand around her neck and slid his open mouth down her throat.

He told himself a hundred logical, lust-dampening things as he pushed her shirt away from her collarbone and over her shoulder and tasted her skin. He envisioned his lands, his tenants, his responsibility and the cold emptiness of Devlin Manor awaiting him on the headlands and crushed his mouth over hers again.

He thought of his title, his father's empty chair. He saw the faces of the tinners, the widows and their children as buttons slipped through loops beneath his fingers and cotton shirt slid over smooth shoulders and fell to the ground in a whisper.

He felt the mantle of centuries of family honor and its legacy on his shoulders and lowered his mouth to the heaven of her full, young bosom.

He thought about the years of training, the grueling torture he'd undergone to prove himself worthy of his title as master over his body as he sank to his knees and lost himself in the taste of her skin, the feel of her flesh in his hands, the vibrant, womanly essence of her. He thought about all of it, kept it plainly in his mind and knew a joyous defeat.

He curled one finger around the ribbon at the top of her chemise, tugged, yanked and heard her intake of breath. Her hands gripped his shoulders.

"Don't make me stop yet." His voice was that of a tortured

man. He slipped first one hand then the other beneath the loose cotton undergarment, and curved his palms around her rib cage. Her skin glowed with the milky luminescence of a pearl. "Sweet perfection." He pressed his mouth to her breasts.

She stiffened, shuddered and sagged against him. Her fingers dug into his shoulders, clutched at his head, and then she twisted away. "I can't."

"You can. You just don't want it now."

Arms over her breasts, she looked at him through the curtain of her hair. "It's not you, Devlin."

"I didn't think it was." He picked her shirt from the ground and stood. She didn't shrink away when he reached out and eased one strap of her chemise up over her shoulder. He rubbed his knuckle over her skin, then handed her the shirt. Their eyes met. Sloan knew a moment of utter despair. "Yes, I remember, you're Brant Masters."

"You have your duty in England."

"Quite right. I'll—" He waved a hand at her, glanced over his shoulder at Edgar. "I'll—" He turned, took two steps, then spun around. "I've got it. An odd thought, but hell. Why not? You could marry me."

Her face was obscured by shadow. Her silhouette remained motionless. She said nothing, simply stared at him.

He took a step toward her, feeling his heart hammering in his chest. "I understand you made a promise, and one's word is, well, his honor. I suppose women feel that way, as well. Reputable women, and you are certainly that. But a promise is not a vow, and it's certainly not a binding contract, complete with consideration and all that. Particularly if you're the only party to the promise."

"Lust is not love, is it, Devlin?" she said softly.

He stared at her. "No." But this was more. He'd known lust, the base, physical need. This was...deeper, a desire for a joining of far more than bodies.

"I thought so. Not after only three or four days."

"Quite right. Impossible, actually. Love, I mean."

"Not lust."

"No, that was there almost immediately."

She glanced down at the shirt she held close to her breasts. "You're offering marriage to make your lust reputable."

Sloan scowled. "That's a hell of a way to put it."

"Is that what they do in England?"

"Men rarely marry for love in England. Or lust, for that matter. Those sentiments are saved for the illicit amours that come after the nuptials."

"Then why marry at all?"

"My sentiments exactly. But duty means heirs and heirs demand good lineage. That sort of thing."

"So you intend to marry?"

Sloan stared hard at her. "The woman won't have me." She turned away, as if she couldn't look at him. "We have to solve this thing with the mine." He watched her shrug into her shirt. "Quickly."

She turned toward him, her profile illuminated by the moonlight, fingers working at her buttons. "So you can return to England."

"So I can find Brant Masters."

The ax whistled through the air and chomped into the log. Wood chips sprayed. Willie turned her head, rubbed a dirt-smudged forearm over her brow, wiped the perspiration from her neck with her hand, then gripped the ax handle tighter.

"You been out here all mornin', Willie-girl."

Willie didn't spare a glance for either Gramps or the enormous pile of split and neatly stacked wood. "Devlin did that."

"You don't say."

Willie swung the ax and with all her might drove it into the log. "It feels good to sweat," she muttered in answer to his unspoken question. She tossed the split wood atop the pile.

"Guess Devlin thought so, too. He was out here before the cock crowed. Now we got enough wood to last us two winters."

"We'll need it. Once Devlin's gone." She felt Gramps's stare and the heat climb from her neck into her cheeks. Blinking perspiration from her lashes, she swung the ax.

"Oh, we got company," Gramps muttered, scratching his neck and giving a cockeyed smile when Willie glanced up sharply. "Bessie Lewis."

"Bessie Lewis? What the hell does that man-hungry, busybody want? I'll tell you what she wants and it has nothing to do with me or my lemon cookies. She and her uppity friends have ignored me ever since Brant and—" She bit her lip. "And now she comes calling and I'm supposed to—"

"Devlin's with her."

Willie felt her stomach sink. "You left them alone?"

"He's tellin' her all about London. I gave 'em some lemon cookies. Devlin fetched some water. Bessie said it was too hot for coffee."

Willie dropped the ax and set out toward the house at a determined march, smacking her hands clean against her thighs.

"You might wanna wash up," Gramps called after her.

She snorted. Bessie Lewis's reasons for being in her house and eating her lemon cookies were no different than Gertie's had been when she'd slithered her way to Sloan's table. When a woman had known desire and wanting she had little trouble recognizing it in other women.

She strode past the water pump without a glance, blood pounding in her ears. She glared at the polished buggy and beautiful bay parked on the front drive and felt fury bubbling inside of her. Her boots thumped on the porch steps. The door thwacked open against the opposite wall at her shove. She stepped into the kitchen just as Sloan stood and turned to her.

Her eyes met his and her heart skipped a beat. He seemed taller today, his legs longer, thicker, his shoes more polished, his topcoat more finely tailored, his hair shinier, his eyes a vivid blue. It seemed she'd been wise in taking great pains to avoid him for the past three days. As he had with her.

And in that time they'd accumulated one hell of a pile of wood.

His gaze fell to her mouth. Willie glanced at Bessie Lewis. Blond, plump and spoiled every day of her nubile eighteen years, she blinked up at Willie with smug satisfaction lurking in her baby blue eyes and sank her small teeth into a cookie. She was a puff of pink satin and creamy white skin, oozing from the top of her gown in lush, overripe abundance. She wore delicate pink lace gloves that matched the tips of the lace slippers peeking from beneath the hem of her knife-pleated gown. Pearl bobs dangled at her ears. She looked every inch the epitome of fashion and womanly charm, a role she'd fervently embraced as the daughter of Douglas Lewis, Prosperity Gulch's general merchant.

Willie had long ago decided that Lewis had stayed on in Prosperity Gulch after the mine blew simply because he was certain of lofty status in the community. He obviously hadn't foreseen the problem of finding a suitable husband for his only daughter in a town with a noticeable lack of available men. Judging by the way Bessie's eyes traveled a slow, consuming path up Sloan's backside, she appeared to be attempting to remedy her predicament with great haste. She'd attempted the same with Brant Masters and had failed, a circumstance which seemed to hover between them in heavy silence.

Willie felt a trickle of perspiration weave between her breasts and licked her lips, tasting grime. A wood chip dangled from a curl at her temple and she flicked it away. "You've met Mr. Devlin."

Bessie licked her lips and powdered sugar fell to her bosom. "He was telling me about traveling over the ocean on a steamer, weren't you, Mr. Devlin?" Eyes coyly lifted at Sloan, Bessie reached for another lemon cookie, a precarious move in a bodice ill designed for a woman of such startling proportions. Of course the wily Bessie knew that and pressed a trembling hand to her bosom as if to help keep it contained.

"Where's your mother?" Willie asked, pouring herself a glass of water from a pitcher.

"She's tending to the sick, as she always does, being the Jesus-fearing woman that she is. Just like me. She knows I'm here." Her eyes shifted to Sloan and she smiled. "And she knows why I've come."

Willie drained half the glass in one gulp. "And she still let you out of her sight."

"Ladies—" Sloan said.

"You're one to talk, Wilhelmina Thorne," Bessie said, her tone rising shrill and thin above Sloan's. "You think because you're a Thorne you can go about as you please, wearing clothes that no decent woman would be seen in, *stealing* men from the arms of their women."

The glass thunked on the table. "I think you'd best leave," Willie said.

"Please, ladies—"

Bessie surged from her chair. "It wasn't only Brant you tricked into proposing to you. Even before he came to town, you were squirming your way into J.D.'s bed. My mama and I could never figure why Lily just up and died so suddenly. One day she's talking fine, poor thing, so confined, the next day she's dead in her bed. I say she knew what was going on downstairs between you and her husband and she meant to do something about it. There's talk she might have been poisoned. Something just found its way into her soup, poor thing. You were cooking for her, weren't you?"

A dull buzz droned in Willie's ears. "If you step a foot on my property again, Bessie Lewis, I'll shoot you. Devlin, show her out."

Eyes wide, bosom surging, Bessie pressed a hand on Sloan's lapel. "Thank you, Mr. Devlin, as you can see, Wilhelmina's a bit—" Bessie gave a helpless smile "—like her father. A bit strange and out of control. Little wonder the tales being told about her. Disreputable tales that could curl a woman's hair. I'd flee for my life if I were you, sir." She slid a plump arm through his. "Come see my new buggy, Mr. Devlin."

Willie turned to the sink, gripped the edge of the counter and blinked away a hot rush of tears. The door banged closed behind them. She squeezed her eyes closed and saw the faces of the townsfolk watching her as they always did when she rode into town and walked the boardwalks with J.D. Her heart twisted. Oblivious to their stares, thinking their thoughts friendly, their smiles genuine, she'd held his arm and walked close beside him for miles along those boardwalks.

Even now she felt his arm comfortingly against her breast, remembered brushing against him a thousand times, leaning close to him, in her blind innocence…kissing his cheek a hundred times, smiling up at him, stopping in to see him at the Silver Spur when no one else was around. They'd drunk whiskey there together, even before Lily had died.

Sweet, tragic Lily, unable to move in her narrow bed, always with a smile on her lips and an anguish in her heart.

"Oh, God." Willie hung her head in her hand and felt a hollow shame for being so foolish. Disreputable. She'd been labeled. Not because of Brant, because of J. D. Harkness.

Shoving a hand across her cheeks, she turned and drew up sharply. Sloan stood in the open door.

"I've known my share of women like Bessie Lewis," he said. "Spiteful, jealous creature, selfish and spoiled to the bone. I pity the man who takes her to wife."

Willie stared at the ashes in the hearth.

"Don't ever run from the truth, Wilhelmina."

"You think that was all lies?"

"Of course, it was. You've no reason to run."

She swallowed and felt her chest compress. "There's such a fine line between truths and untruths."

"Illusion." He stepped into the kitchen and closed the door behind him. "It has to do with intent. People see what they want to see. Women like Bessie see things that aren't there to give themselves something to talk about. Harkness has his own reasons for seeing what he wants. Your only fault in the matter is a bit of naiveté."

"You put a hell of a lot of faith in a stranger."

"We were strangers to each other for about thirty seconds."

"We will be again."

Their eyes met and Willie felt a stab of despair. Shaken, she turned to the table and began to clear it of a scattering of dishes.

"Bessie mentioned something about a town hoedown next Saturday."

Willie turned to the sink and the dishes clattered. "They're held once a month at the church. Gives all the girls like Bessie something to buy a new dress for."

"What about you?"

Willie squeezed a rag. "I don't buy dresses, Devlin. And I don't dance."

"Then it's time you did both."

"Says who?" She spun around, hands gripping the edge of the counter. "You think you're going to take me to some dance?"

He scooted a chair from his path. "It occurred to me, yes." He moved toward her. The counter dug into her back as she pressed deeper against it.

"I don't need dances," she muttered, thrusting her chin up at him, feeling suddenly very small. "And I don't need fancy dresses. I don't need any man holding my hand and whispering sweet words in my ear. I don't need moonlight or stream banks under a warm sun. I don't need anything. Do you understand, Devlin? Most of all I don't need you."

"I know," he rumbled, towering over her. He levered both hands on the counter on either side of her and leaned so close to her she had to crane her neck back. His eyes were glassy, impenetrable mirrors of silver. "But needing and wanting are as different as lust and love."

Willie's throat swelled closed. She felt the brush of his shirt against her breasts, felt the rush of exhilaration that came whenever he was near. His thighs were long and hot against hers, pinning her back against the counter. She tried to ignore it. All of it. Especially the firm, beckoning contours of his mouth. "Take Bessie Lewis to that dance, Devlin. Kiss her under the moonlight. Maybe she wants what you want."

"Tell me what I want, Wilhelmina," he murmured.

She stared at his cravat tied high and perfect around the thick column of his neck and thought her heart would burst from her chest. "You want to be someone's champion. You have pity for the small man. But you can't fix everything. Especially people who don't think they need fixing. People like me."

"You don't know what you need. And as for wanting—" He cupped her face in his broad hands and lifted her eyes to his. "You're right. I need to make it right for you. I need to find out who blew that mine. Maybe more for me than for you and all the people who've suffered because of it. Hell, who can say what drives people to want what they want? Maybe guilt. I don't think anything can chase that away. I thought coming out here would help. All I know is that when I look at you I feel a deep need to protect you."

"Or prove that you can."

His eyes narrowed and his thumbs brushed the corners of her mouth. "Such wisdom from such an innocent."

Willie felt her lips begin to throb. A longing ache settled in her limbs. "You weren't protecting me the other night under that tree. You're not protecting me now."

"No," he murmured, curving his fingers around her head, lifting, tilting her mouth up. "This is wanting. It goes beyond thought or reason. It knows no schedule, remembers no promises to another, or responsibility. It's quite beyond my physical or mental control."

Willie blinked up at him, wanting with a desperation that could have driven memory to the distant reaches of her mind. The smell of him filled her nostrils. The feel of him against her was like heaven.

They would be strangers again when he left.

She pressed a hand to his chest, feeling herself go rigid. "Find the men who blew the mine, Devlin. Maybe then you'll find what you're looking for. I can't give it to you."

His eyes narrowed for a fraction of a second and then he drew back. Willie felt a chill wrap around her heart and loneliness creep into her soul. She almost reached out to him.

"So sorry, my dear," he said, his voice retrieving its smooth tone. All traces of passion were gone. "But I thought I saw something in your eyes. I was, of course, mistaken." He turned, moved to the door, then paused. "If you should change your mind about next Saturday night, let me know."

Long after the door had closed behind him, Willie stood at the window, watching the dust settle once again over the path he'd taken on the road to town.

Sloan tossed the bound pages on Lansky's desk.

"That was fast," Lansky mused, picking up the pages and peering at the headline. "The Iron Horse—Manifest Destiny, Savage Capitalist Irresponsibility or the Frontiersman's Greed?" He glanced up at Sloan. "You're kidding, right?"

"You wanted an editorial."

"Yeah, but not something so damned inflammatory."

"I thought about The Iron Horse Cometh, Blowing Its Steam Breath."

Lansky's brows shot up. "That's good."

Sloan eyed Lansky warily. "How about The Windstorm Sat Down on Its Hind Legs and Howled and Screeched and Snorted?"

Lansky's face fell. "Didn't think you English gents had a sense of humor."

"I don't," Sloan said. "Sarcasm, but not an ounce of humor." Particularly since he'd left Willie in her kitchen. He'd thought he'd exorcised his demons, scribbling out his editorial on the front porch of the newspaper office. It was as inflammatory a piece as he'd written since the opinion he'd submitted to the Cambridge papers. That bit of literary genius had been enough to incite a riot between the tinners and the mine owners near Devlin Manor. With one stroke of his pen, he'd delivered over a hundred tinners, his father included, to bloody, pointless deaths. No, Azato had told him. The riot had been their choice.

Sloan almost reached for the editorial then swung around and ruffled through a stack of *Lucky Miners*. The innocuous headlines jumped out at him. Nothing the least bit inflammatory had been printed in the paper since its inception, from all he'd read of past issues. Nothing worth reading, either.

"This isn't going to please anybody," Lansky muttered. "Didn't you know you're supposed to write something that everybody will read and nobody will remember?"

"That's the point."

"You're looking to start something."

"It started long before I came to town and you know it. Let's finish the business with the mine, I say. And get on with life, without fear of telling the truth and without this damned mistrust of progress. The people in this town deserve it." He strode to the door. "Quit thinking about circulation and free excursions on Union Pacific dining cars."

Lansky yanked open a side drawer of his desk and tossed a silver-barreled pistol onto his desk. "I'll print it, damn you. It'll be in today's paper. But I won't sleep without this."

Sloan narrowed his eyes on the gun. "Blame me. But I think you're more curious than you are afraid of the consequences. It's the curse of a true writer."

"The townsfolk will either burn your house down or elect you sheriff. I wish to hell I could say what the railroad will do."

"It will bring them out if they're around, I can virtually guarantee that. From what I know of Eastern capitalists, they care a great deal about propaganda. Look at it this way, maybe they'll paper the walls of their East Coast offices with the issue." Sloan opened the door. "Think of it as free publicity.

You might wind up behind a desk at a highbrow paper in Boston, wearing embroidered waistcoats over your prosperous paunch.''

"I'm more likely to end up dead. Where are you going?''

"The Silver Spur. I need fodder for my next editorial.''

"If you live long enough to write another.''

But as he headed down the boardwalk toward the Silver Spur, Sloan didn't give Lansky's warnings another thought. He was without fear, determined to rouse the townsfolk out of their mindless acceptance of their fate and rally them behind the search for the truth. If that meant pitting them against a band of ruthless men intent on exploiting the damage that had been done to them by the railroad, so be it. He couldn't idly sit by and allow justice to go unavenged. And Willie to wither and die out on that farm, a casualty of guilt and victimization.

He entered the Silver Spur and paused to allow his eyes to adjust to the darkness. He muttered an apology as he jarred shoulders with a man who mumbled something in reply and continued on toward the door. Sloan stared after the man. Something about the way the man moved, the swing of his tailored coattails, the set of his hat, gnawed at Sloan. Something familiar—

Sloan strode to the bar. "Good afternoon, Harkness.''

From beneath the bar, Harkness withdrew a rifle and pointed it at Sloan. "Get the hell out of my bar.''

Sloan listened to his breath hiss. "Dammit, man, I didn't come here to fight with you about Willie.''

"I'm gonna start counting.''

"Where's Gertie?''

Harkness gave him a strange look. "Upstairs.''

Muttering his thanks, Sloan turned and headed for the stairs.

Chapter Twelve

"Who you plannin' to shoot with that thing?"

Willie folded the sheet over the line and smacked her hands against the cotton to smooth it. A breeze flapped through the row of bedding. The sun rode high in a clear sky. Wildflowers tossed their colorful heads in the wind. The rifle propped next to her basket of wet linen looked oddly out of place. But she'd kept it close since Sloan had ridden to town three hours before.

She peeked at Gramps through the sheets. "We were shot at in Deadwood Run the other day."

Gramps shoved his toothpick from one corner of his mouth to the other and set his jaw. He squinted west toward the mountains. "Devlin must not think you need it or he wouldn't have ridden out these past few mornin's."

"Fine, but I'm not going to underestimate these men. I think they could have killed us if they'd wanted to. They still could. For asking too many questions." Willie bent to the basket.

"Questions needed askin' a long time ago. I shoulda been the one to do it. Who'd bother shootin' at an old man like me?"

Lifting another sheet over the line, she gave Gramps a look that typically brooked little argument from him. "Don't you go poking around now, Gramps. You're not to blame. I am. I thought it would be easier to just leave it alone. To let Pa take the blame. It was easier to sleep nights, thinking the matter had been put to rest. I didn't want to think—''

"That someone murdered him? Or that they mighta had good reason to think about it? Not many folks liked him much.''

"They didn't have to like him to believe in his dream.''

"Yep. He sure talked a fine streak. Always did, 'specially after the war and he came home all decorated like a hero. Anyone would've believed him. Your mama did. I sure did. He was a showman. Always talkin' big. He'd take the boys to the Silver Spur and drink and his mouth would be spoutin' to anyone who'd listen. Cowboys, gamblers. Anyone could've killed him for all the silver he thought was in that mine.''

Willie smoothed her palms over a sheet that fit the bed Sloan slept on. It billowed up into her face like the gentle caress of a man's hand. "That's a hell of a risk for someone to take. To go so far as murder on fool's talk.''

"Happens every day, if you're talkin' about gold or silver.''

"Maybe. But everyone knew Pa was a showman. I think people stopped believing his stories a long time ago.'' A heaviness weighted her heart. "I know I did.''

"Me, too.'' Gramps stared off at the mountains.

Willie's gaze followed. The wind whipped through the sheets. "That mine showed no promise for years. Why would someone go to the trouble of murder if they weren't sure there was silver there?''

"They coulda been sure.''

"How? Unless Pa knew he was about to strike the lode or if he had—'' She thought a moment then shook her head. "He would have told us first, or the boys. Or J.D. He definitely would have told J.D. And he didn't, or J.D. would have told us. It doesn't make sense.''

"Devlin wants to make sense of it for you, Willie-girl.''

She cocked a dubious brow. "Really? Even with Pa and the boys gone the mine still belongs to us. Everyone in town knew that. It'll always belong to us.''

"Unless you sell out to the railroad. Course, you could marry. Then the farm and the mine and any silver down in there will all belong to your husband."

Willie glanced up sharply and felt a chill wrap around her heart. Only two men had asked for her hand since the mine had blown. Brant Masters and Sloan Devlin. Two strangers, so different from each other. Were they driven by compassion and a noble need for justice, or by base lust and greed? She'd learned the hard way that men would say or promise anything to win what they wanted from a woman. Was Sloan an opportunist, deftly manipulating her with fictitious theories and smooth talk, seducing her trust along with her body?

Gooseflesh prickled on her arms. "I think some people know what really happened down there. Gertie suspects something. Dakota Darby knows and she's too afraid to say anything."

"Afraid?" Gramps snorted and shook his head. "Not those women. Money can buy silence, Willie-girl."

"It can buy murder. These men must have a lot of money."

"Not so fast. Around here, folks come cheap. Even Dakota Darby. Course, people been known to change their minds no matter how much money they've taken."

"If Devlin can't wrestle a conscience out of her, no one can." She caught herself, hearing the reverence in her voice. She glanced at Gramps and felt a flush climb up from her shirt collar when she found him watching her with a glint in his eye. Abruptly she turned and fished deep in the basket of wet laundry. "I didn't mean—"

"I know what the hell you mean. You're talkin' to an old man. Hell, I got nothin' better to do than watch you two."

"You'd be better off watching the grass grow."

"Yep. Nothin' out of the ordinary. 'Cept you been flittin' around here like a hummingbird ever since Devlin showed up. And he's been watchin' you like your pa used to watch your mama when he was courtin' her back before the war."

Willie went suddenly still. Yes, she'd felt Sloan's eyes following her as if he wished to memorize her movements. Any woman would get all jittery getting watched like that. She lifted her chin. "I'm not nervous, if that's what you're saying."

"I'm sayin' you didn't flit and your face wasn't always red as a ripe beet when Brant Masters was sleepin' in the front room. And you were gonna marry him, remember?"

Willie poked her head between two sheets and glared at Gramps. "You finished? The horses need to be moved from the north pasture before they eat themselves sick on clover. And there's fence rail to be set."

Gramps flicked his toothpick to one side of his mouth. "Yep. Guess I'll paint the house while I'm at it. Anythin' to keep from makin' you listen to somethin' you don't want to hear. Kinda like the mine, isn't it? Sometimes the truth is damned painful to hear."

"More like an old man's foolish fancy," Willie muttered, disappearing behind the billowing sheets and pulling a tangle of wet chemises from the basket. One by one she strung them on the line and listened to Gramps's chuckle fading as he moved off toward the north pasture. The truth.

Or illusion. She suddenly didn't trust herself to know the difference. Friends had become spiteful enemies, strangers trusted confidants. Was she laying her trust where it didn't belong, driven by bodily yearnings she couldn't control?

Again.

She felt the hoofbeats drumming against the earth before she heard them. One hand gripped the line. The other drew a wet chemise against her belly. The horse was coming fast. One horse from the sounds of it, churning up the road from town. Through the flapping sheets she glimpsed the cloud of dust left in the horse's wake. The sheets fell, billowed again, and she glimpsed the coattails snapping behind the rider, the uncommon breadth of his shoulders....

Her heart jumped. Her pulse skittered along. As much as she might have wished otherwise, a bubbling anticipation flowed through her along with a surge of relief. Relief? Because Sloan was coming back? Because she wouldn't need to keep the rifle within reach if he was around?

Not five minutes ago she'd considered that he might have asked for her hand out of greed. Five minutes ago, he was a slick opportunist, plying her with charm, cleverly leading her on a foolish chase for a fictitious murderer. Truth or illusion. Would she ever look into anyone's eyes again and wholly trust them? And if Sloan Devlin had never come to town, would she have found contentment in her ignorance? She was certain she'd have preferred it to this.

"Hullo, Willie."

She went entirely rigid, then cold, then hot. Her insides began to tremble. Somewhere outside of the billowing sea of white cotton his voice rumbled again, just as it had a thousand times in her dreams.

"Let me see you, girl." The wall of sheet was yanked down. Brant Masters filled her vision. He was bigger than memory had served, thicker, taller, more imposing. More handsome, if it were possible. And more disarming. His dark, deep-set eyes raked over her. "Come here."

Her response clogged in her throat and she tried to take a step back but he was too quick, his arm too strong as it curled around her waist and crushed her against him, pinning her arms to her chest.

"Say you forgive me, sweetheart." His voice was laced with the haunting, silky tone she'd heard in her dreams. The sound of it roused memories and feelings that she'd thought she'd buried forever. She could almost forget the tears she'd shed many long nights on her pillow. She reached deep for her anger, struggled to find it. Where the hell was it? After all, she'd nursed it for six months.

He'd come back for her!

She should be elated. She'd wanted this. It proved she hadn't been taken for a fool. Not that that mattered most. Brant mattered most, being with him, becoming his wife. Not pride.

Mama had always told her it was the woman's place to forgive and nurture. And yet she felt herself stiffen when he drew her deeper against his chest.

"What the hell—?" He reached between them and tugged the wet chemise from her hands. He held it up, his fingers visible through the transparent cotton. His lids drooped over smoldering black eyes and his generous mouth curved into a smile that made something chill deep inside Willie. "I missed you," he said, crushing the chemise in his fist.

Willie braced both hands against his chest, stiffened her arms and met his gaze with a jut of her chin. But her words weren't born of anger, oddly enough, but of a stalwart dose of Thorne pride. "You said two months. It's been over six."

His eyes narrowed a fraction of a second and then he gave her a dazzling smile that would have melted a snowcapped mountain. "My girl's gone and grown up."

"Wiser, is all."

His gaze dipped to her bosom. "That isn't all. You're every inch a woman now."

Willie shoved away from him and headed for the house with brisk strides, wondering why she felt so uncomfortable when he looked at her like that and talked like that. Six months ago she would have thrilled to those words. Now she didn't know what she wanted, or what she felt. And part of her knew why, and it had nothing to do with Brant, or six months worth of wounded pride.

"Whoa, there." He blocked her path, sidestepped when she did, once right, then left, then caught her hand and grinned, a lazy, lopsided smile that made the birds sing in the heavens. "Don't run off just yet. I brought you something." He dug into his topcoat pocket then hesitated. "Unless you don't want it."

Willie stared up into his beautiful face, and felt her heart wrench and her emotions dart in a dozen different directions. "I don't know what I want, Brant."

"Good. I'm here to show you. Close your eyes."

"I don't think that's—" His smooth fingertips swept over her lids. "Fine. They're closed."

"Don't open them until I tell you." He lifted her left hand and slid a ring onto her ring finger. She felt her heart grow weighty. "You know what this is? It's something I promised you a long time ago, that night when we were down by the river."

"You didn't promise me anything that night," she said, remembering his face, her anger. He'd left on the train east that night, without another word to her, left her to cling to the murmur of a promise made in the depths of passion.

"A man knows when he has to do the right thing by a woman. We both made a promise to each other that night when we laid together beside that stream. I always intended to keep to mine. Now open your eyes."

She almost couldn't. The ring felt ominously heavy on her hand. She opened her eyes and felt her throat close up. The diamond was enormous, a perfect oval, set in a wide band that slid easily over her finger. She'd never seen or imagined anything like it. She touched a finger to the stone, expecting warmth. But the diamond was cold.

His fingers gripped hard around hers. "What do you think took me so damned long? It's not as if I didn't try to get here sooner. I had to make the arrangements to leave my business in New York and my home there. And I had to get the ring. You won't find a diamond like that anywhere west of the Mississippi. It was hard to come by, sweetheart, damned hard."

Yes, even to the dispassionate eye the stone was exquisite, almost garish in weight and size. On her sun-browned fingers, with their sensible short nails, the ring almost looked ridiculous. Willie lifted her eyes and saw a desperate hope shining in his. "Brant, I can't."

He pressed his fingers to her lips and stepped closer. "You can't tell me you don't like it. Hell, some women would sell their virtue for—"

"Stop—" Willie threw off his arms. Frustration thickened her voice. "That's just it. I'm not like those women. I can't accept it if there's even a little part of me that thinks you're buying me with this ring."

"It's an engagement ring, dammit. Every woman in the world wants one."

"This isn't a ring, Brant," she said hoarsely, slipping the ring from her finger and holding it out to him. "It's a bribe. Here. I can't wear it in good conscience. Not yet."

Sunlight flashed in the gold, drawing Willie's eye to the scrolled engraving on the inside of the band. Her gaze locked with Brant's and something melted inside of her. She'd thought she loved this man once, desperately enough to sacrifice her pride and pin every hope on his return. She'd also thought she'd hated him at times over the past six months. And now…pride waged a brutal war against a yawning emptiness in her heart that ached to be filled with love and trust.

"Read it," he murmured.

"I'm not going to change my mind." Still her eyes were drawn to the script that wound around the band. "*Angel—For promises made in heaven—BM.* You've never called me 'Angel.'"

"You don't know the half of what I think about you."

"You left without a word. The whole damned town knew—"

He took a step nearer. "I know."

"No. You don't know the first thing about it." She swallowed and glimpsed Gramps standing out in the north pasture watching them. She suddenly felt very young and unwise. "I can't promise you anything, Brant. Not yet."

He stared at her with eyes gone black as pitch then glanced at the house. "You got yourself another man?"

Heat swept to her hairline and she directed her eyes to the ground. "No. I've got a boarder."

"Then there's still room for me. In the house and in your heart." He plucked the ring from her fingers, tossed it once into the air, then pocketed it with a wolfish grin. "A little time is all I need to win you over."

"But—" Her voice caught when he brushed his knuckle under her chin then turned and strode to his horse and the gear he'd stowed on the back of the saddle. He'd traveled unusually light, given that he'd ridden into town six months ago with enough valises for two well-dressed women, and a shiny new buggy to carry it all in. Now he'd come with less baggage than a cowboy.

Willie pressed her palms into her thighs. This wouldn't do. Sloan and Brant under the same roof? Strangers cohabiting could be worse than brothers. She envisioned them lunging over the table for food, the fierce competition for attention, weekly brawls. She'd get nothing done trying to avoid both of them.

"You're sly as your pa was."

Willie jerked from her thoughts. "Quit spying, Gramps. I saw you over in the pasture."

"I tried my damnedest to ignore you." His chuckle jerked his narrow chest. "Like I said you's a sly one, gettin' Masters to stay. Connivin', too."

"I wish I knew what you were talking about."

"Now you can choose the one you want most."

Willie dug deep for conviction. "I don't want either one."

"Mmm-hmm. Your mama said she didn't want your pa 'bout a week before she married him, just like that."

"That's because she trusted pa. I don't know if I trust Brant or Devlin. I'm thinking about throwing them both out."

"Maybe you should—at least one of them."

Willie saw the concern etched deep into the weathered lines on his face. Thornes had never said much about caring for one another. They wore their hackles more comfortably than they did emotion. At least her pa and brothers had. For them, emotion was something for the womenfolk of the world to bear. Their camaraderie had been gruff, their love displayed only through the devotion and respect they showed Pa. Gramps had forever hidden behind his gibes. And mama...she'd poured her love into the meals she'd cooked, the clothes she'd mended and the house she'd kept long after she'd lost faith in her husband's dream.

Something hot stung Willie's eyes and she shoved the back of her hand over them. "I swear, Gramps, something's wrong with me and I don't know what it is."

His hand rested on her shoulder. "I do. You need a husband. And fast. Babies, too. Lots of them, to keep you too busy to connive. But you need a good man first."

Her throat swelled and she stared at the ground through misting eyes.

"Don't fret," Gramps muttered. "Proposals don't come to half the women in Prosperity Gulch." He squinted up at Brant waiting on the steps to the house, a valise in one hand. Gramps lifted a hand in a mockery of a greeting and bared his teeth in a smile. "Guess I have to be nice to him."

"If I can forgive him, you can."

"I don't believe you'll ever forgive him. Not that I'm tellin' you to." He turned and ambled toward the house. "I'll clear out the front parlor before I head into town for the paper," he said. "I can be nice, but I'm not about to let Masters sleep in the upstairs room next to yours. I'll climb those damned steps with a smile on my face to keep him where he belongs." He paused suddenly, turned and flashed a smile. "Course, Devlin could sleep upstairs—"

"Clear out the parlor," Willie said quickly. "I'll get the sheets. And I'll figure out where everyone's going to sleep." She turned toward the line of bed linen but her eye was drawn to the road leading to town. Even now the dust stirred by Brant's horse still hovered over the road. There was no sign of Sloan.

Tom Lansky stepped out of the newspaper office just as Sloan untethered Edgar from the hitching post.

"Better batten down your hatches tonight, Devlin, or whatever it is you English gents do when it storms."

"Skies are clear," Sloan replied, mounting up and glancing west at the glorious twilight skies.

Lansky locked the office door and hefted his loaded walking stick. "I'm not talking about the damned weather and you know it. Paper sold out by four this afternoon. In the ten years I've been here that's never happened. A few dozen gents from Deadwood Run come by and grabbed a handful. I can smell trouble in the air. Look around. Streets are empty. Everyone's inside waiting for something to happen. Or maybe they're oiling up their guns. Where the hell have you been?"

"The Silver Spur."

"I'm surprised you didn't get shot at. Cowboys rode in about an hour ago."

"I was upstairs."

Lansky's brows shot up. "Well, hell, I might have known. Gertie likes you fancy gents. She's always looking for a ticket out of here, something a working man like me can't give her. Hell, she won't look twice at a man who lives in a clapboard house and has ink stains on his hands. I reckon she'd go back to England with you on a flimsy promise."

"I don't make flimsy promises." Sloan touched the brim of his hat and bid Lansky good-night, a sentiment the editor didn't return. Lansky was right. The streets were deserted. The only sounds came from the Silver Spur where the cowboys raised their distinctive brand of fun. Shop windows were dark. As he passed by the general store he spotted Lewis standing at the darkened front window, watching him. The merchant's mouth suddenly jerked with words Sloan couldn't hear.

At the jail he passed Sheriff Cochran beside a deputy on the porch, their ladder-back chairs tilted onto their back legs. From beneath the brims of their hats, they watched him. Edgar's hooves clopped in the dirt. Sloan's saddle creaked with the horse's smooth gait. Silence swelled, and then above it clicked the hammer of a pistol.

''You ain't faster than a Colt, fancy man,'' Cochran snarled. ''Even on that horse.''

Sloan kept his back straight, his eyes leveled between Edgar's ears, and the horse's pace to a slow, smooth trot. For a lawman, Cochran was a bit too accepting of rumor to suit Sloan, and a bit too eager to draw his gun on an unarmed man.

Of course, if the lawman was involved in something underhanded, he wouldn't murder a man on the street for writing an inflammatory editorial. But under the cover of night, any man who knew his schemes were in peril of being exposed would feel compelled to do something. Even an Eastern capitalist determined to preserve his company's good name. Like Lansky, Sloan had a definite sense that something stirred in the air tonight, just as it had the night the tinners had led the revolt that ended in a bloody massacre.

He gave Edgar his head at the edge of town. The horse lunged into the bit. Sloan understood the horse's impatience, just as he understood his own. To get to the farm, to Willie. Not to tell her what he'd learned, or at least thought he'd learned from hours of conversation with Gertie. Not to theorize about motive and opportunity. Not to pour over the suspects he'd lined up neatly in his mind. Just to see her. To share space with her, to breathe the same air with her.

Dusk had faded when he pulled Edgar up outside the barn. When he'd finally cooled the stallion and bedded him down for the night, a full moon had risen over the eastern grasslands. He moved briskly toward the house, Huck loping along at his side, licking his fingertips. He ruffled the dog's ears and lifted his eyes to the dim light in the upstairs bedroom window. Warmth settled in his belly and spread. Damned place felt more like home than Devlin Manor ever had in thirty-five years.

His chest swelled against the confines of his waistcoat. ''Come on, boy,'' he muttered. It was then he saw the movement of a shadow ahead, a rippling silhouette that could only have belonged to one woman. He would know her in a dark room among a hundred women.

He had so much to tell her, so much he wanted her to know. Why in God's name did he feel as if he hadn't seen her in months? His voice rasped from the compression in his chest. "Willie—"

She moved into the splash of moonlight, her hair streaming gloriously to her hips. She wore the white, rose-sprigged dress that gripped her everywhere and reminded him at once that he was a man, red-blooded and potent. She was waiting for him.

"Damn you."

No, he must have heard wrong. He could smell the heady, womanly scent of her skin and his palms burned for her.

"You bastard." She stopped, jutted her chin at him and waved a paper in front of his nose. "I should shoot you."

Sloan reined in carnal thoughts, for the moment, and narrowed his eyes on her full lips. "You don't like it."

"Like it? I hate it." She jabbed him in the chest with her finger, punctuating each word with another jab. "I hate you. Hate. Do you understand what that means? For you to suggest that the settlers were motivated by greed—"

"Give me a better reason."

"Desire for a better life than their fathers and grandfathers had. A better life for their children."

"Better than their neighbor, is more like it. It's the eternal curse of wanting more. Better. Bigger. Never being satisfied. It's inherent to the American spirit. Someone was bound to be exploited because of it."

"That wasn't their fault. They were led out here by slick and flashy propaganda, innocent as lambs delivered to slaughter."

"You're too smart to believe that. Savvy businessmen would be fools not to capitalize on a rabid hunger for land, especially when they could buy that land cheap from the government and turn it over at a healthy profit to anyone who would buy. Maybe you hate the railroad so much because you realize that. I understand your need to place blame somewhere, and who better than a mighty corporation. But the railroad didn't deliver the settlers to their fate, and your father to his death. Their greed did.''

"I'll never forgive you for that."

He caught her arm before she could flee. "You'd be twice the fool to put the blame where the most help can be found."

He could hear her gnashing her pretty white teeth. "I'll never ask the railroad for help."

"That's precisely what you should do."

"I won't."

"And what will you win? Where's the victory? The dream died with your father. You have to take up your own dream now."

"I can't. The railroad killed my pa, my brothers—"

"The railroad had no reason to blow that mine. You know that. Stop putting the blame where it doesn't belong."

Her eyes flashed. "Then why did they form the vigilante group and burn poor—?"

"No railroad men formed that vigilante group. These Eastern businessmen are peaceful men. Hell, they represent one of the most powerful corporations in the country. You tell me why they would put black hoods over their heads and ride around like outlaws? The Union Pacific is mightier than the damned government! They could throw you off your land if they really wanted to. And they haven't, have they?"

"Listen to you!"

"Indeed, you'd better start listening to me."

"I won't, damn you."

"Fine." Before he could think, he grabbed her around the waist and yanked her full and hard against him. Every sweet inch of her burned like a firebrand through layers of clothing and into his skin. He tangled one hand into her hair and forced her head back. Moonlight shone in the tears in her eyes until she twisted her head away once, shoved at his chest and bit out a curse better suited to a miner. He crushed his mouth over hers. She tasted of cinnamon and sweet berries.

She whimpered, squirmed against him and twisted her mouth away. She shoved at his chest and stumbled back. "No—"

He grabbed her hand and yanked her back into his arms. "We're not finished," he rumbled.

"Yes, we are—!"

Again his mouth crushed over hers. It was a savage on-slaught, but he couldn't have controlled it had he tried. And he was past trying. The feel of her wiped his mind of everything but the need to lose himself and find himself at once, and to make her wholly his.

Her name rasped from his lips as he filled his hand with one breast. At the bold thrust of his tongue, her lips swept open again. He brushed his thumb over the peak of her breast and felt the nub tighten and push into his hand. Desire exploded through him like cannon shot.

"We can go anywhere," he rasped from the depths of his passion. His tongue traced the contours of her lips. He swept his hands over the fullness of her backside. "The barn, the pond, the damned woods. My bed. Where's Gramps?"

Her tongue peeked between her teeth, touched his then retreated. "You're not listening to me."

"Yes, I am. You hate me. I remember. We can talk about that at great length, later. Right now I want to kiss you—" He lowered his head and pressed his mouth along the length of her throat. "I want to touch your breasts—" His hand cupped beneath one generous swell and a deeply primal satisfaction shot through him when she seemed to lean against him.

"Devlin, this isn't what I'd planned. Not at all…"

He lifted the fullness to his face and swam in lush desire. "Sweet, Willie—you will give everything to me—"

"It's impossible," she said.

"The hell it is. I'll make it mine to control. I'll make you mine before another man can think to lay claim."

Her fingers bit into his shoulders, she stiffened and drew back. He lifted his head and felt the chill in her stare reach deep and coil around his heart.

"I think you should know, Devlin. Brant's inside."

Chapter Thirteen

Sloan felt the heat leave his blood with great dispatch. Masters had returned. Now it made sense, the dress, her hair, her waiting on the steps for him. Not to greet him. It hadn't been for him at all. She'd been waiting to tell him her fiancé had returned for her, and to lambaste him for his editorial. As for their kiss, he'd all but forced himself on her, like some over-anxious bumpkin who didn't know the first thing about seduction. In his zeal he'd imagined the quivering surrender in her. Mired in his uncontrollable passion, he'd ignored her squirming need to escape him. For Masters.

He felt an overwhelming need to pound his fists into hard oak. He felt an unconscionable desire to apologize to her. Instead he pressed his palms to his thighs and said simply, "Ah."

"Yes," she said, licking her lips. "I agree. He's staying in the front parlor."

"Gramps sleeps in the front parlor."

"I believe Gramps is moving upstairs, or into the barn."

"Fine then. I'll leave first thing."

"That's not—"

"Gramps isn't going to be climbing stairs on my account. I'll find another place to stay." He made as if to brush past her but she blocked his path. He looked down into her eyes and felt his lips twist with wry sarcasm and his hands clench into fists.

His voice rumbled like thunder from the tightness in his chest. "Unless you'd like me up there, sleeping in the room next to yours. The walls are thin, Wilhelmina. I'd be able to hear your clothes rustle when you dress. I'd know when you turn over in your sleep. I have a fierce imagination and a keen memory. I remember what you felt like in that pond without your clothes. I remember that your lips taste like sweet, ripe cherries and your hair smells like a field of warm grass."

Her fingertips reached out and brushed his hand in a soft tentative stroke, seeking his fingers, cajoling a softening from him he didn't want to give. "I'm afraid, Devlin."

He felt his fist loosen, his fingers thread though hers, and something inside him went soft as putty. "You shoot coyotes when they come too close to your property. You don't know fear."

"Men are different than coyotes."

"Indeed. Some of us are not so easily driven away."

"Really? You're going easily enough."

"I thought I was being noble. Into town for the night isn't back East for six months."

Her eyes met his. "You're going to the Silver Spur to sleep, aren't you? To Gertie. Gramps said you were upstairs with her all afternoon. The talk was all over town."

"So even you believe rumor when it suits you."

"It doesn't suit me to think my boarder is spending his afternoons upstairs with Gertie in her—" She waved a hand. "Doing—" She blinked up at him with eyes blazing. "You know—"

"What?" He tugged on her hand and she turned her head away. Satisfaction shot through him like sunlight blasting through a room long shuttered to the outside world. Here was the core of her anger at him, the real reason for her fist-waving greeting earlier. He'd wager it had very little to do with the editorial. "What do you think I was doing all afternoon, Wilhelmina?'' he murmured. "I think you'd be surprised. Gertie is a beautiful woman. The world is full of them. If that's all a man is interested in, he can enjoy a lifetime of feasting. But my interest in her is friendly at best. She knows much."

She glared at him. "You use everyone."

"Not everyone."

Boot heels scraped on the porch and thumped on the steps. "Darlin'?"

The sentiment, a languid drawl in the darkness, roused every protective instinct Sloan possessed. A tall, bulky shadow of a man moved toward them. Willie snatched her fingers from Sloan's and spun toward the porch before he could grab more than a fistful of woman-scented air.

"Brant—" She sounded breathless, too breathless to suit Sloan. And she looked too accommodating as she hurried toward Masters, almost as if she didn't want him to get too close.

"Who the hell is that?"

Sloan stiffened. Memory stirred somewhere in his mind, memory that for some reason coiled his muscles and sparked his suspicions. The voice...the self-satisfaction lacing the drawl...he knew it.

"He's my boarder," Willie replied.

Sloan probed the shadows beneath Master's wide-brimmed hat and searched his memory. Something in the set of the man's shoulders, the flare of his coattails...

The Silver Spur. Sloan hadn't been able to place him when he'd seen him at the saloon earlier that day. If only he could remember where he'd known the man.

"Devlin," he said, extending his gloved hand. "Sloan Devlin, late of Cornwall, England."

Masters went entirely still for several moments. A peculiar smile spread his lips wide over his teeth. They gleamed white and arrow straight in the moonlight, and hinted at wickedness. Sloan took an immediate dislike to the man, for reasons having nothing to do with Willie. With a flick of his hand, Masters tipped his hat back on his head, exposing the familiar classically handsome features, and the eyes that still looked as cold as they had when Masters had shoved his gun into Sloan's ribs and tried to steal his winnings on the train.

Sloan took an invisible punch to his midsection. Willie was engaged to the man Sloan had tossed from a train. Brant Masters was not the smooth and refined East Coast businessman Willie believed him to be, the noble knight who'd ridden away with her heart and left her clinging to a promise. Masters was a two-bit gambler, a down-on-his-luck cheat.

Sloan tasted bile on his tongue. On the train Masters had bragged about the lily-white, land-owning virgins that had turned to him in times of need…the only fortune he'd ever depend on.

Land-owning.

This was the man Willie had lain on that stream bank with, the man she'd granted liberties, and had convinced herself she had to marry because of it. The man who'd had the power to capture then break her heart. And now he'd returned and brought all those dreams and promises back to her. He'd put the wind in her lifeless sails, the hope back into her heart, and crushed six months of bitterness into nothing with one big-toothed grin. He'd proved she hadn't been a fool to believe in promises.

And more than anything else, Willie needed to know she wasn't wrong in believing. As much as Sloan might have wished otherwise, he couldn't bring himself to dim that light of hope in her eyes. At least not yet.

Afraid, she'd said.

Besides, Sloan was somewhat certain at the moment she wouldn't believe anything nasty he had to tell her about Brant Masters. Convincing her would have to be done delicately, subtly, with care and patience, something he didn't think he possessed at the moment, especially since his fists seemed to itch to be put to good use.

She'd lain on that stream bank with Masters.

The air between them seemed to thicken and crackle. Sloan met Masters's stare with unflinching, passive resolve. He recognized the taunt in Masters's gaze, and an irrefutable confidence in his stance. The man hadn't been intimidated by their encounter on the train. He obviously didn't believe Sloan a rival at this juncture, particularly where Willie was concerned. Sloan preferred to keep him under that misconception.

"You know each other." It wasn't a question. Willie looked from Masters to Sloan and back, her copper brows puckered.

"We've met," Masters drawled, his tone goading.

"We were never formally introduced," Sloan assured her, wishing to God she'd quit looking at him as if she suddenly didn't know him. "Has your luck improved, Masters?" he asked with smooth nonchalance.

"What do you think?" Masters slipped his arm around Willie's waist and drew her closer. Willie crushed the *Lucky Miner* to her chest and didn't look at Sloan. Sloan felt his body go rigid. "My affairs are finally tidied up back East," Masters continued. "I've got a ring in my pocket, and a beautiful woman who's going to say she'll be my bride by week's end. Is there any man who'd think I'm not the luckiest bastard standing here?"

"None that I know of," Sloan said, forcing levity to his voice. "It seems congratulations are in order—" Sloan advanced on them like a storm. Willie's head snapped up and he glimpsed the startled look in her eyes an instant before he grasped her hand and drew it to his mouth. "My very best to you," he murmured against her skin.

She frowned at him then folded her hand inward when he released it. He grasped Masters's hand and for the moment denied himself the pleasure of crushing the other man's hand. Forcing a smile, he turned toward the house and felt their curious stares following him.

However best it was to let Masters believe him harmless, it took a strength of will as yet untested for him to climb the steps and leave Willie alone in the moonlight with a man who'd vowed to make her his by week's end.

He muttered a greeting to Gramps as he passed through the kitchen to retrieve his belongings in the front room.

"You goin' to the Silver Spur?" Gramps asked when Sloan returned, valise in hand. The old man leaned against the counter, watching from the window, puffing on his pipe. Sloan wondered how long he'd stood there with the smoke curling around him.

Sloan paused, one hand on the door handle, eyes trained on the slim milky-white shadow in the yard. "What do you think?"

"You don't wanna know what I think. 'Cept maybe that some womenfolk need to be told things sometimes. You can't jest let them figure it out on their own. They might never."

"I don't intend to leave it to chance."

"Didn't think you would. There's a cot in the back room of the barn."

"I know."

"Thought so. You'll find it comfortable. Richard used to spend nights there when he'd come home drunk and Vera wouldn't let him in the house till he didn't stink anymore." Gramps glanced at him. "Don't suppose I need to tell you to be careful."

"You read the editorial."

"Didn't need to. Folks is buzzin'. They tend to forget 'bout an old man. Think we're all hard o' hearin' or just plain dumb. Kinda suits me sometimes to let them think that way. Most folks is sayin' someone's gonna want revenge. There's gonna be trouble tonight. Funny thing 'bout that, sheriff's two deputies rode outta town headin' for Deadwood Run late this afternoon. An' with trouble comin'. Go figure that."

Sloan watched the smoke curl around Gramps's head. "Good night, Gramps."

Gramps gave a brisk nod and turned back to the window. Sloan opened the door.

"Oh, Devlin—" Gramps didn't turn from the window. "Guess I don't get much reason to say it. But ain't nobody come along in a helluva long time who cared if an old man had to climb up those stairs to get to his bed. And I want to thank you for that. I don't feel invisible when you're around, boy."

"No one should," Sloan replied, oddly uncomfortable. As uncomfortable as Gramps seemed to be with the sentiment. He let the door thwack behind him. Willie turned toward him as he headed across the yard. One hand reached toward him then twisted in her skirt. "Devlin, wait—where are you going?"

"To the barn." He touched his fingers to the brim of his hat and lengthened his stride. "And I bid you both goodnight."

Willie rolled to her right side, punched her pillow and closed her eyes. If only she wasn't so hot. If only the sheets didn't smother her and her hair wrap around her neck like a noose. If only the voices in her head would grow silent. If only she wasn't so restless, maybe then she could sleep.

The clock over the hearth in the kitchen downstairs chimed once. The trill of crickets swelled to an almost deafening pitch. Her eyes snapped open. Kicking her legs free of the sheets, she left the bed and parted the lace curtain at the window. The barn crouched in the shadows of an enormous oak.

She touched her fingertips to her lips. *Like sweet, ripe cherries.* Her fingers pressed to the pulse beating at the base of her throat. Beneath a filmy sheen of perspiration, her skin felt feverish. Against her back her hair hung like a heavy curtain. She slid her hand behind her neck, lifting the mass off her nape and let her head hang. Her eyes swept closed and a vision bloomed of broad hands tangling in her hair, cradling her head, tilting her mouth up....

Her lips parted and she tasted the velvety warmth of his tongue against hers. Her back arched and she felt the steely bands of his chest pushing into her breasts. Her thighs brushed together and heat surged into her loins. The ache there swelled with a need to be filled.

Devlin had been wrong. She knew about the dark, dangerous and unknown side of wanting. She knew an animalistic wanting standing there in a splash of blue-white moonlight. She felt the moonbeams on her skin like the brush of Devlin's fingertips.

Turning her head, she saw her reflection in the dressing-table mirror and froze. This was not an innocent girl in the looking glass, a girl who preferred men's clothes, guns and whiskey to dresses, silk stockings and beaded reticules. This was a woman she'd never seen before. She looked like Dakota Darby. Like the portrait above J.D.'s bar. Like Gertie.

She looked soft, feminine, womanly. Her eyes glowed with a wondrous and mysterious allure she'd thought she'd never possess. Her hair fell around her shoulders and cascaded to her hips in wanton disarray. Her damp night rail caught between her thighs, molded the curve of her belly and clung to her breasts. Beneath the cotton her nipples looked large and ripe.

Eager, for a man's mouth, or a baby's…

She sank her teeth into her lower lip as a shudder rippled through her. With trembling fingers she pulled the ribbon loose at the top of her night rail. The cotton drifted apart. Cool air whispered over her skin. Her cheeks burned. She hadn't looked at herself without clothes in months, and never in the moonlight before her looking glass, never through the eyes of a man.

With both hands she parted the night rail. Her skin was white, her breasts milky and moon-splashed, the nipples a pale white-pink. Her waist seemed too narrow for her breasts and flaring hips, and between her thighs a lush triangle of dark copper drew her eye. She cupped a breast, brushed her thumb over the distended peak, and sensation shot to the heaviness between her thighs. Yes, she knew all about wanting.

But where was the logic in wanting a man that was as elusive as any dream, a man who'd said he would be leaving, while another waited, eager to make her his, eager to call Prosperity Gulch home? She could have everything she'd ever professed to want if she married Brant. And with Devlin she would find only broken dreams, and the unknown.

She threaded her fingers through her hair and watched moonlight play through the curls. "Surely it's fickle to love a man while he's gone and then decide to love another when he finally returns."

Love another. No. She couldn't possibly love Devlin. He was odd, eccentric, mysterious, frustrating and elusive. But wanting…yes, she wanted him. The feelings he stirred in her made a mockery of the quivering consent she'd granted Brant Masters on that stream bank. The girl of six months ago was gone. In her place was a woman, full of a woman's wants and needs. This was not an innocent's curiosity.

The night went suddenly still. A shiver crept up Willie's spine. The crickets always grew silent when the wolves roamed. Drawing her night rail closed, she moved to the window and parted the lace. The barn sat in shadow. Her fingers flew to the ribbon at her neck and yanked it into a knot. Something wasn't right.

Cautiously she crept from her room and down the stairs. At the foot of the stairs she retrieved the repeating rifle she'd left in the corner by the door and reached for the door handle. And then out of the corner of her eye she saw a shadow move. She tried to whirl and swing the rifle in blind defense but a hand clamped over her mouth and she was yanked back against what felt like a brick wall.

Her scream clogged in her throat. Only one man felt like a brick wall.

"You should be in bed," Sloan rumbled close to her ear. His forearm wrapped like an iron band around her ribs. Against her back she felt the heat of his bare chest. Along her buttocks his thighs jutted and his loins nestled with disturbing intimacy. The night rail suddenly seemed an extremely thin and ineffectual barrier. Her legs went suddenly weak. From relief. That was it. "Quiet," he whispered. "We wouldn't want to wake Masters."

Her brows met and she slanted her eyes back at him.

"Besides, I think you know we've got some unexpected visitors." He lifted his hand from her mouth and flicked the curtain back over the door window. "Three of them, maybe four. They tethered their horses at the end of the drive and came from the front. They're trying very hard to be quiet. If I'd been sleeping, I might not have heard them ride up."

Willie pressed herself deeper against Sloan. "Who are they?" she whispered, eyes straining into the darkness. She could see no movement in the shadows.

"Vigilantes. Thieves, cutthroats. Someone sent to scare you into selling your farm. Or someone who didn't like what I had to say in that editorial."

"You expected this. That's why you stayed in the barn."

"I never intended to spend the night with Gertie. In fact, I'd like very much to tell you about my afternoon with her. Now doesn't seem to be the time."

Willie swallowed over the lump in her throat and tried to ignore the fluttering in her belly, and the poignant ring of truth in his voice. "Here, take the rifle."

"I didn't come for the rifle, Wilhelmina."

She blinked into the darkness and felt her heart turn over in her breast. "I don't need protection, Devlin."

"I can't seem to remember that." He drew her closer, his hand tightening around her ribs, gently brushing the full underside of one breast. "I'm rather certain I don't trust Masters to see to your safety, seeing as how the man is still asleep. And you're very much awake."

"I couldn't sleep. I feel—restless."

"You're trembling."

She swallowed. "Go out there, Devlin, or I will. Someone has to chase them off my land."

"I was thinking more along the lines of catching them, at least one of them."

"Good idea. Come on."

His arm felt like steel when she surged against it. "You're not going anywhere."

She set her teeth. "We can't catch them in here."

"You hiss like a kitten," he murmured. "Something tells me you can purr just as readily. Ah, there, by the barn."

"What?" She blinked into the night, seeing nothing.

"Shadows move. Watch. There by the back corner. Two of them. The other one must have slipped inside."

"You must have eyes like a hawk. I don't see anything. The horses—"

"They're tethered at the edge of the woods."

He must have moved as stealthily as the creeping of the night to evade two or three men while he secreted the horses. Gratitude tightened Willie's hand over his. Frustration thickened her voice. "I can't just stand here and watch them burn my barn. We can have them arrested for trespassing."

"I want them for attempted murder. Stay here."

"No, damn you—" She clung to his arm as he slipped past her and reached for the door handle. "Let me—"

"Let you what?" His lips twisted wryly. "Trust me, Wilhelmina, if you go out there looking like that—"

She lifted her chin. "I can shoot as good as any man."

"They won't be thinking about your rifle." His knuckle brushed beneath her chin, his lips curved up and then he slipped by the door before she could retrieve her voice. She caught the door before it slammed behind him, threw it wide and surged onto the porch, hoisting the rifle. She blinked, her gaze darting about the yard for Devlin, but she saw nothing. He'd disappeared among the shadows, without even a ripple of movement. Just as she'd seen nothing of the three men...

The hair on the back of her neck suddenly stood on end. A horrifying dread seeped into her bones. Suspicion lurked at the edges of her thoughts. She'd believed Sloan so readily, so instinctively. Surely he hadn't invented the story to perpetuate his fabricated theory that her father had been murdered?

Something moved at the entrance to the barn. A gunshot ripped through the night's quiet.

"Devlin!" Horror-stricken, Willie raced down the porch steps and then the barn exploded in flames.

Chapter Fourteen

The bullet carved through the outer curve of Sloan's left shoulder. He felt the torn flesh beneath his fingers through a sticky flow of blood that dripped from his hand. The pain was jagged and raw, like the slice of a knife, and had come so unexpectedly out of the shadows it had dropped him to his knees. He smelled his blood above the pungent scent of kerosene, tasted rage on his tongue and let the roar explode from his lungs when the black-hooded man bent and touched a match to a pile of hay stacked in the corner of the barn.

Flame exploded around them. The man spun toward Sloan, faceless save for the twin holes in the hood over his eyes. Again he lifted his gun, and Sloan lunged at him. With one fierce uppercut of his leg aimed directly at the man's chest, he knocked the man from his feet just as the gun belched flame. The bullet whizzed past Sloan's ear as he dove at the man. He landed sprawled on top of the stranger on the barn's dirt floor. The man didn't move.

Twisting one fist into his attacker's shirt, Sloan hoisted him from the floor then lifted him over his uninjured shoulder like a sack of flour. He spun, blinking through the smoke, feeling it snake into his lungs. He was met with a wall of flame. He spun again, smack into flames. The smoke blinded him and sent tears streaming from his eyes. He gasped for air and felt the heat of the smoke in his lungs, choking the last breath from him.

He turned again toward the door of the barn, covered his head with his arm and ran headlong into a wall of fire.

Willie lifted the rifle and took aim through a deluge of tears. She squeezed the trigger and choked against the rifle's recoil. "Damn you!" she shouted as the two horses raced away from the house, their black-hooded riders clinging to their backs. She lifted the rifle, took unsteady aim, and fired again, knowing they were beyond range. Shoving a hand across her eyes, she whirled toward the barn and began to run. She tripped on her gown, tearing it. The rifle thumped against her leg. Twigs jabbed into her bare feet. An ache welled in the pit of her soul and anguish writhed in her belly. From fifty feet away she felt the heat of the fire. Flames had consumed the barn.

"Devlin!" she screamed, lifting her forearm over her eyes against the heat. He wasn't in there...he couldn't be....

Then where was he?

Someone gripped her upper arms. She spun then collapsed against Gramps. "He's in there," she blubbered. "Devlin's in the barn...we have to—"

"No, Willie-girl. We can't—"

"No—" She twisted out of his grasp, spun and lunged toward the barn, throwing down her rifle. And then like an apparition, a man emerged through the flames. Smoke billowing from his hair and back, flames lapping at his trousers, he stumbled toward her then fell to his knees in the dirt. He lifted his face and said something indecipherable but Willie saw only the blood streaming from his shoulder, his soot-blackened skin, and raced toward him.

"Water!" she shrieked. "Gramps, we need water!" Skidding to her knees beside him, she flung herself against him, relishing the sooty, heated feel of him. Warm blood soaked into her gown as she swept her hands over the last remnants of flames and cinders clinging to him. "Oh, God, oh, God—"

she whispered, pressing trembling fingertips to the bullet gash in his shoulder. Swiftly she tore off the bottom third of her night rail and began to wrap it tightly around his shoulder. "Damn you, Devlin, you got yourself shot—"

"I got him," he rasped as he let the man slide from his back to the ground.

"I don't care about him," Willie choked, knotting the makeshift bandage. With a shaking hand, she smoothed the hair from his brow. She stared at the blood seeping through the bandage and sank her teeth deep into her lower lip. "We have to get you inside. I'll ride for the doctor."

"I don't need a doctor." His eyes reflected milky moonlight. "I'm sorry, Wilhelmina."

"I'll never blame you for this."

Sloan bent and tugged the hood from the man's head. Willie didn't take her eyes from Devlin's profile. Her heart felt as if it would burst from her chest.

"Looks like your amorous cowboy from Deadwood Run. When he wakes up we'll have a long talk about who hired him."

"You saved his life. He owes you more than a talk."

"He would have killed me. Don't expect him to turn coat without ample persuasion. I take it the other two got away."

She dipped her head and stared at his mighty fists, soot blackened and blood smeared, clenched against his thighs. Her fingertips stretched and brushed over the back of one of his hands. "I can't shoot when I cry. I've never been so scared."

"I'll build you another barn."

She lifted her head and felt the hot sting of tears in her eyes. "I don't give a damn about the barn or the hay."

His eyes glittered with the light of a thousand stars. "Watch what you say in the moonlight."

"Willie-girl, I got water."

Willie jerked around and blinked up at Gramps. "Take it inside. I'll help Devlin to the house." She struggled to her feet. Sloan leaned heavily against her.

"What the hell?" Brant Masters skidded to a halt in the dirt, his shirttails hanging loose, his bare feet peeking from beneath his trousers. In one hand he clutched a pistol. Flames reflected in his eyes as he stared at the barn then at Devlin and Willie. "You're covered with blood. I heard a shot—"

"That was my rifle," Willie said.

Masters blinked. "Why would you shoot your own boarder?"

"No, Brant, I—"

But Masters wasn't listening. He took a step toward Sloan, his brows diving low, mouth twisting, pistol jerking up. "You set this fire. You damned English bastard, you came here to get in on easy take. I should have taken care of you when I had the—" He bit off his last words in a growled epithet.

Willie glanced sharply at Masters. "What the devil are you talking about, Brant? Devlin didn't start the fire."

Masters's eyes glowed. "Don't be so certain."

"And where the hell were you?" Sloan's voice rumbled like distant thunder.

Masters took another step forward, chest puffing, pistol poised at his hip. "I don't like what you're suggesting."

"Just an observation," Sloan said.

Willie glanced between the two men. Animosity hung so thick between them she could have cut it with a knife. But now wasn't the time to probe their shared history, or to further inflame them. She could feel Sloan leaning more heavily on her. "Quit pointing your gun at us, Brant, I can't explain now. That man there, he's part of the vigilante gang that started the fire. He'll have plenty to tell us come morning."

Masters glanced at the cowboy then jerked his head at Sloan. "Take him inside before he bleeds all over you. I'll take care of this one."

"No," Sloan growled as Willie began to lead him to the house. "Don't trust him."

"I don't," Willie assured him, glancing warily at his blood-soaked bandage. "That's why we'll have Brant tie him up. We'll talk to him in the morning."

His breath fanned heat across her cheek. "Wilhelmina—no—"

She'd never liked her name, any form of it, but when Devlin said it, something inside her twisted around itself with longing.

"Get the whiskey," she said to Gramps when they'd managed the porch steps. "He'll need something for the pain until the doc gets here with the laudanum."

Gramps held the door wide. "Take him upstairs."

Willie paused, bit her lips with uncertainty. "I—"

"What the hell's he gonna do to you with a bullet gash in his shoulder?" He jerked his head to the stairs. "Go on. I'll bet Masters's fancy britches Devlin could make it up there on his own if he had to."

Willie thought a moment. "It's the only clean bed."

"Quit tryin' so hard to be a good girl. Go on."

By the time they reached the top of the stairs, Sloan's head hung heavily to one side and he seemed to be leaning his entire weight on her with one arm draped over her shoulders. He was bleeding too fast.

Gasping for breath, praying for strength, she managed to turn and shuffle down the hall, past her own room to the door just beyond hers, to the room her parents had once shared. With the last of her strength, she half dragged him across the floor and tried to ease him back onto the bed. She failed miserably, her burning arm muscles incapable of lowering his two-hundred-pound bulk. Like falling timber, they toppled onto the bed, Willie landing fully on top of him. He groaned.

"Oh, God, I'm sorry—" She tried to shove herself up on her hands and get up. But one arm had wrapped around her and his hand had anchored itself on her bottom. "Devlin." His eyes were closed. His chest rose and fell with swift, short breaths.

"Wilhelmina," he murmured, his voice thick.

Willie saw the blood flowing from his shoulder and felt her

throat constrict and concern turn to dread. "I'm going for a doctor. You need—" Her breath caught. He'd tugged up her night rail and his hand was on her bare bottom and between her thighs with an audacity she found outrageous given his wound and the blood pouring from it. "Devlin—" Her voice sounded oddly breathless, but his hand slid beneath the gown over the lower curve of her back, then skimmed up her ribs and closed over one breast. Willie's breath left her. "Devlin—"

He stared at her with eyes glazed with fever, watching her lips part and the passions flare when he caught the sensitive peak of her breast between his fingers.

"Let me go," she whispered huskily. "I have to—"

With a strength that astonished her, he surged up, grasped her head with one hand and crushed his mouth over hers with punishing force. For one delirious moment she gave herself completely to him, meeting his fever-inflamed desires with her own, drowning in the tender joy of surrender without a trace of guilt or conscience. He fell back to the pillows with a groan that seemed to come from the deep, dark depths of his soul. This time when she pushed herself up, he let her go.

She raced from the room, tearing off her night rail before she reached her room. From her bedroom window she watched the flames leap into the night sky as she hurriedly dressed. With a roar, the barn walls crumbled down on top of themselves and sparks shot a hundred feet into the sky. Less than a minute later she surged into the kitchen, stuffing her hair up under her hat. She threw the door wide and found Gramps on the porch.

Drawing up, she laid a hand on Gramps's shoulder and mustered every last ounce of reassurance she had left. "The fire will burn itself out. The ground's still wet from last week's soaking. Gramps, nothing could have stopped it. We'll rebuild." His weather-beaten face remained blank. "I have to get the doc or Devlin will bleed to death on pa's bed. Tell Brant—"

"Brant rode off 'bout a minute ago."

"What do you mean he rode off? It's too late to try to save the barn with a bucket brigade."

Gramps's chin jerked east. "He ain't goin' after a bucket brigade. Cowboy got away."

Willie's stomach sank to her toes. She tried to make sense of the unthinkable. "That cowboy was unconscious."

"Guess he woke up." Gramps snapped his fingers in front of her nose. "Just got away. Somethin' tells me Masters isn't gonna bring him back anytime soon."

Willie set her teeth, refusing to venture down another path of mistrust at this point. "Yes, he will."

Slowly Gramps shook his head. "Kinda makes you wonder if Masters doesn't want you to talk to that cowboy. Just like I was wonderin' where Masters was when that barn exploded. Took him an awful long time to come runnin' outta the house, longer than me an' I had to get my cane. An' he came from around front, not through the back door. He knew Devlin was sleepin' in the barn, Willie. No one else knew but us. Somethin's not right between them and neither one of them is ready to say what it is. Funny that the barn burned the same night Masters came back. Sometimes coincidence can't be explained away by a shrug and a smile."

A shrug and a smile. She'd certainly fallen victim to that method of persuasion. "Those men were vigilantes, Gramps."

"Someone could've hired them."

"I agree, but it wasn't Brant. He's no murderer."

"That's your fiancé you're talkin' about. I hope you believe what you're sayin'."

For some reason she couldn't meet Gramps's gaze. She turned and started down the porch steps. But as she raced across the yard toward the horses, she couldn't shake the mantle of suspicion that had seemed to settle with disturbing permanence on her shoulders, and an odd feeling that she was being taken for a fool by someone. If only she could figure out who.

* * *

She didn't know he was awake when she tiptoed into his room. Sloan wouldn't have been so certain himself had it not been for the pain radiating from his shoulder. Whatever had left the strange taste in his mouth had also poured lead into his arms and legs and thickened his tongue. They'd obviously drugged him. He felt as if he were waking from a month-long slumber.

He forced his eyes open and tried to focus on her silhouette moving into and out of the sunlight that filtered through the drawn shade. She moved as if she feared making a sound, fiddling with whatever she'd brought on a tray. He listened to her pour water from a pitcher into a washbasin and pondered the odd sense of peace she'd brought to him along with her tray. He had a sudden vision of laying abed for weeks and letting her tend to him with her slender woman's hands, something no master of mind-over-body principles should even consider. But strange as it seemed the idea flooded his soul with warmth.

She turned toward him but her features remained obscured by shadow. He wanted her near, wanted her hands on him.

He willed his tongue to form words. He managed a hoarse rasp. "Come here."

The air stirred with her scent. She pressed a glass to his parched lips. "Drink this."

Cool liquid trickled over his mouth, past his throat. He swallowed then wrapped his fingers around her wrist, already feeling like a new man. His eyes sought hers, focused, blurred, then refocused. "No more drugs."

"You don't have to be brave on my account, Devlin," she said in a tone that held little tenderness. "I've changed your dressings, washed the soot from your skin and soothed you while you thrashed with fever for two days and nights."

Two days? "I am brave. I am a master."

"You feel no pain."

"None."

Brows knit, she leaned over him, fingers probing the bandages over his wound.

He felt as if she plunged a knife into his shoulder and twisted. He sucked in a breath and forced a grim curve to his lips when her eyes met his. She was all business this morning, buttoned-up stiff, brow appropriately stern, hair pulled severely into one thick plait—the look of a governess, cold and impenetrable. But no governess he'd ever known had a mouth that begged to be kissed, with lips full and pouty even when pursed. No governess had a body that made a scandal of any clothes she wore. He found her utterly charming and completely, illogically irresistible.

The pain was little burden to bear if she continued to lean over him and grant him full, unbridled enjoyment of her bosom on his chest. Women thrived on nurturing. He might as well be the fellow to provide it for her.

He watched her top teeth sink into her lower lip. "I'll leave the dressing for a few more hours," she said, looking as if she were about to turn away. His hand sneaked to her elbow.

Unease stirred in his belly when her eyes refused to meet his and her fingers fiddled with smoothing the sheet. She wasn't normally a nervous woman. "What is it?" he asked.

She swallowed. "The cowboy got away. Brant chased him all the way to the river but he lost him." She lifted her eyes. "I know what you're thinking."

"You don't know the first of what I'm thinking."

Her chin inched up. "I won't fight with you about Brant."

"We're not fighting." He glanced at the open door, well aware that sound carried through the wooden floors like the deafening echo of a drop of water falling in a cave. No doubt it was Masters's French boots he heard wearing a path in the kitchen floor. "He let you come up alone."

"He let me sleep up here with you." Her eyes angled to the chair drawn close beside the bed. "No man tells me what to do."

"Only a fool would try to tame you, Wilhelmina."

A flush crept up from her collar. Her fingers resumed their fiddling. "Fine, then." She lifted her upturned nose and drew up so stiff her breasts bobbed. "You'd best know Sheriff Cochran was here first thing after the fire. He promised to catch the vigilantes. His posse's going after them."

"Ah. The venerable sheriff knows where to look."

She gave him a strange look. "He'd better. The townsfolk are getting plenty fed up with this sort of terrorizing. They want someone in jail. They want to sleep nights."

"And Cochran wants to stay sheriff."

"The election's in less than a week. He'll have no job if half the town pulls up stakes and moves on."

"Or if the remaining half decide to elect someone else." Sloan felt his mouth twist with sarcasm. "Then it's a fine time for him to placate the populace."

"Half of them are spitting mad at you for writing that editorial. Some thought you might have deserved something, but burning the barn wasn't what they had in mind." She paused. "Those men didn't burn the barn because of the editorial. It was another warning to stop asking questions."

"Or a nudge to get you to sell out without too much fight. Maybe a little of both."

"Are they going to burn the house next?"

"They'll kill for what they're after, Wilhelmina. And they won't stop until they get it."

Her mouth tightened. "All this for land? Land that the railroad won't pay much for? For some mine that's barren?"

"How many times have you heard that? I've heard it at least a dozen times. After a while I started to wonder why people keep bothering to tell me anymore."

She blinked. "Why should you? Everyone knows there's no silver down there."

"Everyone? It might suit someone to allow the townsfolk to believe there's no silver in that mine. Indeed, what if people suddenly knew differently?"

She hesitated then said slowly, "They'd storm the mine.

Ownership wouldn't much matter. We've all heard the tales of the gold-rush frenzy. Men were brutally killed for their fraction's share of a strike.''

"It would be chaos."

"Madness." Her brows quivered. "Everyone knows that."

"If someone struck silver then, he'd be a fool to announce it. Even a man who loved to talk big would think twice about telling just anyone that he'd struck."

Face draining of color, she sank onto the bed and stared blankly at the window across the room.

"No one would bother with a useless mine, Wilhelmina," Sloan said, watching the tightening of her profile as realization swept over her. "Virgil Brown was looking for something in the mine when he was killed, or he was following someone who knew precisely what they were looking for. It wasn't coincidence that we stumbled on them down there. I'd wager they've been going down to the mine frequently for some time to judge its safety, to forage a new path, or to get to all that silver. There's so much of it down there it was in the dust I brushed from your cheeks."

Her lips parted with a defeating breath. "Pa found silver."

"I'd venture to say he struck the lode."

She lifted trembling fingers to her lips. "I didn't know."

"Someone obviously does."

She closed her eyes and shuddered. "Who? Only pa and the boys were down there near the end, and one or two other miners. Gertie's husband, I think. No one else. But why would any of them say anything if they knew it would jeopardize the find or even get them killed?"

"Why do people talk, Willie, when they damned well know they shouldn't? Some men will do anything to win the women they love or want in the heat of the moment. They make promises they have no intention of keeping. They boast, especially young men. Your brother Wes—he knew Dakota Darby."

She looked at him with eyes wide with disbelief. "No—" Slowly she began to shake her head. "He told me he loved her. And I—'' Her throat jerked. ''I told him she wanted a man who could buy her things. I told him she didn't want the good, earnest things he could offer a woman. Things of real value.'' Agitated breaths lifted her chest. ''Oh, God—Wes— he told her they'd found silver, to impress her. And she—she sold that information to someone, didn't she? She got him killed—''

''Wait.'' He clamped his hand around her wrist. ''If she believed him why would she tell anyone anything? She'd be much better off keeping it secret, waiting for him to cash in on his share and all those promises he made her.''

She looked doubtful. ''Maybe. But I think you're giving her too much credit. She's ruthless.''

''A side of her, yes, perhaps.''

Wariness lit her eyes. ''You think someone else betrayed them.'' She bit her lip. ''Someone they would confide in without fear of being betrayed.'' She glanced sharply at him. ''Gertie.''

''Or Lansky.''

She shook her head. ''Pa and the boys never liked him much. None of the miners did. They wouldn't trust him.''

''What about Harkness?''

''No.'' He could almost see her erect a wall of defense. ''J.D. would never betray my pa.''

''Maybe not knowingly.''

''Not even then.''

''His wife was killed because she knew something. Gertie says there was poison in her soup.''

''Gertie's looking for vengeance for her husband's death. That's all she cares about. The doc says Lily's heart just gave out. I believe that.'' She tossed her head. ''Gertie probably took her tray up to her that day. Maybe Gertie's so certain Lily was poisoned because she knows damned well what she put in that soup. You should be talking to her not me. Let go of my arm.''

''Not until you listen to me,'' Sloan hissed through his

teeth. "Gertie didn't poison anyone. As much as you'd like to believe otherwise, Gertie's not looking to capitalize on her husband's death. She wants revenge, all right, just as you do."

"I don't want it enough to cast blame willy-nilly and see where it sticks."

"You'd rather put blinders on and blame yourself. Lily Harkness was killed for what she knew, for what she over-heard and was certain to tell Bessie Lewis and her mother when they came to see her every afternoon. She would have known they'd spread the word around town, faster than anyone could have stopped it."

"I don't believe it. I took lunch over to Lily every day and visited with her. She mentioned nothing to me."

"Of course, she didn't. Lily didn't trust you, Wilhelmina. She blamed you for stealing her husband's heart while she lay helpless in her bed."

"I can't listen to this. It's fiction. Overblown fiction."

"You know damned well it isn't. Dakota said a woman had been killed because she knew too much. I think that woman was Lily Harkness." An invisible knife seemed to twist in his heart when tears pooled in her eyes and pain embedded itself on her features. He curled his fingers around hers. "Willie, no one ever said the truth was easy to hear."

"The truth?" Her lips parted over bared teeth. "I'll never believe J.D. killed his wife. He loved her, he was a faithful husband to her. He brought in every doctor he could find to make her well and almost lost the Silver Spur because he couldn't pay his bills. He didn't kill her. No one did. Quit spinning your tales. It was her heart. Do you hear me? Her heart just stopped beating." With a vehemence that startled him, she yanked out of his grasp and backed away from the bed. "Next you'll be telling me that Brant had something to do with all this."

"The thought has occurred to you, too, hasn't it? Lily died the night Masters left town. And if there's silver in that mine, and you don't sell out, who but your husband would benefit the most from that? Everything that's yours will become his.''

"No, damn you—'' Tears spilled to her cheeks and trembled on her lips. And deep in her troubled eyes, mistrust flared like a newborn flame.

No. He wouldn't allow that.

Sloan shoved himself up and swung his legs over the edge of the bed, planting his feet wide on the floor. The room tilted then righted itself and remained steady. The drug was fast leaving him, but the effects lingered in his muscles like the ache after a brutal hand-to-hand fight. In several hours he would be fine, every trace gone. With one hand braced on the bed, he shoved himself upright. He swayed. Her face blurred then refocused. Strength seemed to flood into his limbs.

Her eyes flew wide with alarm. "What are you doing?"

"Get over here before I come get you."

"You'll topple like a felled oak if you try."

His lips curved. "I wouldn't wager the farm on that, my dear.''

Her hands pressed into her thighs. "Get back in bed. The doctor said you have to stay in bed for at least another day.''

"Never listened to them," he muttered, reaching a hand toward her. "Sweet, earnest, innocent Willie—I'm no stranger to you. Quit looking at me like I am.''

He started toward her, ignoring the ringing in his ears, the tilting of the floor beneath his bare feet. She took a hesitant step forward then backed right into the wall when he advanced on her like a storm billowing out of a coal black sky. He fell against the wall, hands braced on either side of her. Pain spiraled through his shoulder in white-hot spasms. His breath left him in a hiss and he hung his head close beside hers, willing away the pain, focusing on the singular pleasure of her body pressed against his.

"Willie, none of this matters to me…none of it but you—''

He turned his face into her neck and breathed in her essence, filling his lungs, letting it seep into his soul and sweep away everything else. His hand gripped her jaw. He brushed two fingers over her mouth, back and forth, and felt her stiffen, her lips part.

"No," he rasped. "Don't say anything. Feel it here—" Fingers spread, he slid his hand down the length of her neck, over her collarbone, lower, lower, until he felt the fluttering of her heart beneath his palm. "Look here. Tell me what you see here. And you'll never again look at me like you don't know me."

A sigh drifted from her lips as he curved his hand over her breast. "I don't want to believe you. You've made me doubt everything, everybody—" She turned her head toward his and lifted her mouth. "Do you hear me, Devlin? I don't want to trust you...."

His lips touched hers, tenderly, a hesitant stroke, as if playing with a fire that could leap out of control. Fingertips brushed over cotton, pushed buttons through loops, delved beneath the fabric and slid against warm, filmy cambric.

"I have thoughts of devouring you," Sloan rasped against her mouth. "I think of you as I lie in my bed. The fever heats my blood. It consumes me." A groan rumbled from his chest when his fingertips pressed against the engorged peak of her breast. "I know what it's like to want against every bit of logic, to want even more when you tell yourself you shouldn't, you can't possibly—to awaken every day and hope that the wanting has diminished, not grown, has faded, not ripened—"

He felt her hands gripping at him, pushing and clinging at the same time, and lowered his head to her breast. Fever raged and consumed and he became the flame lapping at her skin. With a savagery before unknown to him, he hooked his fingers into the cambric and split it wide.

"I have to—" he gasped, sinking to his knees, drinking of all of her with mouth wide and tongue laving. She was a gentle haven, perfumed by nature, an exquisite bit of fool's heaven. His will weakened by fever, he gave full rein to his desires and knew a different pain as noble intent crumbled.

He heard the sob break from her lips, felt her arms clasping at him with an urgency that inflamed him. His fingers yanked at the buttons of her denims.

"The door—" she gasped.

"Yes—" One more button popped, then another. He pulled at the coarse fabric, deepening the vee, fingertips brushing her belly, full and white and smooth.

"Devlin—the door—"

"I know—" He lifted her cotton shirt and she grabbed it and jerked it over her head. The remnants of cambric undergarment followed to the floor and then she was there, pearl white, lush belly and breasts and men's denims riding open and low to a nest of copper curls. He pressed his lips there.

She sagged lower against the wall. "Oh, God, the door—"

"The door—" He turned and stretched to reach the door, flicking at it. It creaked on its hinges, swung and failed to catch in the latch. But Sloan was tugging taut denim with one arm over a woman's full hips and extravagant backside. Everything about her was abundant.

He felt as if he'd plunged into a hidden garden bursting with delights. His mind spun. His body went up in flames.

He tugged the denims over her thighs and tugged her down with them. Mouth crushing over hers, he fell to the floor with her and fumbled with the buttons of his britches. His manhood burst through the parting fabric and leapt into his hand, heavy and full with need. If she touched him, he would explode.

She was kissing him wildly, trying to kick one leg free of her pants and squirming deliciously all over him. Blood rushed in his ears, pounded in his shoulder like a cannon. He tasted his sweat on her neck, her shoulder, saw it glistening on her breasts as he pressed his mouth there and lifted his loins intimately against hers. Desire exploded through him when her thighs parted. He didn't hesitate, couldn't…there was no stopping…until he surged into her and encountered the taut barrier.

Chapter Fifteen

Willie stiffened. Sloan went completely still. She opened her eyes and found her voice through the thickness in her throat. "You're bleeding—"

"It's not that—" He was looking at her strangely. "Damn." He rolled off her, a wince slicing across his features as he came to rest on his back. He stared at the ceiling, and Willie looked at him lying there, magnificent in his full-blown desire. No, she shouldn't look at him. This was debauchery. This was depravity. This gave a whole new meaning to disreputable. What had transpired on that stream bank had been but a shadow to this and yet that episode with Brant had left her bitter and filled with self-contempt. So why didn't she feel contrite or ashamed now?

His Adam's apple worked in his throat. "This is—not that I didn't expect you to still be—I did. That was never in question. What astonishes me is my—" his eyes fell to her breasts, darkened, then slid over her belly to the juncture of her thighs "—my sudden, unwelcome surge of restraint." He scooped her shirt from the floor and handed it to her. "Get dressed. This isn't going to happen."

He might have dumped a bucket of icy water over her. Gripping her shirt, she struggled to her feet alongside him. Denims sinking to her ankles, she shoved her arms into her shirtsleeves and set her fingers to the buttons just as he did to his own. A chair's legs scraped against the kitchen floor downstairs. Willie waited for a deep guilt that never came.

"I forgot myself." He shoved a hand through his loose hair. "It won't happen again. You deserve far better than a—" He waved a hand vaguely at the floor and his scowl deepened.

Turning, Willie drew her denims up over her hips, achieving this with her usual shimmy, tug and yank. "I don't suppose it should happen again."

"It shouldn't and it won't." He lingered behind her as she hooked more buttons. She felt his eyes on her and her fingers fumbled. "Nothing could foul matters up more. I've said it before. The trouble is I can't seem to remember anything when you and I— You see, I've this inescapable thing called duty hanging over me. And you've this—" his breath left him swiftly "—this matter of an anxious fiancé."

"Yes," she said, feeling a hollow ache in her belly and a need to thrust up her chin. "You know him."

"My prior experiences with him were far too brief for me to feel an obligation to try to change your mind."

"So you would advise that I don't marry him."

"No. I wouldn't wish to sway you either way. No wise man has ever set out on a noble course to change a woman's mind about another man. You agreed to marry him. You're not a woman who easily parts with her heart."

"No, I don't suppose I am...anymore." Wondering why she felt like crying, she half turned toward him, startled that he loomed so close to her back. Her words sounded trite but it was all she could think of to say. Anything else and she might dissolve into useless tears. "You should get in bed."

Seconds ticked past. He didn't move. "I suppose you should know that I don't make a habit of this sort of thing."

She lowered her eyes. "What sort of thing?"

"Sex."

"On floors in particular?"

"In general, dammit. You must know that. I suppose attacks of conscience are common in men who don't—"

"Make it a habit?"

"Precisely."

Her breath trapped in her chest. "Are you apologizing?"

"You'd be mistaken to think that I'm regretful." His breath fanned warmth on the back of her neck. "But I know a regret so deep it aches in my bones every time I look at you. A regret of circumstances, of responsibilities and duty and promises made and determined to be kept."

"Circumstances can be changed," she whispered softly. When she turned, he was sitting on the edge of the bed. His face was drawn and shadowed beneath two-days' growth of black stubble. He looked untamed and wary, with his hair hanging past his shoulders and his eyes glowing silvery white. Her gaze dropped to the juncture of his thighs and the irrefutable evidence that his desires still raged. When he'd thrust her clothes at her she'd thought he'd found her lacking. It seemed she'd been wrong.

She moved to the door, aware of a heaviness in her chest that made looking at him almost impossible. "You should rest."

"I can't lie here," he muttered.

"I'll get fresh bandages to change your dressing."

"We haven't time." He grabbed a roll of bandage from the bedside table. "Where are my clothes?"

She indicated the valise at the foot of the bed. Panic gripped her. "You can't leave alone. I'll come with you—"

"I need to go alone."

She stared into eyes gone bleak as a winter's sky and a chill wrapped around her heart. "If that's how you'd prefer it."

"I would." He rose from the bed and started toward her, hips jutting, thighs bunching, features drawn and tight. He'd never seemed so unreachable, so foreboding, even with a bandage wrapped around his shoulder. She'd never seen a more dangerous looking man. He stopped just inches from her.

Willie stared at the ridges of his belly and the line of dark hair tapering into the top of his pants.

"Go," he rumbled, "or I'll do something we'll both regret. And there won't be any taking it back. Only guilt and confusion and heartache. That's the only promise you'll get from me." He reached around her for the door handle and tugged it wide. She felt the heat of his arm as it stirred the air over her skin. "Run," he said. "Run before I make you disreputable as hell."

And she did. For the first time in her life Willie fled from a man and all his wicked promises.

"Sheep," Brant Masters said, spreading his arms as if to embrace the whole of Willie's property. "And cattle. Enough to eat the grass clean of the land and plenty to breed, sell and ship out. With the acreage here, we could raise a thousand head. Damn, but we'll be rich. Did you hear me, Willie?"

Over Brant's shoulder, Willie watched the last traces of smoke curl skyward from what was left of the barn's dying embers. She felt a thousand miles away from the only home she'd known for the past ten years. "Yes, I heard," she replied, idly rubbing Huck's head and pondering lost dreams.

Planting one boot between Willie's on the porch steps, Brant leaned so close she could smell his spicy cologne. For some reason she felt no need to inhale deeply. Her fingers tightened together when he covered her hand with his. "You'll have dresses from Paris and fine china and jewels...anything you want. Come a time we can even move to Denver, have a big house built there. Become one of the rich city folk."

Willie looked up at him silhouetted against the sun, his smile wide and full of hope and dreams. His dreams. But were they hers, as well? Her dreams had never been filled with clothes and jewels and houses and things. But did they really have to be if he was giving her what she'd professed to want, or at least had been somewhat certain she needed? A future, security, children, here on the farm in the town her father had died trying to build. Brant painted a picture both broad and irresistible. It should have been easy for her to lay aside the last of her misgivings and quiet the nagging voice in her head that kept whispering that he'd broken her heart, and he could again.

Yes, it could be easy. While with Devlin, everything was difficult…everything except the wanting. His duty lay in England. Hers lay here. His interest in her would end the moment he solved the mystery of the mine.

The door thwacked closed behind her. Polished heels tapped out a staccato rhythm across the porch. Willie felt as if all the air was instantly sucked out of her lungs.

"Ah, Masters," Sloan said, pausing just behind Willie. "Just the fellow I was looking for."

"I am?" Brant eyed Sloan warily over the top of Willie's head. Willie had her doubts, as well, but did her very best to keep from swiveling around and gaping up at him. Sloan sounded a touch too accommodating for a man who'd just come out of a laudanum-induced haze and nearly seduced another man's fiancée on a bedroom floor. If he didn't like Brant, he was certainly making an effort to appear friendly, at ease, as if he presented no threat whatsoever to Brant's carefully laid out plans. Or to their engagement. Her throat seemed to swell closed.

"It's come to my attention," Sloan began, "that the monthly hoedown will be held this Saturday evening near the church."

Brant squinted up at him. "So?"

"I thought I'd pass that along to you. More nuptials have come of dance-floor interludes than any amount of grand philosophizing and hand-holding on a young woman's porch. Good day to you." Impervious to Brant's heightened color, he tipped his top hat at Willie and marched down the steps. Burgundy coattails flapping behind him, he took three strides, drew up short, lifted a gloved index finger and spun around. "Masters. One more thing. I nearly forgot, but it was rather odd, so I thought I'd mention it. You see, I've always adhered to the notion that a man ought to know if he's being followed.''

Brant straightened and gave his roguish half smile. "Followed? That's not likely."

"Indeed." Sloan grimaced and rubbed the tip of one gloved index finger against his temple as if rousing his memory. "I suppose I'm too damned quick to doubt coincidence. But strangers are so rare in Prosperity Gulch, and then to have two in one day, within minutes of each other, and both in the Silver Spur while I was there yesterday? It just seemed rather curious to me."

"Curious," Masters repeated. "Who was this gent?"

"I'd say he was from the East, judging by his clothes and his manner. He had a travel-weary look about him. Natty brown bowler all dust covered. Whiskers in need of a trim. A cosmopolitan-looking fellow though somewhat shabby. Eyeglasses. Stern looking."

"Doesn't sound familiar. What did he want?"

Sloan shrugged and Willie detected the merest hint of a wince tighten his features with the movement. He was making a grand effort to conceal his pain, and his feelings for Masters, beneath a harmless facade.

"I didn't speak to him," Sloan said. "He came in about five minutes after you left. He spoke with Gertie, drank one sip of his water and left."

Brant grinned. "Nothing curious about that, Devlin."

"The man was probably lost," Willie offered, sensing an ominous undercurrent in Sloan. His transformation from savage into linen-crisp gentleman was almost eerie, and she found herself staring at him and wondering what message he was laying out for her with this performance.

"I'd wager the fellow wasn't lost," Sloan said. "He had no horse. A man doesn't walk or hire a wagon to take him this far off the railroad line for no reason."

"Who says he came by rail?" Masters asked.

"He had a Union Pacific ticket in his inside coat pocket."

"Nosy gent, aren't you?" Masters said slowly.

Sloan smiled. "Observant."

"You don't miss much."

Sloan's laugh was full, genuine and struck a lonely feeling in Willie, as if she'd already watched him ride down the road to town for the last time, and knew she'd never see him again.

"I'm quite certain I miss plenty," Sloan said, completely self-effacing. "I believe his ticket was stamped from New York. You hail from New York, don't you, Masters?" The look in his eyes made Willie go entirely still. She looked at Brant.

"Not anymore," Masters replied.

"Ah. Business all tidied up, I take it."

"All tidied up."

"Very good. You'll need more than a fistful of dollars from a sold-out New York business to make a go of it raising cattle and sheep. But you've thought of that, of course."

"Of course," Brant said, watching him.

Sloan's smile lit stars in his eyes and again transformed him into the innocuous oddity no man could find cause to quarrel with. His motives remained frustratingly unclear. "Too damned curious for my own good, I suppose," he muttered, tugging his top hat lower over his eyes. "Take it for what it's worth." He waved his hand. "Carry on."

Willie felt her insides tangle as Sloan turned on his heel and strode toward the horses tethered at the edge of the woods. She gripped the porch steps to keep from running after him.

"I don't trust that bastard," Brant muttered.

Willie angled her eyes at him. "Where did you meet?"

Masters's cheek twitched. "On the train from Omaha. Over a poker game. We had a disagreement about the outcome of a hand."

"Someone was cheating."

Brant looked quickly at her. "Accusations were thrown around. No man takes kindly to being falsely accused."

Willie's eyes followed Edgar as Sloan trotted him past the house then reined him toward the road to town. Much as it would have suited her to think otherwise she knew in her heart Sloan Devlin was an inherently fair man, and an honest one. He wouldn't accuse anyone of anything without ample reason.

"Odd that Devlin didn't tell me anything about it," she mused.

Brant snorted. "Of course, he didn't. He was in the wrong and he knows it. Bastard's probably waiting for me to claim what's mine."

"Winnings."

"Damned right."

Willie looked hard at him. "Why haven't you?"

His full lips tightened then he swung a disarming grin on her and reached for her hand. "Why stir up trouble?"

Before he could grasp her hand, she shoved off the porch steps and thrust her hands into her back pockets. "I'd want what's mine, especially if I'd been swindled out of it."

"That's just it." Masters stared off into the distance where the dust clung to the road in Sloan's wake. "I'm not sure if I was swindled at all. Hard to tell with a gent like him. He looks all pretty and talks real fancy about nothing and you start to ignore him and then something happens...."

"And you realize he's bigger than life." Willie blinked. Brant was staring at her with eyes as hard as black marbles. She swung around before he could see the heat climbing into her cheeks. Why the devil had she said that? The words had just jumped off her tongue. "I—I need to—in the kitchen—" She raced up the steps before he could stop her.

Several minutes later Willie watched from her kitchen window as Brant rode off toward town at a murderous pace. Hurriedly she rinsed the last of the dishes and set them to dry, then smacked her hands on her thighs.

"You'd better go after him," Gramps said, appearing in the doorway to his room. "Ain't no tellin' what he's up to."

Willie glanced around the kitchen. "I lost my hat." She

looked under the table, in several cupboards, on the mantel then sighed with frustration. "Yes, I'm going after him. He has no business riding anywhere with a shoulder half torn away and a town full of spitting angry folk ready to paint him with sorghum and feathers. Besides, I have to talk to J.D. Aha!" She reached into the corner where her hat sat on the nose of the repeating rifle.

"I wasn't talkin' about Devlin or J.D."

Willie shoved her hat on her head. "Brant needs no looking after."

Gramps smacked his lips in obvious disagreement.

Willie laid the rifle on the table. "I thought you'd sleep until dinnertime after all the recent commotion."

"With all the racket, even a tired old man can't hope to sleep."

"Racket?"

Gramps jerked his thumb to the ceiling. "All kind of scrapin' and thumpin' up there, like Devlin was wrestlin' with a wild coyote on his floor."

Willie blinked in stunned silence. "I—I didn't hear anything." Certain that her cheeks glowed crimson, she spun so quickly to the sink her elbow jarred a bowl perched on the top of the dishes. She caught the bowl by the tip of one finger just before it fell to the floor. "Keep the rifle with you and shoot anyone that looks suspicious."

"That include Masters?"

Willie set the bowl on the counter and ran her thumb along the rim. "Brant says we're going to raise cattle and sheep. A thousand head. He says we'll be rich, Gramps."

"And he knows." Sarcasm dripped from his voice.

"He should. He's done business back East."

"Most of the folks out West did business back East sometime in their lives, Willie-girl. Shoddy business mostly. If you ask me, most folks who come out here are runnin' from somethin' and it's somethin' they're hopin' you don't find out about." Gramps's lips spread wide over his teeth. "Way I see it Masters was runnin' and lookin' until he bumped into you, landin' in a pot o' silver.''

Gramps shook his head. "I'm tellin' you, you leave Devlin alone for now. He can take care of himself. It's Masters you oughta be worryin' about. He rode outta here like his fancy coattails was on fire. Now an old man like me, hell, I cain't think of a reason why Masters would be stompin' mad like that all of a sudden. Can you?''

Yes, she could. For all of Devlin's efforts to appear innocuous, Willie had given it all away in one simple statement. At least she'd given away her half of the story. And Brant was quite obviously not pleased.

"Quit looking at me like that," Willie grumbled. "You get all twinkly-eyed like you know something.''

"Course, I know something. And so does Masters. I'm just wonderin' when you and Devlin are gonna figure it all out.''

"Dammit—'' Willie shoved away from the sink and faced Gramps, hands on her hips, eyes spitting fire. Anger and frustration surged up in her like water boiling up and over the edge of a deep pot. The words leapt from her tongue like hissing steam. "There's nothing to figure out. Whatever it is you think you see, whatever you think went on upstairs on his floor, it doesn't matter. None of it means anything beyond that moment. Because when Devlin finds the men responsible for killing pa and the boys, he's leaving. He's going back to England. He's an earl, Gramps, he holds a title. He has duties to himself, his family and his tenants. Those responsibilities are stronger and deeper and more meaningful to him than anything that could hold him here.''

"You're still thinkin' like a good girl.''

Willie scowled. "What the hell does that mean?''

"Think with your heart, dammit all. Just like your pa did.''

"Really? You know where that kind of thinking got him.''

Gramps surged into the kitchen, his dark eyes glowing with a long-ago lost vitality. His fist thumped on the table, rattling the rifle. "I know he didn't die a bitter, unfulfilled old man,'' he said hoarsely, emotion coursing from him. "He didn't die nursing the forgotten dreams of his youth and wishing with all his might that he could turn back the clock. He died with a pickax in his hand, with a soul unburdened and a dream alive in him. He might have been all kinds of a fool but he wasn't when he chose to follow his heart."

Willie swallowed and felt the bite of tears at the backs of her eyes. "You were right to be proud of him."

"Damned straight I was proud, even when folks were talkin' about him and thinkin' he was half-crazy."

"But there's a lesson to be learned from his mistakes."

"I'm tellin' you this, Willie-girl—make sure the dreams you chase are yours and no one else's tales spun of silver. Or you're gonna end up like your pa might have."

"Bitter and unfulfilled."

"Shoot, no man'll want you then." Gramps's mouth twitched upward. "Except maybe Devlin."

An ache swelled in Willie's chest. Shoving her hand over her eyes, she murmured, "Thanks, Gramps. I—"

He jerked his head to the door. "Go on, then. I promise I won't shoot Masters no matter how much I might want to. You gotta figure this one out on your own."

The crowd surrounding the jailhouse bulged into the street, blocking all the buggies and wagons attempting to move past. Traffic snarled as the curious abandoned their wagons and horses and descended on the jail. Sloan pulled Edgar to a halt at the rear edge of the crowd.

"I say hang 'em!" one fellow shouted. Cheers rose up.

"Git yer wood, Elmer," another bellowed. "We'll build ourselves a scaffold by nightfall. We can hang 'em then."

Another ripple of agreement passed through the crowd.

Dismounting, Sloan looped Edgar's reins around a hitching rail and peered over the heads of the townsfolk at the door of the jail. Extreme height had certain advantages. He saw noth-

ing but bobbing heads and the unmistakable back of Sheriff
Cochran filling the open doorway to the jail.

"I knew it was the railroad behind those vigilantes," a
woman close beside him said to another from behind the wide
brim of her bonnet. "They should be strung up and shot, then
hung and left for the crows."

Sloan gave the carnivorous female a wary glance just as she
turned to scan the crowd. He didn't swing away from her
quickly enough. Gloved fingers pressed into his sleeve.

"Sloan Devlin, good God, you're here!"

"Bessie Lewis," he murmured, forcing a smile and a cour-
teous nod for both Bessie and her hovering mother. "Mrs.
Lewis."

"We heard you were shot," Bessie breathed, huge baby
blues skimming over Sloan from head to toe and back.
"Thorne's barn burned to the ground by a vicious gang of
vigilantes and yet here you are looking fit as any man I've
ever seen."

"Hush your mouth, Bessie," her mother hissed, nothing but
her nose poking from the deep rim of her bonnet.

Bessie dissolved into her smile and wriggled her arm
through Sloan's. "Hush, nothing." Saucy eyes slanted up at
him, and Sloan could almost hear the nubile young woman's
mind scheming away as she rubbed a finger over his sleeve
and tried to pout. "You might think I was a tiny bit angry
with you after your editorial came out the other day. And
maybe I was, for about a minute. But I got to thinking about
what you wrote, same as all the folks did, once they stopped
huffing and puffing and stomping around. Folks don't like the
sound of the truth sometimes."

"Apparently someone didn't."

"It takes them a couple times reading it through to think
about it. I know my pa didn't like it, not one bit, especially
the greedy part about taking advantage of folks with unfair
prices. He yelled all night at my mama and—ow!" Bessie
jumped as if she'd been poked in the behind then glanced over

her shoulder and gave her mother a sugary smile. Leaning closer to Sloan, she whispered, "You knew the railroad men wouldn't like what you said either. You're so smart, Sloan Devlin."

"Wisdom has very little to do—"

"And brave! Why, if you hadn't written what you did, I reckon they wouldn't have been mad enough to burn your barn. And Sheriff Cochran wouldn't have been able to catch the men who did it. And them just sitting all peaceful at the Devil's Gold Saloon in Deadwood Run, drinking their whiskey like they did nothing wrong. Ha! They'll be lucky to get a judge here before we hang them. You risked your life for us and I for one am going to make certain the entire town knows it. So, for helping to catch those vigilantes and making the streets of Prosperity Gulch safe once again, I thank you, Sloan Devlin, from the very bottom of my heart." Rising on tiptoes, she laid the entirety of her bosom on his arm and pressed a smacking kiss on his cheek.

"Elizabeth Margaret Mary Lewis!" Her mother yanked Bessie around, leveled Sloan with a glare that would have curled a less stalwart man's hair and elbowed through the crowd, dragging her yelping daughter behind her.

The crowd erupted into a roar and surged toward the jail. Sloan spotted Cochran and several of his deputies emerging from the jail, dragging two men between them. The men were gagged, their ankles and wrists chained in irons, and they stumbled several times, falling to their knees. This roused a chorus of lewd epithets and cheers from the crowd. The deputies hauled each prisoner to his feet by the hair then shoved them forward, yanking their heads back and their faces full into the sun.

Sloan swore under his breath. Their faces were puffy from a beating, purple bruises already beginning to show beneath the swollen skin. Their clothes were torn, the finely made waistcoats blood splattered, their crisp linen neck cloths soiled with dirt and hanging limp. But he recognized them just the same. Hyde and Strobridge.

Chapter Sixteen

Sloan pushed through the crowd and stepped onto the boardwalk. The crowd fell suddenly silent. "Nice bit of lawmanship, Sheriff," he said. "Chained and gagged is a bit excessive, isn't it, seeing as how you found them sitting peacefully in a saloon in Deadwood Run?"

"They're vicious vigilantes," Cochran spat. "Hell, they got you shot and a barn burned, Devlin. I reckoned you'd be as pleased as the rest of the folks."

Sloan arched a brow. "Not hardly. You've let one escape."

A murmur rippled through the crowd.

Cochran shot a nervous glance at the crowd then narrowed his eyes on Sloan. "These are the gents you want hung, Devlin."

Sloan kept his gaze level, his tone deceptively soft. "I saw neither of these two gentlemen last night. They didn't shoot me. And they didn't set the fire. I want the man who did."

Color climbed from Cochran's collar. "If he's got himself any brains he's long gone."

"Maybe he wasn't paid handsomely enough. He could still be somewhere near town, waiting for more."

Cochran gave him a strange look. "These are the gents who hired him. They're responsible for folks not sleepin' nights."

"You've proof, of course."

"Proof enough to hold 'em. And all the proof a hangin' judge'll need to get them the proper justice by hemp."

"And what proof is that?"

Cochran's chest bulged. "Confessions."

"Beaten out of them?"

"A judge won't much care how we got it. Get off your high horse, Devlin. And while you're at it, get the hell outta town."

Sloan let his lips curve. "And here I thought you'd be thanking me for helping you nab this vicious, nasty gang of cutthroats." Sweeping a hand to the crowd, he added, "Your electorate is foaming-at-the-mouth pleased with you, just as you expected they'd be. Odd, that after all these months of vigilante terrorizing you're suddenly able to find someone to throw in jail to pacify the townsfolk, and not a week before election time."

Sloan jerked his head at Hyde and Strobridge. "A bit of bad timing on their part. Then there's their share of Dakota Darby's affections, which I'm certain you're aware of. An East Coast businessman holds a hell of a lot more charm for a woman than the sheriff of a town going belly-up. But hell, a man's got his pride. And politics are politics. Reelection seems certain at this point. No one would dare challenge you."

Cochran stepped up, chest puffing, toe-to-toe with Sloan. "I earned it, you uppity English bastard," he snarled, his breath reeking of stale whiskey and cheap tobacco. His lips peeled over long, brown-stained teeth. "We're gonna have ourselves a hangin' once Judge Mason gets here from Copper Glen in two days. Then I'm gonna ride you out on a rail for what you just said to me."

Sloan slanted Hyde and Strobridge a quick look, his voice so soft only Cochran could have heard him. "You'd better hope you have the right men, Sheriff. You hang innocent Union Pacific employees, you'll have more trouble with the railroad than you could ever imagine. And no job to speak of. More Eastern capitalists and their highbrow lawyers will descend on this town than you'll be able to count. You can count, can't you?''

Cochran's nose turned a vicious crimson.

Sloan sensed the movement the instant the idea sprang into Cochran's head. "Don't draw your gun, Sheriff," he purred. "I wouldn't want to embarrass you. You'd do well to remember that the Union Pacific has more power than the United States government, or any hanging judge. I can only wonder why I feel so compelled to remind you of that." With that, he turned on his heel and disappeared into the crowd.

Willie looped Beau's reins around the hitching rail in front of the Silver Spur and glanced up the street as the crowd gathered in front of the jail erupted with a roar. Curiosity piqued, she ventured several steps up the boardwalk and squinted into the distance. Was Devlin being driven out of town by an angry mob? She dismissed that instantly. For some reason she found it impossible to imagine anyone making Sloan Devlin do something against his will.

She paused to cup one hand around her eyes and peek inside the Silver Spur's windows. Whatever had drawn all the townsfolk to the jail hadn't lured J. D. Harkness from his duties. He stood behind the bar, hamlike arms swaying as he polished glasses. Willie turned to push open the door to the Silver Spur when a movement out of the corner of her eye stopped her cold. She never would have noticed the movement had she not been aware on a deeper level that this end of town was strangely deserted today.

She squinted against the glare of sunlight. There, in front of Lewis's general store, a man sat in a chair on the boardwalk, watching her. Brown bowler pulled low, hands clasped over his waistcoat, he regarded her through small oval spectacles with such a calm, unconcerned yet forthright stare Willie caught herself staring back. Bewhiskered and travel weary, he looked as conspicuous as Devlin had when he'd ambled into town. He looked as if he intended to sit there all day, waiting.

For what? Was this the man Devlin had suspected of following Brant? Had it been mere speculation or a thinly veiled warning to her?

"Hey, Miss Wilhelmina, you comin' in?"

Willie turned and found J.D. filling the doorway. Unable to look directly at him, she attempted a smile, but her heart was nowhere close to being in it. She jerked her head at the gentleman across the street. "Do you know him?"

"Thought *you* might."

"I've never seen him before."

"Figure that. He came in yesterday. I would have given him a room but he left and never came back. Gertie talked to him. Told him the only places that let rooms are here and your place. I figured he was staying out by you."

Willie looked at the man. "He's not. He looks like he hasn't slept in a bed in weeks. I wonder what he wants."

"To stir up trouble. That's what all the strangers been wantin' lately."

The uncharacteristic bite in his voice made Willie stiffen and roused all the suspicions she'd shoved to the back of her mind, the suspicions she wanted to ignore and couldn't any longer. They needed to be faced. So why did the thought of talking to J.D. suddenly seem so daunting? Maybe because she didn't know if she wanted to hear the truth.

Brushing past him, Willie moved into the shadowy saloon, not surprised that the place was deserted. "Gertie down at the jail?" she asked as J.D. closed the door behind him. Levering herself up onto a bar stool, she watched in the mirror over the bar as J.D. ambled toward her.

"Yep." He paused at her back, seemed to sway on his feet then braced one hand against the back of a chair. "My guess is that Cochran caught the vigilantes that burned your place the other night."

Willie waited for a surge of relief that oddly enough never came. "That was quick." She frowned. "Almost too quick."

Her eyes met J.D.'s in the mirror. "You wanted them caught more than anyone, J.D. Why aren't you down there?"

J.D. shrugged and continued around the end of the bar.

Willie's chest compressed as she watched him reach for a glass he'd left behind the bar. He drained what was left. Before he lowered the glass he reached for the whiskey bottle to refill it. She almost lunged over the bar for the bottle, but he gripped it tight and angled his eyes in warning at her. A chill crept through Willie and it took her a moment to label it. Fear.

"I thought you'd come by," she said, hearing her voice crack. "You had to know about the fire."

He drained the glass. His lip curled savagely with his words. "Why you askin'? You want me to believe you're suddenly missin' your old Uncle Jeremiah?"

Despair crept into her heart. Tears stung her eyes. "We've known each other a long time. You've stood by me. You stood by Pa when no one else believed him."

His laugh cut like a blade. "Stood by him. Yeah, I was there, all right. Believin' every word."

"He trusted you with all his secrets."

"All of them." He tipped the bottle to his lips, drank deeply, then gave a guttural growl and swiped the back of his hand over his mouth. "Go on home, Wilhelmina. You're not safe here. I can't keep you safe anymore—anywhere—"

"Safe from who?" Willie shoved out of her chair and moved around the bar. She knew she wore her despair and her grief recklessly. She felt emotion welling up uncontrollably out of her and didn't think to stop it. She reached for J.D. and he backed away.

"What's happened to you, J.D.? You're like a stranger to me and I can't stand it. You're too dear a friend. Whatever's done this to you, whatever you think can be fixed with that—" she swept a hand at the whiskey bottle dangling from his hand "—it's not hopeless. We can make it right."

His breath released in a short grunt. "If I can't forgive myself, Willie, you never will."

"Yes, I will," she whispered. "I'll try—"

His face went hard as cut glass. "I wanted her dead. Did you hear me?" He took a step toward her, and another, until he loomed over her with eyes blazing a torturous fire. "I didn't want a woman I couldn't be a man to up there waiting for me anymore. She just lay there and looked up at me and smiled, every day, and didn't know that it was eating at me, little by little, every day.

"And then there were the doctor bills I couldn't pay...mountains of them...bill collectors knocking on my door, threatening to take my saloon. I could only water the whiskey so much before folks started to suspect. It was too much for me to look at every day without thinking that there had to be a way out—some easy money somewhere—" His eyes probed into hers. "Betrayal comes easy when you think you're going to lose everything. And then it doesn't take much in the way of cash to keep your mouth shut after."

Tears coursed over her cheeks. "You betrayed Pa."

"I did. I got him killed. I got the mine blown."

Willie could barely find her voice. "You couldn't have known—tell me you didn't know, you didn't plan this."

"Plan it? Hell, I still betrayed my friend. I betrayed his boys. I betrayed you." He drank again from the whiskey, then stared out at the empty tables as if the memories took vivid shape.

"It was the last night your pa ever came in. He'd left the boys at home and we got to drinkin' too damned much—and then he told me." His voice rang hollow and bleak as an empty well. "There's silver down there, he told me. The last bit of charge he set drove through a wall of rock and there it was. Just sittin' there, waitin', just like he always said it was. A fortune in silver. He talked about givin' it away to the folks who needed it most. He talked about movin' on and findin' another mine."

J.D. blinked quickly. "I didn't see him again after the sun came up. Hell, I should have seen it comin' but the whiskey got to talkin' in me. It made me evil that night. Maybe I wanted to tell somebody. Maybe I knew deep down I was lookin' to sell what I knew. When the mine blew the next day and your pa was killed, God, I saw what I'd done. I sold out my friend. I murdered him for my own gain. And I kept my mouth shut because I knew what they would do to me if I talked. I had no choice. They paid me. I was going to lose my saloon. What kind of man does that make me?''

Willie clenched her fists. "Who are they, J.D.? You have to tell me who murdered my family."

J.D.'s head swung back and forth. "I murdered them. Hate me. I promised to protect you, Willie, and I've tried my damnedest. I saved you once from them...." His voice trailed off and he shook his head. "No. Tellin' you would get you killed."

"But Devlin would—" The pained look on his face stopped her cold.

"Devlin. He's all the protection you'll ever need, isn't he? If it hadn't been for his meddlin', none of this would have come out...none of it. Maybe it would've been better that way—" His mammoth body seemed to shudder. The whiskey bottle crashed to the floor, spraying liquid and shards of glass, and his hands gripped like steel bands around her arms. "I was a faithful husband to Lily. For years I turned away the other women—kept myself a loyal husband and then one day you walked in here, same as you always did for years, but it wasn't the same for me anymore. I didn't see the little girl who fell off the back of her pa's wagon. I saw a woman who made me want to be a man to her in every way."

Willie closed her eyes. "Don't say any more."

"No, you'll hear this. It's what you came here for."

She forced her chin up and stared into his eyes. "I came for the truth about Pa and Lily. I want to hear you tell me you didn't kill her."

He shook his head with disbelief. "I might as well have."

"I came to tell you that I could forgive you for your betrayal because I know you had no intention of putting Pa in danger. I know you."

"Do you?" He yanked her full against him with punishing force. "You don't know me. You know nothing about wanting what you can't have. Do you know what kind of hell it is for a man to find himself in love with a woman he promised to protect like a daughter? A woman who will never love him back the way he wants her to? I look into your eyes and see that mine blowing, and I know that I killed your father. As much as I love you, I know it'll never be between us—" He crushed her in his arms, driving the breath from her lungs with the force. "Willie—my Willie—" he rasped, burying his face in her neck. But the shudders rippling through him were like those of a child in desperate need of love.

Willie wrapped her arms around this fierce, tortured man and felt her heart swell to near bursting with a deep sadness for all the injustices J. D. Harkness had been thrown in his life. She clasped him close, felt the trembling in his lumbering body and whispered, "I forgive you, J.D. It's a great man who can somehow see his way to forgiving himself."

Willie felt the air stir an instant before a deep shadow leapt over the bar with the agility of a mountain lion.

"Unhand her!" Sloan's voice rang out in deeply strident tones. Before Willie could shout out that he had it all wrong, Sloan yanked Harkness around and delivered a punch to his jaw so powerful the behemoth of a man toppled to the floor and lay there motionless.

"Devlin!" Willie shrieked. And then he yanked her against his rock-hard chest with a force that drove all speech from her.

"Are you hurt? If he touched you, by God—" His voice rumbled thick and hoarse from his throat and for an instant her mind swam with the languorous effects of being held so near to him, so safe in his arms, and her body responded beyond her will, curving up into him with a need that was staggering.

Gritting her teeth, she shoved with all her might against his shoulders and stumbled back a step against the bar. "Damn you! Don't you even pause to think? You killed him!"

Devlin glanced at J.D., sprawled motionless on the floor. "No, Wilhelmina, I didn't. But if you'd like I could—"

Willie scowled up at him then slipped past. She knelt beside J.D. and touched her fingertips to the lump swelling along his jaw. "Whatever happened to a peaceful settling of differences, to mind-over-body principles?"

"I can't seem to remember any of that when I see you in the arms of another man." In the ensuing silence, his words echoed with a bleak honesty that tugged like coaxing fingers at Willie.

"I wasn't in his arms. He was in mine." She bit her lip against the fresh threat of tears as she stared at J.D.'s face. "You misjudged him, Devlin."

"The hell I did." Long fingers wound around her upper arm. "Come with me. Gertie's here. She can tend to J.D."

Something in his voice, his hovering, overprotective manner, would always touch the lost and lonely part of her, the woman part of her that had been ignored and in need for so long.

Only a child would cling to dreams of fancy, spun of silver in the gilded days of youth. And she wished to be a child and a fool no longer. She'd faced J.D. as a woman. She would face Devlin and her future the same.

With no resistance she let him lead her from the saloon. "Masters is at the jail," he said. "Cochran and his posse marched into Deadwood Run this morning and found Hyde and Strobridge sitting in the Devil's Gold. The fact that they're Union Pacific employees was enough to get them beaten and locked in a cell for burning down your barn. He'll hang them in two days if we don't do something about it."

Two days. In two days Devlin would ride out of town for good. Willie mounted up, looked down at him and felt destiny

crashing around her. Her toes curled in her boots with anticipation. "Then we've got time. Follow me."

"Follow you?"

"If you're game."

Flames leapt into his eyes. She felt the heat sweep over her
and an intense trembling take root in her limbs.

"Lead on, my lady," he rumbled.

Before she dissolved into butter right there on the street, she
reined Beau west and dug her heels into his flanks. Less than
an instant later, Edgar thundered after her.

Three miles west of town, still bent low over Edgar's pumping neck, Sloan realized that Willie was leading him on a game
of cat and mouse, straight up into the mountains. Just as Edgar's pumping forelegs pulled even with Beau's flanks, Willie
suddenly reined Beau sharply right and down a steep path that
led into a narrow canyon at the base of the mountain range.

Yanking back on Edgar's reins with a force that brought
the stallion skidding to his rump, Sloan spun the horse around
and urged him after her.

The trees and brush grew wild and undisturbed there, ef-
fectively blocking his view of the path ahead. Male pride sufficiently pricked, he set his jaw and kept the reins frustratingly
taut. Wisdom prevailed over pride, for the moment. Willie
knew the terrain, where he didn't. She also knew where she
was going. Judging by the seductive sparkle he'd glimpsed in
her eyes, he'd be all kinds of a fool to lose her now.

She was baiting him. She knew he'd follow her to hell and
back to catch her, and the tougher she made it for him, the
more enflamed he would be to capture her.

Primal satisfaction flowed through Sloan when he spotted
Willie an eighth of a mile ahead, Beau's tail streaming behind
him like a ship's pennons. Willie rode proud and sleek in the
saddle, her hair a liquid copper curtain billowing in the wind.
Sloan's blood fired as she drew up suddenly and spun Beau
around. She paused, breasts heaving with her exertion, round

thighs and plump buttocks hugged by her denims, as if to remind him of the prize once more. As if he needed reminding.

With a shouted command, she reined Beau around and charged recklessly for the base of the mountain ridge.

"What the hell—?" With a certain admiration, Sloan watched her negotiate the narrow path that led almost straight up and disappeared among the taller pines blanketing the base of the ridge. In an instant she'd disappeared from his view.

Driving his heels into Edgar's sides, he followed her, charging up the rock-strewn path at a pace that would have tested the best bloodlines England had to offer. The stout-hearted Edgar negotiated the path brilliantly, without an ounce of grace, stumbling once, grunting and spewing and emerging at the top of the hill with a furious snort. Sloan scanned from left to right, eyes probing the shadows beneath the dense pines. She couldn't have moved far on this terrain. The grade was still steep, the ground littered with rock and brush. Even an experienced horseman who knew the area would have to pick his way carefully—

"Damn." About a third of the way up the mountain, well above the pines, well beyond where she should be, he spotted a glimpse of copper curls and a flick of Beau's tail before she disappeared again. His lips parted into a grim smile. "Ride on, my lady. I'll find you. And there will be no escaping me then."

Blood thundering in his ears, desire leaping like tiny flames in his veins, he drove Edgar after her. At the top of the hill, he paused to consider his course then plunged Edgar into a shadowed ravine between two steep, rock-smooth ledges. Ahead he could hear the whisper of water rushing over rock. Edgar's hooves slipped on the rock path, their echo reverberating through the canyon. A lonely echo that lured him deeper along the winding path that seemed to go nowhere but into darkness.

And then suddenly he emerged into a sun-dappled valley that swept from the base of one mountain range to another.

Like a thick, verdant blanket, grass and wildflowers grew among the pines. A narrow stream wound like a woman's hair ribbon through the center of the valley, spilling into a small lake that glittered like a fine jewel about a quarter mile ahead. Nestled beside it was a small house.

There was no sign of Willie. All looked deserted.

It was a private heaven, a refuge against the outside world. Perfectly chosen. Tugging his hat over his eyes, he urged Edgar toward the house.

Chapter Seventeen

Willie heard the latch lift. The door creaked open on its hinges. Sloan stood silhouetted against the sunlight, tall as the doorjamb and just as broad. Willie's throat went dry. The door thudded against the opposite wall. Shivers swept over her arms despite the airless heat of the place and the sheen of perspiration dampening her skin. She'd ridden hard and fast, at a pace so reckless she'd thought he wouldn't find her.

She should have known better.

She stood motionless, felt his darkened eyes on her breasts, knew her shirt clung to her damp skin and outlined the swells of her bosom. Satisfaction surged through her along with a wave of desire so potent she trembled. Her hair lay like a suffocating blanket against her back. Her denims gripped tight around her thighs and seemed to press high and deep between her legs, where the heat had begun to pulse from her.

She licked her lips and tasted the perspiration dotting them. It was too late to turn back, too late for conscience.

"Close the door," she said.

The door squeaked closed, plunging them into semidarkness. Dust danced in the sunbeams blasting through the window at his back. Silence swelled between them. He took a step toward her, and another, until he loomed over her and sucked all the air from the room. Their eyes locked.

She reached up and flicked his hat from his head. He stared with a palpable hunger at her mouth then at the open collar of her shirt where it gaped low. Her fingers plunged into his hair, freeing it of its thin leather strap to spill to his shoulders. He lowered his head and her eyes swept closed when his mouth pressed to her skin at the deepest vee of her shirt. It was a gentleman's form of seduction, a moment meant to be savored by both, and treasured forever by an innocent on the verge of womanhood. But this was Sloan, and beneath his fine clothes and elegant demeanor, the fires burning were not those of a gentleman.

His mouth took hers in a savage declaration of possession. He claimed her from the first thrust of his tongue to the sweep of his hands over her shoulders, over her breasts and waist to her hips and buttocks. He breathed her in and gave new life to her. She knew no purer joy, and no greater impatience when the buttons of her shirt popped beneath his fingers, cotton shoved wide and cambric rent to lay her bare from neck to waist. Beneath her hands, broadcloth was pushed wide, and brocade and linen pulled and tugged apart until her palms slipped over warm, male skin and her naked breasts were crushed against his chest.

He murmured hoarse love words, drank of her skin from her neck to her belly in a long, openmouthed exploration that made her go hot from the inside out. His fingers brushed low over her belly, working to free the buttons there, stroking the ache between her legs to a feverish pitch until she gasped for breath and dug her nails into his shoulders. She felt her denims peel away from her hips, felt the brush of air on her thighs, then the claim of his callused hands, and stepped out of her pants and boots only to dissolve to the floor, cradled in his arms.

He rose up on his knees and stripped off his coat. Without taking his eyes from hers, he yanked his shirt over his head then flicked open his britches. Boldly he drew her hand to his manhood and pressed her fingers around him, moving them in an age-old rhythm that brought a rumble of appreciation from his lips. Inflamed by his reaction, Willie arched up and met him as he fell upon her, crushing his mouth over hers and pressing her deep into the floorboards. With a heart unburdened by remorse or innocent delusion, she surrendered to him.

She was suddenly, wondrously attuned on every sensory level. She relished the feel of the coarse wooden floorboards against her bare buttocks, smelled the musty scents of a place left untended for years, heard the distant call of a hawk circling high overhead. She breathed every breath Devlin drew, responded to the slightest brush of his fingertips over her skin, smelled the leather and spice scent of his skin, and tasted the salt on his beard-stubbled throat.

When the pain inevitably came, she clasped him close and let the hushed intimacy of his voice and his tender kisses soothe her. When the skies burst with pleasure, she cried out with the spasms against his mouth, heard the satisfaction in his murmurings and knew a singular fulfillment. And when he lifted her up into him, his body one long, sinuous instrument of physical pleasure, and found his own shuddering surcease, she knew an inner peace and satisfaction she'd never dreamed possible.

For some time, she stared at the beamed ceiling overhead, smoothed her palms over his back and relished the feel of two hundred pounds of male on top of and embedded deep within her.

Devlin's breath fanned against her neck in deep even measure. She thought he slept. Until one large hand moved in a slow circular motion over her breast and drew the nipple long and taut between his fingers.

Her throat felt thick. "Devlin—"

"I'm not ready to talk yet." Lowering his head, he took her nipple into his mouth. For him, conscience remained beyond the closed door. He displayed none of the sudden shyness she felt, no recriminations. Part of her suddenly yearned to shield herself from consequences as she took the time to gather her thoughts. The other part of her, the part that had brought her there on a whim in the first place, arched her back and offered herself into his hands and his mouth for as long as he wished. That part of her offered no resistance when he rolled with her onto his back, spread his hands around her waist and, with a slight flex of his arms, lifted her astride him.

He was right. No words could be spoken. Nothing could be said to capture the pleasure and the exquisite pain of this union.

His face was drawn tense and taut, his body rigid and bathed in a sheen of passion, his eyes dark and fathomless as he took her again to wondrous heights of sensation and left her suspended there without mercy, for long, breathless moments when the pain and the pleasure became one, until she demanded her release, and she was at last the lioness set free.

He joined her there at the pinnacle and they found an endless mutual surcease until Willie finally collapsed against him.

"How did you get this?"

Sloan opened his eyes. He could have lain there content for the rest of his days with her sweet little body poured all over his. Talk was beyond him, and composing a logical thought a feat worthy of knighthood. Still he couldn't resist her.

She'd propped her chin on her hand against his chest and was running her fingertips over the inside of his forearm, where the skin had long since shriveled with the brand's scar. For all her prior innocence, she wore her sexuality like a beacon. Her eyes were sultry and heavy lidded, her lips swollen. Her hair was a lustrous tangle of curls that rippled over his skin like raw silk. Her skin was hot and moist from their exertions, and she smelled like sex and sunshine in the grass, a peculiar, most intoxicating combination.

He felt himself at once go rigid. Her eyes slanted at him. She was waiting for his reply. He would have preferred to pounce on her again. Squelching the urge, in favor of her tender sensibilities, he replied, "I got it in England...many years ago, in a test of courage."

"You passed, of course."

His chest seemed to swell. "That certain, are you?"

Again her palm smoothed over the scar as if she wanted to memorize it. Odd. Every woman he'd known had made it clear she thought the brand revolting, and had seemed to employ great effort to avoid touching it. Willie harbored no inhibitions about any part of him. Her hand continued over his wrist. Fingertips brushed against his palm then entwined with his. "It could only be the mark of a true master," she said softly.

He slid one hand low over her back where it met with the fullness of her bottom, and he felt a great compulsion to anchor her there, forever. "It is. Azato set me to my final test. I had to find my way through a specially designed labyrinth filled with traps and obstacles designed to test my skills. If I'd failed, I would have died in the tunnels."

She looked startled. "This Azato is a friend of yours?"

"He could never be my friend."

"He would have let you die in the labyrinth. When you went in, you knew you could die. You were very brave for a young man."

"Not so young. I was eighteen. Old enough to be a master."

"And when you made it through the labyrinth?"

"I emerged at the front gate and found it blocked by a smoldering urn. To gain freedom, I had to move the urn. Because of its weight, I had to grasp the urn in my bare arms to lift it out of the way and trigger the front gate to open."

"So as you lifted it you were branded by the metal." Her voice dropped off in a whisper. He felt her quick breaths push against his chest. "You were very brave."

"To face the pain? Anyone can retreat from physical pain."

"I was talking about the unknown."

"We all face it every day, to some degree. Take our current circumstances—" He glimpsed a telling shyness skitter across her face and rolled her to her back before she got any ideas about getting up. Gathering her in his arms, he pressed his lips to her brow and murmured, "The time for regrets has passed, Wilhelmina. We are as indelibly etched into each other as this scar is in my skin. Neither one of us can lightly consider what happened here. We would be fooling ourselves to think otherwise. Surely you knew that when you rode up here."

Color stained her cheekbones.

"Ah. You were driven by reckless, wanton thoughts—" He heard her breath catch and lowered his mouth to hers. Their lips touched, parted, tongues met, retreated. "You made me mad for you, chasing you like that. I didn't give much thought to anything else." He couldn't resist the lure of her bosom, thrusting up at him in glorious abundance, and brushed his lips over one peak until it distended fully. "But the having is far better than the chasing, isn't it?"

"Much better—"

"Tell me about this place."

"I can't, not when you're—" Her fingers dug into his scalp. Her loins squirmed against his. "We really shouldn't—"

"We make the rules, my dear. Remember that." He levered himself up, grasped her hand and assisted her from the floor. He swept her hands aside and laced her chemise while she looked to the side as if she found something of great interest in the corner. He felt a pang of conscience when he saw the bloodstains dotting the floor and flecked across the front of his britches. A bit of shyness was to be expected. He left the buttoning of the shirt to her. Affording her a bit of modesty, he turned and tended to his britches then swept his shirt and topcoat from the floor. He shook them free of a year's worth of dust and glanced at her. "You haven't been here in a while."

She looked sharply up at him. "I've never been here with a—that is, you're the first to—" She bit her lip and looked so out of sorts he pulled her into his arms.

"I know I'm the first," he rasped, feeling an odd compression in his chest. "I'd prefer to think I'm the last."

After several moments she said, "My mama used to come here. She brought me only twice but I'll always remember the way. I'm sure Pa never knew about this place. Whenever she went off by herself for a day, and it wasn't often, he and the boys thought she went to visit a friend who lived up in the mountains. I knew different. She came up here."

Dark emerald eyes lifted to his. "She didn't come alone. After she died, I came up here one day and saw a man standing in the door. I knew he was waiting for her. He was big, tall and young, younger than my mama. He had long, golden hair..." She reached to smooth his hair against his shoulder. "Long, like yours. He wore buckskins and furs and carried a long rifle. He had a great thick beard and moved like a mountain lion. He must have lived in the mountains, alone. I think he was her lover."

"And if he was?"

She pushed away from him, her chin inching up. "I'm not ashamed for her, if that's what you're asking. I can't possibly judge her. I don't think I ever understood that part of her...until now. She needed to live her own dream, even if it was only for an instant in time. She loved my pa. Her life and her duty was with him. But I think she loved this man, too."

"You'll have more than that," he murmured, shrugging into his shirt and quickly tending to the buttons.

She shook her head. Her eyes flashed with reckless self-confidence and Sloan had a sudden sinking feeling in the pit of his belly. "Gramps says I have to live my own dreams. I think that's why I brought you here." Rising up, she kissed him full on the mouth. "Thank you, Devlin...."

He yanked her hard against him, forcing her head back and her eyes to his. Anger surged through him in great rhythm. "Don't thank me, dammit. I did you no favors here. Whether you like it or not, you're going to marry me."

She blinked at him, black, copper-tipped lashes sweeping clear to her innocently arched brows. "I beg your pardon, Devlin, but I brought you here to fulfill my own little dream.

And you did, marvelously. Marriage had nothing to do with it. If I remember, you were the first to point out to me that the granting of certain favors is a pitiful poor reason for accepting a man's offer of marriage.''

He almost laughed aloud at the absurdity of her suggestion. That she would think to refuse him! He clamped his teeth before he reminded her that he had been referring to Brant Masters when he'd said that, not to himself. And that certain favors were definitely not the same as her virtue. By God, the woman was acting as cavalier as a man about the whole affair! Chest puffing with his ire, he said, "So sorry, my dear, but your little dream just bumped into my reality. I intend to do the right and honorable thing.''

"Not on my account, you won't. I'm not your responsibility.''

"The hell you're not. You're mine now.''

"Yours?" She drew a swift breath and twisted out of his arms, agilely sidestepping him around a table and chairs before he could lunge after her. "Because of a few minutes of shared passion on a mountain shack floor? Not hardly.'' Cat eyes slanted up at him and he felt the bite of her words deep in his bones. "Whatever happened to your duty in England?''

Shoving a chair aside, he advanced around a corner of the table, shirttails billowing behind him. "I have every intention of fulfilling my duties there.''

Backing away from him and around the opposite corner of the table, she blinked at him as if she thought him half-daft. "And I'm supposed to docilely follow you and forsake everything here?''

"You won't want for anything, I can assure you.''

Her lip curled with derision. "Don't attempt to buy me.''

"I'll leave that to Masters.''

"I'm not a child.''

"I need no reminding.''

"Really?'' She tossed her head defiantly, hands planted on her hips, eyes blazing with the full force of her female ire. "It suits you to think of me as a woman only when your lust overcomes you. Any other time, you behave as if I need the protection and care of an infant. I need to be told what to do, what to think, and then I'm kept in the dark about anything of importance, including the murder of my own father. I won't have it anymore. Not from J.D. Not from Gramps. Not from Brant. And certainly not from you."

"You damned well know I don't treat you like that," he growled. "Call me a bullheaded lout, but in my experience I've found that enlightening a woman to something she had been blind to will only achieve a swift and vicious denial. Oddly enough, women enjoy being wrong about things even less than men, and tend to despise any man who tries to teach them anything. It goes to the heart of their damned intuition. They want to figure it out on their own. Highly admirable, I say, but they sometimes need a gentle hand guiding them. It seems you resent guidance of any kind."

"I suppose I do."

"Then do forgive me if I haven't sat you smartly in a chair and rubbed your nose in the truth."

"About Brant?"

"Masters will dig his own hole. I don't need to help. I was thinking about J. D. Harkness."

Her eyes flashed with challenge. "You're so drawn to the needy, the beleaguered and the exploited. You're driven by duty and an uncompromising sense of right and wrong. First in England with the miners, and now here. You were drawn to Prosperity Gulch for a reason, for the difference you could make in people's lives here. And when your duty is up, the challenges met, and the wrongs righted, you will have to move on. After we catch my pa's killers, there will be no cause left here to champion, no one left to save."

"I've never pitied you, dammit."

"Maybe. But you can't deny that you think of me as chattel, as just another one of your tenants requiring tending, or a miner's widow needing comfort."

"I think of you as belonging to me." He took another step and shoved the table aside with the sudden savagery of his anger. It teetered on two legs then toppled over with a thud. Willie backed straight up against the wall. Just as she turned and lunged toward the door, he pounced on her, pinning her arms on either side and looming over her, full of a churning rage that came with a feeling of complete ineptitude.

"Don't ever run from me," he rumbled through clenched teeth. "As my wife, you would have the full measure of my protection and all the security and comfort I could provide you as your husband. What is mine would be yours, all of it, generations' worth. There isn't a woman in the world who'd find fault with that."

"Yes, there is," she hissed. "I won't be any man's duty because of a moment's weakness."

"Dammit, you're not—you're—" Sloan closed his eyes and listened to his teeth slide together. He felt as if her fist had plunged into his chest and grabbed his heart. He wanted to put into words his conflicting desires to crush her in his arms and make love to her and yet strangle her at the same time. She'd done nothing but confuse and tangle the simplest of issues and, in the process, had tied him in knots. "This isn't going well."

"What do you expect when you bully someone?"

"You consume me." He forced his fingers to loosen their grip on her arms and willed a calmness to his voice he didn't feel in the least. "What do you require of a husband?"

Her forthright stare made him feel centuries old and very foolish. "What every woman wants, of course."

He was at a total loss. Every lesson he'd ever learned in his life, from the most grueling of physical skills to his experiences with women, couldn't have prepared him for her.

"Love," she said.

His throat went dry. "Love."

She watched him. He thought her chin quivered, but then she thrust it up at him and he felt as if an invisible shield went up around her and knew his window of opportunity had slammed closed. "Yes, that's what I said," she said crisply. "Now let go of me. We've my father's killers to find. Or did you forget that your friends Hyde and Strobridge are in jail?"

Yes, he'd quite forgotten. About everything except wiping the distant look from her eyes. If he couldn't find the words to say what lurked in the shadowy recesses of his soul, if he couldn't label the emotion welling up inside him, then hell...

He gripped her jaw, tilted it and brought his open mouth down on hers, thrusting his tongue deep, sweeping, tasting, claiming until he felt the moan tremble through her. It was all he wanted from her, more of the same uninhibited feast of a response she'd given him on that floor. The physical combustion occurring between them had nothing to do with responsibility...and, for that matter, neither did his desire to spend the rest of his life with her, making love to her, listening to her breathe as she slept in the deepest hours of night, growing very old and wise with her.

The thought, that instant of realization, made his head spin, and he crushed her in his arms and fit his mouth deeper against hers. Consumed with the thought of having her beside him for all his days, he knew there was only one way to convince a woman as stubborn as she of something she was keeping herself blind to.

Sloan lifted his head and stared into her eyes. For an instant she looked so desperately in need of something he could have turned himself inside out to make it right. And then as suddenly as it flared, the fire turned to ice and she withdrew into herself. Her hands pushed into his chest. "Devlin—"

Relishing the breathlessness in her voice perhaps a bit too much for a man determined to make her see reason, he released her then bent to retrieve his forgotten topcoat and hat. He held a hand to the door and cocked a brow at her.

"Ready for the world once again, my lady?"

"I always was," she said crisply. Shoving her hat on her head, she turned and strode out the door.

* * *

It was with some dismay that Willie noted the lengthening shadows of dusk creeping across the yard when she pulled Beau to a stop by the porch steps and dismounted. She heard Devlin's saddle creak as he dismounted behind her and tried her best to act normal when Gramps shoved out from the shadows and reached for Beau's reins. Swinging her head away, she handed them to him.

The problem was she didn't feel the least bit like herself. Her face felt hot, her lips swollen, and her loins raw and achy. Devlin's scent still filled her nostrils and emanated from her skin. She might as well have been wearing a sign around her neck that proclaimed her Prosperity Gulch's newest deflowered virgin.

She watched Gramps lead the horses away. Worse yet, she felt deeply, despairingly sad. Not regretful. Not even guilty. Sad, as if she'd lost her heart irretrievably in those mountains, the instant Devlin had looked at her when she'd said "love."

She recognized the hot burn at the backs of her eyes for what it was and gritted her teeth. If she was going to recklessly go after a moment of physical fulfillment, surrender to her passion, and profess herself satisfied with simply that, she'd better stay satisfied. Particularly since Devlin was quite obviously acting out of obligation.

Not love. No, there wasn't a hint of that from him.

Warm hands cupped around her upper arms and drew her back against a sturdy chest. Cigar smoke wrapped around her. "I'm glad you're back," Brant said.

Willie resisted the urge to cringe and turn away from him, very much aware that Devlin saw everything, despite his fussing with unsaddling Edgar.

"Come inside." Brant turned her toward the house. "Dinner's still warm."

She immediately disappeared upstairs and splashed water over her face and neck to clear her thoughts. She'd never lived a lie. She didn't think she could look Gramps square and not blurt everything out for him. But as she watched from her window as Devlin headed out over the fields toward the woods and the quiet haven of the bathing pond, she knew a longing grip her like a man's fist squeezing. She would have to get quickly comfortable with concealing her deepest feelings, not so much from Gramps or Brant, but from Devlin.

Until he left. Yes, maybe the sadness would go with him.

She spent the rest of the evening waiting for Brant to ask where she and Devlin had spent the better part of the day. He wasn't a stupid man. He had to suspect something. She should have done the noble thing and told him. But how did a woman go about telling her fiancé that she'd lived out one last fantasy that afternoon, and that it had nothing to do with him?

She barely ate. Throughout dinner Brant remained charming and gracious. He talked about his plans for the farm and smiled at her across the table with a warmth in his eyes that made her want to crawl out of her skin. Guilt crept closer around her as the mantel clock ticked. Devlin and Gramps remained conspicuously absent, well into the evening. She supposed that was for the best.

By the time Brant led her onto the porch, she could barely think clearly. Sitting on the porch steps beside him, she stared out into the moonless skies. The night was silent, but to Willie's ear the hush was expectant, as if the very trees were waiting for her to speak before they allowed their leafy limbs to bend with the cool breeze.

His hand closed over hers. "Don't say anything."

Willie swallowed. "I've never been able to lie."

He turned to her, handsome as any woman could hope for in a man, eager as an expectant bridegroom, brimming with hope, faulted, too, just as she was. He drew her hand to his mouth. "All I want to hear from your sweet lips are these words—'Yes, I'll marry you.' That's all. No explanations. No excuses."

Willie was stunned into silence. She felt the weight of the ring sliding onto her finger and the heat of his mouth on her cheek. His breath was laced with cigar smoke and something else…whiskey.

For a man who most probably suspected himself wronged by another man, he was taking it most nobly. Almost too nobly. When had she ever known a man to sacrifice his pride to another man without any kind of fight? Brant Masters had never seemed the self-sacrificing sort, or the type to so quickly forgive. Then again, perhaps she didn't know Brant Masters as well as she thought she did.

"I love you, Willie," he rasped against her cheek. "I want you as my wife. I'll do my damnedest to make you happy. One day you'll find that you love me, too."

Her heart wrenched. Would she? Had her mother reconciled her need for the love of her mountain man with her obligation to her husband and family? She hadn't found complete fulfillment in either. Would she be sentencing herself to the same fate?

But as she looked up into Brant's eyes, she found herself considering that she could find contentment with him. Her mind swam with conflicting thoughts and unwelcome memories of that afternoon. Her heart ached with confusion.

True love. Was that the fantasy, the dream she was destined to chase without success? Her father had chased a dream and had made it his. Would he have told her to find happiness with the one man who loved her, even if she loved another?

The words crept to her tongue and poised there. *Yes, Brant, I will marry you.…* "I—" Her breath released in a rush. "I'll give you my answer tomorrow. I promise."

She didn't want to ponder why she left him smoking his cigar on the porch and scurried up to her bed. She didn't pause to consider why she left the bedside lamp burning low as she crawled beneath the sheets. She was overcome with a strange impatience to find herself safely tucked away in bed, where she could stare up at the ceiling, listen to the night creep, to the wolves howl, and twist the heavy ring around her finger. To wait. To wonder. To remember.

Deep into the night, she waited for the footfalls in the hall outside her door. She waited for the muffled sounds of movement from the next room, the scrape of a chair, the rustle of linen and brocade peeling off muscled shoulders, the thunk of shoes hitting the floor, the creak of the bed ropes. She waited for her door to squeak open on its hinges and a broad silhouette to fill the doorway. She waited for a lover she'd created out of her own romantic delusion, a man who never came.

With a start, she awoke to midmorning sunlight blasting through her window. Surging from the bed, she opened her door and listened to the silence filling the house. Quickly she checked Devlin's room and found it empty, the bed untouched. She found the kitchen deserted. Nightgown billowing around her legs, she raced from the house. She met Gramps and Huck halfway across the yard.

"Where is he?"

Gramps slowly set down the bucket of feed. Leaning heavily on his cane, he replied, "Funny, you never know where your fiancé is. Course, it's probably Devlin you're askin' about, eh?" Working the chew around in his mouth, he said simply, "He left."

Willie felt the blood drain from her face. "He left?"

"You looked damned scared, Willie-girl. You think he'd leave town with those poor railroad gents locked up for somethin' they didn't do?"

Willie wrapped her arms close around her, suddenly weak with relief. Her voice trembled from her throat. "He went to town."

"Nope." Gramps jerked his head west. "He rode out thataway, toward the mine. With Dakota Darby."

Willie blinked at him with disbelief. "She was here?"

"Standin' right beside me in this yard, skirts aswishin'. 'Bout an hour ago."

"And you didn't wake me? Dakota knows, Gramps! She knows who's behind the murder."

Gramps looked deeply affronted. "Now, Willie-girl, I wasn't thinkin' much about you when she rode up in her fancy wagon with the pink spokes and her pink feathers in her pink hat. That's a mighty fine lookin' woman, even in the early mornin'. Devlin seemed to know what to do with her. She wasn't too comfortable stayin' here and sayin' whatever it was she wanted to say to him. Course, she got that way when Brant Masters walked out onto the porch. Yep, she got all jumpy all of a sudden and wanted to leave real quick. She didn't even want Devlin ridin' in the wagon with her. She just 'bout fidgeted herself silly while he saddled up Edgar."

Willie's mind flew. An hour ago. A hell of a long time. Anything could have happened. Anything could have been said. The chances of finding them were slim, considering that Dakota was acting like she didn't want to be seen or found. Willie chewed at her lip. "Where's Brant?"

"Funny you should ask. Even before Dakota and Devlin disappeared around the side of the house he was saunterin' across the yard, sayin' good-mornin' and talkin' 'bout nothin' to an old man he don't even see half the time much less like, thinkin' I won't notice that he's all shifty-eyed and fidgety. Then he saddles up his horse. I never seen him move so fast. He was goin' somewhere. And with you upstairs, ready to come down any minute to tell him if you're gonna marry him. Thought he'd be pacin' a hole in the kitchen floor. But off he went."

Willie was suddenly certain she didn't want to know where Brant Masters had gone. She felt cold, from the inside out. "He followed them."

Gramps's thin lips compressed. "You tell me, Willie-girl. You tell me what business he's got pokin' his nose into all that? I tell you, he's too damn smug, that one. Too damned sure of himself. Hey! Where the hell you racin' off to with your tail on fire? You better not be chasin' after Masters."

"I've got to find Devlin." Fists balled into the sides of her nightgown, hair flapping like a curtain behind her, she growled, "Damn him for being right."

"You act like you don't want him to catch the men who blew the mine," Gramps called after her as she stomped up the porch steps. "Thought you'd be damned happy to see the murder solved. Thought we all would be."

"Damned happy," she muttered as she raced up the stairs. So damned happy. Vindicated, yes. Avenged, certainly. But happy to see Devlin pack his valise and move on?

She wasn't sure but at that moment part of her would have been content to let the mystery remain unsolved, perhaps for good.

Chapter Eighteen

Some things in life were just too damned easy. Take card cheating. When the moment was ripe it was a simpleton's trick. The talent lay in recognizing the moment when his opponents were the most unsuspecting and convinced beyond a doubt that they held the winning hand, and their guard slipped just enough to let him in. A card up his sleeve, concealed in his palm, a flick of his wrist as he lit another cigar.

He wasn't sure which he enjoyed more, scooping up a wrist-deep pile of coin and bills at the end of an evening's work, or recognizing the look a man got in his eye when he realized he'd been robbed blind. A look of utter, empowering dread.

Dakota Darby had made the mistake of being too confident. She had to be thinking she held the winning hand to risk coming anywhere near Prosperity Gulch and sniff out a meddling bastard like Devlin. She should have stayed in the Devil's Gold, counted her money and kept her mouth shut. That was the problem with women. They didn't know how to control themselves. Dakota and her mouth.

Willie with Devlin. Women got a look in their eyes after they'd been tumbled. He'd seen it often enough to recognize that look, particularly on a woman like Willie. He'd even smelled it on her, through the whiskey and the cigar smoke. She'd reeked of Devlin's scent.

Anger pumped through him, demanding a swift and brutal revenge. He shifted in his saddle and curved his fingers around his silver-barreled Colt. Through a tangle of brush, he stared at the broad back and black top hat just a hundred yards beyond, the figure standing tall and still beside Dakota Darby in a clump of willows.

Lifting the pistol, Brant squinted and took aim at Devlin's back. Perspiration dripped into his eyes. He blinked, focused, tasted the bile of rage on his tongue. He'd never been possessed of such an urge to kill. His finger trembled on the trigger.

He should have shot Devlin on the train when he'd had the chance. Instead, like a coward, he'd allowed the foppish Englishman to get him stranded on the Nebraska prairie with no horse, no gun and bruised ribs. He wasn't about to let him foil his grandest scheme yet. He was going to get the real prize. The easy take.

Or would he? Devlin had gotten Willie gun-shy and bedded. So, now she wasn't a virgin. He could drown his wounded pride in his silver-stocked mine. And if he ever got hungry for something unused, he was certain he could find what he was looking for in Deadwood Run, at the Devil's Gold with some fresh-faced, down-on-her-luck, orphaned cutie. The West was full of them.

As for Willie and her skittishness, the English bastard would be leaving town soon, with a bullet or two in his back. With him gone, she'd be seeing reason soon enough, especially since she was now used goods. After all, it hadn't taken him too long seven months ago to turn the cool, redheaded beauty into hot, snow-white putty in his hands. The seduction had been almost too easy. But hell, when a man knew how to play a woman's vulnerabilities against her like he did, seduction was just another simpleton's trick. With Devlin gone she'd be damned grateful to find any man who'd marry her. Grateful, obliging, humble, and sitting on a pile of money. Just the way he'd liked each of his wives.

Lowering the pistol, he swiped a forearm over his brow and shifted his gaze to Dakota Darby. She'd recognized him. She obviously didn't trust him. And to think he'd spent long nights seven months ago whispering his own silver-spun promises in her ear while they rode the creaking bed ropes together. She hadn't laid any hopes in him then and he'd known it, just as he'd known someone else had been plying her with bigger promises. With money. Not sex. He knew for a fact whoever it was hadn't satisfied her in her bed. She'd always been too eager for him.

Briefly he wondered if they'd ever reckoned she'd turn traitor on them. Some stupid, boastful bastard was about to learn a tough lesson in keeping his tongue in check around a beautiful woman. He was also about to learn that women were always looking for bigger, fatter fish.

He watched Devlin hand Dakota into her buggy. They exchanged a few words. Devlin reached into his breast pocket. Brant's lip curled. The payoff. He wondered how much she demanded for telling secrets and turning traitor. He scowled as Devlin pulled a white handkerchief from his pocket and handed it to Dakota. She dabbed at her cheeks. A pink glove waved Devlin off. He hesitated, then turned and mounted up. Again he paused, said something to her, but she shook her head and sat in the buggy with her head down and her pink feathers fluttering in the wind.

Several minutes later Devlin raced by. The man was in a hurry. Brant had little time to waste if he intended to use Dakota Darby and her secrets to his best advantage. Keeping one step ahead of Devlin was a daunting prospect. He'd been taken for a fool once. He wouldn't be again. With a grim smile, he eased his horse from the brush and headed toward Dakota Darby.

Willie drew Beau up in front of the jail where a dozen men scrambled about with hammers and wood erecting the hanging scaffold. Already someone had affixed a line of thick hemp to the structure. The looped end stirred in the breeze, waiting.

Dismounting, Willie stepped onto the boardwalk and pushed the jailhouse door open. A deputy dozed beneath his hat in one chair against the wall. Cochran sat with boots crossed on a desktop, a *Lucky Miner* spread under his nose. Eyes narrowed, he read silently, his lips moving as he read. He glanced up when the door slammed.

"Keeping the peace, Sheriff?" Willie said, peeking down the hall at the jail's lone cell.

The paper snapped closed. "Cain't say that fer yer boarder, Willie Thorne. Time's ripe fer him to move on."

Willie inclined her head and folded her arms over her chest, well aware of the threatening undertones in Cochran's voice. "Now that's curious. Here I was thinking you'd be pinning a deputy's star on him for all the help he's given you. Why, if it hadn't been for his editorial you would have been baking cookies and selling lemonade to get folks to vote for you next week. And you still might not have gotten elected."

Cochran's fleshy upper lip quivered with his sneer. "Your pa shoulda cut yer tongue out when you was a little girl."

Willie smiled. "Talk too much. Think too much. Funny how that bothers you, Sheriff."

"It'd bother any man."

"If he had something to hide, maybe." Willie jerked her head toward the front window. "Scaffold's near done. You send for the judge?"

"You tellin' me how to do my job, girlie?"

"Just wondering. Who'd you get?"

Cochran's lips peeled back over long, yellow teeth. "Mason."

The most notorious hanging judge in the county. Willie's teeth compressed. "It'll take him a couple days to get here from Copper Glen. You could have sent for Judge McKay. Twisted Nickel's a lot closer than Copper Glen."

Cochran's eyes narrowed on her. "I didn't want McKay."

Of course, he didn't. McKay wouldn't necessarily give Cochran the hanging he wanted, because McKay was known to be an inordinately fair judge. Willie turned and headed straight down the hall toward the back of the jail.

Chair legs jerked against the floor behind her. "Hey!" Cochran shouted. "Git back here. Them's dangerous prisoners."

"I can see that," Willie muttered, moving close to the cell. Hyde and Strobridge, the swank East Coast capitalists and figureheads of the mightiest corporation in the country, the men she'd turned away from her land a half-dozen times with a solid shake of her head, the dangerous prisoners, lay curled up on threadbare cots sleeping. Blood stained their elegant clothes. Bruises marred their faces. Eyes bulged purple, and their smooth pink hands were dirt smeared.

She remembered the last time they'd ridden up to the house in their shiny buggy. They'd shaken her hand, looked at her squarely and treated her like they would have any man, without the pat-on-the-bottom kind of patronizing most men had for landowning women. It hadn't mattered how much they'd offered her to sell and she'd told them that. They countered by raising the offer substantially. They'd even offered to subdivide the land with her.

She closed her eyes and remembered them finally turning back to their buggy, shaking their heads and clamping cigars in their mouths. She remembered the wind that day whistling through the trees, flapping in their coats. She remembered thinking they looked prosperous and soft, as if they'd lived cushy lives in cushy chairs. Their bellies had ridden well over the tops of their trousers.

She opened her eyes. They'd carried no guns in their waistbands or inside their coats. They'd come peacefully. She hadn't wanted to believe it then. She'd wanted someone to blame for the terrorizing. But she knew it now.

She breezed past Cochran without a word, strode out the door, head bent with her thoughts, only to jostle headlong into a man watching the scaffold go up. She glanced at him, an apology poised on her lips, and was met with a bespectacled gaze beneath a worn brown bowler. She recognized him immediately as the man Devlin suspected of following Brant.

Up close she could see the lines around his eyes, and something else, something that made her instantly certain he missed very little. Something that made her suspect she hadn't stumbled into him as much as he'd put himself directly in her path. For a reason.

"So sorry, miss." His mustache twitched up and down. Then before she could summon a thought, he touched his gloved fingers to the brim of his hat, turned smartly on his heel and ambled off down the boardwalk.

She watched him go, certain that she'd received a thorough inspection and not liking it in the least. But whatever he was up to would have to wait.

Mounting up, she reined Beau toward the Silver Spur and charged past the mustached stranger. Devlin could mount a stunning array of witnesses and evidence, but all of it would amount to nothing with a hanging judge and a bloodthirsty sheriff calling the shots. And she intended to do something about it before more innocent men paid with their lives.

"I'll tell you what I'm going to do," Brant Masters said to the man. He followed him around the back corner of the building, well beyond earshot of the street and out of sight of the busy bodies. "And I'll tell you right now I'm not leaving you much choice in the matter."

"That so?"

Glancing around, Brant said, "And we'll both get what we want. Maybe not as much as we'd thought but, because of that bastard Devlin, we have no choice." He deepened his stare. "I just had a conversation with Dakota Darby. Right after she had a conversation with Sloan Devlin. Seems she's all torn up about those two railroad gents getting hung for something she knows they didn't do. Seems she's got a soft spot for fancy

East Coast businessmen and a young Thorne boy who wore his heart on his sleeve for her. So soft she couldn't live with your secrets any more. Guess you didn't count on that when you decided to brag a little about your scheme and make promises to her about all that silver you were going to find."

"Dammit." The word sizzled on the afternoon air.

"Seems she knows who really blew that mine."

"That so?"

Brant bared his teeth. "What is it you don't understand? I'm on to you. You and your boys. I know about that schoolteacher you paid to go down there and blow the mine. Damned clever of you, hooking up with a con artist eager for a quick buck. Even if he fingered you, folks wouldn't have believed him. Especially after you went charging in to rescue those poor miners, knowing damned well they'd been instantly broiled with the amount of charge he used. No one suspected you were behind it.

"Then when they left and the talk died out for a while you formed the vigilante gang to scare folks into thinking the railroad would do anything to get them to sell. All the while blaming the railroad when they had nothing to do with it. None of it.

"The plan worked a while. Some folks sold. But those weren't the folks you were really after. You blew that mine to get Thorne and his boys out of the way. You thought a woman with an old man to take care of would scare easy. You thought she'd be packing up after you got her almost kidnapped and shot at in Deadwood Run. You were wrong. You thought she'd be running after the barn burned and selling to the first unlucky cuss who came along.

"And that cuss was going to be you. Because you know about the silver down in that mine and you want it so bad you're thinking about killing me right now to shut me up."

Silence swelled. Brant felt the triumphant surge in his blood, the singular feeling of power over another man. "The problem was that Devlin showed up and everything started to go wrong. Virgil Brown was murdered. Folks got all stirred up. Devlin started asking questions and thinking too damned much about things that just wouldn't make sense to a stranger, and talking about it, too. And when talk gets stirred up, folks start feeling guilty about things they know. Devlin's no fool. I suspect he had his hunches about you but he knew he couldn't prove anything. He just laid bait and waited to see who'd take it. And now, thanks to Dakota, he knows." Brant let his lips slide into a grim smile. "One more thing you didn't count on. I came back. And that land and that mine are going to belong to me when Willie becomes my wife."

"Thought that wasn't going to happen?" The insolence was palpable. The gibe dug and twisted like a knife.

Brant balled his fists against his thighs. Heat swept from his starched collar. Lunging, he twisted his fist into the man's shirtfront. "Listen to me, you fat bastard—"

A wagon clattered past on the street. A child's ball rolled between the buildings and ricocheted off Brant's boot. A moment later a small boy ran between the buildings, saw them and skidded in the dirt. Blinking through his bangs, he reached for his ball, then turned and hightailed it back to the street.

Releasing a pent-up breath, Brant untwisted his fists and stepped back, tempering his rage. "I got a plan," he said finally. "You want part of the mine. I want Devlin taken care of and out of the way. For good. But I don't want a body. I want folks to think he just up and left town for good. You do that for me, with nothing pointing at me, by the time the hoedown starts tonight out by the church, and I'll give you a one-third share in the mine."

"Half."

"A third."

"Half, or I can't guarantee there won't be a body to find."

Negotiation tasted bitter on Brant's tongue. He didn't like giving up any more than he had to. The trouble was that Willie had to believe that Devlin had left town, for good, without even telling her goodbye, which meant that Brant had to find her quickly, before Devlin got to her. She hadn't been at the house. She was somewhere in town. Impatiently he spat the word. "Fine. But you'd better take care of Devlin quick. He's on to you. And he's got a good hour's head start. Something tells me he's laying you a fat trap."

"He's only one man. And he don't carry a gun. Don't think we'll have much trouble with him."

"Think again," Brant muttered. "I've seen Devlin fight without his gun."

"I've heard the talk."

"Good. I hope you've been listening." Tugging his hat over his eyes, Brant turned to head back to the street.

"Where's Dakota?"

Brant's step didn't falter. "Where all fickle women should be. In a place where no man will have to put up with her."

Willie's boot heels clicked on the floorboards. Nibbling on a thumbnail, she glanced at the clock over the bar, then scowled at Gertie draped over a bar stool in scarlet satin. Gertie polished glasses and watched her from beneath heavily kohled eyelids. They'd exchanged chilly glances since Willie had marched into the saloon ten minutes ago looking for J.D. A thump came from the back room and then the double doors that led from the kitchen banged open.

"There you are!" Willie hurried over to J.D. "Where've you been?"

Lowering a tray of glasses to the bar, J.D. grunted a greeting, barely glanced at her and moved behind the bar. "I was out back. Taking inventory." He grabbed a whiskey bottle from beneath the bar, thunked it down and heaved a sigh that sounded like it came up from his bones. "I'm sellin' out, Willie."

"No." Willie's hand shot out to still the bottle as he slid the neck against an empty glass. "Don't. That would be giving up, letting them win."

"They've won."

"They will if you let them. Listen to me. Dakota Darby came to see Devlin this morning. She told him who murdered Pa and the boys."

J.D.'s eyes narrowed. "You heard this?"

"No. I was—" Asleep. Willie swallowed. "They went somewhere—"

J.D.'s massive chest jerked with a bitter laugh. "Miss Wilhelmina, I think you're foolin' yourself. Only one thing men do with Dakota when they go off with her. Talkin' isn't it."

Willie went instantly cold.

"You seen Devlin since, Willie?"

Willie swallowed. "N-no, but I thought he'd come to town."

"I haven't seen him. You sure he didn't just decide to take Dakota back with him to England, just like that? She's been looking for a ticket out of here for years. And Devlin could have just about had it with burning barns and folks who don't much care for him. Think about that before you go off assuming he's going to come charging into town with the United States Army like some kind of damned hero and fix it all up for us. The man's human, just like the rest of us."

Chagrin slammed through Willie. Her face went instantly hot. Doubts…doubts…surely she hadn't been wrong in assuming what Dakota had come to Sloan for.

No. She'd had an instinctive faith in Sloan Devlin since the moment she'd met him. Now when she needed that faith most she wasn't about to lose it.

"He won't come with an army," she said stoutly. "He thinks he's invincible. Listen, J.D., I know you have every reason to dislike Devlin."

J.D. rubbed a paw over his bruised jaw. "It's gone well beyond dislike, Willie."

"You have to understand why he—" Willie swallowed "—hit you. He thought you were—and he was—he thought he was protecting me. He's actually a very peaceful man—and very wise. But how you feel about Devlin shouldn't matter. Two innocent men will hang tomorrow if we don't do something. I have a plan."

"And you came here for help."

"Of course, I did."

"Go home." J.D. abruptly turned his back on her, bottle clamped in one hand, a glass in the other. "Go, before you make a fool of yourself."

Willie felt herself shake with disbelief. "I thought I'd never see the day that you turned coward."

"Don't you call me that, woman."

"You're afraid of them—whoever they are, afraid enough to keep their identity from me. I'm giving you an opportunity to right some wrongs, to stop them now, before Hyde and Strobridge hang. We have to try or we're all cowards. It's one step toward forgiving yourself, J.D."

Moments passed. Willie barely breathed.

"I think every day about goin' out and shootin' them and I can't," J.D. said finally. "I'm not usually a killin' kind of man. But that doesn't mean I don't dream about revenge. I taste it and breathe it every waking moment. But I figured I deserved to pay my penance this way. I never thought I deserved a chance at making anything right."

"You do," Willie whispered. "You have to do this, J.D. What I'm asking has nothing to do with Devlin...well, not completely. Those railroad men don't deserve to die and you know it. You've got to help them."

"Your pa sure would have." His words barely registered in the silence. J.D. hung his head, lifted the bottle, looked at it and set it on the bar. "What's this plan of yours?"

Willie could almost hear jubilation singing in the empty saloon. Another moment passed before she could steady her voice. "Cochran sent a deputy to get Judge Mason and bring him back quick for a speedy hanging."

"No one like Mason to get a cuss hung without a trial."

"Exactly. I was thinking Judge McKay would see a lynching for what it was, and at least give Hyde and Strobridge a fair hearing. And what with McKay being so much closer, not even a two-hour ride away, say, if Judge McKay were to get here before Judge Mason, and free those men—''

J.D. swung around slowly. His lips twitched and color seemed to flood into his face. "Course, we could make damned sure of that, couldn't we? In fact, we could make damned sure Mason *never* gets here."

Willie could barely contain her excitement. "Fastest route to and from Copper Glen is through PickAx Gorge. You know that area of the mountains."

J.D. scratched his chin, but the glint in his eye betrayed him. "Seems to me folks been tellin' tales about the PickAx Gorge, lately. Somethin' about a masked gunman holdin' them up and scatterin' their horses so they have to walk to the nearest town. Could take them near to a week to walk all the way here. Any sane man would turn around and head back to Copper Glen." J.D. smiled, and Willie suddenly realized she hadn't seen his gold-toothed grin in months. "Guess that means I'll have to saddle up Mack."

Willie couldn't contain herself another minute. She threw her arms around J.D. "Thank you."

"Whoa, now!" J.D. grabbed her arm as she spun around. "Where you runnin' off to?"

"To Twisted Nickel, to get Judge McKay. Pa knew him from the old days, when Prosperity Gulch was a tent city, and the cowboys were looting every time they came through. McKay put a quick stop to it. Pa always thought he was a fair man." Her heart seemed to swell a little with each pulse. "And I believed my pa."

Before the tears defied her, before another minute passed, she turned, slipped around the corner of the bar and headed toward the door. She would have made it, too, clear to Twisted Nickel and back without a hitch had she not run into a large body blocking the doorway.

"Hold on there," Brant said, swinging her around. He grinned, looked at her mouth, her breasts, then finally into her eyes. "I'm right here. Tell me I'm the one you're so hot to find."

Something inside of Willie cringed at his words. Or maybe it was simply the way he said them. The way he said just about everything. There was no emotion beneath the bronzed and groomed veneer, nothing of value that a soft rub of a fingernail wouldn't expose. All her feelings for him had been born of guilt over what she'd thought had transpired on the stream bank.

He looked suddenly very cold, his eyes shallow pits, his smile a much-practiced slice of white across his handsome face. She didn't love Brant Masters and she never would, no matter how she felt about Devlin.

His grip held firm when she tried to wrest her arm away. "Actually, Brant, I've an errand I have to do."

His smile hardened. "But I got a surprise for you, honey. Something real special for tonight. If you want, it can wait, and I'll come with you."

"No—" She bit her tongue, knowing she'd responded too quickly simply by the narrowing of his eyes. "You don't have to do that. It's quite a ride."

"Fine. Let's go."

Watching him, Willie had a sudden horrific thought that Brant Masters knew far more than he was letting on. Was he daring her to deny him? A shiver whispered up her spine.

Her skin crawled where his palm smoothed over her arm. "What's the matter, honey? You keeping secrets from me?"

Her chin inched up. "Why would I need to do that?"

"Why, indeed!" From the corner of the saloon came a furious rustle of crimson skirts and the click of high-heeled shoes. Gertie sashayed, with ample cleavage bobbing, toward them, her dark eyes skewering Willie. "Go on, why don't you just tell him where you're going?"

Willie gulped and blinked at Gertie as if she'd just seen her for the very first time. "Tell him," Willie echoed, quite certain that Gertie held their plan in the palm of her tiny hand. The months of cool exchanges, the friendship that they'd let deteriorate because of one man's fickle affections, stood like a fortress between them. Impenetrable, unless differences could be put aside to achieve a common goal.

One dark brow poking upward, Gertie glanced at Brant. "See there. You've got the poor girl all atwitter." Her tone suddenly turned icy. "I hope you're pleased with yourself, Brant Masters. Like my mama used to say, there's some things a woman should be able to do on her own without her husband gettin' all in a fuss over it. And buyin' her husband somethin' special for their weddin' day should be one of them."

Brant lost a bit of his bronzed glow. "I—I didn't think—"

Gertie's eyes flashed. "Of course, you didn't think. Men seldom do." With one last glance, Gertie dismissed Brant Masters. "It's okay, Willie. I'll take care of it for you. Really—" Her gaze deepened, searched and glowed with forgiveness. "I'd be happy to do it."

Gratitude welled up in Willie. Her voice cracked. "You know where to find it."

Gertie dissolved into her smile and looked as pleased as a plump cat in cream. Fingering the black lace trim along her plunging neckline she had the effrontery to blush, and purred, "Oh, my goodness, yes. That particular fellow and me go way back. I'd reckon he'd do just about anything to help me out. Don't you worry now. You go on and let Brant give you that surprise." She glanced over her shoulder. "J.D. I'll need some help harnessing up the buggy." Gertie's fingers gently squeezed Willie's arm. "I'll see you later tonight at the hoedown."

Willie watched her disappear into the back room, J.D. at her heels.

"Didn't think you and Gertie much cared for each other," Brant muttered, clearly befuddled.

Willie gave him a wide-eyed innocent look that was intended to augment his confusion. "Now why would you think that? Just because you seemed sweet on her for a while and then suddenly sweet on me—really, Brant, women don't let just anything come between them.''

The stunned look on his face at being dismissed as trivial brought a smile to her lips. Her victory was to be frustratingly short-lived.

"By the way, you seen Devlin?" Brant asked, shoving the door wide and guiding her onto the boardwalk.

Her step faltered. "I—not yet today I haven't. Why do you ask?"

Brant shrugged and loosed Beau's reins from the hitching rail. "Just wondering. Last I heard from Gramps he was heading out of town with Dakota Darby. And her with bags packed in her buggy. Hope he was paid up. I don't like to think anyone's taking advantage of my woman's generous nature."

Willie's jaw tightened as Brant helped her mount up. "He didn't go anywhere, dammit."

Brant glanced sharply at her then bent to tighten her saddle cinch. "I wouldn't count on it." He moved around his horse and mounted up. Oddly enough, he felt some compulsion to lay one hand on the butt of the Colt riding in his saddle scabbard. "You ready for your surprise now, honey? It's over in Deadwood Run."

Willie glanced up the street. A breeze churned the dust. People ambled along the boardwalks. Only a handful of horses stood at hitching rails. A typical day in Prosperity Gulch. No sign of Devlin or Edgar. Her stomach churned with something close to doubt and despair. A good three hours had passed since he'd ridden out with Dakota Darby. Why hadn't he come to town?

No. She refused to believe that Devlin had left for good. He was preparing to capture the men who murdered her pa and brothers. He would outwit them, unmask them, save the town...and come back for her.

In front of the newspaper office she spotted Tom Lansky bent in earnest conversation with the mustached man in the brown bowler. "Do you know that man with Lansky?" she asked, jerking her head toward the newspaper office.

"Never seen him."

She turned and looked squarely at Brant.

Beneath her stare he shifted in his saddle and scowled. "What? I got no reason for anyone to be following me."

"I didn't say anything about him following you."

"Yeah," he muttered, reining his horse around. "You've been listening to Devlin for too long, honey. I for one am damned glad to see him go. C'mon."

They were so certain, all of them, that Devlin had moved on. Why wasn't she?

Because she believed that his sense of purpose was as strong or stronger than hers. Because he wouldn't leave a town or a woman in the lurch. Because he would never take a woman's favors and disappear without a word. Because he was noble, he was a gentleman, and he was, in many ways, invincible.

Because she loved him.

Maybe it was that deeply held faith that made her follow Brant out of town and toward Deadwood Run without another word. If Devlin was laying a trap for the murderers, he didn't need anyone alerted to it. He needed Willie to keep up appearances.

It was for Devlin's sake alone that she plastered a pleasant look on her face, kept Brant's ring on her finger, and determined to let Brant Masters believe it was all because of him.

Chapter Nineteen

Sloan hauled back on the reins when he spotted Dakota's wagon beneath the willows where he'd left her. But the wagon was empty and Dakota nowhere to be seen. Dismounting, he began retracing his steps along the road that led past the mine entrance and looking for any clue as to where Brant Masters might have taken her. Instinct told him Masters wouldn't have risked riding into town with her.

In a tangle of brush and willows that marked the entrance at the top of the mine tracks, he spotted a fluttering pink feather. A quarter mile down the overgrown track, he found her pink feathered bonnet. Another quarter mile farther, where the track leveled off, he found her pink shoes and a torn, blood-splattered portion of her pink satin dress.

Deep within a freshly dug tunnel of the mine, he found her. Her wrists and ankles were bound with torn strips of her dress, her mouth gagged, and she wore nothing but the tattered remains of a shift and French-made stockings. Judging by the blood on her thighs, belly and hands, and the bruises on her face, she'd been beaten.

At first Sloan thought she was dead. But when he knelt beside her and released the gag, she cried out hoarsely.

"Don't talk," he muttered, freeing her hands and ankles.

He shrugged out of his topcoat, drew it around her, then gathered her into his arms. "It was Masters."

The word hissed from her. "Yes."

His chest swelled with a snarl as he lifted her and moved swiftly toward the entrance. "I never should have left you there alone."

"It's not your fault—"

"The hell it isn't. After we talked, I went to the house to find Willie, to tell her everything. Gramps told me she'd left for town. He also told me that Masters followed us this morning. Dammit, I was too anxious to know, too eager to figure this thing out—for my own reasons—and because of it, I made myself vulnerable. And you. I didn't think it through. When you act on emotion—" his breath wheezed through his lips as he exited the mine and started up the steep tracks "—you don't see it coming. You give your opponent an edge. Dammit, I knew Masters was capable of something like this."

"Y-you should have gone to find Willie first."

"I intend to. Right after I get Gramps and find a safe place for both of you. If Masters knows everything, he's going to use what he knows as leverage to cut himself a bit of the action. And part of that action will be getting me out of his way. The farm won't be a safe place for anyone."

She turned her face deep against his chest. He could almost feel the guilt washing over her.

His face hardened. "You had no choice but to tell him. He would have killed you. No secrets are worth your life."

"Are they worth yours?"

"I'm not dead yet."

"What about Willie?"

His vision seemed to blur with the sudden depths of his rage. The brush fringing the path glowed with an ominous red haze. At first he labeled it more anger, anger he'd never before experienced. But then he knew. This was fear he tasted on his tongue. This was fear not exertion making him hot and slick with sweat. This was fear galloping through his veins. Fear.

Something he'd never been allowed to know. Fear for someone he loved...

In the middle of his chest an invisible knife twisted into his heart. The words came from an unknown part of his soul. "Willie's not going to die."

"She's more important to you than catching those men."

"Yes." His thigh muscles strained as he leaned into the steep grade. Heat seared through his arm muscles. The mother-of-pearl buttons on his linen shirt dug into his skin as his chest strained against them and cloth stretched taut. But the ache he couldn't rise above, the ache he couldn't separate himself from, was beyond physical.

"You'd give your life for her."

"And leave her in Masters's hands? No chance of that."

"He's got her now."

Sloan's teeth met. "If he's smart he's got her as far away from town as he can get her. But she's safe, for now, even from him...until he gets what he wants from her. Until she marries him and the mine becomes his. And that isn't going to happen."

"You sound sure of that."

His laugh was crisp and brutal. "You're talking to a true master, Miss Dakota. And masters always have a plan."

"Let's hope it works."

Dakota Darby's words still echoed in Sloan's head thirty minutes later when he drew Edgar up at the edge of the woods that flanked Willie's property. He stared at the house and felt the hair on the back of his neck slowly rise. Everything looked as tranquil and sun dappled as it had the day he'd first ridden up the drive. Yet instinct told him something wasn't right.

They'd already laid his trap.

Dakota had slumped against his back twenty minutes before. He dismounted and gently shook her shoulders to rouse her.

"Take the reins," he said, twisting the leather around her bloodied hands and propping her higher in the saddle. "Edgar's got a tender mouth," he said. "Remember to use a light touch."

She blinked at him through eyes puffy and bruised but her voice rang strong with conviction. "I know how to ride, Devlin. Are you going to tell me what's going on? Something's wrong, isn't it? That's why you kept to the woods. You think I'm going to have to go for help."

"I'd prefer to think I can manage the situation alone and with grand aplomb. Don't be too concerned if I come out of there a prisoner. I've found the best way to catch an opponent is to let him think he's caught me first."

"Dammit, Devlin, you should have ridden straight for the nearest judge and let me be down in that mine. But you're too damned good, aren't you? I tell you I don't want your blood on my hands just because you were fool enough to save my life."

He looked up at her and felt a deep admiration for her bravery. "You'll have no men's blood on your hands once this is over. You did a noble thing to come to me with the truth, Dakota. We're going to get those men."

"That sounds like a promise, Devlin."

"I only make the ones I can keep."

Her hand reached for his and gripped tight. "I came to you because I wanted to do the right thing by Wes Thorne, and for Hyde and Strobridge. I wasn't thinking one bit about the theater in London...it might seem like it and folks might think it but—"

"I'll never think it, Dakota. You'll get to that theater in London anyway, in first-class cabin accommodations aboard a Cunard steamer. Now keep to the woods and out of sight. Then get yourself to the nearest doctor. I can handle those men. I won't need help. Besides, I'm still not certain who we can trust. You'd best keep this between us."

"And if you don't come back?"

Sloan reached into his pocket and pressed a wad of bills into her palm, curling her fingers around it. "I'll be back."

Her lips trembled and a tear slipped onto her cheek. "Then what's this for?"

"Your peace of mind."

He'd made it halfway across the field when he realized what was wrong. The shaggy dog Huck should have been loping across the yard to greet him. Gramps's dog Huck, who followed the old man and kept him company when he sat on the porch and watched the sun sink over the mountains. It would kill Gramps if they'd done anything to Huck. They'd murdered a father and his boys. A dog wouldn't matter.

Fists balling and blood beginning to thunder in his ears, Sloan lengthened his stride. He swung around the corner of the house and saw the three horses tethered under a nearby sycamore. He turned to mount the porch stairs and then he saw the black dog lying as he always did by the back door. Peaceful, as if he waited for Gramps to awaken from his midday nap. Only Huck didn't lift his head and sweep his tail over the floor when Sloan's footsteps sounded on the stairs. He just lay there, his head twisted at an odd angle from his neck, his black eyes staring blankly out toward the mountains.

Huck would have barked at a stranger, alerting Gramps, even from a sound midday sleep. The poor animal had died trying to protect his master. If they'd harmed Gramps...

Anger barely reined, Sloan shoved the door open, stepped into the kitchen and drew up short.

"Afternoon, Devlin," Sheriff Cochran drawled. He sat at the kitchen table, legs propped and muddied boots crossed at the ankles on Willie's fine white linen tablecloth. He had a jug of what Sloan knew to be whiskey in one hand and an enormous pistol in the other. The sheriff's gelatinous girth quivered as he belched. "We've been waitin' on you, Devlin. An' kinda hopin' the old man wouldn't see to wake up. Seems we got lucky on both accounts."

Sloan glanced at the door to the front parlor where Gramps obviously still enjoyed his midday nap. The door stood slightly open, the room beyond it dim. The man peeking into the room turned to Sloan, nudged his hat back and spread his lips into a gap-toothed sneer. Sloan immediately recognized him as the cowboy who'd set the fire and shot him. He'd come ready to kill this time, complete with two pistols in the gun belt riding low over his hips and one very long rifle gripped in his hand.

Sloan glanced at the third man slouched against the wall. One of Cochran's deputies, indistinguishable, nameless. The man sneered at Sloan then continued sifting through the basket of freshly folded clothes Willie had left on a stool there. Watching the man's grimy finger poking through Willie's clean shirts and undergarments, Sloan was flooded with an incomprehensible possessiveness and rage. It took a strength of will he hadn't tested in years to keep from dropping the man to the floor in a soggy, lifeless heap.

"I think you know why we're here, Devlin," Cochran said slowly, as if he savored the victorious moment and every word a bit too much. "And you're gonna go peaceful like or Billy there's gonna empty his rifle into the old man while he sleeps. Course, he could break his neck. Just the right hold and a quick snap—" Cochran snorted. "Be easier than the dog was."

Lurching to his feet, Cochran braced his legs wide. His head wobbled on his thick shoulders, back and forth as he gave Sloan a satisfied smirk. "Thought you were smarter than me, eh, gettin' Dakota to turn tail? Bet you thought you'd just ride into town and walk up to me an' say 'I knowed what you did.'"

Sloan kept his face impassive. "Actually, I planned on letting you catch me first."

Cochran went perfectly still, turned a shade paler, then glanced at the deputy and jerked his head at Sloan. "Tie him up, dammit. What the hell you waitin' for?" Cochran waved his pistol. "An' no fancy fightin', Devlin. We got our guns."

"You sure you have enough of them?"

Cochran's nostrils flared. "We'll put enough lead in you to kill twenty men."

Sloan arched impressive brows as the deputy jerked his hands behind his back and began wrapping rope around his wrists. "You can ill afford any more mistakes, Cochran. I can't help but wonder if you've thought this out completely."

Cochran shoved his nose into Sloan's face. "I know what the hell I'm doin', mister. Case you didn't notice, I'm the one who's got him a prisoner. Not you. No, dammit—" Cochran bent and snatched the rope from his deputy. "Don't tie his feet till we got him on the back of the horse. Then we'll hog-tie him." Again he thrust his nose at Sloan. "I been smellin' your blood since the minute you stepped foot in my town."

Sloan quirked one brow. "Your town? Odd choice of words, Sheriff, considering that your reelection, hell, your life at the moment is in the hands of one very contrite and justice-minded woman who doesn't seem to harbor a bit of loyalty toward you. Just thought I'd mention that Dakota Darby's not the kind of woman to keep a secret once she decides to spill it. I'm not even sure if I was the first to know."

"Dakota's been taken care of," Cochran sneered.

"That was your first mistake," Sloan replied. "Trusting Masters."

Sloan could hear the great amounts of air Cochran sucked in through his bared teeth. "You're lyin'."

"A terrible habit, common to weak-minded men whose plans are going awry." Sloan narrowed his eyes. "What's Masters promising you? A quarter share of the silver in that mine, maybe a third if you get rid of me?"

Cochran had the audacity to look smug. "I got half. And no body."

"And he was sloppy with Dakota." Sloan shook his head. "You'll be going to jail whether you kill me or not. And Masters plans to be sitting on that silver mine all by himself. Of course, you've thought of all this already, a smart man like you."

Cochran ground his teeth then smashed his fist into Sloan's midsection. The force drove the breath clean out of his lungs.

Sloan coughed, struggled to get his breath and braced for the next punch. It caught him in the ribs. Raw pain spiraled through his midsection. Cochran must have fought his way to become sheriff, Sloan thought.

"Now keep yer damned mouth shut," Cochran snarled. He turned and muttered something to Billy. Sloan saw all the opportunity he needed to bring Cochran to his knees with one well-aimed upward slice of his leg. But Billy stood across the room, only ten feet from where Gramps still slept. At that range, the gap-toothed cowboy wouldn't miss shooting in the dark. What Sloan had in mind required that they hog-tie him on that horse and take him out into the grasslands or up into the mountains.

A place where Gramps wouldn't be in danger. A place where Sloan would best be in communion with nature and the elements, and where he could harness the flow of energy required to outmaneuver three men and seven guns.

He separated his mind from his body and focused beyond himself when they shoved him from the house, threw him down the steps and drove their boots into his ribs to keep him on the ground. His mind and spirit soared high, into the mountains, over a canyon, up a pine-studded mountain ridge and into a valley carpeted with meadow. It sought haven in the rough-hewn cabin where untold pleasures had been found, with a woman that would soon be his.

Chapter Twenty

As the day wore on, Willie felt more and more like an unwilling participant in a bad play. Throughout the afternoon and into the early evening, she kept pasted on her lips a smile which she hoped made her look like an eager bride-to-be, with little to worry her save for the fit of her new dress.

They'd found it in Deadwood Run's general store. When she modeled it for Brant, the ivory-and-emerald-striped taffeta lost most of its original luster from the day when Devlin had taken her there and she'd spotted it in the window. The neckline seemed to plunge too low, the bodice gripped too tight around her waist and ribs, and the bustle seemed to indecently accentuate her backside. She'd said so, only to have the shopkeeper produce a pair of ivory silk gloves that covered her bare arms clear to her elbows.

Brant beamed as he counted off crisp bills and handed them to the shopkeeper. Willie did her best to evade his hands and reminded herself that no charade was too burdensome to carry off if it was for Devlin and the success of his plan.

But despite these reminders, her patience wore thin and her apprehension mounted, reaching startling heights when they returned to the farm late in the afternoon and found Gramps burying Huck near the edge of the woods. No, he hadn't seen Devlin.

She went through the motions of getting dressed, slid French silk stockings onto her legs and secured her hair on top of her head with an emerald taffeta ribbon. When she looked in the mirror she saw nothing but a pale woman whose nerves were stretched unmercifully taut. She held her eyes wide to keep the tears back in her throat with the lump swelling there.

Where was Devlin?

Before she left her room she slid her gun into one silk garter and smoothed the dress over it.

If Brant took notice of her crisp responses to his conversation, he offered no remark. As he steered the wagon into town, his mood remained obscenely gay and lighthearted compared to the turmoil she felt. But instead of coaxing her from her distraction, his bravado scraped like a dull blade on her nerves.

Her smile began to quiver at the corners. Her responses became more and more an edgy silence. And when they arrived at the churchyard, where lamps glowed around the perimeter of the makeshift dance floor and a crowd had gathered around a fiddle and harmonica, Willie leapt from the wagon before Brant could even begin to assist her.

Distress brimming over, she shouldered past several couples, aware that they stared at her coming out of her dress with mouths popping open. If the dress was enough to get them all buzzing, what would they all do when Devlin rode into town with his bagged villains?

He was coming. She could feel it.

"Punch?" Bessie Lewis popped up into Willie's path and waved a glass of pink liquid in front of Willie's nose. "My—" Bessie blinked furiously and stared at Willie's bosom. "Y-you're—that is—I don't think I've ever seen such a sight on you."

Willie stood on tiptoes and glanced quickly around the throng. "Have you seen Sloan Devlin?"

"I wanted to talk to you about that. I heard a rumor."

Willie's teeth slid together with impatience. "About Devlin and Dakota Darby." Before Bessie could do more than open her mouth, Willie snapped, "It's not true. None of it."

Bessie's plump shoulders seemed to sink into their sockets. "Not even the part about them knowing each other from the theater in London? Someone said that she was his mistress when he was barely a young man. Then it all made sense, him scurrying off back to England with her. Not that I give talk any credence, ever. It's Mama who likes to chew the fat. Are you saying he hasn't left town for good?"

"Not yet he hasn't," Willie muttered. She'd seen no sign of Devlin, J.D., Gertie or Judge McKay. Her eyes swept again over the sea of faces. No Lansky, Cochran or his deputies. And come to think of it, no brown-bowlered, mustached stranger.

Her stomach churned. The air crackled with tension. Something was about to happen. Didn't anyone else sense it? For a moment the earth seemed to vibrate beneath her feet. She hadn't been wrong about Devlin. She hadn't.

"Let's go, darlin'," Brant drawled, grasping her by the arm and swinging her out into the swarm of dancing couples before she could brace her feet and refuse. She yanked her arm away. Fake smiles and petty conversation were one thing, when she felt like she did. Dancing was something else altogether, as was allowing herself to be manhandled another minute.

"Hey there, don't you go running off on me." Brant lunged for her arm, grasping only air when she sidestepped him then headed off the floor. He caught her at the edge of the dance floor and yanked her around so violently her head snapped.

"You're gonna do as I say," he growled through his smile. His eyes plunged down her bodice. Lust spread over his features, hardening them, wiping clean the boyish handsomeness. "I say it's high time I laid my claim to you, Willie."

Willie felt her restraint snap like a brittle twig. "The hell it is. There's nothing left to claim."

"Still thinking about Devlin? It's what you've been thinking about all day. He's gone, honey, and he's never coming back. Don't worry, I'll get you free of him. C'mon.''

Had she been wearing Levi's and boots she easily could have escaped and outdrawn him. In two-inch heels and a narrow sheathe, with no gun riding in her waistband, it was all she could do to walk, especially when he hauled her almost out of her shoes and half dragged her alongside him through the crowd, toward the back corner of the church, where the lantern light didn't penetrate the shadows.

Spinning her around, he yanked her head back by her hair and forced her eyes to his. ''Look at you,'' he sneered. ''Eyes spitting fire like you hate me. That's fine. Nothing like a woman in need of taming to get me hot and ready. There was a time, sweet Willie, when you liked the feel of my hands on you. I think you need some reminding, especially since you think you tasted something better.''

A strange smile split his lips. ''Devlin's gone. You're nothing but another man's leftovers now. I think you'll need some reminding of that from time to time. Just might make you grateful that I'll still marry you.''

''I'd rather rot in hell than marry you.''

''You'll change your mind. All women do. They have no choice.'' He crushed his mouth over hers with punishing force then leapt from her with eyes bulging and blood trickling down his chin. He pressed a hand to his tongue, stared at it and roared, ''Damned bitch, you friggin' bit me!''

''Be thankful I don't shoot off that thing between your legs.'' Tugging off the ring, she threw it at his feet, unable to dam the tide of anger and resentment surging through her. Unable to keep up the charade another moment if it meant physical surrender to Brant. ''Grateful? For your bribery and emotional blackmail?''

His chest heaved as he seemed to make a great effort to control himself. ''I love you, honey.''

''You love something but it isn't me. A man in love doesn't have control over his emotions. A man in love isn't able to look the other way when he knows his woman has been with another man." Hands finding her hips, she advanced a step toward him. "How long have you known about the silver?"

Brant took a step toward her. "Willie, honey—"

Quick as a flash, she bent, hoisted her dress, and whisked the Colt Peacemaker from her garter. Jerking upright, she pointed the gun at Brant's chest. Satisfaction curved her lips when his face fell and his hands jerked slightly skyward.

"How long have you known about the silver?" she repeated

"You're not going to shoot me."

"If I think you had something to do with blowing that mine, I'd shoot you dead. And I'm starting to think it. Especially since I've got good reasons."

"You've got nothing on me."

"Really? You're being followed. It's also mighty suspicious that the barn burned the night you arrived."

"Whoa, there. I didn't have anything to do with that."

"And you didn't let the cowboy go, either, eh?"

"Now, listen, honey, I had to let him go. He knew that I knew about the silver and I didn't want him telling you before I did. Simple as that."

Willie's laugh was short and cold. "You waited seven months too long to tell me. You keep standing there and lying to me and I'm likely to get a slippery trigger finger."

"Hold on now! I didn't blow that mine. I've never killed anybody, and that's a fact."

"Odd that you feel so compelled to tell me that."

He blinked at her, momentarily uncomprehending. "Listen, I overheard a couple fellows talking about the silver they knew was down in the Lucky Cuss when I first came to Deadwood Run about seven months back."

"Before you came to Prosperity Gulch. So you thought you'd get yourself in on the take by seducing the unsuspecting owner of that mine who you knew was a woman."

"You're seeing this all wrong."

"No, I'm seeing it all quite clearly for the first time. Keep your hands away from your coat. Your first mistake was to underestimate me once. Don't do it again or I'll kill you.''

Brant's hands visibly shook as he lifted them higher. Rage ignited in his eyes and twisted in his lips into a snarl. ''You can't do anything about it by yourself, honey.''

''Not true. I can go after my dream, all the way to Cornwall England if that's what it takes.''

Face tight, jaw ticking, boots fidgeting, he stared hard at her. ''Listen to me, Willie, put down the damn gun and listen. I've got a plan. It'll all be ours. We won't have to split an ounce of the silver with anyone. But you can't do it alone. There's too many of them. You've got to trust me.''

''If you say another word I'm going to shoot you.''

''Hold it right there, Wilhelmina Thorne!'' The shout came out of the darkness behind Brant. An instant later moonlight reflected off oval spectacles half-hidden by the worn brim of a brown bowler. ''Put the gun down, Miss Thorne.''

Willie kept her arm steady and her aim true. ''Not until you tell me who you are, mister.''

''David Green, Special Investigator, Pinkerton National Detective Agency out of New York.'' His card flashed in the moonlight as he handed it to her. He jerked his head at Brant. ''I've been on his tail since a certain Angelina Quinn Masters was robbed in her New York town house. Funny thing, her husband here disappeared the same night all her jewels were stolen.''

Willie felt her jaw sag. ''Husband? He has a wife?''

''Only one currently that I know of. He divorced the other two. She's the daughter of a very wealthy Eastern industrialist, Edwin Quinn. Masters here is a con artist, Miss Thorne, slick as they come. Gambler at heart, always looking for the big easy take. He posed as a businessman to gain Quinn's favor then seduced Angelina when he knew her father would discover them. That guaranteed a quick wedding and a settling of all his debts. Then came a little dabbling in the family business, skimming off some of the profits, until he was caught and Edwin Quinn promised to ruin him unless he left town and divorced Quinn's daughter.

"He came out here, heard about the mine, met you and tried the same operation. Only Angelina wanted him back to reconcile, promised him the world, all the money he wanted. He couldn't resist. But things didn't work out. Maybe things looked too good out here. So he staged a phony robbery, lifted the jewels and caught the first train west."

Willie bent and scooped the ring from the ground. "I believe you're looking for this, Mr. Green. It's Angelina's." Her eyes met Brant's and held until he looked away. "He used to call her Angel." She handed Green the ring, surprised when he grasped her hand.

"My apologies, Miss Thorne. When I bumped into you earlier today, I meant to see if you were wearing the ring. I never meant to cause you distress, but from the looks of it here, you were on to Masters long before I—"

Before Willie could think to squeeze off a shot or Green could utter another word, Brant grabbed Willie by the neck, yanked her back against him and shoved a cold steel muzzle against her temple. Willie froze.

"Drop the gun, Willie," he growled. "Hold it right there, Green. Keep your hands up, away from your coat, and your feet still. Fine bit of detective work there. Sorry I can't oblige you or sweet Angel."

Green looked completely unfazed. "I'll add kidnapping and attempted murder to the charges, Masters. That could guarantee you a hanging out here."

"I won't be waiting around to find out. No tricks, Willie honey. We're going to find ourselves a preacher and nobody's going to stop us." He inched backward away from Green, around the back of the church toward the horses and wagons. Darkness instantly swallowed them. The crowd milled not twenty paces away, voices raised above the fiddler's tune, punch swilling. Willie stumbled back in front of Masters. Attempting escape or a shout for help at this juncture could be tantamount to suicide. And she had no desire to test Brant's determination to escape at any cost.

"Good evening, Masters. Having a bit of a problem with your fiancé?"

It was as if the heavens opened above her and showered her with joy. *Devlin.* Her limbs went weak. With a curse, Brant yanked her around and shoved the gun deeper against her skull. "You move, Devlin, and you live with her blood on your hands for the rest of your sorry life."

Tears blurred her vision and then Sloan sprang into focus against a silver moon rising behind him through the trees. Shadows obscured his features. A light breeze ruffled through his unbound hair. He wore nothing but his trousers and boots.

His nonchalant tone had been brilliantly deceptive. He was all animal tonight. Willie could smell it on him. He'd discarded all traces of the gentleman with his clothes. It was as if he'd harnessed all of nature's energy and it flowed out of him through his eyes. Those starlit depths glowed hot silver the instant they focused on her. The ground quivered beneath her feet. The air crackled as if shot through with lightning.

Brant was either too desperate or too stupid to realize how dangerous Sloan was. "I'm not falling for your fancy tricks a second time, Devlin. Things are a bit different this time around. I've got your woman and there's no train to toss me off of. I don't care how fast you move, you're not quicker than a bullet. And you don't got yourself a gun. I'm wondering how you think you're going to keep me from taking Willie anywhere I want—" Brant's breath fanned hot on Willie's cheek even when she twisted her head away "—and doing whatever I want with her."

"You're going to get hurt, Masters."

Willie could almost hear the great compression of raw energy focusing in Sloan, fusing, imploding. Brant started to say something but the words never got past his tongue. Sloan exploded in a blinding series of movements. Something whizzed past Willie's ear. Sloan's foot. An instant later the pistol discharged into the sky with a roar. Above it, rising into the night like a wolf's cry, she heard Sloan's savage scream. And then, Masters crumpled to the ground with a painful moan.

Before Willie could draw a breath she was crushed in Sloan's arms. She blubbered against his chest, mouth open, tasting the salt and the blood on his skin, her soul wrenching with joy, until he cupped her jaw and lifted her mouth to his. She tasted her tears then the rough and wondrous plundering of his mouth and the claim of his hands.

She surrendered to him as she always would, wholly, with every piece of her soul, fitting her body deeper into his, sinking her fingers into the raven thickness of his hair.

"I hate to be the one to do this—"

Sloan lifted his head but his eyes never left Willie's. "Then don't, Lansky." His thumb brushed over her mouth, parted her lips, and he lowered his head again only to be thwarted when Lansky's voice rose an octave higher.

"They need you over at the jail, Devlin. Judge McKay just showed up with Gertie. There's a slight prob—well, we, er, we need to know what we should do with Hyde and Strobridge and the three prisoners you've got hog-tied on that horse."

Willie slanted her eyes at Devlin and felt a smile well up from her heart. "You *are* invincible."

His eyes glowed. "I have a deep need to prove that to you in a very special way, my dear Wilhelmina." He glanced sideways as Lansky gave a sheepish grin. "Can't you figure it out?"

"I suppose I could. But actually, what I was most curious about is how you managed to disarm three men, and them lawmen! I tell you I've never seen anything like it. Willie, maybe you would have believed it. I know I didn't. Devlin here came walking into town not fifteen minutes ago leading Sheriff Cochran and his two deputies—"

"Cochran?" Willie exclaimed.

Lansky nodded. "There's just no trusting lawmen anymore. Like I said, all three on a horse behind him with a rope around their necks. Looked as dumb as oxen to me with their heads hanging, docile as could be. Not a speck of blood on them. No bruises. But when Devlin just looked at them there was fear in their eyes the likes of which I've never seen even on the faces of dead men."

"You sound like a damned headline," Sloan muttered.

"I'm seeing it on the front page of the *Lucky Miner*." Lansky spread his palms wide. "English Gentleman Solves Murder Mystery, Becomes Sheriff."

"Let's go," Sloan snarled, sweeping Willie along beside him as he turned to head toward the jail. "Anything to get him to shut the hell up."

"I'll take care of Masters," David Green said. He shoved his toe into Masters's side and got a groan in reply. "He'll be calling a jail in New York home for the next ten years or so."

It was only when they stepped fully into the moonlight that Willie saw the blood caked over Sloan's brow, the purple bruises swelling along his jaw and cheekbone, the blood-encrusted lashes crisscrossing his chest and arms.

She laid a palm on his chest, fingertips trembling on the lacerations. "Why did you let them do this to you? You could have stopped them."

"They had me at the farm, in the kitchen, and Gramps was sleeping in the front room."

Willie looked up into his beautiful face with misting eyes and felt her heart swell near to bursting. "You protected him. You let them do this to you because of Gramps. And they could have killed you."

His eyes angled down at her and a seductive half smile tipped his lips. "Two minutes ago I was invincible."

"I don't want 'invincible,' Sloan Devlin. I want a flesh-and-blood man."

"Yes, and that's exactly what you need."

The hushed intimacy lacing his voice sent delicious shivers down Willie's spine. There was promise in his words, a promise of a lifetime. They approached the jail where Cochran and the deputies lay on their bellies, hog-tied to a horse. Judge McKay stepped out of the jail, Gertie and J.D. following at his heels. The judge, a white-haired, barrel-chested man with sweeping whiskers and a twitch that affected only one eye, stood his ground until Devlin stepped onto the boardwalk and introduced himself.

"Devlin," McKay muttered, squinting up at him. "From what I can gather, you're the fella who's going to tell me why the sheriff of this damned town is hog-tied to that horse with his deputies."

"I'd rather the sheriff tell you, sir," Devlin replied, glancing over his shoulder at Cochran. "That was the arrangement, wasn't it, gentlemen?"

Cochran squirmed and muttered something that sounded like an affirmation.

Devlin turned back to the judge. "They'll be happy to confess to blowing the mine and terrorizing the folks of this town. They also killed Lily Harkness by poisoning her." Devlin nodded toward the rear of the jail. "Hyde and Strobridge are peacekeeping men. They were wrongfully imprisoned by Cochran."

"You saying they were framed?"

"The town has no quarrel against them."

The judge squinted at Devlin. "I suppose the sheriff here will fill me in on that, too, eh?"

"He'd be happy to, sir."

The judge glanced at Lansky and jerked his head toward the jail. "Let them go, then. We don't need the Union Pacific breathing down my neck." Lansky hurried into the jail. "One more thing—" McKay said, glancing at Devlin. "Can the good sheriff explain why he killed his own deputy Virgil Brown?"

"I ain't the fella what did that," Cochran shouted. "It was someone else, I tell ya. Someone who knew Willie was goin' down to the mine that night. Someone who knew what Virgil Brown would have done to her if she found him diggin' away into that mine for our silver. It was someone who wanted to protect her, that's the way I see it.''

Over Judge McKay's shoulder Willie's gaze locked with J.D.'s. Only J.D. and Gramps had known that she and Devlin were going down to the mine that night. But only J.D. had known that Cochran and his men were secretly digging farther into the mine, searching for the silver he knew was there.

J.D. He'd been protecting her even then. *I saved you once*, he'd told her. *I can't anymore*.

His mouth opened. He laid a hand on McKay's shoulder. He was willing to die because of his guilt, hang for murder....

''I killed him.'' All eyes riveted on Willie. She swallowed, drew a deep breath, glanced at Sloan, then faced the judge. ''I found Brown on my property. He drew on me. I had no choice.''

Sloan watched her. J.D. stared at her. McKay squinted at her for so long in silence that Willie felt the heat start to climb up from her collar.

''That the way it happened?'' McKay finally asked Sloan. ''You were there.''

Sloan's hand slid around Willie's waist. ''That's the way it happened, sir.''

McKay gave a swift nod of his head. ''Then that's the way it happened. Ain't no crime in self-defense.'' McKay waved a hand toward Cochran. ''Someone get those men off that poor horse and into a jail cell.''

''Happy to do it,'' J. D. Harkness piped up, bolting off the boardwalk toward Cochran. He paused as he passed Willie but kept his eyes fixed in front of him.

''Don't you dare thank me,'' Willie said softly.

J.D.'s Adam's apple jerked in his throat. ''I was going to wish you well, Wilhelmina. And all the happiness you deserve.''

Willie reached for his hand, but he moved on and proceeded to herd Cochran and his men off the horse and into the jail.

''Sloan Devlin, by God, you saved my life!'' Hyde and

Strobridge surged out of the jail and began to furiously pump both of Devlin's hands at the same time.

"Anything the Union Pacific can do for you—" one said.

"Heard there was silver in that mine," the other chimed in. "We'll lay track through here and haul out all the ore you can mine for rock-bottom freight rates. Hell, we'll do better than rock-bottom rates. We'll bring in all the goods and services the fine folk of this town will ever need. Six months from now you won't even recognize this town. It will be the new Denver. Civic opera will be making regular appearances here—"

In short order a crowd surged around them as word spread fast and soon folks were jostling for an opportunity to shake Sloan's hands and those of Hyde and Strobridge. Bessie Lewis proclaimed herself nominating chairwoman and promptly took up a chant, "Devlin for sheriff!" Others joined in with raucous cheers. Without anyone realizing, Sloan broke out of the crush. He found Willie sitting against the hitching rail in front of the Silver Spur, her high-heeled shoes dangling from one hand.

"Sheriff Sloan Devlin," Willie said softly after he settled beside her, hip to hip, thigh pressed against thigh.

"Lady Wilhelmina Thorne Devlin, Countess of Worthingham."

Their gazes locked.

"You look damned fetching in that dress," he murmured. "I love you, Wilhelmina Thorne."

Willie slid her hand over his. Hope and joy and love burst through her and she saw her dream there and her future, for the first time, in the love shining in his eyes. "Tell me about Cornwall, England."

Epilogue

The door to the bedchamber closed softly. Willie glanced up into the gilt-edged dressing-table mirror as a shadow stirred the darkness untouched by candlelight. A warm hand cupped around her shoulder and eased the sleeve of her silk dressing gown off her shoulder. In the glow of the candle on the dressing table, the gold band encircling his long finger burned a warm yellow.

"Wife." He bent his lips to her shoulder. "Have you been dutiful today?"

The letter Willie held trembled in her fingers. In the mirror she watched high spots of color bloom on her cheeks as his hand cupped one breast. Beneath the silk, her nipples tightened in anticipation.

"Yes, my lord, quite dutiful."

"Mmm." He moved into the deeper shadows. Broadcloth rustled as he shrugged out of his topcoat. Buttons whispered free of their moorings as he doffed his waistcoat. His shirt was a splash of white in the dark as his fingers drifted down the buttons. "What does the letter say?"

"It's from Gramps." Willie lifted the letter closer to the light and averted her eyes when those fingers made quick work of trouser buttons. The diamonds and emeralds on her left ring finger winked with a precious brilliance in the soft light.

"Chock-full of news. It seems Dakota Darby has established herself on the stage at Her Majesty's Theatre in London. The reviews are filtering all the way to the pages of the *Lucky Miner*. Folks are hoping she'll make a return engagement to the newly opened Civic Opera House in Prosperity Gulch. J. D. Harkness was elected Sheriff. Tom Lansky was offered a position with a giant newspaper conglomerate in Boston, which he promptly turned down to marry Gertie. She's opened a milliner's shop and sells the latest in Paris fashions. Apparently Tom has three presses and six men working for him now. The mine's exceeding everyone's expectations. Its subdivided shares are selling for an incredible sum now."

Willie paused, growing thoughtful. "There's a definite tone in Gramps's letter."

"A tone." His voice seemed to tremor through the ancient rafters high overhead.

Heat washed over Willie as the air rippled behind her. She stared into the mirror as her husband materialized out of the darkness behind her, proud, untamed, the savage shed of all gentlemanly accoutrements. She admired the magnificence of his bare chest, felt the ridges of his belly pressing against her back, caught a glimpse of bare hip, long-muscled thigh—

Warm hands cupped around her neck, fingers splaying over her collarbone, palms pressing flat against her skin as he hooked his thumbs in the banded collar and slipped the dressing gown over her shoulders to her elbows.

Desire flooded through her. The pages of the letter fell from her fingers. Her eyes swept closed. "I see him sitting on the porch at the farmhouse, with his new dog beside him. He's content." A sigh escaped her lips as the gown slipped over her breasts and dropped to her waist. She turned toward him as he bent to her, sinking to his knees and lowering his head to her breasts. She plunged her fingers into his hair, freeing it of its leather cord and arched her back as he drew one nipple deep into his mouth.

"Dutiful wife," he murmured. "You haven't been riding about the countryside—"

"Never."

"In britches and boots—"

"I've a closetful of gowns to choose from."

"Tasting beer and pilchard in all the brew houses from here to Falmouth—"

"Azato watches over me like a mother hen."

"I'm hearing tales from my tenants. As for Azato, I can't be certain, but I believe you've charmed him into some sort of secretive pact about the whole damned thing."

"Secretive pacts? Really, Devlin, I'm a countess now."

"You're in confinement."

"I don't like that word. It sounds too—"

"Tamed." His broad hands splayed over the mound that was her belly, caressing the budding life beneath the taut skin. He lifted his head and his eyes leapt with silver flame. "And you are anything but tame. Much more of this and they'll be talking about you in Parliament, my dear."

She arched a saucy brow and lovingly traced the firm contours of his mouth. "They're not already? After all, my husband is responsible for spearheading all the new mine reform laws. Indeed, were it not for your genius and powers of persuasion, mine owners and tinners would never have gathered at the same table and talked, much less come to a mutual agreement."

He caught her finger between his teeth. "If they only knew the depths of your powers, they'd be as enamored of you as the tenants and Azato are."

"And you?"

"I'm enslaved," he breathed, brushing his lips over hers, breathing his life into her, taking hers into him. She curled her arms around his neck and offered herself up to him. He drew her into his arms and bore her to the bed. The silk gown fell to the floor in a forgotten whisper.

"Now, dutiful wife," he rumbled, laying her back on the

goose-down mattress and stretching out beside her. He claimed her with one slow sweep of his hand over her body. "You will please your lord."

"Dutiful and untamed," she murmured, as he rose above her in masculine magnificence.

"I'll have you no other way."

Her lips curved with a knowing smile. "As you wish, my lord."

* * * * *

**Harlequin Historicals presents
an exciting medieval collection**

THE KNIGHTS OF CHRISTMAS

With bestselling authors

Suzanne
BARCLAY

Margaret
MOORE

Debborah
SIMMONS

Available in October
wherever Harlequin Historicals are sold.

*Harlequin®
Historical*

Every month there's another title from one
of your favorite authors!

October 1997
Romeo in the Rain by Kasey Michaels
When Courtney Blackmun's daughter brought home Mr. Tall,
Dark and Handsome, Courtney wanted to send the young
matchmaker to her room! Of course, that meant the single
New Jersey mom would be left alone with the irresistibly
attractive Adam Richardson....

November 1997
Intrusive Man by Lass Small
Indiana's Hannah Calhoun had enough on her hands taking
care of her young son, and the last thing she needed was a
man complicating things—especially Max Simmons, the
gorgeous cop who had eased himself right into her little boy's
heart...and was making his way into hers.

December 1997
Crazy Like a Fox by Anne Stuart

Moving in with her deceased husband's—*eccentric*—family
in Louisiana meant a whole new life for Margaret Jaffrey and
her nine-year-old daughter. But the beautiful young widow
soon finds herself seduced by the slower pace and the much-
too-attractive cousin-in-law, Peter Andrew Jaffrey....

**BORN IN THE USA: Love, marriage—
and the pursuit of family!**

Available at your favorite retail outlet!

From bestselling Medieval author

Suzanne Barclay

comes another tale in her popular Sommerville Brothers series

Knight's Rebellion

Romance and intrigue abound when an outlaw knight rescues a beautiful aristocrat, who bewitches his heart!

KNIGHT'S REBELLION (ISBN 28991-X) will be available in November.

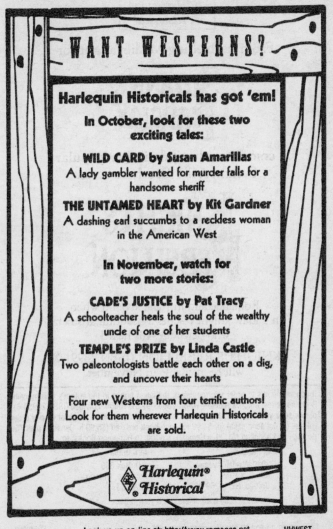

WANT WESTERNS?

Harlequin Historicals has got 'em!

In October, look for these two exciting tales:

WILD CARD by Susan Amarillas
A lady gambler wanted for murder falls for a handsome sheriff

THE UNTAMED HEART by Kit Gardner
A dashing earl succumbs to a reckless woman in the American West

In November, watch for two more stories:

CADE'S JUSTICE by Pat Tracy
A schoolteacher heals the soul of the wealthy uncle of one of her students

TEMPLE'S PRIZE by Linda Castle
Two paleontologists battle each other on a dig, and uncover their hearts

Four new Westerns from four terrific authors! Look for them wherever Harlequin Historicals are sold.

◇ *Harlequin®*
Historical

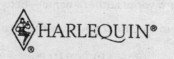

Coming in August 1997!

THE BETTY NEELS
RUBY COLLECTION

COLLECTOR'S EDITION

This August start assembling the
Betty Neels Ruby Collection. Six of the
most requested and best-loved titles have
been especially chosen for this collection.
From August 1997 until January 1998,
one title per month will be available to avid
fans. Spot the collection by the lush ruby red
cover with the gold Collector's Edition banner
and your favorite author's name—Betty Neels!

Available in August at your favorite retail outlet.

HARLEQUIN®

COMING NEXT MONTH FROM

HARLEQUIN HISTORICALS

DON'T MISS THESE FOUR GREAT TITLES AVAILABLE NOW!